Praise for

JENNIFER ROBSON

'Jennifer Robson pens a tale of devastating simplicity
and poignant sweetness, superbly grounded in the
horrors of fascist Italy'
Kate Quinn, *New York Times* bestselling author

'*Our Darkest Night* is a rich, atmospheric Italian journey
of survival from an ancient city to the rustic countryside
to the concentration camps. With poignant precision,
Robson tugs at the heartstrings . . . in this beautiful
tale of love, survival, and triumph'
Stephanie Dray, *New York Times* bestselling author

'A powerful, emotional, and unflinching story of love, sacrifice,
and resilience during one of history's darkest moments'
Chanel Cleeton, *New York Times* bestselling author

'Jennifer Robson's superb storytelling balances heartrending
events with hope and humanity for a moving story of courage,
integrity, and love amidst danger'
Janie Chang

'With stunningly intense and intimate prose, Jennifer Robson
shines a light on the lesser-known fate of Italian Jews during
World War II . . . Robson has penned an extraordinary tale of
family sacrifice, resilience, and love'
Lynda Cohen Loigman

'Jennifer Robson is a master storyteller who will sweep you
away with this wartime tale of the importance of family and
above all, the enduring power of love'
Stephanie Marie Thornton,
USA Today bestselling author

'With nuanced characters and beautiful, evocative prose,
Robson weaves a compelling tale of bravery, perseverance,
and the immeasurable power of love in the face of adversity.
Haunting and inspiring, heartbreaking and hopeful,
this novel is unforgettable'
Kristin Beck

'Heartbreaking and heartfelt, Jennifer Robson's new novel is her best yet. With powerful prose and vivid characters, this unflinching novel shows not only the horrors of war, but the unshakeable power of love against hate. A must read'
Bryn Turnbull

'*The Gown* is marvelous and moving, a vivid portrait of female self-reliance in a world racked by the cost of war'
Kate Quinn, *New York Times* bestselling author

'An unforgettable story of friendship, hardship, and hope. Robson has managed to craft a story that is personal and universal, timely and timeless. *The Gown* soars!'
Pam Jenoff, *New York Times* bestselling author

'A moving story about the power of female friendship and renewal in the face of adversity . . . Perfect for fans of *The Crown*!'
Lauren Willig, *New York Times* bestselling author

'*The Gown* is a heartwarming story of friendship, resilience, and the power of heirlooms to connect people through generations, sometimes in the most unexpected ways'
Kristina McMorris, *New York Times* bestselling author

'Embroidering a magical moment in royal history, Robson tells a heartrending story of friendship, loss, love, and redemption'
Leslie Carroll

'A fascinating glimpse into the world of design, the healing power of art, and the importance of women's friendships'
Kirkus

By Jennifer Robson

Fall of Poppies
Somewhere in France
After the War is Over
Moonlight Over Paris
Goodnight from London
The Gown
Our Darkest Night
Coronation Year

CORONATION YEAR

JENNIFER ROBSON

REVIEW

Copyright © 2023 Jennifer Robson

The right of Jennifer Robson to be identified as the Author of
the Work has been asserted by her in accordance with the
Copyright, Designs and Patents Act 1988.

Published by arrangement with William Morrow,
an imprint of HarperCollins Publishers.

First published in Great Britain in 2023
by HEADLINE REVIEW
An imprint of HEADLINE PUBLISHING GROUP

1

Cataloguing in Publication Data is available from the British Library

ISBN 978 1 0354 0421 6

Designed by Diahann Sturge
Crown illustration © Maxx-Studio/Shutterstock
Blue Lion and map illustrations © Charisma Panchapakesan

Offset in 11/15 pt Plantin Std by Jouve (UK), Milton Keynes

Printed and bound in Great Britain by Clays Ltd, Elcograf S.p.A.

HEADLINE PUBLISHING GROUP
An Hachette UK Company
Carmelite House
50 Victoria Embankment
London EC4Y 0DZ

www.headline.co.uk
www.hachette.co.uk

For Matthew and Daniela
(how fortunate I am to be your mum)

CORONATION
YEAR

MARBLE
ARCH

OXFORD STREET

EAST CARRIAGE DRIVE

PICCADILLY

CORONATION
PROCESSION OF
HM ELIZABETH II

June 2, 1953

BUCKINGHAM PALACE

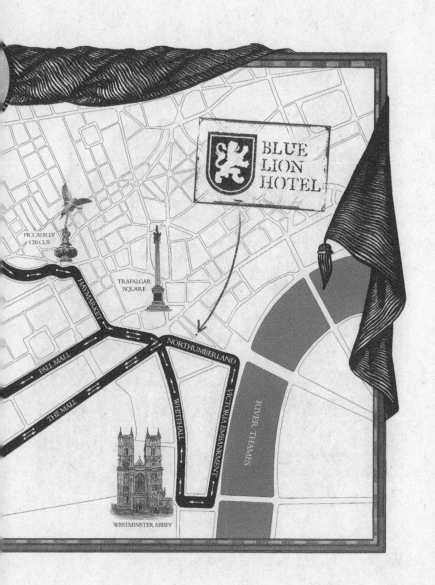

JANUARY

Chapter One

EDWINA DUNCAN HOWARD

Thursday, January 1, 1953

Agale from the east had swept across the city late the
evening before, scouring away the worst of the smog,
and the rare sight of London's night sky had inspired
Edie to open her curtains and raise the fraying blackout
blind. She'd tucked herself into bed, her spectacles still on,
because what was the point of looking at the stars if she
couldn't make them out?

But she'd been tired, so awfully tired, and she'd fallen
asleep straightaway. And now it was a quarter to seven in
the morning, the stars had faded from the still-dark sky,
and before she was even fully awake she remembered it all.
Nothing tragic or calamitous; nothing she would dream of
sharing with any of the people who worked for her. Just worries, an impatient and none too polite queue of them, each
demanding her attention, her time, and every last penny of
the Blue Lion's ever-diminishing supply of capital.

She threw back the covers, sat up straight, and set her feet on the cold floor. Time to be up, past time to stop fretting and fussing, for it was a new day—a new year, the year of the queen's coronation, and in six months the world would be coming to London, and by the greatest stroke of good fortune she and her guests at the Blue Lion would have front-row seats for at least part of the festivities.

Even now, months after learning the coronation procession from Buckingham Palace to Westminster Abbey would pass by her front door, Edie still marveled that some bureaucrat in Whitehall had made the fateful decision to send the procession along Northumberland Avenue, never for a moment considering the effect it would have on the historic, if often overlooked, hotel that Edie's ancestor had founded in 1560.

A knock at the door put an end to her musings. "Miss Howard?"

"I won't be a moment." She fumbled for her spectacles, which she fortunately hadn't crushed in her sleep, pulled on her robe, stepped into her slippers, and glanced at the overmantel mirror to ensure her hair was tidy. Only then did she unlock and open her door to the hotel's night manager.

"Good morning, Mr. Swan, and Happy New Year."

"The same to you, Miss Howard. May I bring in your breakfast?"

"Yes, thank you. How were things overnight?"

"Nicely quiet. Not a peep from the rooms."

Well. There wouldn't be, given that only seven guests were in residence, among them their three long-term boarders, and none were the sort to stay up late. By midnight they had likely been abed for hours.

"Any trouble with the Queen Bess?" The public house down the street made for good neighbors most of the time, but bank holidays occasionally meant messes to clear up and, intermittently, broken windows when its patrons turned into amateur pugilists.

He set her breakfast tray on the desk by the window, straightened it with care, and turned to face her. "Not as bad as Boxing Day. Quieted down long before last orders."

"Good, good. I always sleep well when I know you're at the front desk."

"Thank you, miss," Arthur said, his ears reddening at the compliment. "I'll see you this evening, then."

The particulars varied, but the essentials remained the same. In the fourteen years Arthur had been night manager, neither he nor Edie had deviated from the established formula for their morning conversation. She knew he was married and that his wife's name was Florence but he called her Flossie. She knew he had two children, Arthur Junior and Gawain, the latter name a startlingly poetic choice for such a placid and practical man, and she knew his address and of course exactly how much he made, since she was the one who paid his wages. But she'd gleaned nearly every scrap of information from overheard conversations and secondhand exchanges with other hotel employees. Not once had she and Arthur spoken of his life beyond the hotel, and if she were ever to unbend herself and ask after Flossie and the children, she was almost certain he would faint on the spot.

She never called him Arthur to his face, though she thought of him that way. She thought of all her employees as family, though she could never allow herself the luxury of friendship with them. *Be friendly,* her father had liked to remind her, *but remember that you're not their friend. You're not meant to be friends.*

Edie had remembered that advice, together with everything else Pa had told her, when she'd been left with the hotel. A few months shy of twenty-one, still in shock after the death of her parents, suddenly responsible for the livelihood and well-being of eighteen full-time employees, she'd clung to her memories of Pa and Mum and the generations of Howards before them. Her family had kept the Blue Lion open and modestly profitable for almost four hundred years. She had only to follow in their footsteps.

Pa had loved to tell her stories of the hotel, so while other girls fell asleep to fairy tales or stories from *Schoolgirl's Own,* Edie's bedtime fare had been the unfolding saga of the Blue Lion and its glorious past.

"It was our ancestor, Jacob Howard, who founded this hotel," her father would often begin. "Mind you, it was an old building even then, never mind the Victorian coat it wears now, and ever since then, for seventeen generations, there's been a Howard at the helm. Your mother and I have the running of it now, just as your grandparents did before us, which means . . . ?"

"It will be mine one day."

Left unsaid was all that had happened before she was born. Her brothers, killed during the Great War, lost in the mud and blood of the Somme, and Edie the replacement, conceived so the Howard name would not die along with them. The disappointment of her being a girl was never mentioned, of course.

"Think of it, Edie—every timber and flagstone and scrap

of plaster and stick of furniture in these buildings will be yours. And that makes you the luckiest girl in London."

She had believed him then, but now? Now she wasn't so sure. It all depended, she supposed, on what one accounted as luck.

The little clock on her mantel trilled the hour. Seven o'clock already, her breakfast growing cold, and the entire day yet to get through. One day she would lounge in bed until noon, and she would eat her breakfast without getting up, never mind the crumbs, and she'd spend all afternoon reading. One day, after the coronation, when she had restored the hotel's fortunes and the weight of it all didn't sit quite so heavily on her shoulders.

Today, however, she could not afford to linger. Instead she ate her toast and marmalade, poured her tea and gulped it down, and then set about getting dressed. She always wore the same thing, excepting the odd evening out, for it saved time in the morning and, more importantly, made her instantly recognizable to both her guests and employees. A white poplin blouse with detachable collar for easier laundering, a charcoal-gray skirt that grazed the top of her calves and was scarcely fuller than the Utility skirts she'd worn during the war, a tailored jacket to match, and sensible lace-up shoes with a low heel. On her left lapel was a blue enamel badge, its edges delicately gilded, that read *Miss E. D. Howard* and, below it, *Proprietor*. She wore no jewelry apart from her mother's wristwatch.

After making her bed, Edie collected the tray to take downstairs. Her room was on the top floor at the back of the hotel, with a northerly aspect and an unremarkable view of the surrounding roofs. The largest of the staff bedrooms, it was half the size of the best guest rooms at the front of the building, and its furnishings were the same as they'd been when her parents had taken over the chamber at the turn of the century.

She locked her door, neatly balancing the tray on one arm, and walked to the end of the corridor, through the staff-only door, and down the back stairs to the kitchen. There she deposited the tray and greeted Cook, Ruth the assistant cook, and Dolly the scullery maid.

"Happy New Year, ladies."

"Good morning, Miss Howard, and a happy New Year to you," Cook answered brightly, though she didn't look up from the bowl of eggs she was whisking.

"Happy Coronation Year, Miss Howard!" burbled Dolly, who was a fervent devotee of the royal family. Everyone at the Blue Lion had heard, most more than once, how the late king himself had visited her street in Stepney Green after it was blitzed, and even though Dolly had only been four years old, and her right arm had been in a sling, he'd reached out and grasped her left hand, and given it a proper shake, and he'd been so gentle and nice and hadn't cared one bit that she'd been all over with dust. When his death had been announced, almost a year ago now, Cook had needed to sit Dolly down and fortify her with a mug of well-sugared and lightly brandied tea.

Edie had also been sad, for the king been a good and decent man, and everyone knew the war had more or less killed him. And she had an idea, too, of what it was like to be weighed down by duty and expectations and centuries of compliant ancestors.

"Only six months and a day, Miss Howard, and then

the gold coach and the queen herself will be passing by our front door!"

"It is exciting, yes," Edie agreed, "although we do have a while to wait until then, and in the meantime rather a lot of work to get through."

On the great day itself, they'd be working from dawn to the wee hours, for the hotel would be bursting with guests for the first time in years, and everyone, Edie included, would be run off their feet. All the same, she resolved to find a way for her staff to watch the procession as it rolled past. What difference would a half hour make in the grand scheme of things?

Edie continued on through the dining room, occupied at present only by the Hagerty family—a middle-aged Australian couple and their teenage sons, all of them pleasant, undemanding, and unfortunately only staying for two nights—as well as Miss Polly and Miss Bertie, now in their third decade of residence at the Blue Lion and lingering over their second pot of tea. She offered nods and hellos and just the right amount of a smile, with an expression that suggested she would love to chat but was hurrying along to deal with something terribly important.

Professor Thurloe was waiting for Edie in the front hall, just as she'd been expecting, since it was the first of the month and he was nothing if not a creature of habit. After handing over his monthly report, which consisted of a detailed list of the occasions when he had been bothered by excessive noise, together with a summary of his complaints on a range of subjects that invariably included the food served at breakfast and tea (not enough butter for his toast, not enough tea leaves in his teapot, not enough cress in his egg-and-cress sandwiches), he trailed after her in his usual hangdog fashion, only stopping short when she opened the door to the front-desk alcove and her office beyond.

"Is anything the matter?" she asked in as polite a voice as she could contrive. "I'll read your report as soon as I have a spare moment, but I am really quite busy this morning."

"It will only take a moment for me to explain. I've made some fascinating discoveries, you see."

"About the beams in the cellar and tunnels?" She hoped she didn't sound as weary as she felt. "I've already told you, more than once, that I cannot allow you to go rummaging around down there. Not until I've had a surveyor in to check that it's safe."

Every month the professor had something new and, to his mind, utterly fascinating to share with her; and every month, without exception, in the twelve and a half years he'd boarded at the Blue Lion, he had regaled her with arcane facts about the ancient building techniques used to construct the hotel. But she had a soft spot for the man, who had no one else in the world to look out for him, and who wasn't so very annoying in comparison to some guests who had stayed at the Blue Lion over the years. So she smothered her honest reaction and instead allowed him a glimmer of hope.

"Perhaps once the coronation is over and things are a bit less busy? I could have the surveyor in then."

"Oh, yes, please. That would be splendid. Only . . . you're *quite* certain I can't have a peek in the meantime?"

"Quite. Now, tell me: Have you had your breakfast this morning?" The poor man was looking even more frail than usual.

"Well, no. I'm afraid I've been rather wrapped up in my reading."

"Come along with me to the dining room, then. I'll have Ginny bring out your breakfast straightaway."

"Dear girl. I'd waste away without you. And you will consider my request?"

"When things aren't quite so busy, yes. I'll consider it then."

Edie settled the professor at his usual table in the far corner of the dining room, and then returned to the front hall, intent on greeting Mr. Brooks, the hotel's assistant manager, who had been patiently waiting for her to finish her conversation with the professor.

But then her attention was caught by a flickering light-bulb in the wall sconce to the left of the stairs. It took only a moment to tighten, her fingers smarting from the heat of the glass, but the fleeting discomfort was worth the satisfaction of solving at least one problem that morning, no matter how trivial.

"That's done," she said. And then, belatedly, "Good morning, Mr. Brooks. Happy New Year."

"The same to you, Miss Howard. The morning papers are on your desk. No post, of course, on account of the bank holiday."

"Any telephone messages?"

"Nothing overnight."

"Very well. Give me half an hour, and then we'll go through the reservations for this coming week."

There weren't many to discuss. The Australians were leaving tomorrow, and after that no one was expected until Monday, when three regular guests were due to check in. A salesman from Manchester who always asked for the cheapest room, and a retired couple from Southend-on-Sea, up for three days and two nights so Mr. Tippett might have his annual appointment with his Harley Street heart specialist. She'd have to remind Cook that he'd be wanting his eggs without the yolks, and every bit of fat stripped from his bacon. Then she'd have to listen to complaints about ingrates who wouldn't recognize a decent plate of food if it bit them on the nose.

Edie shut her office door, grateful for a moment of quiet before the day began in earnest, and went to sit at her desk. It was satisfyingly tidy, just as she preferred, with her notebook to the left, the old metal tray that held the post and messages to her right, and before her a neat stack of the *Times*, the *Daily Telegraph*, and the *Daily Mail*.

Nearly everything in the office was as her father had left it: the same furniture, the same ancient and threadbare carpet, the same black-framed photographs of her brothers in their uniforms. The only significant addition was the typewriter on an adjoining table. Pa's secretary had retired just before the end of the war and Edie, determined to rein in costs, had shouldered the extra work herself rather than find a replacement. One day soon, once there was a little money to spare, she would train up someone new for the work. Until then, the secretary's old office was a useful spot to stow luggage and parcels and bits of furniture that needed mending.

Opening her notebook, she began her daily list. *Mr. T food remind Cook*, she wrote. *C day staff view Qn coach. Typewriter ribbon. BOILER*. That last item had been part of her daily list for weeks now, but she'd been avoiding what was sure to be a disagreeable conversation with the curmudgeon who'd been maintaining it since she was a girl. She would call Mr. Pinnock that morning, she resolved.

The newspapers were thin, with the usual sort of warmed-over stories that dominated on a bank holiday, but she went through them carefully, alert to any sort of news that might affect the hotel—a looming coal strike, the prospect of reduced income tax in the forthcoming government budget, an unexpected turn in the weather—and found nothing alarming, nor even terribly interesting. She paused to skim through a rather smug editorial in the *Telegraph* about the coming coronation and the new Elizabethan age it would surely herald, and didn't even bother to inspect the included map of the route the queen's procession would take.

Only one point on the map mattered to her: the stretch of Northumberland Avenue that, by some happy accident of geography, was only yards from the spot where the Blue Lion had stood for centuries. The hotel wasn't directly on the procession route, but its position mere yards from the avenue, with nothing but a stretch of open pavement between it and the route, was close enough as made no difference and, crucially, the view from its upper floors across the avenue was clear and entirely unobstructed.

Only once before had a coronation procession passed by the hotel, and that had been in 1937, when the queen's father had been crowned. Edie couldn't remember much from that day, apart from the crowds and cheering and general air of celebration at the hotel; she'd been too busy to even spare the time to watch the gold coach pass by. The hotel had been full to bursting, but that had been in the old days, before the war, and if her parents had been excited by their proximity to the festivities they certainly hadn't said as much to Edie.

In the months after the queen's accession, as she and the rest of the world waited for details of the coronation to be announced, Edie hadn't allowed herself to hope that Northumberland Avenue would once again be part of the official route; the anonymous men who made such decisions might easily decide to send the entire parade up the Mall and straight down Whitehall to the Abbey instead. Yet the official route had included Northumberland Avenue after all, and the queen would indeed pass by the Blue Lion, and Edie had eight guest rooms at the front of her hotel with excellent views—she'd run upstairs and checked, just to be absolutely certain. In that instant last July, seeing the map in the newspaper for the first time, she had known one thing straightaway: She and the Blue Lion had been given a chance.

Now it was 1953 and six of those eight rooms were booked, each of them at the monstrous sum of seventy-five guineas a night with a minimum stay of one week starting the Saturday before the second of June, and none of the people who had written and cabled and even rung up the hotel had balked at the cost. Only later had she learned that other hotels, and indeed anyone in possession of windows with even a half-decent view of the procession's route, were asking hundreds and even thousands of pounds for a single day's rental of a well-situated room.

All the same, the profits from those few days would be enough to carry along the Blue Lion for some months. Enough to put off any dispiriting conversations with the bank for a while. And maybe, just maybe, it would allow her to save the only home she had ever known.

Chapter Two

STELLA GIOVANNA DONATI

Tuesday, January 6, 1953

Stella was not *un*happy.

She loved Rome, even though it was noisy, loud, smelly, and occasionally almost too much for a girl who had spent the past seven years living on a farm in the Veneto. She enjoyed her work at Signor Rosato's foreign-language bookshop in the Piazza del Spagna, where the customers were interesting, the work was rarely taxing, and her wages were generous enough to pay her rent, eat well, buy pretty clothes, send some money home, and keep her camera, the only truly valuable object she owned, loaded with film.

She loved the neighborhood where she lived, only a few hundred meters from the shop, in a shared flat on the top floor of a decrepit palazzo on the Vicolo del Babuino, and while her room was only big enough for a bed and table and a folding chair, it was, all the same, hers alone. It even had a view, for if she leaned out her window and looked to the right, she could just spy the squared turrets that topped the Villa Medici.

Life in Rome was wonderful, but Stella was lonely, and more than a little homesick, too. She missed her zia Rosa and nonno Aldo and the rest of her adopted family. She missed the sounds and smells of the farm and its animals, and the chores that had become as familiar as her next breath. She missed the softly huffing dialect that everyone used in Mezzo Ciel, its words and cadences so different from the formal Italian her parents had spoken at work and home alike.

But she had learned to live with loneliness, just as she had learned to endure the absence of her parents. Their deaths were an old wound, imperfectly healed, that would never stop aching. Painful, yes, but not enough to prevent her from recognizing moments of joy in the new life she had created for herself. She would not, *could* not, betray their memory by allowing herself to be unhappy.

So Stella was not unhappy, but she could not say, either, that she was truly content. Her work at the bookshop was pleasant enough, but it did not inspire her, nor did she believe it would lead anywhere beyond her little room with its scrap of a view and her not-quite friendships with flatmates who knew nothing of the life she had once lived.

Anna-Maria, Sofia, and Bruna were friendly girls, and were generous in their efforts to include Stella in their conversations and evenings out. She'd learned the names of their beaux, and heard about where they'd grown up, how they'd come to live in Rome, and their plans for the future. In return, she had shared a little of her own stories. Not enough to upset them, nor enough that they would look upon her with pity. Only the bare bones of her life, or rather lives, before she had come to Rome.

The other girls knew Stella's parents were dead, but as she never elaborated, and they were too polite to ask, or possibly uninterested, she was spared the burden of sharing the truth. That her life, the life she ought to have lived, had been stolen from her, and even now, nearly eight years after her liberation, she still had not discovered where she was meant to go and who she was meant to become.

She had been set adrift on a wide and empty sea, and though her raft had reached the opposite shore, the world she now inhabited felt, at times, like a foreign place where she understood the language, could make sense of the customs, but would never quite belong.

More than once, Stella had begun a heartfelt letter to her friend Nina, who had saved her at Birkenau, and had cast herself in the role of elder sister from then on. It was Nina's family who had taken Stella in after the war, but in the years since, her friend had moved away from the farm in Mezzo Ciel and was now married, studying for a degree in medicine, and busy with two small children. Nina was happy in the life she had made for herself, and Stella could not bear the thought of stealing so much as a gram of her joy. So she kept her silence, and when Nina or Zia Rosa asked if she was happy Stella told them she was.

And then she told herself it was not a lie, but rather a prediction. One day she would be happy again. One day she would be content in the life she had made for herself.

When she had first come to Rome some eight months ago, Stella had visited nearly every newspaper, magazine, and news agency with offices in the city and asked if they were hiring photographers. Each time she had left behind an envelope of her best pictures. Precisely three of her attempts had resulted in polite but formulaic replies that had thanked her for her interest before conveying their profound regret at being unable to offer her a position. The remainder had simply ignored her, and the knowledge that her photographs had likely been dropped in a bin was disheartening enough to prevent her from persisting.

She would simply have to become a better photographer. She would study the newspapers and magazines to see what they were publishing, and she would improve her technical skills—she had already read and practically memorized every book on photography that Signor Rosato carried in the shop—and she would, in time, assemble a portfolio of work that would impress even the most discerning editor.

"WHEN YOU'VE FINISHED wrapping up the orders to go out by post, my dear, could you set out the newsmagazines from America and England?"

"Of course, Signor Rosato," Stella replied, though she had already begun the latter chore.

"I'll go upstairs for my dinner and a nap, I think. Are you all right to keep the shop open? The tourists never seem to bother with a proper meal and rest."

"I don't mind at all," she said, briskly sorting the magazines into neat piles. The new issue of *Picture Weekly* from London had arrived, its cover an eye-catching photograph of the pretty English queen in a strapless gown, and she set it aside to read while she ate her own modest lunch of bread, cheese, and dried figs, the latter now quite squashed, which Zia Rosa had sent in her latest parcel.

It took hardly any time at all for Stella to set out the magazines and newspapers on their racks, ready for the foreign tourists hungry for news from home, and once that was accomplished, and the rest of the shop returned to a state of perfect tidiness, she retreated to the back room, her ears alert to the arrival of any customers, and ate her lunch at a pace that would have horrified her zia. All the better to allow her a few minutes of leisure to perch on Signor Rosato's stool behind the front counter and look through *Picture Weekly* without fear of marring its pristine pages with crumbs or greasy fingerprints.

She read through it quickly, focusing on the photographs before returning to the opening pages. The editor's letter touched upon the coming coronation of Queen Elizabeth as well as other newsworthy events in the months ahead, and at the bottom of the page, unusually, there was an advertisement.

PHOTOGRAPHER WANTED

We are looking for a news photographer to join our staff. Experience in magazines or daily news preferred but not essential. Apply in writing with samples of your work (include explanatory captions) to:
Walter Kaczmarek, *Picture Weekly*,
87 Fleet Street, London EC4

She lost track of how long she sat there, staring at that single paragraph of text, wondering and hoping and warning herself there was no chance, not a single chance, that a magazine as well-known and respected as *Picture Weekly* would be interested in her humble photographs. Her favorite subjects were ordinary people doing, for the most part, ordinary things: an elderly man reading a newspaper as he waited for a tram; a young couple wandering around the gardens at the Villa Medici, their faces tilted toward the thin winter sunshine; a nun, her habit flapping in the wind, chasing after a handful of pamphlets she'd dropped while crossing Piazza San Pietro.

The bell above the door jangled as a gaggle of American tourists came into the shop, likely in search of copies of *Time* or *Life* or the *Herald-Tribune*. She directed them to the appropriate rack, gave them directions to the Keats-Shelley house only a few meters away, and, when they came to pay, patiently counted out the coins they found so unfamiliar.

It wasn't until Signor Rosato had returned from his nap and taken charge once more that she was able to retreat into the back room and copy out the advertisement on a scrap of wrapping paper. Later, when she wasn't so busy, she would allow herself to think about it, and to consider whether it was worth the small cost of sending a packet of her photographs to England, where they would be appraised and judged and likely found wanting.

Yet she knew they were good, and she felt hopeful that Walter Kaczmarek would like and appreciate her work. Perhaps not enough to offer her a job; such imaginings required a feat of imagination far beyond her capabilities. But she would regret it if she did not try.

Stella was tired by the time she got home from work. Her flatmates had eaten earlier, but they'd been kind enough to set aside a bowl of pasta e fagioli for her. She didn't bother to warm it, nor did she bother to sit, instead gobbling it down as she stood by the sink. Then she did the dishes and swept the floor and made a cup of coffee in the battered old cafetière that had come with the flat.

Only then did she go to her room and take out the box of photographs from beneath her bed. She would select half a dozen—she already knew, without looking, which ones she would choose—and send them to England, and she would be honest in the letter she wrote to the editor of *Picture Weekly*.

January 6, 1953

Dear Mr. Kaczmarek,

I wish to apply for the position of photographer as advertised in your magazine. The photographs I enclose were taken on my Sirio Firenza Elettra camera in natural light with a 50-mm lens on ASA 100 film. As requested, I have described the subjects and setting on the reverse of each.

Although I do not have any formal training as a photographer, I am prepared to work hard and learn quickly. I speak and read English competently and I also have a good working knowledge of French, Spanish, and Dutch.

I thank you for your consideration and I eagerly await your reply.

Yours very truly,
Miss Stella Donati
c/o Liberia Rosato
Piazza Spagnolo
Rome, Italy

Chapter Three

ALEXANDER JAMES GEDDES

Monday, January 19, 1953

Jamie had slept poorly, although that was nothing new, and then he'd drunk too much coffee on an empty stomach, and now he was feeling queasy and hungry and headachy all at once. What he needed, now, was breakfast and some aspirin tablets and a short nap, and then he'd be ready to face what promised to be a not-so-good day. It was, depressingly, the latest in a long string of not-so-good days.

But then the morning post arrived with a message from Hugh. A surprise, to be sure, for Jamie didn't often hear from his art dealer, and when he did it was more in the way of badgering reminders that artists who didn't regularly produce salable work also tended to be artists who had difficulty in paying their bills.

Hugh meant to be encouraging, but the refrain had become tedious. "Bugger the voice in your head that says you're a hack," he'd told Jamie when they'd last met in

December. "Get to work and stop whingeing. And enough with the doom and gloom. Paint some flowers for a change. Or a beautiful woman."

This time the message was succinct: "Ring me as soon as you get this." And that meant Hugh had news. Exciting news—perhaps a sale? Fortunately there was a phone box outside the newsagents' at the end of the street.

"Campion Galleries, Miss Halliwell speaking."

"Hello, Meg. It's James Geddes. Hugh asked me to ring him straightaway."

"Oh, right. He's not in his office, I don't think . . . let me track him down. Won't be a moment."

His headache was becoming exponentially worse. If Hugh didn't—

"Jamie? That was quick."

"You did ask me to ring straightaway."

"Yes, because I've some good news for you. A letter from the Master of the Worshipful Company of Cartwrights and Wainwrights—"

"The what?"

"One of the city's livery companies. Sounds like something you'd read about in Pepys's diaries, but they're real enough."

"Are they still in the business of making carts and wagons?"

"I think they run more to charitable works these days. Helping widows and orphans, I suppose, and paying school fees for a deserving few. That sort of thing. I will say their endowment is rumored to be enormous. More capital than the queen herself, and their wine cellar is the stuff of legends."

"That's well and fine, but what does it have to do with me?"

"I was about to tell you. Archibald Owens, the fellow who wrote to me, wants to speak with you about a commission. A significant one, in his words. I gather he saw your work at the R.A. last summer and was impressed."

"You're sure it isn't a mistake? It was my painting he saw at the Royal Academy? *My* work?"

"Yours indeed. I rang him up, just to make sure of it. I think they're celebrating their five-hundredth anniversary? Or something like that."

"Did he mention how much?"

"No, but you should ask for at least a hundred pounds. That is, if you agree to it."

"As if I'd turn down such an offer."

"You have before, or do you not recall your impassioned speech about how you'll never allow your vision to be compromised by the empty promises of commercial success? Or words to that effect?"

"I do, although I'm fairly sure I was three sheets to the wind at the time. The thing is . . . I'm not sure I can afford my scruples this month. Not when we're talking about a hundred pounds. How did you leave things with them?"

"He wants to meet with you. Can you manage tomorrow afternoon at half-past one?"

"Yes. Yes, of course."

"I'll let them know. Try to get a decent night's sleep. And be on your best behavior."

"Whenever am I not?"

"Come on, Jamie. You know how it works. You pay the bills with commissions like this, and you take them on even if you have to hold your nose and plug your ears. If Rembrandt could do it, so can you. Tell me you understand."

He'd known that it wouldn't be easy. He'd known all along, and he'd made his peace with it, mostly, but it had begun to wear him down. The paintings he sold through Hugh's gallery brought in enough to keep the wolf from the door, just, but he was thirty-three years old and as poor as a church mouse, and he was tired of it.

"Yes, Hugh," he said. "I understand."

"Good. Now write this down so you don't forget: Cartwrights' Hall, number eight Northumberland Avenue, half-past one tomorrow. And don't be late."

"Wood Green isn't all that far. It'll only take an hour on the bus. Shall I ring you after I'm finished with—what was his name again?"

"Owens. And, yes, let me know how you get on. Good luck."

A DAY LATER, give or take a few hours, and Jamie found himself in an uncomfortable chair in a gloomy anteroom in a not-so-ancient pile of soot-etched stone on Northumberland Avenue near Charing Cross. He'd already weathered the incredulous reaction from the master's secretary, but that was nothing new. Instead he ignored her acidic stares and turned his attention to the dreadful portraits of past guild worthies on the opposite wall. It was only an assumption, though. Given their subjects' pink and well-fed appearances, the paintings might just as easily have depicted a collection of boiled hams.

"Mr. Geddes? The master and wardens will see you now. Through the door to my right."

The room he now entered was a surprise. It was absolutely enormous, as airy as a ballroom, and enviably bright, too, with tall south-facing windows that began at hip height and soared to the ceiling. To his left was a desk with the approximate acreage of a barge; to his right, a long and sumptuously polished table. Three men were seated at its far end, one at its head and the other two on the side closest to the windows. A fourth chair sat empty on the near side of the table.

As Jamie came forward, he realized the portraits in the waiting room had not lied, for the trio at the table shared the rather porcine features of men accustomed to lives of undisturbed comfort and repose. The man at the head of the table now stood and reached out to shake Jamie's hand.

"I'm Archibald Owens, Master of the Worshipful Company of Cartwrights and Wainwrights. Welcome to Cartwrights' Hall, Mr. Geddes."

"A pleasure to meet you, sir."

"Allow me to introduce two of our wardens, Philip Warburton and Richard Mallory." The others nodded, but neither offered to shake his hand. Instead they exchanged alarmed glances, not troubling to hide their reaction behind a veneer of civility.

If Owens noticed, he gave no sign of it. "Do sit," he said instead. "Would you like something to drink? Some tea? A glass of sherry?"

"No, thank you." Jamie sat in the empty chair and placed his portfolio on the table. It held color photographs of his larger paintings, as well as the sketchbook and bundle of pencils and vine charcoal he always carried.

"Very well. I suppose I'll begin by saying that I saw your painting at the summer exhibition last year—"

"*Trafalgar Square*?" Jamie finished.

"Yes. That's the one. Thought it was terribly good, you know."

"Thank you, sir."

He was surprised that anyone had seen the thing, given its relegation to one of the lesser rooms amid painfully sincere portraits of rosy-cheeked debutantes and formulaic homages to Constable and Turner. "What did you like about it?" he asked, too curious to resist.

"I, well . . . I was out of the city on VE Day. Staying with friends in the country. And I suppose your painting made me feel as if I'd been there, too, celebrating with half of London. I rather think it reminded me of how I felt that day. How we all felt."

"Thank you. I appreciate the compliment."

Hugh had insisted he submit *Trafalgar Square* for the summer exhibition. Jamie had protested, certain it would be rejected. But Hugh had been sure it would lead to good things, and the painting had been accepted, and now, months later, it had brought him here.

"What did you do during the war?" one of the other men asked, his chins wobbling above a too-tight collar.

"Bomb disposal with the Royal Engineers. In London to begin, then North Africa, then Italy." Jamie squelched the urge to ask how the man, whose name he had already forgotten, had himself spent the war. He doubted it had involved anything more dangerous than the occasional paper cut.

"You had a long war," Owens said approvingly.

"Yes, sir."

Such an anodyne way to describe the worst years of his

life. Something like fifteen hundred days, though he'd held back from ever counting them definitively. Most had been forgettable; most had faded from his memory. But the bad ones, the ones marked by bursts of heart-stopping terror amid the tedium of his long, long war . . . those days had etched themselves into the marrow of his bones.

"And before that?" the third man asked, his bland face made memorable by a nicotine-stained moustache that crept north into his nostrils and south past his upper lip.

"I was at Oxford," Jamie said. "Modern Greats."

"College?" Wobbly Chins asked.

"Merton. Following my father and grandfather." Not that it mattered. Not that it shed any particular light on Jamie's character or accomplishments. But men like Wobbly Chins and Revolting Moustache seemed to think it would.

"Splendid," Owens said. "Simply splendid. Now, if we've finished with introductions, I suppose I ought to tell you why you're here."

"Hugh Campion mentioned a commission. Something in connection with the company's five-hundredth anniversary."

"Exactly that, but as it also coincides with the coronation of Her Majesty the Queen, I had the notion you might combine the two."

"I'm not sure I understand."

Chins and Moustache all but rolled their eyes at this, but he ignored them. Owens was the only man in the room he needed to impress.

"Of course, of course—you likely wouldn't know. The coronation procession will pass by this very building, and I want a painting of that exact moment. Obviously I'm not an artist like yourself, but I can picture it quite clearly. Our hall in the background, and the queen herself, in her gold coach, right in the front."

As a composition, it wasn't particularly original, but it could become a striking one. "I see. Only . . . you do mean *this* building? It can't be more than fifty or sixty years old."

"Our original hall was destroyed in the Blitz. All that old timber, you know, but rather luckily we found this place going cheap not long after. Rather unheard of to move so far from the city, but the gunmakers guild is over in Whitechapel and no one's ever kicked up a fuss about *that*. Still. We've been here for nearly ten years, and as our anniversary lines up with Coronation Year, I thought we ought to mark the occasion with a painting. A really big one. And we'll put it there." Owens pointed across the room to a beautiful landscape that hung on the wall behind the great desk.

Astonishingly, Jamie recognized the scene of a hay wagon laden with exhausted farm workers, though only from a description and rather poor photograph in the artist's catalogue raisonné. "But that's a Gainsborough."

"Damned gloomy thing. We'll find somewhere else for it."

"I don't know what to say," Jamie hedged, knowing that he ought to display some degree of enthusiasm. "Apart from thank you, of course. I'm honored."

"We're prepared to offer a considerable sum as your fee. I thought, perhaps, two hundred guineas?"

Two hundred? It was difficult to maintain a neutral expression, let alone formulate a dignified response.

"Is that not satisfactory?" Owens asked, his air of bonhomie beginning to waver.

"I beg your pardon. It is, yes. More than satisfactory. It's only that . . ."

He wanted the commission, wanted it quite badly, but he had to know if the image in his mind's eye was even possible. "I have to see for myself," he said abruptly. He stood, his chair skittering back with a screech, and retrieved his sketchbook and pencils from the portfolio at his elbow. "I'll be back shortly."

Ignoring the volley of whispers at his back, he strode past the vinegary secretary, down the swath of marble stairs, and across the road, dodging cars and buses rather than waiting for a break in the traffic. Only then, once he was safely on the far pavement, did he turn to survey the unremarkable frontage of Cartwrights' Hall.

It wasn't far enough; his view of the building was too cramped, too hemmed in. Swinging around, he noticed an open area where a second, far more narrow street joined the avenue at an angle. He retreated until he was almost on the doorstep of a small hotel, opened his sketchbook, and flipped to an empty page.

He captured the view quickly, with sure, swift lines of charcoal, checking his wristwatch from time to time. Another few details, one last look, and he was done. It took only seconds to return to the cavernous ballroom-turned-office across the way. As he'd suspected, the men he'd left behind were engaged in an agitated conversation, but they quieted as soon as he set the drawing before them.

"Is this what you have in mind?" he asked. "Not the sketch itself—it's only the work of a few minutes. I mean the way I've set things out. Can you see? Your hall will take up most of the canvas, as I've shown here, and in the foreground will be the queen in her coach, and because it's not a solid thing—the coach, I mean—it won't block the view of Cartwrights' Hall."

"So the queen here, and our hall behind her . . . ?"

"Yes. Think of the coach as a frame for a portrait of the queen. Then that portrait, in turn, will also be part of a larger view of the hall. Does that make sense? Her face will be turned in your direction, and she'll be waving"—here Jamie mimed the upturned hand and serene wave he'd seen in newsreels—"and you, the observer, will feel as if you are there, too. As if it's Coronation Day all over again."

"Oh, yes," said Mr. Owens. "Yes, indeed. That is *exactly* what we want."

But Chins was frowning. "You speak of depicting the queen, but have you actually done any portraiture?"

"I have, though it hasn't been exhibited widely. I'm confident the queen in my painting will look just as you'd expect." Even as he spoke, Jamie turned to a fresh page in his sketchbook and began to draw. A few swift lines, a swipe or two of his thumb to rub back the charcoal here and there, and he was done. "There," he said, pushing it back across the table. "Will that do?"

The young queen was smiling as she looked over her left shoulder, her eyes widening in delight. It was just this side of a caricature, and really no more than a party trick, but he'd captured her likeness well enough.

Now he only had to wait for Chins or Moustache, or indeed both of them, to voice some version of the protest he'd been expecting all along.

"Are you certain, Archibald?" Chins asked.

"I am. And I do wish—"

"But he's a *foreigner*," Moustache hissed.

At last, there it was.

"True enough," Jamie admitted. "I am a Scot. But then, so is the queen mother. Or perhaps I have it wrong. I mean, I am a Presbyterian. Is that the problem?"

The man's nostrils, and the oily yellow broom of hair beneath them, flared with distaste. "You know very well what I mean."

"If it's my nationality that concerns you, I was born and raised in Edinburgh. But I think we all know you're referring to my ethnicity." He paused, hoping it might add to the discomfort of the men who saw fit to question his existence. "My mother is Indian by birth. She met my father when they were both undergraduates at Oxford. Is that what you wanted to know?"

Only Owens was brave enough to meet Jamie's gaze. "Please take no notice of my colleagues' antediluvian notions. I very much wish for you to take up the commission. To that end, I've drawn up a contract. It's signed and dated, and I've also had a check drawn up for the first half of your fee."

Jamie looked over the contract, for once glad of the years he'd spent as a law student after the war. There was nothing concerning, so he added his signature, pushed it back across the table, and accepted the proffered check from Owens. This he placed in his portfolio, along with his sketchbook and pencils, before leaning forward to shake Owens's hand.

"Thank you, sir. I'll keep you apprised of my progress."

And then he was outside again, standing on the pavement, willing his hands not to shake. Reminding himself to breathe.

Two hundred guineas was a handsome fee. That was something to think of in the long, lonely, doubting hours before dawn. He'd won the commission for an important piece, and soon he'd have money in his pocket, and he wouldn't have to think about what came next for a good, long while. His headache had vanished, too, and the sun was shining, and he could almost remember what it felt like to be happy.

It was a good day.

Chapter Four

EDIE

Monday, January 26, 1953

Edie closed her office door, intent on avoiding interruptions, but when the telephone at the front desk rang a few minutes later, she let her attention wander. She could hear Mr. Brooks speaking, his voice an indistinct murmur, and then the telephone on her desk began to trill. She crossed her fingers, hoping it was a guest in search of a reservation and not an irate vendor in search of payment for an overdue invoice.

"Good afternoon, the Blue Lion, Miss Howard speaking."

"Miss Howard. David Bamford here. I'm in London for the week, and I thought perhaps you might agree to join me for supper tonight. I thought the Grill at the Savoy? Or Quaglino's if you're game to venture farther afield?"

It had been some time since she'd last seen Mr. Bamford, so hearing his voice was a pleasant surprise. He was a fellow hotelier, though the string of properties he owned was far more profitable than the Blue Lion, and he had first approached her, back in October, with a request for advice on the challenges of managing a historic property.

He'd collected her for lunch in a motorcar of jaw-dropping proportions, complete with an impassive driver who had opened her door and only nodded when informed of their destination. Its cavernous interior had smelled of leather and expensive cologne and rather more faintly of cigar smoke, and the engine had purred like a contented tiger.

He'd taken her to lunch at his club in Belgravia, the sort of place she'd only ever read about, with footmen in livery and a ladies' lounge where female guests might dine without wounding the tender sensibilities of the club's more antiquated members. She'd felt a little out of place at first, and more than a little cowed by the hushed tones and rarefied atmosphere of the place, but after a glass of delicious claret and an enormous serving of tender roast beef and featherlight Yorkshire pudding, she had found it much easier to unbend and enjoy herself.

When Mr. Bamford had then asked if she would sell him the Blue Lion, she hadn't understood, not right away, for the wine and rich food had left her feeling rather sleepy.

"I beg your pardon. Did you say you wished to buy the hotel?"

"I did."

It had been years since anyone had shown an interest in the hotel—since before the war at least. She remembered that her father had dismissed the offer out of hand, and had counseled Edie to do the same if ever presented with the opportunity, no matter how tempting.

"Are you serious?" she'd asked. Perhaps he was joking.

"I am. I really do wish to buy the hotel, Miss Howard, and I'm prepared to be very generous."

"I don't know what to say. Apart from no, of course. The Blue Lion has been owned by my family for nearly four hundred years. I couldn't possibly sell it."

"I understand your reluctance, but I'm sure we could come to an agreement that would suit us both. The history would not be lost, nor would I change the name, or indeed remove any of the period features that make it such a charming place."

"All the same, I assure you that I am not interested." She'd pushed back her chair, ready to leave, but Mr. Bamford had caught hold of her hand before she could stand.

"Do stay. We haven't finished our lunch, and I would like to get to know you."

"All the better to convince me to sell up?"

"No, Miss Howard. Only because I find you interesting, and I've enjoyed your stories of life at the Blue Lion very much. I won't say another word today on the subject of buying it. I promise."

She had stayed, and by the time he'd dropped her off at the Blue Lion, she had, again with the help of his club's excellent food and wine, all but forgotten his offer to buy the hotel. So much so that she had readily agreed to accompany him to dinner at the beginning of December.

Once more he had asked if the hotel was for sale, and once more she had refused. He had been perfectly civil about it, but the renewal of his offer had rankled. He had said, more than once now, that he wished to get to know her, but she suspected—in fact she was all but certain—

that his interest was driven solely by his determination to acquire her hotel.

She had said as much as they'd wished each other a good night in the front hall of the Blue Lion after their dinner in December. "You've been very kind, Mr. Bamford, and terribly generous, but you're wasting your time. I won't sell my hotel, not to you or anyone else, and I won't change my mind. I think it's only fair that I let you know before you waste any more of your time or money on my account."

"I know. And it's not a waste."

He had left without proposing a further evening out, which rather belied his insistence that time spent in her company was worthwhile, and after some weeks of silence she had assumed, not without regret, that she had seen the last of him. Until today.

"Dinner tonight? That is indeed short notice," she protested.

"Shall we say half-seven?"

"If you'll let me finish, Mr. Bamford. While I am happy to hear from you, I was about to say—"

"I'll see you tonight." With that he rang off, leaving her to stare at the buzzing telephone receiver.

Drat the man. What if she'd had plans?

And she did. After supper with her staff, she intended to go over the following week's menus with Cook and together draw up the orders for the butcher, grocer, and greengrocer. Then she would inspect the corridors and staff areas for any damage that needed repairing. Last of all, just before bed, she would wash her knickers and brassiere and stockings in the sink in her room, since it was too dear to send them out to be laundered. If she wasn't too tired once she was done with her chores, she might even read for half an hour.

And yet . . . she hadn't had an evening out since her dinner with Mr. Bamford in December, and the prospect of eating at a really fine restaurant was rather tempting. It would be easy enough to meet with Cook that afternoon, and the other chores might wait a day or so.

Her father would certainly have shut the door in David Bamford's face, as would her grandfather before him. Both had turned down offers to sell up; both had refused to believe that the Blue Lion might ever be owned by anyone other than a direct descendant of Jacob Howard himself.

But they were dead and gone, and she had been left to go on alone, and she fancied an evening out. It was not a betrayal. It was only dinner, nothing more, and she had more than earned a few hours of leisure.

IT WAS ALMOST seven o'clock when Edie finished the last of the day's paperwork and returned to her room to change. She only had three frocks that would pass muster in a first-rate restaurant, and Mr. Bamford had seen her in two of them. The blue wool it would have to be.

It was three years old, and though in pristine condition was no longer quite as smart as when she'd first bought it. Its skirt still swirled prettily around her legs, though, and it was made of a dark blue wool—ocean blue, she liked to think of it, rather than a more prosaic navy blue—that was ever so flattering. She put on her mother's pearls, stepped into the same black leather court shoes she always wore, and set her best hat on her head. It was a simple black felt crescent overlaid with a swirl of dotted veiling, and she'd always thought it becoming, if not precisely chic. Her hair was still neat, with only a few ringlets escaping from her low bun; these she pinned back severely. Her lipstick had faded since the afternoon, so she dabbed on more. The color suited her, she supposed, though the name was ridiculous. *Rascal Red*, indeed.

She put on her coat, still presentable after five winters, and gathered up her gloves and handbag, and only then did she stop to survey her appearance in the looking glass that sat on her dresser. She looked fine. Decently dressed, neat as a proverbial pin, with ordinary hazel eyes and medium-brown hair and a good complexion with scarcely a wrinkle to show for her thirty-two years. She had never been thought of as a pretty girl; not even when she'd been young and hopeful and happy had anyone complimented her looks beyond a general assertion that she looked well or nice or fine. But she would do.

She was waiting in her office, or rather pacing back and forth, when she heard the front door open, followed by Arthur's greeting and promise to fetch her. A deep breath for courage, another for good measure, and then she entered the hall.

"Good evening, Mr. Bamford."

"Good evening. You look smashing."

It was kind of him to say so, and he did seem sincere enough. Either that, or he was a criminally accomplished liar. "Thank you," she answered, resolved not to let the compliment go to her head.

Turning to Arthur, she offered an explanation. "I'll be out for a few hours, but I certainly won't be late. If there's an emergency of any sort I'll be"—and here she turned to Mr. Bamford—"Where will we be?"

"The Grill at the Savoy."

Arthur was too well trained to offer anything but the most neutral reaction. "Very good. Enjoy your evening, Miss Howard. Mr. Bamford."

The rather vulgar motorcar she remembered from her previous outings with Mr. Bamford was idling outside, its driver as stone-faced as ever, and without thinking Edie allowed herself to be guided into its plush interior. Only then did she recall their destination. "Didn't you say we're going to the Savoy? It's hardly more than a five-minute walk."

"It wouldn't do to arrive on foot. It's raining, besides."

"It's winter. It always rains."

"I hate getting my feet wet," he countered. "And I wasn't lying before. You really do look splendid." His smile, a flash of gleaming white in the dark of the car, was mildly startling.

"Thank you."

"I'm not trying to make you uncomfortable. Only to offer you an honest compliment."

"I suppose most women like to be complimented on their appearance. And it's not that I don't. Only, I suppose, that I would rather be praised for things that matter to me."

"Such as?"

"My work. The work I do in running the Blue Lion."

"You do a fine job of it. As I've told you more than once."

She was still formulating an answer that wouldn't seem as if she were fishing for compliments when the car turned off the Strand into the entrance of the Savoy. The driver pulled up on the right-hand side of the laneway—a hold-over from the days of carriages, her grandfather had once told her—where a grandly liveried attendant opened her door and ushered her onward.

The maître d'hôtel stood waiting at the entrance to the Grill, all smiles and practiced charm as he greeted Mr. Bamford by name, took their coats, and guided them across the neoclassical splendor of the dining room. Nearly every table was occupied, with many of the diners, likely theatergoers, dressed to the nines; but others, she saw with some relief, wore less formal attire. Never mind that most of it was bespoke in origin and cost the earth.

After helping Edie with her chair, furnishing them both with menus, and promising the imminent arrival of their waiter, the maître d'hôtel took his leave.

"Cigarette?" Mr. Bamford asked, opening an engraved silver case and offering it to her.

"No, thank you," she answered, though she had already told him, several times, that she didn't smoke.

"I hope you don't mind that we're in a quieter part of the dining room," he went on, once he was finished with the business of lighting his cigarette and exhaling a showy plume of smoke across the table. "It's impossible to carry on a conversation if you're in the middle of things. Forever being interrupted by people who want to say hello."

"I quite understand." She supposed she did, after a fash-ion. When was the last time, after all, that she'd eaten an entire meal undisturbed?

"What do you think?"

"It's beautiful," she answered, for it was. Heartbreak-ingly beautiful.

The important thing was to ignore the quality of everything she saw and touched, for if she allowed herself to truly consider the beauty and luxury that now surrounded her, she would surely despair. Even the snowy perfection of the napkins and tablecloth was depressing, for she couldn't help but compare them to the linens in use at the Blue Lion. Though pristine in their cleanliness, they were worn thin from age, along with everything else her guests touched, ate from, and sat or slept upon.

"Have you been before?" he asked.

"Yes. When I was little. My grandfather would bring me for lunch on my birthday. He liked to say he was keeping an eye on the competition."

At the time, she hadn't realized it was a joke, and a self-deprecating one at that. To her mind, the Blue Lion had been perfect, entirely perfect. So she had believed her grandfather.

She couldn't remember, now, when she had stopped believing. When the weight of it all had fallen upon her, and she had finally seen, and understood, and accepted her fate as the last of the Howards.

He nodded, his expression coolly assessing, and then his attention was drawn to a spot over her shoulder. Edie glanced around, following his gaze; their waiter was standing at a discreet distance, his face a genial blank.

"Good evening, Mr. Bamford, madam. Welcome to the Grill Room."

"Thank you. I'm afraid we haven't so much as opened our menus."

"Perhaps a cocktail to begin?"

Mr. Bamford nodded. "Excellent. A manhattan for me. Miss Howard?"

"I'll have a Mary Pickford." Her grandfather had always ordered them, she remembered, and once he'd allowed her a small sip. The cocktail had tasted of pineapple and something much stronger that had made her eyes water and her tongue sting just a little.

"Very good, madam."

She waited until the waiter had departed before opening her menu. "Is there anything you recommend?"

"I always have the beefsteak, so I can't speak to anything else. Sorry."

Edie was still trying to decide when the waiter returned with their drinks. She accepted hers gratefully and took a fortifying sip.

"And?" Mr. Bamford asked.

"Lovely," she managed, for her cocktail seemed to be concocted entirely of spirits. If she didn't drink it slowly she would be pickled through before their first course arrived.

"Has madam decided on what she would like to order?" the waiter prompted.

"Oh, yes. I'll have the smoked trout to start, and then the saddle of lamb."

"Very good. And Mr. Bamford?"

"The potted shrimps, if you please, with the sirloin to follow. Rare, with shoestring potatoes and whatever you have that's green."

"Of course. The sommelier will be over presently."

The sommelier arrived only seconds later, and after a

brief conversation Mr. Bamford ordered a bottle of what she suspected was a fearfully expensive claret.

"There. With any luck the interruptions will be at a minimum from now on. I want to begin by apologizing for my behavior when we first met."

"Go on," she said, chancing another sip of her alarmingly potent cocktail.

"I ought to have warned you that I was interested in buying the Blue Lion. Been more explicit when I first spoke with you."

"More explicit than a fellow hotelier seeking advice?"

"Yes, well. I didn't want to scare you off. My offer was sincere. It still is. And I think it's time you set your emotions aside and considered it seriously."

"Who's to say that I didn't?" Edie countered. She took another, rather larger, sip of her drink, which would undoubtedly have knocked the real Mary Pickford off her feet. "I know, better than anyone, what I'm facing."

"Do you truly? Because I'm not certain you fully comprehend just how precarious a footing you're on. You've a property, a very valuable property, which has increased in value by an exponential factor since your grandfather's day. We both know that. But it's an ancient building, and it needs constant attention, and in the meantime your capital has been whittled away to nothing, first by death duties—that's a matter of public record, let me remind you—and more recently by repairs and general upkeep."

True. All true. She gulped down the last of her cocktail, praying it would armor her against the rest of his indictment.

"But the costs of running the place keep growing, and your guests are fussy. To attract them you need all the mod cons, but three of your best rooms are occupied by old dears who have scarcely more than their pensions to pay for their room and board. The guests you do attract are penny-pinching businessmen or provincials in from the Home Counties for a day or two of shopping and theater. And each year, each month, there are fewer of them. I've done my research. We both know it's true."

It was. Every last word of it.

"Miss Howard. Edwina. Won't you look at me?"

So she did. She met his gaze squarely, and only when she sensed that his discomfort had begun to match her own did she respond. "Things are not as hopeless as all that. We are on the procession route for the coronation, you know, with every room booked up from the middle of May onward."

"Yes, but for how long? No—I don't expect you to tell me. Only consider what comes after. How often can you expect a coronation? Perhaps once every thirty years or so? And if we're honest, the uptick in bookings is only because you happen to be on the parade route. I doubt you saw a bump in bookings for the Festival of Britain or the Olympics."

He had softened his voice. He was trying to convince her that he was her friend. That he understood. "I'll say one last thing on the subject, and then we'll talk of something else. All of these difficulties and troubles? They're only going to get worse."

After such a statement, what else was there to discuss? Never mind that he was absolutely, horrifyingly, correct.

"Mr. Bamford. The Blue Lion is more than a ledger

sheet to me. More than a building I can sell. It is my livelihood and that of the people who know me best. It is my *home*. And here you sit, and talk to me as if I'm an ignorant fool who is blind to the truth. I assure you, I know every bit of that truth, for it's all I see when I close my eyes at night. The Blue Lion is everything to me, and I will do everything I can to save it."

It was a fine speech, if rather too grand for anywhere other than the House of Commons, and nothing she might say or do that evening could hope to top it. So she pushed back her chair, gathered up her handbag and gloves, and stood. "I have heard enough. Good evening. I can see myself home."

She swept past the waiter, who had been about to unveil their first course, and by the time she reached the foyer the maître d'hôtel, presumably an old hand at managing stormy exits, had retrieved her coat. She shrugged it on and kept walking, out onto the Strand and in the direction of home.

She refused to run, and she certainly would not allow herself to cry. Tears were a luxury she could only allow herself in the privacy of her room.

"Miss Howard—"

She would not look around.

"Miss Howard—Edwina. Won't you stop for a moment and listen? I'm sorry. Truly sorry."

She did not look back, nor did she answer, but she did slow her pace. Only a little. Only so he might complete his apology.

"Do come back to supper. I won't say anything more about the hotel. I swear I won't."

She stopped short and spun round to face him. "Why should I wish to spend my evening in the company of a man who holds me in contempt?"

"That's unfair, and you know it. I thought we might be friends. That you might wish to listen to what I have to say."

"I don't. None of it is news to me. Nor are you the first man who has tried to convince my family to sell up."

"Then let us speak of other things, and part as friends. Our food is waiting. Please tell me you'll come back."

She was hungry, and it had been a long and wearying day. "Very well. But no more talk of the Blue Lion. Not one word."

"Upon my honor," he promised, and he smiled his toothy smile, and she allowed him to take her arm and lead her back to the dining room.

FEBRUARY

Chapter Five

STELLA

Friday, February 6, 1953

She wanted to like London. She wanted to love the city, but it was loud and dirty and surprisingly ugly, and the few people she'd spoken with so far were distinctly unfriendly. None had any patience for her accent, even though her command of English was excellent, and now the officer in the Customs Office who was inspecting her passport and visa and her offer of employment from *Picture Weekly* had started to grumble under his breath about foreigners taking work away from decent people and what was the point of even winning the war if the eye-tees were just going to take over anyway.

He waved her on with a grunt, not once having looked her in the eye, and she suppressed the sudden urge to tell him what she thought of small, unpleasant, and entirely forgettable men. It would only make her late, besides, and it would run contrary to her resolve to make the best of every situation in which she found herself.

Instead she smiled brightly, picked up her case, and went in search of the bus Edie had told her to take. To her delight it was a double-decker, just like she'd seen in photographs, but as the top level could only be reached via a set of steep and twisting stairs, she prudently moved to the nearest window and tried to orient herself.

The view from the bus was an unremarkable stretch of drab office blocks on either side, punctuated every so often by temporary walls papered over with advertisements. Perhaps there were ruins behind the flimsy barriers, or the beginnings of new structures to replace the ones flattened by bombs. She had expected the ruins, but not the dreary streets and impassive facades that might be found anywhere.

"Westminster!!" called out the conductor from his spot by the rear door.

The bus swung to the right, and the tedium of the past few minutes was instantly erased by the sight of Westminster Abbey and the Parliament buildings and the tower with its great bell. So different to her eyes, schooled as she'd been in the genius of Palladio and his spiritual ancestors, but pleasing, too, in their steadfast stolidity. She would have to return for a visit as soon as she had a day off.

"Whitehall!"

The bus turned onto a broad avenue, and here the buildings were truly monumental, set square to the road, and far newer than the ancient abbey. The bus stopped, disgorged a handful of men in dark suits, admitted a greater number of the same, and as it pulled back into traffic she caught sight of the open piazza ahead, its lions keeping steadfast watch over a lonely statue left marooned at the top of a nearby column. A long-dead king, she supposed, or one of his generals.

"Trafalgar Square!"

As she moved toward the exit at the back, Stella struggled to keep her footing among the throng of departing passengers. She was just able to keep hold of her suitcase, but in the commotion the little map Edie had drawn up was torn from her grasp. No matter, for she had memorized its every detail.

She crossed over Whitehall, watching carefully for cars, for Edie had warned her to be cautious. Now she crossed Northumberland Avenue and continued along a few more meters to the junction with Northumberland Street. She looked to her left, suddenly nervous that she might have remembered wrongly, but the Blue Lion was there, waiting for her, just as she'd expected and hoped. Not a grand building, nor very beautiful, but she liked it all the same. She liked it very much.

Built of faded red brick, it had worn stone lintels and a classical pediment over the front door that was possibly a little too large for the building. A swinging sign, set at an angle on the corner wall, bore the brightly painted image of a blue lion standing on its hind legs. The same lion appeared on a carved plaque set into the wall by the door, and as Stella drew near she was able to read the date inscribed beneath its worn stone paws: 1560.

The entrance hall was small and low-ceilinged and smelled pleasantly of lemon and beeswax. A coal fire was burning in a modest hearth to her left, with deep-cushioned upholstered chairs arranged at either side. A staircase was straight ahead—she supposed the hotel was too small for a lift—and to her right was an alcove that contained the reception desk. It, along with every vertical plane in the room, was paneled in beautifully polished wood that gleamed under the soft light of the wall sconces.

It seemed a friendly sort of place, and while very different in appearance from her zia Rosa's home back in Italy, it had the same sort of warmth and unpretentious charm.

"May I help you?"

Only then did Stella notice the man at the desk, his gaze assessing, his smile wintry. How long had he been watching her?

"Good afternoon. I am Stella Donati. Miss Howard is expecting me."

"Ah, yes. The Italian girl. She wasn't expecting you until this afternoon."

"I am early," she explained, and she smiled at the clerk even though he was far from welcoming. "I caught an earlier train from Folkestone. Is she busy? I do not mind waiting."

The man smoothed his necktie and straightened his shoulders, and some of the chill faded from his expression. "As it happens, she is away from her desk. Why don't you wait in her office? It's just through the door there. I'll come around and show you through."

"Thank you, Mr. . . . ?"

"Brooks. Ivor Brooks. I'm the assistant manager here."

"I am very pleased to meet you."

He led her into the office, reached by a near-invisible door set into the wooden paneling to the left of the alcove, and indicated with a wave of his hand that she should sit at one of two chairs drawn up before an enormous desk.

"If you'll wait here until Miss Howard returns."

She kept her back straight and her hands folded neatly in her lap until he had retreated to the reception desk. Only then did she allow herself to relax and let her mind go blank for a few precious minutes. She would think of nothing, worry about nothing, and rest in the knowledge that she had reached her destination and was, for the moment, safe. Hungry, yes; weary and more than a little anxious, but none of these afflictions would harm her. She knew what suffering felt like, and this did not even come close.

After an interval of no more than ten minutes, she was pulled from her reverie by voices in the entrance hall. A flurry of footsteps sounded, and then Edie was at the door, an apology on her lips before Stella could stand to greet her properly.

"Oh, here you are—at last, at last! I am so sorry to have kept you waiting. I gather your train arrived a little earlier than expected? And I would have sent our doorman to fetch you, but Mick has Fridays off. I hope you didn't have any trouble finding your way here."

Stella and Edie Howard had never before met, but they had been corresponding with each other for some years, and had even exchanged photographs of themselves a few months earlier. In the picture Edie had sent, she'd looked serious and rather earnest; in person, she was pretty and engaging and warmly welcoming.

"Please do not apologize. I enjoyed seeing a little of your city."

"Why don't we get you something to eat?" Edie suggested. "And then we can get you settled in your room."

"My case . . . is it all right to leave it here?"

"Certainly. We'll take it upstairs when we're done."

Stella now followed Edie across the hall to the dining room. There were sixteen tables in all, only four of them occupied, and the bountiful array of food being set before the diners was more than she'd seen, let alone imagined, since long before the war.

"We're in time for afternoon tea," Edie explained as she led them to a table in the far corner. "We only serve the two meals, breakfast and tea, but they're quite filling. If you have to miss either because of work, you must let me know and I'll have Cook set something aside for you."

A woman about Stella's age emerged from a set of swinging doors only seconds after they sat down. "Good afternoon, Miss Howard."

"Good afternoon, Ginny. This is Miss Donati, who has just arrived from Italy. Could you bring out the usual?"

"Right away, Miss Howard. And welcome to England, Miss Donati."

Ginny came back moments later, setting out a plate of sandwiches cut into triangles, a small loaf that might have been bread or cake, and a basket of craggy buns that, by their tempting aroma, had just emerged from the oven. She returned a second time with a brown-glazed teapot, a jug of milk, and a little cut-glass dish filled with jam. Such a feast would have served Stella's entire family back in Italy, yet here it was meant for only two people.

"Would you like me to explain what I meant by 'the

usual' just now?" Edie asked. "Since I expect some of this will be unfamiliar."

"Yes, please. Unfamiliar but delicious, I am certain."

"That it is. Well, the sandwiches rather depend on what Cook has on hand. Let me see . . . hmm . . . I think there's salmon, and some egg mayonnaise, and this looks like ham. Or perhaps tongue? It's rather difficult to tell by just looking. Go on—take as many as you like."

Stella dutifully took three triangles, one of each type, and at Edie's prompting also helped herself to one of the buns.

"A scone," Edie explained, "and best if you split it open and add some jam. No need for a fork and knife. You're meant to pick it up."

Stella followed her instructions, careful to not use too much jam, and took a modest bite. It was . . . she had no words. It tasted of butter and sugar and comfort. She took a second bite, this one embarrassingly greedy.

"Even with butter still on the ration, Cook manages to make these taste heavenly. What do you think? Is it good?"

Stella could only nod, her mouth full of jam and sultana-studded scone. She would likely have a stomachache if she ate the entire thing, but she was very hungry, after all, and it would be wasteful not to finish.

"Do have some gingerbread as well," Edie urged, cutting a thick slice of the loaf and setting it on Stella's still-full plate. "We've been serving it here at the Blue Lion for generations. Not bread, as you can see, but rather a dark and quite rich cake. Terribly nice with tea. Oh—let me pour you a cup. It should be strong enough by now."

Before Stella could protest, or think of any reasonably polite reason to decline, her teacup had been filled. "How do you take it?" Edie asked.

"I am not sure," Stella admitted.

"Then why don't you try it black? That's how I like it, and you can always add some milk and sugar if it's too strong."

Stella took a tentative sip, then another, and was amazed to discover it was not the insipid drink she'd been steeling herself against. "I like it very much," she said, directing a smile over the top of her cup. "At home Zia Rosa gives us chamomile tisanes when we are ill. I have never cared for them, but this . . . this has a good taste. A strong taste."

"'Builder's tea,' we say when it's like this."

"Yes. My nonno Aldo would say it hits you on the head. 'El pesta sto tè.'"

"That it does," Edie agreed. "Now, tell me—how was your journey? I do hope it was pleasant."

"It was. Thank you for suggesting that I book a sleeping berth."

"Not at all. You were traveling on your own, and you certainly wouldn't have got any rest sitting out in an open carriage. When did you leave?"

"It was yesterday afternoon." Only a day ago, though her farewells to her family felt far more distant.

"Were you able to go home for a visit before you left? Your last letter said you were hoping to manage it."

"I was, but only for a few days. They were excited for me, but I think Zia Rosa will worry now that I am so far away."

Edie reached out, the gesture oddly hesitant, and patted

Stella's arm. Once, twice. "I'm sure you will have a marvelous time, not only here at the hotel but also at work. Just imagine the people you'll meet there. Perhaps you might be asked to photograph a film star—or even the queen!"

"I am not sure what Mr. Kaczmarek will ask me to do. His letter only said that my photographs were very good and that he thought I would do well at his magazine."

He had also told her she would be paid the astonishing sum of six pounds and ten shillings at the end of each week, and that he could recommend several economical and safe boarding hotels within walking distance of the magazine's offices.

She had written back right away to confirm her acceptance of his offer of employment, which by mutual agreement would begin on Wednesday, February 11, and had explained that she would be living at the Blue Lion hotel, which was owned by friends of her family. Her next letter had been to Edie to ask if she might come to live at the hotel as a long-term boarder.

"I hope it is not an inconvenience to you," Stella now said. "Having me here. Looking around the hotel, and seeing how nice it is, I worry that I will not be paying you enough for my room and meals. Are you certain you only require two and a half pounds each week?"

"Quite certain. I would charge quite a lot more to a stranger coming in off the street, but you are a friend. I'd rather not charge you anything at all, but with things so dear right now every shilling coming in will make a difference."

Stella smiled, and felt the last of her worries melt away, at least for the day. "I am most grateful, and I promise I will not forget your kindness."

"Well, for my part I am honored that you thought of me and the Blue Lion. And I do want to say, to let you know, that is, how very fond I was of your parents. I only met them a few times, but my father always spoke of them with real affection. And of course we were terribly grateful that they rated the Blue Lion so highly in their wonderful guidebooks. I am truly sorry that you lost them in such an awful way."

Stella nodded. Tried to thank her friend, but the words stuck in her throat.

Her parents had not been lost. They had been stolen. They had been murdered. They had been erased from the world by the remorseless machinery of the death camps and the dead-hearted men who ran them.

Her parents had vanished and she would never know the truth of their final hours. Gone, gone, and all she had to remember them, now, was a few battered copies of their once-famed *Guide di turistiche Donati*. No photographs. No mementos. Nothing apart from their words and her memories.

There was no point in telling Edie any of this, for no one, with the exception of Nina and her family in Mezzo Ciel, seemed to care about what had happened to her during the war. No one wanted to remember.

And so she would use the same careful phrases that she always employed, and she would smile even if it made her feel ill to do so. If she smiled hard enough and long enough, she would be happy again. It was simply a matter of practice and persistence.

"Thank you, Edie. You are very kind. I am sure I will be happy here."

Chapter Six

JAMIE

Thursday, February 12, 1953

Jamie had put off the inevitable long enough. He needed a place to live and work that was clean and quiet and free of distractions, and that meant he needed an escape from the grubby house in Wood Green and the indolent and frequently repulsive habits of his aimless housemates.

Geoffrey and Lester, fellow artists he'd met at the Slade, were younger than him by five years or so, and had still been schoolboys for much of the war. At first he'd enjoyed their company, which was blissfully free of the misery-guts rehashing of wartime exploits that men of his age seemed to use as a kind of currency. He'd liked them enough to move to their lodgings in the greener climes of Wood Green a little more than a year ago, but he'd quickly regretted his decision.

He was thirty-three years old if reckoned by traditional means, about a hundred and fifty if one took into account how he felt most mornings, and he'd had enough of the filthy kitchen, even grimier bath, and endless parade of strangers that Geoffrey and Lester saw fit to invite around at all hours. His own room was spotless, a legacy from his years as an officer, but the rest of the house was almost beyond redemption.

But now he had the commission to consider, and he was finding it almost impossible to make any headway on his preparations. For almost a month he'd been trying, and failing, to work up some decent drawings. For reference he had the hurried sketch from the day of his meeting at Cartwrights' Hall and several more that he'd since ventured into town to make, along with a set of photographs he'd taken with the same ancient camera he'd been lugging around since his schooldays, but it wasn't enough.

What no sketch or photograph could capture, he knew, was the way the hall would appear at close quarters and from across the avenue, how it would look in fair weather or on a rainy day, and how the late-morning light would fall across its facade. All of that would take time, and he couldn't very well set up an easel on the pavement. Nor did he relish the tedious journey from Wood Green every time his memory or imagination demanded prompting.

But then he remembered the little hotel across the way from Cartwrights' Hall. He couldn't recall its name, but it had seemed a pleasant enough place from the outside. Modest and quiet, inexpensive if his luck held out, and in exactly the right spot for his purposes.

Jamie packed his notebook and pencils into his satchel, changed from his paint-spattered working clothes into his most presentable suit, tidied his room, and locked the door.

He'd installed the lock after returning home from a visit to his parents and finding a stranger asleep in his bed.

His housemates were having a slow start to their respective days. This involved approximately a gallon of coffee, enough cigarettes to leave a fug of noxious yellow smoke hanging at shoulder height, and some hours spent in quiet contemplation of the art world's ills.

"I'm heading into town," Jamie told them, not waiting for a response, for he was eager to get away from the stale smoke and smell of damp and the faintly nauseating tang of unwashed dishes cluttering every horizontal surface.

The bus from Wood Green to central London took an age, but since nothing could induce him to take the Underground, it was the bus or a bicycle. He alighted at Trafalgar Square about an hour later; a few minutes' walk took him to Northumberland Street just opposite Cartwrights' Hall and, set back about fifteen yards from the wider avenue, the hotel he'd noticed back in January.

A plaque set into the brickwork told him he'd arrived at *The Blue Lion, est. 1560*, which was puzzling as the exterior was solidly mid-Victorian. Not that he really cared about the history of the place, or even much about it in the present day. All he required was a view of Cartwrights' Hall and a tolerably comfortable room in which to work and sleep.

Now he only had to hope they'd have him. He looked down, reminding himself that he was dressed respectably, and he spoke like a gentleman, and he carried himself like the officer he'd once been. Beyond that there was nothing else he could do. Either they would admit to having a room available and then invite him to stay, or they would show him the door.

Once he was inside, the mystery of the hotel's history unraveled a little, for the innards of the building were far more ancient than its exterior would suggest. It reminded him, in the best possible way, of the library at Merton, with the same age-worn oak paneling, glazed tile floors, and determined indifference to modern technology.

A few steps and he was across the entrance hall and standing in front of the reception desk. The clerk had noticed when he entered, his frosty gaze taking stock before darting away, and he now took his time looking up. No matter. Jamie had all the time in the world.

The clerk closed the ledger he'd been pretending to read, straightened it on the desk, and took a step back, his hands clasped behind him. Putting distance between them.

"Good morning," Jamie said. "I'm interested in taking a room here. Preferably with a view of the avenue."

"May I ask for how long?" The man had a faint northeastern accent beneath a skim-coat of King's English.

"If possible I'd like to take a room starting now and stay on until after the coronation."

"I see. Typically it's Miss Howard, our proprietor, who manages reservations for guests planning on a longer stay, but she is not in her office at present. If you'd care to leave a note, I will certainly ask her to ring you back when—"

"If you'll allow me, Mr. Brooks?"

A woman had emerged from an office behind the reception desk. *Miss E. D. Howard, Proprietor,* according to the badge on her jacket lapel. She was smiling, her hazel eyes friendly behind gold-rimmed spectacles, and she promptly extended her hand so Jamie might shake it.

"I'm afraid I missed the first part of your conversation with Mr. Brooks. Is there any way I might help you, Mr. . . . ?"

"Geddes. I was saying that I'd like to take a room here. I understand you offer weekly rates for longer stays?"

"That we do. Two pounds ten for a room, or three pounds ten with breakfast and afternoon tea daily."

"And do you have rooms available?"

"We do indeed," she said, then looked to the waiting clerk. "I'll take over now, Mr. Brooks. Perhaps you might wish to take your break?" Her voice was pleasant, but there was an unmistakable edge of steel to it.

Brooks's features were composed, but his gaze, now focused on Jamie, was contemptuous. If Miss Howard hadn't appeared, Jamie suspected no space at all would have been found for him at the hotel. "Very well. I'll be in the staff lounge if you need me."

She now returned her attention to Jamie. "As I said, Mr. Geddes, we do have rooms. Several, in fact."

"I particularly need one with a view of the avenue. Specifically a view of Cartwrights' Hall."

At this she frowned a little. "Cartwrights' Hall?"

He didn't blame her. Likely no one had ever come asking for a view of the uninspiring heap of masonry across the way. "Yes. For Coronation Day."

"Three and a half months ahead of time? You must be terribly fond of the royal family."

He chanced a smile. "Not so fond as that. I'm an artist, and I've been asked to paint a view of the hall on Coronation Day. Since there's quite a lot of preparatory work to do beforehand, I thought it would be sensible to base myself here."

"Oh, I see. How clever of you. Well, I can certainly let you a room. I have several free on the second floor, all with excellent views of the hall. Only . . ."

"Is there a problem?" he asked, hoping very much that she was not having second thoughts.

"The difficulty is that they are already reserved for other guests on Coronation Day itself. Would you mind moving to another room for that week? Except . . . hmm. I do have another room that *might* do. It has an excellent view of the hall, only it isn't one of our usual guest rooms. Perhaps you'd like to see for yourself?"

At his nod, she set out a bell and a little sign on the desk—*Kindly Ring for Service*—and then locked a drawer below the desk. A moment later she emerged from a door that was set into the adjacent wall. "It's just this way. I'm afraid we don't have a lift."

"I don't mind. I grew up in a town house in Edinburgh that was all stairs."

"Oh, yes. I could tell from your accent that you're a Scot."

"That I am. Born and bred."

He waited for her to demand that he clarify his answer. *Yes, but where are you* really *from?* Or *But where are you from originally?* Instead she continued to climb, and after a moment, glancing back, she smiled again.

"I've never been to Scotland, though I would love to visit. The hotel keeps me awfully busy, you see." And then, a few steps later, "We're almost there."

They reached the top of the stairs and she led him through a fire door and into a dimly lit and rather low-ceilinged corridor. Here and there, he noticed, age-darkened beams cut through the plaster above. He'd have to watch his head.

He followed her a few strides to a door at the end of the hallway. There she fished a ring of keys from her jacket pocket, selected one, and unlocked the door. After switching on an overhead light, she waved him forward.

"Here it is, but please bear in mind that it needs a good clean. We can bring in whichever furniture you need, apart from an easel. Though I suppose I might—"

"Don't you fret about that. I've one of my own."

He moved farther into the room, taking in the space, and was gratified to discover it was far, far nicer than the dank and gloomy garret he'd imagined. "It's perfect," he said.

The room wasn't all that big, and his head cleared the ceiling of the window dormer with only an inch or so to spare, but the view of Cartwrights' Hall, in all its uninspiring solidity, was entirely unobstructed. And the window was not the only source of light, for there was an enormous skylight set into the ceiling. Even on cloudy days the light would be good.

"It really is perfect," he repeated.

"You're sure you don't mind being up here?"

"Not at all. The light is ideal, and the view of the hall couldn't be better. When may I move in?" Geoffrey and Lester would find someone to take over his room easily enough, and he'd paid up his rent until the end of the month.

"Would Monday be suitable?" At Jamie's nod she pulled a wee notebook from her jacket pocket. "I only need a few days to put everything here to rights. I'll just take some notes so I don't forget anything. Table and chair, dresser, double bed . . . do you need a desk?"

"The table will do. I wouldn't mind an easy chair if you've one to spare."

"I do. A wardrobe?"

The room didn't have a closet, but there was a double row of hooks on the back of the door. "Those are fine," he said, nodding in their direction. "What's the rate for room and board again?"

"Three pounds ten if you take breakfast and afternoon tea. We call it that for the tourists, only it's more of a high tea. I promise you won't go hungry. We don't serve lunch or supper, but the Queen Bess across the way does sandwiches and has pies and such in the evening."

"That's more than fair. Thank you, Miss Howard. I feel certain I'll be happy here."

As HE'D HOPED, his leave-taking from Lester and Geoffrey was perfectly pleasant. They wished him well, reminded him not to be a stranger, and he left. Jamie wasn't sure if he would ever see them again.

He'd balked at the cost of a taxi, instead arranging with the mechanic at a nearby garage to deliver his battered old army trunk to the Blue Lion for only two-and-six, along with an impromptu sketch of Jerrold & Sons Motors. Jamie had taken the drawing home, neatened it up and added a color wash, and Mr. Jerrold, declaring himself best pleased, had collected the trunk that morning.

A doorman was on duty when Jamie arrived, but rather than query him on his business at the Blue Lion, the man smiled and wished him good morning and opened the door. It was a fine omen, Jamie decided, for the months to come. The sign asking one to ring the bell had been left out at the reception desk, so Jamie rang it, and was gratified when a smiling Miss Howard emerged from her office.

"Mr. Geddes. So lovely to see you again."

He considered replying in the same vein, but thought better of it. "Thank you."

The telephone began to ring. "Would you mind terribly if I answer this call?" she asked.

"Not at all."

"Good morning, the Blue Lion, Miss Howard speaking. Oh, hello. Yes, I'm quite well, thank you . . . and the same to you, Mr. Bamford. Oh . . . well. That's very kind of you, but I'm not certain . . . Of course. Water under the bridge, as they say. I am sorry, but I have a guest waiting— perhaps you might ring back another time? Yes, do. Very well. Good day."

She set the telephone headset back in its cradle and stared at the thing as if it, rather than the caller, had annoyed her, and Jamie, having listened to her half of the conversation without making any great effort to distance himself, was tempted to offer a penny for her thoughts. Tempted, but not so foolish as that.

"I do beg your pardon. Particularly since I was about to offer you the grand tour. It needn't take very long."

He wouldn't mind if it lasted all day. "I would love a tour."

She led him through the dining room, indicating the kitchen beyond, and then to the lounge next door. A pair of old ladies sat on either side of the fire, busy with their knitting, the Light Programme playing on the wireless.

"Good afternoon, Miss Polly, Miss Bertie. This is our new boarder, Mr. James Geddes. He's an artist, and he's staying here while he works on a very important painting of the queen."

"How tremendously exciting," said one of the ladies. "Come all the way from India, have you?" The question stung, as it always did, but he wasn't about to make a pill of himself on his first day in residence.

"No, ma'am. I'm from Edinburgh, though I've lived here in London for some time."

Now the other lady chimed in. "A painter, you say?" she asked. "My sister and I are terribly interested in the fine arts. Our late father, the Baron Crane of Hopworth, had a marvelous collection of equine portraits, including one by Master Stubbs himself. Unfortunately, it was auctioned off after his untimely death by our dreadful cousin Dominic."

"I'm very sorry to hear it, ma'am."

"Mr. Geddes and I must be on our way," Miss Howard now intervened. "But you'll have a chance to speak with him again at teatime."

As soon as they were back in the corridor, and the door to the lounge had been safely shut, Miss Howard turned to Jamie, a faintly conspiratorial gleam in her eye. "Now you've met the Crane sisters, although I think of them as the Hons."

"The 'awns'?" Jamie asked, not understanding.

"My pet name for them. Officially they are the Honorable Leopoldine Crane and the Honorable Albertine Crane, though they've given us leave to call them Miss Polly and Miss Bertie. I'll spare you the full story, but they've lived here since their father's death in 1927. They're, ah, waiting for a legal proceeding to be resolved."

"That does seem a very long time," Jamie replied, not knowing what else to say.

"They're rather eccentric, but they're also quite sweet. In their own way, I do think they try not to give us any trouble. Never mind that they can't help but be rather difficult. They had a rather old-fashioned upbringing, you see."

The next room was evidently the library, a small and rather dark chamber with a sturdy table at its center, a pair of leather club chairs flanking its single window, and floor-to-ceiling shelves packed with volumes both antique and recent. It reminded him of the used bookshops in Edinburgh where his father loved to linger, with the same odor of warm and not entirely unpleasant papery mustiness.

An older man, well into his sixties, sat at the table, his attention focused on a large map that he'd weighted down with stacks of books at each corner. He looked up, smiled at Miss Howard, frowned briefly at Jamie, and resumed his inspection of the map.

"Professor Thurloe," Miss Howard explained in a whisper. "He's the only person you're likely to meet in here, although we have an excellent selection of books. Do feel free to borrow anything you like."

"The professor is another boarder?"

After beckoning him into the corridor, she closed the library door and led them back in the direction of the front hall. "Yes. He's a retired archivist and historian. The library where he worked for many years, along with his flat, was destroyed near the end of the war by one of those awful V-2 rockets. He came to live with us after that."

The doorman who'd been so friendly to Jamie was coming through the front door when they returned to the hall.

"Morning, Miss Howard."

"Good morning. Mick, this is Mr. Geddes, our newest boarder."

"Pleased to meet you. I'm Mick Nelligan, the doorman and driver here." Mr. Nelligan had the face of a pugilist, and the frame to match, but his expression was gently welcoming as he shook Jamie's hand.

"I'm pleased to make your acquaintance, Mr. Nelligan."

"No need to be so formal, sir. I'm just Mick to everyone here. I don't bother with any of that commissionaire nonsense, either."

"I know, Mick. I know," Miss Howard acknowledged. "Mr. Brooks was only trying to help. He thought it might seem more modern."

"I'm a doorman, plain and simple, and when I've a bit of time to spare I turn my hand to anything else you need doing. Don't need some silly title I can't even spell to make me feel important."

"Of course not," Miss Howard soothed. "I've made it quite clear that you are our doorman, just as you prefer."

"Thanks. Well, I'd best get meself back outside. Nice meeting you, Mr. Geddes."

Miss Howard pressed her lips together, almost as if she was suppressing a laugh, and only after Mick was safely outside did she return her gaze to Jamie. "Well. That was Mick. Such a dear man, and quite indispensable. Now—

may I show you your room? I must say I am very pleased with how it's looking."

Again he followed her, his long legs taking the shallow steps two at a time. "The bath is across the hall, just there," she explained when they reached the top floor, "with the WC just next to it. And here is your room," she announced. "Mick brought up your trunk earlier."

Miss Howard and her staff had worked miracles in the space of only a few days. The floors and furniture gleamed with polish, the window and skylight were so clean as to be invisible, and everywhere there were thoughtful and homey touches—a standard lamp next to the requested easy chair, a faded Persian rug that softened the floor by his bed, and even a little pot of primroses on the windowsill.

"This is wonderful," he said after he'd taken it all in. "Thank you."

"Do let me know if you need anything. Oh—I almost forgot. Tea is at half-past four."

"I missed my breakfast and lunch, so I'll be glad of it."

"Then I'll see you there. Welcome to the Blue Lion, Mr. Geddes."

He began to unpack, reckoning that the sooner he was settled in, the sooner he'd shed the lingering urge to retreat to the house in Wood Green or, worse, his parents' home in Edinburgh. It had been nearly eight years since he'd lived when he ought to have died, and a little more than five years since he'd abandoned his law studies and moved to London. If he failed now, if he let inertia and fear bear him back to the safety and security of life in Edinburgh, working alongside his father and brother, unsurprised and uninspired by the pattern of his days, then he'd have failed at everything that mattered to him.

A knock sounded, startling him, and then a softly questioning voice came from the hall. "Mr. Geddes? Hello?"

He opened the door to a young woman in a starched white apron. She was holding a tray, its contents hidden by a linen cloth.

"Good afternoon, Mr. Geddes. Is it all right if I bring this in?"

"Of course," he said, stepping aside so she might pass. "Only I think there may have been a mistake. I didn't order anything from the kitchen. For that matter, I wasn't aware it was even possible to have food brought up."

"Normally it isn't, but Miss Howard said you hadn't eaten anything today."

She set the tray on the table and removed the cover, revealing a bowl of soup, a stack of sandwiches, a wedge of cake that smelled of treacle and spices, a flask of coffee, and a small jug of milk.

He opened his mouth to thank the girl, but a rush of emotion, unexpected and unfamiliar, stopped his throat. He coughed, waited a moment, and then, at last, was able to speak. "This looks wonderful. Shall I bring the tray downstairs when I'm done?"

"Oh, no. I'll collect it. Just leave it outside when you're done. Miss Howard says that you aren't to be disturbed."

"That's very kind of her, but I'm not so delicate as that. There's no need to walk on eggshells on my account."

"Very well. Enjoy your food, sir. And welcome to the Blue Lion."

Chapter Seven

EDIE

Wednesday, February 18, 1953

No. I'm afraid our answer is no."

"Miss Polly—"

"We cannot move. We *shall* not. It is quite, quite impossible."

The Crane sisters sat shoulder to shoulder on the settee in their sitting room, their expressions every bit as mulish as Edie had expected. She'd been putting off the conversation for weeks—months, even—and from the start it had gone exactly as she'd feared. Badly.

"For you to ask such a thing of us is cruel," Miss Bertie said.

"Quite monstrously cruel," her sister echoed.

It was nothing of the sort. Edie had calmly and clearly explained her dilemma to the Hons. They had waited for her to finish, their matching frowns growing ever more pronounced, and they had reacted exactly as she had known they would.

"That is quite enough," she now said, adopting the tone she used with Mr. Pinnock when discussing the lamentable state of the hotel's boiler. "It is the opposite of cruel, and you both know it." Ignoring their protesting chirps, she soldiered on. "You have lived here for many years, and I certainly do not wish for you to go elsewhere, but you must understand several things. First—the going rate for room and board at the Blue Lion is three pounds and ten shillings a week. *Per person.* Yet you occupy two rooms and between you are charged only two pounds a week."

"Highway robbery, that's what—"

"Miss Bertie. Allow me to finish. For the weeks before and after the Coronation I am charging a premium for rooms with a view of Northumberland Avenue. A significant premium."

"Just as my sister—"

"I am not asking you to pay that premium for your rooms. Nor am I asking you to pay the ordinary rate that every other guest, Professor Thurloe included, is charged. I am, instead, asking you to move across the corridor, to a set of rooms that are in every particular the same as your current rooms, so that I may charge other people the higher rate."

"Such upheaval, and after all these years . . . I simply cannot bear it. Can you, Bertie?"

"I cannot, Polly."

Edie was fond of the sisters, and she did have some sympathy for their circumstances. When their father had died suddenly in 1927, squashed by his horse in a hunting accident, the cousin who'd inherited had ignored the modest provisions for the sisters set forth in the baron's will, and had, instead, shown them the door. The will, and their cousin's failure to provide for Miss Bertie and Miss Polly, had been the focus of a series of legal proceedings ever since.

What little savings the Hons had once had were long gone, swallowed up by *Crane v Crane*. Between them they owned little of value, for their cousin had retained all the really valuable artwork and furniture. In the decades since, however, they had managed to cram their rooms full of framed photographs, embroidered pillows, ceramic figurines, dried flowers, and an assortment of bric-a-brac that took the maids forever and a day to dust. Simply thinking about the effort to move the sisters and their possessions across the hall was enough to give Edie a headache for days. Yet it had to be done.

"You know how we have suffered since cruel Cousin Dominic took possession of the family estate. The courts are certain to decide in our favor, and when they do—"

"As they are *certain* to do—"

"We will naturally compensate you. Has that not always been the understanding? It was your father's suggestion, after all."

Edie's father had, unfortunately, been rather more susceptible to the aristocratic wiles of two terribly self-indulgent old ladies than she was now, or indeed had ever been. A dose of unvarnished honesty was in order.

"I'm afraid that I cannot wait for the lawsuit to be settled. Miss Bertie, Miss Polly—the hotel is in trouble. Ever since the war, it has been a struggle to make ends meet. I won't burden you with all the details, but the situation is dire."

"Dire, you say?" Miss Polly asked tremulously.

"It is quite, quite dire. The hotel has been running at a loss for some years now, but with the coronation I have a chance to save it. *We* have a chance. Visitors from abroad are prepared to pay quite shocking amounts for a room with a view of the coronation procession, and your rooms, overlooking the avenue as they do—these are the very best rooms in the hotel. I might be able to ask as much as two hundred guineas a night for each of them, or even more, and that will help enormously. Do tell me you understand."

"If you need our rooms so badly, then why not toss us out?" asked Miss Bertie, always the more dramatic of the sisters.

Edie took a fortifying breath and prayed for composure. "I would be very sorry to see you go, of course, but I must warn you that it is very difficult to find anywhere to stay in central London—anywhere respectable, that is—for two pounds a week. Of course you might wish to consider Bayswater, or perhaps one of the ladies' hotels near King's Cross . . . ?"

A long, grumbly sort of silence hung in the air as the sisters absorbed the horror of Edie's suggestions, their noses wrinkling as if confronted with a very disagreeable smell.

"Your father would be appalled if he knew what you were asking of us," Miss Bertie said at last.

It was her father, bless him, who was responsible for much of this mess. He had run the hotel at a constant deficit, blithely assuming trouble would never catch up with them, but it had. The day her parents had been killed, Edie had discovered just how rocky a foundation the Blue Lion rested upon. She had been trying to shore it up ever since.

"Perhaps he would be," she conceded, "but he is not

here. I am. This is my hotel and I am doing my best to keep it open."

Another long and grizzling silence ensued, punctuated only by Miss Polly's sniffles. "It would only be across the hall?"

"Yes. Mere steps away."

"But what about our things?" Miss Bertie asked. "You don't suggest that strangers sleep in *our* beds and sit on *our* settee and chairs?"

Somehow Edie managed to refrain from pointing out that none of the furniture actually belonged to the sisters. "No, no. Everything will go across the hall to your temporary rooms."

"We cannot be expected to move our things on our own. Neither of us is young, nor are we strong."

"I will take care of all that, Miss Polly. It is not something you need to worry about."

"Of course we will worry," Miss Bertie protested, her chin quivering. "All this dreadful upheaval and anxiety is simply too much to be borne, and together with everything that cruel Cousin Dominic has done to us . . ."

Not for the first time that day, Edie felt a twinge of remorse. It wasn't the sisters' fault they'd been indifferently educated and raised in an atmosphere of such privilege that even the most ordinary demands of daily life would wilt them faster than a bouquet of hothouse gardenias.

"I promise we'll keep the upset to a minimum," she said. "You can even wait in the lounge while everything is being moved over."

Miss Bertie snorted. "Just so we can be robbed blind? No, thank you. We will need to watch those movers like a hawk."

"Indeed we will," said her sister.

There would be no movers, only Mick for the heavier things and the maids for everything else. The same girls who had been in and out of the sisters' rooms day after day for years, without so much a single hairpin ever going astray. But that was a conversation for another time.

"Now that we have everything settled, I'll have Ginny bring up a pot of tea for you," Edie offered, feeling magnanimous in victory. "Along with some of those lemon biscuits you like so much."

THE EVENING PAPERS had arrived while Edie was upstairs with the sisters, and although the account ledgers needed her attention, and there was a pile of post to get through, and she'd crossed off only one item from the list in her notebook—*persuade Hons move*—she picked up the *Times* and sat down to leaf through it. Five minutes of leisure was all she needed, and then she'd get back to work.

There was a photograph of the queen on the front page, taken at a ribbon-cutting for something or other that had been grand enough, in its planning and construction, to earn a visit from the monarch to celebrate its opening. It had only been a year since the king had died, but Edie would wager his daughter was already sick to death of at least some of the duties she'd inherited. Or maybe she wasn't? Perhaps she enjoyed it all.

Perhaps it truly gladdened the young queen's heart to know the rest of her life would unfold in an endless succession of plaques to be unveiled, cornerstones to be revealed, ships to be named, trees to be planted, ribbons to be snipped, and thousands upon thousands of strangers to be dazzled by their momentary connection with the most famous woman in the world. Unlikely, Edie thought, but perhaps there were consolations enough.

The queen was wealthy and admired and treated with deference, awe, and real affection wherever she went, but was it enough to outweigh her lack of freedom? She'd been a little girl when her father had become king, and she had become his heir without ever being asked if it was something she wanted, and with the stroke of a pen the entire course of her future had been laid out for her. She'd only been ten or so, far too young to have realized, or understood, what it had truly meant.

Edie had been young, too, when she had first understood that she was to be her father's heir, and that the gift and burden of the Blue Lion was to be hers, and that she would never be allowed to do anything but follow a path laid out since before her birth. She would never go to university, even though she was always top of her class in school, and she would never have a home, or life, that did not locate the Blue Lion at its center.

And now she was thirty-two years old, six years older than the queen, and it had been years—decades, even— since she'd spent a night away from the hotel, or gone to the pictures, or had a proper evening out, with the sole exception her one lunch and two dinner dates with David Bamford. She was surrounded by people, some of them very dear to her indeed, but she was lonely. Lonelier even than the queen, who had a husband and children and mother and sister to love her.

She was still caught up in this unhappy train of thought when someone tapped at her door.

"Miss Howard?" She looked up to see Mr. Brooks edging into her office. "How did it go with the Misses Crane?"

"More or less as I expected," she answered, not bothering to hide her gloomy mood. "But in the end they gave in." She closed her eyes and began to rub at her temples.

"What is it?"

"Only a headache." A headache and what felt like the weight of the world. That was all.

"You stayed up late again. Were you going over the accounts? Your light was on past midnight."

"How would you know that?" she asked, a little unsettled. Mr. Brooks lived out, and he had finished work at six o'clock the night before.

"It was calling for rain today, and I remembered I had left my umbrella here. When I came back to fetch it, I saw the light was on in your office. Didn't you hear me speaking with Mr. Swan?"

"Oh. I see. Of course."

He took a small step forward. "You can confide in me, you know. How bad is it?"

"My headache? I'll survive. Some aspirin will—"

"I meant the hotel. How bad are things here at the hotel?"

For years she had confided in no one. Not a single soul. And then, in the space of only a few weeks, she had admitted at least part of the truth, first to David Bamford and then to the Hons. What harm could there be in answering Mr. Brooks's question?

She met his gaze and discerned no spark of guile, no half-hidden delight in her misfortunes. Only calm acceptance and, she hoped, understanding from a man who had proven his worth time and time again in the years he had worked for her.

"Do you swear to keep what I tell you in the strictest confidence?"

"I do. On my honor, I do."

She couldn't help noticing that his Geordie accent was stronger than usual, which only happened when he was tired or worried. Such a dear man to take her concerns so much to heart.

"Thank you. It is . . . not good. You've seen the accounts, so you'll be aware of how little revenue the hotel is generating. That alone is troubling, but nearly all of my capital is gone. Not that there was much left after I paid up the death duties when my parents died. And when it's gone . . .

"I've been careful, so careful, but the repairs are endless, and everything is so dear right now, and there are only so many economies one can take without the guests noticing. No matter how often I go through the accounts, and search for ways to save, it's never enough, and the worry of what will happen when the last of my savings are gone is so deflating. And talking with the Hons, trying to convince them to help me in this one small way, was simply exhausting."

"Didn't they agree to move?"

"They did, but they'll still put up a right royal fuss when we do move them across the hall, and when the coronation is over and we move them back I'll still have two of my best rooms let at two pounds a week to two hopelessly sheltered old ladies who have no notion of what it truly costs to live in London."

Mr. Brooks came round her desk to sit in one of the

guest chairs. He was frowning, rather as if he had a head-ache, too. "How bad is it?" he asked once more.

"Bad enough that I don't take a salary for myself. How could I? We only have the income from the guests, but the outlay for wages, taxes, rates, insurance, maintenance, and supplies is . . ."

"Considerable?"

"Yes. That's the nice way of putting it. Crushing would be more accurate. Each year, everything is a little bit more dear, and I keep having to dip into my capital. But that's meant for real disasters—burst pipes, or a fire. Not the greengrocer's bill."

"Shouldn't insurance cover the costs of anything truly unexpected?"

"Some, but never all. We learned that in the Blitz." The hotel hadn't been hit directly, but there'd been small fires from incendiaries, and one of the outbuildings had needed rebuilding. Insurance had only paid for a fraction of the repairs.

He leaned forward, his hands clasped on the desktop, his eyes soft with concern. "All this work you do, never tak-ing a day off, and you don't pay yourself anything at all?"

"A very little. Enough to keep myself looking decent. It wouldn't do the hotel any good if I were walking around in rags." It would have been funny if it weren't so pathetic. Even Dolly had nicer clothes for her days off. For that mat-ter, Dolly had days off. Edie hadn't taken any time off from work in . . . she couldn't remember.

"But a night out?" Mr. Brooks asked, as if reading her mind. "A day at the seaside?"

She shook her head. "No. Not since before the war. I did go to dinner with David Bamford those few times, but he was . . . well. He's really only interested in buying the hotel."

"Surely you would never consider selling it?" he asked, clearly aghast.

She ought not to have said anything. Now Mr. Brooks was worried, too. "Of course not. I mean . . . it could conceivably come to a point where I've no choice but to sell up. But I'm not there yet."

"It's a shame you have to face this alone," he said. "Without any family, that is."

"I suppose so. It does feel strange to be the only Howard left. I think there were some cousins a few generations back, but I've never met them. For all I know, they may have died out as well."

He frowned at this, his distress for her evident. "Yes. It is a shame. Though I was wrong to say you are alone. Since you do have all of us at the hotel to help."

"It's kind of you to say so." She smiled, and he smiled back, though it was clear he was troubled by her revelations. "I do hope I haven't upset you with all this."

"Not in the least. I am the assistant manager, after all, and part of my role, surely, is to support you. Besides, I'm certain we can think of some ways to improve the hotel's prospects. There's the coronation, for a start. Above and beyond charging a premium for rooms, there must be other things we can do to bring in some revenue. What about afternoon tea? I know we offer it to nonresidents, but it's been an age since anyone came in off the street."

"I know," she agreed. "It doesn't help that there's a Lyons just around the corner. Most people would rather have a quick cup of tea and a bun and be done with it."

"Ordinary Londoners, perhaps, but not the tourists. And definitely not the foreigners. They have an idea of what afternoon tea ought to be like, and it isn't a cuppa at a Lyons. They want to sit in a historic dining room in an ancient building, and they want sandwiches and dainties and scones that taste like they've been made with butter. All of which we have at the Blue Lion—and don't forget the legend of how the first Elizabeth took refuge here during the great blizzard of 1564. That's a draw if ever there was one."

"Do you think so? I've never quite believed it. The notion that the queen of England could find no other place to shelter than a small coaching inn? Don't forget that the palace of Whitehall was only a few hundred yards down the road. If she and her party had pressed on they'd have been home in another half hour."

"It doesn't matter if it's true," he insisted. "The legend is enough. And we still have the chair she used. Why don't we bring it out of the lounge and set it up in the dining room? We can put it on a little platform, but roped off so people don't sit on it."

"That's a good idea. We'd need to do some improvements to the dining room," she mused, "although I doubt I'll be able to chase down so much as a single pint of paint that isn't battleship gray."

He smiled at this. "I don't think you'd need to go that far. The hotel is perfect as it is. We simply need to rearrange a few things."

"Thank you, Mr. Brooks. I do hope I haven't worried you."

"Not in the least. It's only . . . if I seem at all preoccupied, it's only because my mother has been poorly. It's hard not to worry, you see. What with her being so far away."

"Am I right in thinking you're from the northeast?"

"I am. I grew up in South Shields. Haven't been home for an age, though. After my father died, we lost the lease on his chemist's shop, and I had to find work that would support both Mother and myself."

His admission squeezed at Edie's heart. "Oh, Mr. Brooks. If only I'd known. You haven't taken any holiday for . . . well, for longer than I can remember. You *must* go and see her."

"I'm all right. I'll go once the coronation is over and things are more settled here."

"That's very unselfish of you."

"Not at all. The hotel needs me, you see, and it won't be long before I've time for a visit. I only have to be patient." He smiled again. "I wonder . . . would you object to calling me Ivor? When it's just the two of us? And if I might be so bold . . . may I address you by your Christian name?"

"Please do. It's Edwina, but I prefer Edie."

"Edie, then. Thank you for confiding in me. I won't let you down."

He retreated to the front desk, closing her office door behind him, and Edie was left alone with her thoughts. Her headache had subsided, she realized, and along with it the thrum of panic that was as familiar, and constant, as her own heartbeat.

She had admitted the worst to another person, and the hotel had not collapsed upon her. She had shared her worries, and rather than recoil from her, as she'd half expected him to do, Ivor had understood, and he'd offered to help, and he'd confided in her in return. She might be the last of the Howards, but she was not without friends.

Chapter Eight

STELLA

Wednesday, February 25, 1953

"Good morning, Miss Berridge—am I late?"

"You've five minutes still. What caught your attention this morning?"

The receptionist at *Picture Weekly* enjoyed hearing of the sights that diverted Stella on her walk to work each morning. The day before it had been a workman clinging to a tall ladder as he briskly glued an enormous poster of Vera Lynn to the hoarding on the front of the Adelphi Theatre; today it had been the unexpected splendor of a baroque church marooned upon a traffic island in the middle of the Strand. "I'll tell you after the meeting!" she called back, all but sprinting past Kaz's office, along the corridor, and upstairs to the photographers' quarters. It was a large open space made bright by skylights and a run of south-facing windows that took up most of one wall; in winter it was very pleasant indeed, though she suspected it would become infernally hot in the dog days of summer.

In the center of the room a jumble of tables were pushed together, their tops laden with cases of photography equipment, swathes of contact sheets, back issues of the magazine, and the assorted detritus of a lived-in and none-too-clean workplace: mugs of tea gone cold, overflowing ashtrays, old jam jars stuffed with pencils, and a typewriter so rarely used that its keys had filmed over with dust. At one end of the room's north-facing wall was a makeshift studio that consisted of a tattered paper backdrop hedged round by a small forest of lamps, reflectors, and tripods; at the other end was the darkroom, its door crowned by an unmistakable red light, its walls garlanded with freshly printed photographs.

Although the weekly editorial meeting was about to begin, Stella dumped her camera bag and satchel on one of the tables and went in search of the pictures from her previous day's assignment. She'd been tasked with photographing Norman Hartnell's new designs for the robes to be worn by lords and ladies at the coronation, as well as gowns for less exalted guests, and the experience had left her feeling strangely unsettled. The photo-call had been set up as a sort of fashion show, with models parading back and forth in ermine-trimmed velvet and bridal-white satin, their arms swathed in kid-skin gloves that rose past the elbow, their hair crowned with rhinestone tiaras. She'd liked the designs well enough, but the Hartnell showrooms had been so coldly elegant, and the models so otherworldly in their beauty, that Stella had felt ill at ease the entire time.

Upon closer inspection her pictures were fine. Just fine. Not terrible, but not memorable, either, and she was still consumed with this realization when the red light blinked off and Win Keller emerged abruptly from the darkroom.

On her first day at *Picture Weekly*, he'd been introduced to her as the darkroom assistant; in the weeks since, she had come to regard him as the darkroom overlord. Her photographs had never looked better, but he was ruthlessly frank in his criticism of all the photographers' work, hers most of all, and she had quickly learned to be wary of his sharp tongue.

For all that, she had decided she liked him. He was a young man still, but he had an old soul, just like her; and his thorns, she suspected, were defensive ones. She didn't know anything about him, but she felt sure that he, too, had been marked by his past, and that he, too, carried invisible burdens that others could not, or would not, be bothered to notice.

"Those turned out well enough," he now said. "Don't gape at me, Stella. This shot, here—what were you trying to do with it?

At the end of the photo-call, the group of models had formed a sort of procession, and as they'd left the showroom one of the women, taller than the rest, her gown an elegant column of white satin, had turned her head and raised one arm in a regal sort of wave. Stella had slowed the shutter speed on her camera and, relying only on the light from the overhead fixtures and wall sconces, had caught the model's face and shoulders in perfect focus; the rest of the image remained a blur of ghostly figures and receding shadows.

"I wanted to find a moment of stillness in the middle of all the . . . I'm not sure how to describe it."

"The noise?" he offered.

"Yes. I used a shutter speed of one-twenty-fifth of a second. That is the slowest setting on my camera."

"Hmm. I've a Leica you can borrow. Try that instead. Ignore the noise and find those points of stillness."

"I will," she said, astonished at his generosity. "Thank you, Mr. Keller. I promise to take good care of it."

"I know you will." He swung round to face her, and for a moment his expression softened into something close to a smile. Likely thinking better of it, he retreated into the darkroom and shut its door firmly behind him.

A moment later, Frank called to her from the stairs. "Stella, dear—are you joining us?"

The most senior of the staff photographers, Frank had invited her to follow him around for her first week at *PW*, and from him she'd learned how to set up and use the Speed Graphic that he favored for indoor photo-calls. In return, he only asked that she fetch him the occasional cup of tea so his bad knees could have a rest from the stairs.

"I'll be right there!"

On her first day at the magazine she'd been horribly late, not realizing that the front door for the office was located on a laneway rather than Fleet Street proper, and consequently had been both flustered and out of breath when she'd burst into the waiting room. The receptionist had regarded her calmly, not in the least disconcerted by Stella's abrupt arrival.

"Miss Donati?"

"Yes. I am sorry. I was lost—the door . . ."

"It happens to nearly everyone. He's waiting for you."

"Mr. Kaczmarek?

"Yes," the woman had said, smiling, "but don't let him catch you calling him that. He's Kaz to everyone here."

"Where . . . ?"

"Along the corridor, first door on your right."

The door to Mr. Kaczmarek's office had been open, but rather than knock she'd paused at the threshold. A broad-shouldered, fair-haired man had been at the desk, his shoulders hunched as he briskly annotated a typewritten manuscript. "Miss Donati?" he'd asked, his gaze never moving from the pages before him. "Do come in. I won't be a moment."

She'd inched forward and perched on the very edge of a wooden guest chair, and while waiting for him to finish she'd inspected his office. It was small and dusty and terribly messy, with framed photographs and paintings hanging askew on the walls, and not the slightest bit grand. Not the sort of office she had expected for the editor-in-chief of a magazine as respected and widely read as *Picture Weekly*.

"There. That's done," he'd said, setting down his pencil and pushing back in his chair. He'd taken a long look at her, his pale blue eyes made owlish by his spectacles. "Miss Donati. May I call you Stella?"

"Of course."

"I suspect Miss Berridge out front has already warned you that I'm Kaz to everyone here."

"Yes, sir."

At this he'd smiled. "Just Kaz will do. How was your journey from Rome?"

"It was very pleasant, thank you."

"You grew up there?"

"Well, no. Originally I am from Livorno."

"Ah. Beautiful city." And then, unexpectedly, "What led you to photography?"

No one had ever asked, not even those who loved her most. "My mother. She was a photographer." He had made no comment, though his gaze had been intent and unwavering, and in it she'd found the confidence to elaborate. "I wonder if you might have heard of the *Guide di turistiche Donati*?"

"I certainly have. Splendid guides, and so well written they were worth reading for pleasure alone. Are you related to the people who published them?"

"They were my parents. My father wrote the guides and my mother took the photographs and drew the maps. But they were killed in the war."

"I am very sorry to hear it."

"Afterward, I went to live with some friends. They gave me some money for my twenty-first birthday, and I used it to buy a camera. It's the Elettra I still use. I'd had the idea, you see, that I would try to become a photographer like my mother. It was hard, at first. I knew nothing. But I practiced, and I learned, and before very long I started to understand, and the photographs I took began to match the pictures I imagined. I hope that does not sound strange."

"Not in the least. You have a wonderful eye."

"Thank you."

"The photographs you sent were good. Very good. But you need to learn more than how to take an interesting picture in broad daylight with fast film. Frank will help you out—he's our ranking staff photographer. Everyone here will. For my part, I want you to carry your camera wherever you go. Even when you're not at work. Take pictures of anything that catches your eye, and not just a frame or two, either. The whole roll, if that's what it takes. Keep going, and experiment while you're at it, and when you hand over your film to Win Keller upstairs, listen to his advice after he's developed it. Then I want you to bring the prints to me and explain what you saw in your head while you were taking each photo. Does all of that make sense?"

"It does. Thank you."

TWO WEEKS ON, Stella and most of her colleagues were squeezed around the enormous round table in the main part of the newsroom downstairs.

"Morning," Kaz began. "Let's have a round of updates."

He listened attentively, asking the occasional question but leaving most of the commentary to Emil Bergmann, the assistant editor. When the last of the staff writers had weighed in, Kaz nodded decisively. "Good. What's next?"

Everyone was allowed and even expected to offer suggestions at this point, from Mr. Bergmann to Larry Elton, the most junior of the staff writers, and while Stella's confidence had grown since her arrival at *PW* she still found the experience more than a little nerve-racking. All the same, when it was her turn to speak she managed to find her voice.

"I was still in Italy in December, when you had the problems with the smoke in the air here—what did you call it again?"

"The Great Smog," Mr. Bergmann answered. "Dickens himself couldn't have improved on it."

"It was only a few months ago, but I have not read of it in your newspapers or magazines since I arrived in London. Surely there must be many who are still sick, or who are mourning those who died. Could we not do a story about them? With portraits of their faces? And along with the photographs," she continued, though with less certainty, "there might be an editorial that asks what the government is doing to help those who still suffer?"

"Aren't you a ray of sunshine," Larry muttered, but Kaz was already nodding.

"Yes. A welcome break from coronation-related treacle. Who wants to work with Stella on this? Ruby?"

Kaz now looked to the most senior of his staff writers, an American woman who had worked for the magazine longer than almost anyone else excepting Kaz, Frank, and Miss Berridge. Stella had yet to exchange more than occasional good mornings with Miss Sutton, but she seemed friendly enough.

"Sure, I'll do it," Ruby said. "Let me start at one of the East End hospitals. See if I can get some nurses to talk to me. There's usually a chippie or café nearby where they congregate when they come off duty. I'll see where that leads. Might take a week or two to run people down and get their stories."

"That's fine," Kaz said. "In the meantime, Stella, have a word with Win about the portraits themselves."

It was close to five o'clock before Stella worked up the courage to knock on the darkroom door. "Mr. Keller? It's Stella. Kaz told me that I should speak with you. I am to take some photographs, some portraits, of people who are sick because of the Great Smog. Do you have a few minutes?"

He came out of the darkroom, blinking hard in the light, and beckoned her closer. "I do," he said, "but not with you standing halfway across the room."

He was exaggerating, but Stella obliged all the same, taking several steps toward him. "Is this all right?"

"Yes, but only because it's a good way for me to explain what you're doing wrong."

"What I'm doing wrong? I haven't even—"

"You don't get close enough. How far are you from me? You still think in meters, so let's say two meters? Maybe a little less? It's too far. That's what's wrong."

"I don't understand."

"It's human nature to keep your distance from people you don't know well. It's comfortable. It makes you feel safe. And it's a mistake, because it will lead to second-rate work. I guarantee it will."

"I haven't done any portrait photography for the magazine, so how can you know this?"

"I know it because most photographers are guilty of it. You hold your camera to your face, and you look through the viewfinder, and it tricks you into thinking you're close to your subject. But you're not, and the pictures you take will show that distance. I can crop them, certainly. Enlarge them so they have the *appearance* of closeness. But it's extra work for me, and there's a chance the prints will be grainier than either of us would like. For those images to look their best, you need to stand as close as you dare to your subject. Do you understand?"

"I think so? Only . . . what will people think? Will they not be annoyed?"

"It's not your job to worry about what they think. It's your job to take good photographs. Now, imagine that I'm your subject. Hold up your hands as if they're a camera. Like a mime might do, yes. Now take a big step toward me. I'll tell you when to stop."

She took one step forward. Another. Then another. She was close enough to reach out and touch his shoulder. So close she could see the lines at the corner of his eyes, even though he couldn't be more than thirty years old. She could see that he was tired and far too thin, and that the collar on his shirt had begun to fray.

"Stop. Do you understand now?" he asked.

"Yes. I think so."

"Good."

"What sort of name is Win?" she asked, surprising herself.

He stepped back, away, and out of focus. "It's short for Winton."

"After your prime minister?"

"No. Another man entirely. And it's Winton, without an *s*. No one ever gets it right." He turned away, ready to retreat into his darkroom again. "Tonight, once you're home, take some portraits of the people you live with. Get as close as you dare, and then move even closer. Bring me the film when you're done, and I'll tell you if you've bridged that distance."

MARCH

Chapter Nine

JAMIE

Tuesday, March 3, 1953

It was past six o'clock when Jamie returned home, and though he was hungry, having missed tea at the hotel, he was also aware that he smelled quite strongly of the stables where he'd spent much of the day.

The problem of the horses in the coronation procession had been weighing upon him, for he was dissatisfied with his first attempts at drawing the Windsor Greys who would be hauling the enormous gold state coach. To his mind his attempts looked strangely artificial, as if a man who had never before seen a horse had depicted one with the aid of only a secondhand description; and with only three months remaining until the great day, he'd decided an intensive course in equine anatomy was in order.

To that end, Jamie had spent the morning at the National Art Library in the V&A, poring over an original edition of George Stubbs's *Anatomy of the Horse*, not stopping until he had a decent understanding of how the creatures, broadly speaking, were put together. Then he had gone in search of actual horses, which was rather more challenging in 1953 than in Stubbs's day. Fortunately, there were still a number of riding stables in the mews surrounding Hyde Park, and for the cost of a one-hour lesson he'd been allowed to sit in one such establishment's yard all afternoon and draw as many horses as he liked.

He'd enjoyed himself, and he'd learned a great deal over the course of the day, but he badly needed a hot bath before going in search of supper. All the same, rather than head straight upstairs, he continued along the corridor to the library. Miss Howard had promised a good selection, after all, and it was late enough that he was unlikely to disturb Professor Thurloe at his work.

As he'd hoped, the library was empty, though the professor's books and papers were scattered across the table in the middle of the room. Ignoring the leather-bound volumes in glass-fronted cases on the far wall, Jamie made a beeline for the shelves of paperbacks on either side of the fireplace. They held, delightfully, a bookshop's worth of popular novels, Penguin Classics, guides to London, and histories of the city and Britain itself. He selected a murder mystery that his father had recommended in a recent letter, as well as a guide to Wren's churches, and had just left the library when someone came around the corner and bumped into him before Jamie could step out of the way.

He steadied the other man, who was slight of build and none too steady on his feet, and stooped to collect the bundle of books and papers that had fallen to the floor. Only then, stepping back, did he realize he'd collided with Professor Thurloe.

"Are you all right?"

"Yes. Quite all right," the man answered, squinting up through smeary spectacles. "You must be the new boarder."

"I am, yes. James Geddes. I'm sorry I haven't introduced myself before now. We keep missing one another at mealtimes." He held out his hand and the professor shook it readily enough, though he didn't trouble to hide his inquisitive stare. "Is anything the matter?" Jamie asked, resigned to the questions that were sure to follow.

"Not at all. It's only that I hadn't realized you were Indian. Saw you at a distance, and as you don't have a foreign sort of name I assumed you'd been on holiday. Bit of sun and all that."

Now there was an explanation Jamie hadn't heard for a while. "That depends on what you consider foreign. I'm a Scot, but my mother grew up near Bombay."

"Yes, yes. Tremendous place. India, that is. Have you been to see the Amaravati marbles yet? They've gone back on display at the British Museum. Heaven only knows where they were stashed during the war. I'm friends with the Keeper of Oriental Antiquities. If you like I'm sure he'd be delighted to show you around."

"That's very kind of you. Perhaps one day when my work permits."

"Ever been to that part of India?" the professor asked.

"Er, no. Bombay is on the western coast and Amaravati is a good six hundred miles or so to the southeast." Trying to explain that India was no more a monolithic entity than

Europe or Africa was, he had long since learned, a fruitless task.

"Oh, yes," Professor Thurloe agreed. "Quite, quite."

"I gather you've been living here at the Blue Lion for some time?" Jamie asked, hoping to steer the conversation into neutral waters.

"Donkey's years. Bombed out in the war. Can't imagine ever moving on. Although"—and here he pitched his voice to a carrying whisper—"it has been hard going at times, what with the Crane sisters being the only other boarders. Splendid women, but their conversation is not what one would call serious-minded. Quite relieved to have another man here to, ah, balance things out."

"I understand," Jamie said, having endured more than one tedious breakfast with the sisters. He now managed to avoid them, most mornings at least, by appearing in the dining room at the dot of seven o'clock.

"Do come and fetch me if you're ever around for tea," the professor offered. "I tend to forget, you know. Get caught up in my work."

"Perfectly understandable."

"Merton man?" the professor asked suddenly. "Your scarf."

"Oh, right. Yes."

"I'll forgive you for it. Balliol man myself. Well, I had better get back to my work. Good to have met you."

When Jamie returned to the hall, he was surprised to find Miss Howard on the point of leaving for the evening. A man stood next to her, and though he had yet to hear the fellow speak, or even look him in the eye, Jamie disliked him on sight. The stranger wore an expensive suit and handmade shoes, and on the little finger of his left hand was an enormous gold signet ring. His hands were manicured and his hair had been ruthlessly shellacked into place. Likely he was drenched in some expensive cologne, too.

Miss Howard didn't see Jamie, for she was busy putting on her gloves, and before he could blink, let alone say a word, she and the stranger were gone. Off for an evening out, leaving Jamie alone, hungry, tired, and desperate for a hot bath. Now he just had to hope the boiler wasn't on the fritz.

AN HOUR LATER, Jamie was clean, tidy, and very, very hungry. It was late enough that Brooks had been replaced at the hotel's reception desk by the affable Arthur Swan, and though he knew he was likely being unfair to Brooks, who had been faultlessly polite since Jamie's arrival, he couldn't quite shake his memory of their first encounter. Jamie might have imagined the flash of rage in the other man's eyes; it was certainly possible he'd been mistaken, given Brooks's unobjectionable behavior since. All the same, he was glad to see that Mr. Swan was on duty instead.

"Good evening, Mr. Geddes. May I help you with anything?"

"You may indeed. I missed my tea, and I wouldn't mind a pint of beer along with some supper. Which of the nearby public houses would you recommend?"

"That's easy enough, sir. The Queen Bess down at the end of the street should suit you to a tee. Landlord's a friendly type, and you'll probably find Mick taking up room at the bar."

"Is the food decent?"

"Not so good as what Cook makes for us here, but it'll do. Won't leave you with a bellyache, and it's not too dear."

"Thank you. I'll head there now."

The Queen Bess was an ordinary sort of place, with few pretensions to decor apart from a large and badly faded reproduction of the Armada portrait of Elizabeth I. Jamie ordered a pint of lager and took it to a small table in the corner, grateful when the barman said nothing beyond the price of his beer and a brief thank-you for the sixpence Jamie left behind as a tip. The place was as smoky as a kippering shack, but after heaving open a nearby window, he was able to breathe with some degree of comfort.

He'd taken a few sips of beer, and was mulling over the possibility of something more solid for his supper, when a shadow fell across the table. He looked up, suddenly wary, and was relieved to see Mick Nelligan had come over to say hello.

"Mr. Swan told me you might be here. How are you, Mick?"

"Well enough, Mr. Geddes. Mind if I join you?"

"Not at all. Only I do wish you'd call me Jamie."

Mick scratched at his jaw, considering the invitation. "I suppose I could. Not at the hotel, mind. Not sure as Miss Howard would approve."

Jamie doubted that she'd mind in the least, but he nodded all the same. "I understand."

"How're you liking it?" Mick asked once he was seated in the chair opposite Jamie.

"The beer or the hotel?"

"Both."

"The beer is good. Not a patch on a pint of Tennent's, but it'll do. And the hotel is excellent. I couldn't be more pleased."

"I'm glad to hear you say so. Miss Howard's worked ever so hard to keep it going—oh, hold on. Is that Detective Inspector Bayliss I see? Get yourself over here, man!"

"Let me get my order in!" the man protested, his Brummie accent as thick as tar. He had dark auburn hair and a freckled face, and as he approached Jamie could see that he was tired but doing his best to appear cheerful.

Jamie stood and they shook hands. "James Geddes," he offered. "I'm boarding at the Blue Lion."

"Gordon Bayliss. Mind if I join you?"

"Not one bit."

"Gordon's at Scotland Yard," Mick explained, "but not so high-and-mighty that he can't sit down and share a drink with old friends."

"How are you liking the Blue Lion?" Bayliss asked. "I used to stay there during the war."

"It was open?"

"Too small for the government to commandeer. And it was handy for those of us at the Yard."

"You lot were working all hours back then," Mick said. "Expect it was easier to stay put than try and find a way home in the wee hours."

"That it was," Bayliss agreed. "You know, I complain about being run off my feet now, but it was twice as bad in those days. Now we all rabbit on about making do and carrying on and pulling together, and to be fair some did, but . . . well. To my mind, it brought out the worst in people. You name it, I was dealing with it. Assault, rape, murder, and on top of that all the usual stuff. Burglary, affray, vandalism. It was all I could do to keep up."

"I don't doubt it," Jamie said.

"I expect you were still in school during the war," Bayliss said, and since Mick had to be at least sixty years old Jamie knew the policeman was talking to him.

"Only at the beginning. Joined the Royal Engineers in the summer of 1940. Bomb disposal." Only two words, yet they still had the power to shake him.

Bayliss nodded in approval, as did Mick. "Surprised you made it through in one piece."

"So am I." Jamie's hands, tellingly, had begun to tremble. He ignored them, focusing instead on the way the light fell on his glass of lager. He considered how he would paint it; how he would capture the bubbles rising to the surface of the beer. He took one long, deep breath. Then another. And calm, or something close to it, descended again.

"I'm off now," Mick said, heaving himself to his feet. "I'd stay for another, but then young Jamie here would have to carry me home. Night, gentlemen."

They wished him good night; that accomplished, they sat in silence for a few minutes.

"So," Bayliss began. "Now that Mick is safely away, what do you think of the hotel?"

"It's a decent place. Quiet. Good food. Clean rooms."

"How do you think Miss Howard is managing? I've always felt a bit sorry for her, you know. She couldn't have been much older than nineteen or twenty when her parents died and she was stuck with the place. How she's kept it going since then I've no idea."

"If she's struggling, she does a good job of hiding it."

"I don't know as I'd say that. The cracks are showing if you bother to look. Was there any hot water the last time you ran a bath?"

Jamie thought of the tepid bath he'd had that morning. "I gather they've been having trouble with the boiler," he admitted.

"That boiler's been giving them trouble since her grandfather was at the helm. And if it isn't the boiler, it's something else. Only a matter of time before she sells up."

"Can you honestly see her doing that?" Jamie asked, uneasy at the turn their conversation had taken. He'd almost prefer a return to talk of the war. "It's been in her family for centuries."

"If anything's kept her going, it's that. And she does tend to collect waifs and strays. She'll try to keep it open for them, if not for herself."

Jamie couldn't suppress his smile. It was almost charming, really, the notion of Edie Howard as some sort of shepherdess with a flock of lost lambs. "I rather like that about the place," he said.

"Are the Crane sisters still there?"

"The Hons? Oh, yes. They buttonholed me at breakfast the day after I moved in. Regaled me with the story of their cruel cousin Dominic and his thievery. I was tempted to ask about the lawsuit, but sanity prevailed."

"What about the mad professor?"

"Thurloe? I only met him properly for the first time today, but he seemed harmless. A bit oblivious, to be sure."

"That's a nice way of putting it. Obsessive is another. Did you know that he submits monthly complaints to Miss Howard? He tots up all the times he's been annoyed by noise, or hasn't been best pleased with the food or service, and hands it over like a schoolmaster passing out exam results. I don't know why she puts up with it."

Jamie didn't know Miss Howard very well, but he had a good idea of why she would allow such a thing. Or, rather, force herself to endure a monthly recitation of the Blue Lion's failings. She needed the assurance of the professor's continued rent, and she also knew there was no other place for the man to go.

"Never mind me," Bayliss said, perhaps regretting his candor. "I've been dealing with security for the coronation for weeks now, and it's got me on edge. Can't wait until the damn thing is over and done with and I can go on a proper holiday."

Jamie nodded, not knowing what else to say. He'd finished his beer, but was wary of drinking even another mouthful of lager on an empty stomach. "What's the food like here? I missed my tea."

"It's not bad. Try the steak and mushroom pie. If you're lucky, you'll even find some bits of beef in the thing."

"I will. Can I stand you another pint?"

"That you can. Then you can tell me how you ended up at the Blue Lion with the rest of Edie Howard's waifs and strays."

Chapter 10

EDIE

Monday, March 9, 1953

Edie had always been a light sleeper, so the knock at her door, soft as it was, brought her awake in a heartbeat. "Who is it?" she called, already up and searching for her robe.

"It's Mr. Swan. It's the boiler, I'm afraid. I noticed it was colder than usual, so I popped down to the cellar and had a look."

"And?" she prompted.

"I think, perhaps, it's gone out?"

Not disastrous news; not yet. "Did you knock on Dolly's door?"

"Yes, but she didn't answer. I'm worried she may be poorly. Cook said as much when I saw her last night."

That would explain the slumbering boiler, for Dolly was ever diligent in her duties. "I'll check in on her, and then I'll see to the boiler."

"Are you sure? I don't mind trying my hand at it."

"No, that's fine. I don't want to send you home as grimy as a sweep. Mrs. Swan wouldn't thank me for it."

Arthur Swan was excellent at most things, but absolutely hopeless when it came to the boiler. Even Dolly, whose first job of the day was to rise at five A.M. and deal with the wretched thing, excepting only her day off when the chore fell to Mick, had taken weeks to learn how to rake out the cinders, feed it with fresh coal, and bank the fire so it would burn steadily. She also stoked the boiler with fresh coal before going to bed each night, and that last chore of the day ensured the boiler would not go cold in the long hours before dawn.

Edie went down the hall to the room that Dolly and Ruth shared, knocking first, then opening the door when there was no answer. Ruth was snoring gustily in her bed, but Dolly, poor thing, was huddled under her blankets. What looked like her overcoat was draped on top, but beneath, Edie could see, the girl was shivering.

She drew back the covers and saw, with dismay, that Dolly's face had gone quite blotchy with fever, and her hair was damp with sweat.

"Dolly? It's Miss Howard," she whispered, and ran a soothing hand over the girl's brow.

Dolly opened her eyes and blinked hard at the light coming in from the corridor. "Oh, Miss Howard," she managed, her voice cracking. "I'm so sorry. I know I'm past my time—oh! The boiler!" She struggled to rise, but Edie eased her back against the pillow.

"It's in good hands. I'm more concerned about you. Is it your throat?"

"Yes, and my head, and, well, everything. I ache all over. Cook gave me some aspirin last night, and a drink to help with my cough, but then I woke up in the night and I couldn't get warm."

"It was very clever of you to use your coat. I'll have a nice, warm eiderdown brought up, and I'll ask the doctor to stop by if you're still feeling poorly later on."

"I'm so sorry to be a bother," Dolly fretted.

"You're nothing of the sort. Today, your only job is to lie in bed and get better. Would you like something to read? I could pop out and get you some magazines from the newsagent at the station. Is there anything you'd like in particular?"

Dolly's wan face brightened, and she even managed a smile. "If it isn't too much trouble, I'd love the new *Woman's Own*. The one with Princess Margaret on the cover."

"*Woman's Own* it is. I'll also have Cook send up a pot of tea, and some more aspirin, too. That'll help with your head and the fever." Abruptly remembering the still-snoring girl in the other bed, she asked, "Do you think Ruth has caught it?"

"I hope not. She was right as rain last night, though."

"That's a bit of luck, then, isn't it? I doubt we could manage if both of you felt poorly."

Edie returned to her room, but instead of her usual uniform she put on a zip-up siren suit that had originally belonged to her father. It was so baggy that she might easily be mistaken for Churchill himself in poor light, but it was far better suited to boiler maintenance and repair than her usual clothes. On her feet she wore a sturdy pair of boots that she kept for such occasions; over her hair she tied an old scarf. She looked ridiculous, but it was early enough that there was little chance of her running into any of the guests.

The door to the cellar was located off the kitchen corridor; it had originally been tucked into the paneling under the main staircase, but after one guest too many had mistaken it for a coat closet and nearly come to grief, her grandfather had blocked it off and had the stairs moved to the other end of the building. Unfortunately, he had insisted on economizing by reusing the original flight of steps, which were so steep as to require the aid of handrails on both sides; and even with the help of a strong electric light at the bottom, Edie always was a little nervous when navigating the descent.

As cellars went it wasn't so bad, for it had once been the site of the hotel's kitchen, scullery, and storerooms, and consequently had reasonably high ceilings and a good amount of light from deep-set windows. When the boiler had been installed some eighty years ago, her great-grandfather had decided to modernize the hotel. The kitchen had been moved to an adjacent outbuilding, toilets had been installed on each floor, hot and cold running water had been plumbed into sinks in the guest rooms, and central heating had been added via enormous radiators in each of the bedrooms.

The cellar had been used as a shelter during the war, and some nights they'd had so many guests, many of them detectives from Scotland Yard and civil servants from Whitehall, that Edie's father had expanded the shelter area into a tunnel that, centuries ago, had once led to the grounds of Northumberland House, but now ended a few hundred yards to the south.

Edie had never been very confident in the structural integrity of the tunnel, and had been only too happy, after the war, to see it blocked off behind a barricade of surplus doors, broken chairs, boxes of Christmas decorations, and anything else that was too awkward or bulky to be stored elsewhere. The chore of putting that end of the cellar to rights had been on her *Things to Do (Rainy Day)* list for some years, but as few people ever saw the mess apart from herself, Mick, Mr. Brooks, Dolly, and the tiresome Mr. Pinnock, it managed not to bother her overmuch.

She reached the bottom of the stairs and, after switching on the light, was astonished to see that the mess had been cleared away. At some point over the past fortnight, someone had stacked the boxes on either side of the tunnel entrance, and had also disposed of every last piece of rubbish. To her relief, the door itself was still shut, and when she opened it and peered inside, the area beyond appeared to be undisturbed.

It might have been the professor, intent on exploring the tunnel despite her insistence he stay away, but she doubted he'd have been so meticulous in clearing a path to the door. Most likely it had been one of the staff. She would have to ask around and ensure she thanked the person who had taken care of the task for her.

Setting aside that small mystery, she turned her attention to her nemesis. The boiler was made of cast iron, as bulky as an elephant, its elements so large and heavy that they'd been hauled into the cellar piece by piece and riveted together in situ. It was set into what had once been the hotel's original kitchen hearth, then further fortified by layers of brickwork, and nothing short of exploding dynamite or an earthquake could hope to dislodge it. Edie had, variously, imagined both, though in highly localized forms that only affected the boiler and no other portion of the Blue Lion.

As it wasn't long past the usual time to stir up the banked coals, Edie very much hoped that a low fire was the beginning and the end of the boiler's complaints. She set a hand on the flue door, and was relieved to find it warm. Not hot, or anything close to it, but it was far from stone cold.

Before investigating further, Edie collected two scuttles of coal from the adjacent storage bin, which was filled at weekly intervals via a chute that opened onto the back courtyard, put an empty bucket for the ashes and cinders to her right, and last of all set a low stool in front of the boiler's central flue. With everything arranged, she opened the flue door, peered in, and all but shouted out her relief when she saw the fire was still burning, though very feebly. A little encouragement would soon have it going again.

She spent the next half hour shoveling out ash and cinders, adding in fresh coal, layering on the still-glowing embers she'd raked to the side earlier, and then, when the fire had begun to burn in earnest, banking the coals to ensure a slow and steady level of heat. Last of all she swept up the mess she'd made. The ash buckets were too heavy for her to manage, so she left them for Mick, who carried them up each morning and evening, and made her way back upstairs and into the kitchen.

Cook regarded Edie with sympathy. "Were you able to get it going again?" she asked.

"Oh, yes. It knew better than to put up a fight."

"I checked on Dolly before I came down. Expect she'll be in bed for another day or two. D'you think it's flu?"

"I hope not. Probably it's just a nasty cold. I did promise I'd fetch her some magazines to keep her occupied."

"Don't you bother with that. I'll send Ruth out. How about a cup of tea?"

"I'd love one. I'd love a bath even more, but it'll take ages for the water to heat up."

"I'll draw off a pitcher of hot water from the range. Not enough for a bath, but you'll be able to wash your face and hands. Sit tight with your tea while I lay everything out for you."

"You're so kind to me."

"You deserve it, Miss Edie. Forever taking care of the rest of us, you are. Nice to have the chance to do something for you. And it'll perk you right up, it will."

So Edie sat and waited for Cook, and she let herself think of nothing more than how wonderful the hot mug felt in her hands, and even though she was chilled to the marrow and so tired she was ready to tip over sideways, she resisted the urge to slip into somnolence. Instead she watched Cook bustle back and forth, and she sipped at her tea, and she remembered other visits to the kitchen over the years, other times that Cook had mothered her, and she felt a surge of gratitude that was dizzying. It was almost enough to make her cry.

Of course she wouldn't dream of crying, for it would only alarm Cook. Instead she drank her tea and thought of how lovely it would feel when she washed the grit from her eyes and the coal dust from her hands.

"It's all ready for you," Cook called out from the scullery. "There's a fresh facecloth and towel, and some of the nice soap we used in the guest baths."

It was an effort even to stand, which was alarming given that the day had scarcely begun. Somehow she managed to stagger over to the scullery, where Cook had arranged two bowls of steaming water on the draining board. "Thank you."

She rolled back her sleeves, opened the collar of her siren suit and tucked it back, and picked up the little bar of soap. It smelled of rose petals and geranium leaves, and it lifted her spirits instantly.

By the time she finished with her hands and face, both bowls of water were gray, the facecloth and towel were in need of a good bleaching, but she felt like a new woman. Edie was emptying the first bowl of water into the sink when Cook plucked it from her hands and sent her packing. "Off you go—it's past six already and Mr. Swan is waiting to give you his report."

"Of course. Would you mind having my breakfast sent through to my office? I'll eat at my desk this morning."

As keen as she was to change, she didn't wish to keep Mr. Swan waiting, for he'd want to see his children before they headed off to school. She had just emerged from the still-dark dining room into the front hall, and had hoped to make it into her office undetected, when someone called to her from the stairs.

"Is that you, Miss Howard?"

She stopped short, resigned to the mild embarrassment of being seen in the unflattering siren suit. "Good morning, Mr. Geddes," she answered, for she'd recognized the soft burr of his accent straightaway. "Please excuse the way I'm dressed. We had a spot of trouble with the boiler this morning."

He descended the last few steps to join her in the hall. "A practical woman," he said admiringly. "I'm beginning to think there's nothing you can't do."

"Oh, I can think of any number of things. Painting, for a start. I can draw a very fine cat, but that's all."

"I may ask for proof, you know."

Never in her life had she spoken to a guest in such an unguarded fashion. "Will you? Then I may ask for help with the boiler."

In an instant, the merry expression was wiped clean from his face. "I wish I could," he said, his voice laced with regret. "I can't bear to be belowground. I'll gladly fix anything for you in this building, from the floor we're standing on to the slates on the roof, but I'm not sure I could ever force myself to go down into your cellar. A legacy from the war, I'm afraid. Sorry."

"Don't apologize. I was only joking, you know—I'd never dream of asking a guest to help in that way."

"What about a friend?" he asked softly.

"Oh, friends as well. I've few enough, and I don't dare lose one to the wrath of that damnable boiler. Excuse my language, but it's been trying my patience this morning."

"I don't doubt it. Where are you off to now?"

"Oh, I . . . well, Mr. Swan is just waiting to give me his report, and then I'll run upstairs to change, and then I suppose I'll get on with my day." Emboldened, she dared a question of her own. "You're up and about quite early. Is that usual for you?"

"Oh, aye. Easier to think when it's quiet. Streets are quieter, too." At her questioning look, he added, "If the weather's fine, I go for a walk most mornings. Usually I start at the river and walk south to Westminster, across the river to the south bank, and then back across the Bailey bridge they put up for the festival. It's only about a mile, but it does me good."

"All at the crack of dawn?"

"Earlier, if I can manage. It helps with my work, you see. Makes it easier to concentrate if I've emptied my mind of my worries. I hope that doesn't sound too farfetched."

"Not at all. I do try to take a walk every day, though it's usually after lunch. And I always seem to spend it fretting about something or other."

"Then don't," he said, and the look he gave her was both understanding and concerned. "The moment you leave the hotel for your walk, from your very first step, leave all of it behind."

"I can't. I mean . . . how could I? It's all I . . ."

It's all I think of, she wanted to say. Worry and fear and the near-paralyzing certainty that she was running out of time, and that she was failing, sinking, drowning, and had drifted so far from shore that no one would hear her cries for help, or even notice that she was gone, and—

"Miss Howard. This isn't a test, and I'm certainly not judging you, but I think you and I might be a little alike." He offered this last suggestion hesitantly, as if she might recoil from the notion. "Because I worry, too. I always have. Hence the walks."

"Is it really that simple? Leaving it all behind? How do you do it?"

"I suppose I try to stop thinking and start looking."

"Looking?" she echoed, not understanding, for didn't he spent his days engaged in looking at things and then painting them?

"Yes. I look at the color of the sky, the faces of the people I pass, the leaves on the trees, the wind on the water. Sometimes I listen for birdsong. It's almost always there if you search for it. Even in the busiest parts of the city, it's there. I promise."

"Thank you, Mr. Geddes. I . . ."

He nodded. And then, quietly, though they stood alone at the bottom of the stairs, "I'll listen, you know. Not because I expect anything in return. Not because I want anything from you. Simply because you deserve it."

"A listening ear?"

"Yes. And a friendly one, too."

Their eyes met. The seconds marched past, marked by the ticking of the clock by the front desk, yet neither looked away.

He had the most beautiful eyes. He'd taken a step toward her, close enough that she could see the colors that striated his irises. Tortoiseshell, she thought. His eyes looked exactly like tortoiseshell held up to the light.

A delicate cough from the reception desk brought an abrupt end to her musings. "Miss Howard? I'm ever so sorry, but I'll miss my train if I don't leave soon."

"I'm so sorry, Mr. Swan. I'll be right there." And then, to Mr. Geddes, "I must go, but I won't forget what you said. I hope you have a lovely day."

HER OWN DAY was singularly unlovely. The Hons were, naturally, affronted by the chill in the air and the lack of hot water, but she managed their complaints by having fires laid in their bedroom and sitting room, and a pot of tea and lemon biscuits sent up for elevenses. Then, when Dolly's fever did not come down with the help of rest and *Woman's Own* and regular doses of aspirin, Edie called for the doctor. Fortunately, he was able to stop by on the way to his afternoon surgery.

"Looking like strep throat," he pronounced after examining the girl. "I took a swab. If it comes up positive I'll send along some penicillin tablets. They'll clear it up in no time."

"Is it catching?" Edie asked.

"Not compared to some bugs. All the same, keep her isolated until she's better, and let me know if anyone else begins to feel poorly."

Now it was long past midday and Edie had barely touched her breakfast and lunch, she had a headache brewing, and she had yet to cross off so much as a single item from her list. It had been a wretched day, with hours yet to endure, and she badly needed a few moments of peace.

But not quite yet. The telephone began to ring in the front hall, and she listened, bracing herself internally, as Ivor answered. A moment later the phone on her desk began to trill.

"Good afternoon, Miss Howard speaking."

"David Bamford here. How are you?" And then, without waiting for her answer, "I'm in town tonight. Have a pair of tickets to *Paint Your Wagon*. Thought we might make an evening of it. Could dine at my club. What say you?"

What, indeed, did she have to say? It had become a sort of habit to accept his invitations, and while he was amusing and generous and generally pleasant company, she hesitated.

It was the conversation she'd had with Mr. Geddes that morning that gave her pause, and the memory of the rare moment of peace it had afforded her in a long day filled to the brim with tedious conversations and unfulfilling obligations. That memory alone was enough to propel a single word past her lips.

"Why?"

"What do you mean, 'why'?" he sputtered.

"Why are you asking me out?" she clarified, as much for herself as for him. "I feel quite certain that it's not because you have any romantic interest in me. You don't, do you?"

"Hold on—"

"I don't mind, only I don't think we're friends, either. Would you say we are friends?"

"Where is all of this coming from?"

A listening ear, she thought. "I don't think you especially like me, or find me interesting or amusing. The only thing about me that you do like, and which I know you want for yourself, is my hotel."

"Edwina, my dear, I am shocked you would say such a thing. More than that, I am affronted. Truly affronted."

"Perhaps you didn't believe me when I told you I would never sell the Blue Lion. I expect you thought I just needed to be wined and dined a little more thoroughly. And I did enjoy our evenings out. I did. But I would rather not go out with you again. Good-bye."

Edie returned the telephone's headset to its place on the cradle, extinguishing the last of Mr. Bamford's incoherent protests, and at once a feeling of clarity came over her. She sat at her desk a moment more, then she put on her coat and hat and gloves and marched to the front door before she could change her mind. "I'll be back in half an hour," she called back to Ivor.

Leave all of it behind, Mr. Geddes had said.

Edie stepped out onto the pavement, into the late-afternoon sunshine, and began to walk toward the Thames. She followed the same route she always took, but this time she looked at the sky. She noticed how its pale blue was shaded through with gray, how the clouds were mere wisps of swansdown, as insubstantial as dreams, and how the wind seemed intent on chasing them ever westward, its invisible broom sweeping the sky clean.

She turned onto the gardens along the Embankment, and she admired the arching tracery of the lime trees, their leaves still firmly in bud, and in them, for she was listening now, really listening, she heard the merry chirping of house sparrows, the chatter of blue tits, and the staccato whistles of a rotund little robin. Beyond their song was the ceaseless hum of traffic, the clatter of trains as they came and went from Charing Cross, and the mournful lowing of the tugboats on the Thames.

London was beautiful, and not just in the way that visitors thought it beautiful. There was delight to be found in smaller things, too. This pleasant park, for instance, with its tidy beds of fragrant blooms and its soothing fountains that muted all but the loudest of the traffic barreling along nearby roads.

Her life was beautiful, too, but she'd allowed the tedium of tiresome obligations to obscure that truth for far too long. She had forgotten how to live, just as she had forgotten there were birds in the trees whose song, sweet and joyful, had been there all along, waiting for her to remember, and to listen, and to love. She would not allow herself to forget again.

Chapter 11

STELLA

Wednesday, March 18, 1953

The Leica IIIf that Mr. Keller had lent her was a revelation. It had taken Stella a week or so to overcome her initial anxiety that she would lose or break it, for the camera's body alone had to be worth close to a hundred pounds; but she'd soon discovered that it was wonderfully easy to use, with a rangefinder that made it almost impossible to take out-of-focus pictures, along with controls that were both elegant and intuitively designed. She was already dreading the day when he would ask for it back.

Her first photographs with the Leica had been utterly forgettable, for she hadn't quite learned the knack of capturing a subject that was moving at speed, and the distraction of the rangefinder had led to some perfectly focused images without a single identifiable point of interest. All the same, day by day, frame by frame, her work had steadily improved.

"This lot of pictures is good," Mr. Keller had told her last week. "Not great, not yet, but good all the same. Past time for you to make a start on those portraits I asked for. Don't tell me you've forgotten."

"I haven't, no." She paused, wary of irritating him with excuses or long-winded explanations. "I live in a hotel," she began, "and although I am friends with the woman who owns it, and I know the names of the people who work there, and the other boarders, too, it is only enough to say good morning and to talk about the weather. So that is why I have not started. Not yet, I mean."

"I understand, but I still want you to do the portraits. Not least because taking a person's photograph is a pretty good way to get to know them. You aren't planning on staying silent the whole time you're taking their pictures, are you?"

"Well, no . . ."

"Then talk with them. Like as not, they'll be a little nervous, and part of your job is to put them at ease. And the best way to do that is to strike up a conversation. Nothing too weighty, of course. Ask them how long they've worked at the hotel, what they're planning for their next day off, what they saw the last time they went to the pictures. Questions like that are more than enough to get most people started, and by the time you're done you'll know your subjects a lot better. I expect you'll have taken some fine photographs, too."

Stella had been tired and hungry by the time she'd returned home that afternoon, and though she ought to have gone to her room and dropped off her bags and washed her face and hands, she'd been unable to resist the siren call of freshly baked scones coming from the dining room. She had just settled into an empty table in the far corner of the room when Edie had appeared at the kitchen door, a pot of tea in one hand and a tiered plate loaded down with sandwiches and cakes in the other. Rather than deliver it to one of the other guest tables, she had marched straight over to Stella.

"Here you are. I saw you come in, and I had a feeling you were more than a bit peckish."

The term was unfamiliar but Stella had understood Edie's meaning all the same. "Thank you. I am indeed very peckish." And then, knowing that Mr. Keller would expect an answer when she saw him tomorrow, "Would you like to join me? I have something to ask you. A favor."

"I'm all ears. Just let me fetch myself a cup and saucer, and then we can talk."

By the time Edie had returned, only a few minutes later, Stella had wolfed down two triangles of cheese-and-pickle sandwich, and had made a good-sized dent in the slab of gingerbread cake. The scones she would save for after their conversation.

"I need to practice taking portraits," she'd begun. "Mr. Keller at the magazine wants me to practice on the people I live with." As an explanation it was rather opaque, but Edie hadn't been fazed.

"You would like to take photographs of the other guests? Is that what you are asking? I can tell you that the Crane sisters will be delighted, but the professor will probably fuss."

"Not the other guests, no. I would like to take your picture, and Cook's, if she will agree, and some of the others who work here. Only so I may practice—the photographs will not be published. But I can ask Mr. Keller to make copies if you decide you like them."

"I don't mind at all," Edie had said. "And I'm sure the others will love having pictures to share with their families." She'd sipped at her tea, then, setting down her cup, had fixed her gaze on Stella once more. "Who is this Mr. Keller? Your editor?"

"No. He is in charge of the darkroom. Of all the photography. He is . . ." How was she to describe the man? She didn't know him well at all, didn't know the first thing about his life outside work, had yet to have a single conversation with him on a subject that didn't revolve around her photographs. "He is a good teacher," she offered. "He understands what I am trying to do."

"I'm glad to hear it. Where were you thinking of taking the pictures? The lounge might be nice. Or what about here in the dining room?"

"I would rather use natural light. Perhaps outside?"

"There is a nice spot by the kitchen door in the back. Shall I show you?"

Stella went with Edie to inspect the cobbled backyard of the hotel, and then they had gone to the kitchen and talked to Cook and Ruth and Dolly, and with everything settled they had decided upon Saturday afternoon for the portrait session.

Stella had borrowed a chair from the dining room and set it in front of the hotel's ancient back wall, its faded brick obscured by the spidery seed heads and glossy leaves of a winter-flowering clematis. The weather had been fine, the sun hanging low in the western sky, and there'd been a wonderful softness to the light in the yard.

Edie had sat for her first, and one by one the others had followed, each of them touchingly eager to help, and also a little nervous at the uncommon experience of having their picture taken.

"There's a street photographer who used to work along a stretch of Mile End," Dolly had explained, her wan and rather homely face brightening as she talked. "He took the nicest picture of me and my mum when I was little. My dad said it was too dear, but Mum said we had to have it. All these years, and it's still up on the wall in the kitchen at home."

STELLA NOW SAT at her usual place at the table upstairs and waited for the red light above the darkroom door to blink off. It wouldn't do to interrupt Win Keller, not even with a soft knock on the door. Not when he was developing her portraits from the Blue Lion.

She'd handed him the rolls of film without a word, for she'd already been late for the weekly editorial meeting; and once the meeting had finished, nearly an hour ago, she'd run back upstairs and begun her watch at the table. Of the meeting itself she had almost no recollection. For all she knew, Kaz had told her to knock on the door at Buckingham Palace and ask if the queen might possibly be available for a photo shoot that afternoon.

At long last the light clicked off and Mr. Keller appeared, a stark silhouette at the darkroom door. He didn't so much as glance at her, his attention focused on the prints he was hanging up to dry.

"What are you waiting for?" he asked.

She walked over to him and forced herself to ask the one question that had been on her mind all morning. "What do you think?"

"I'll tell you in a moment. First I want to know what you think. Are they good?"

"Yes. Yes, I think so."

"Why?" He still hadn't turned to look at her.

She answered with the first thought that came into her head. "They are honest."

It was true. They were an honest representation of what she had seen with her own eyes. Her eyes, and the true afternoon light, and no more. Perhaps, she had to admit, they were too honest. Edie was a pretty woman, but her portrait didn't hide how weary she'd been on Saturday, the delicate skin under her eyes shadowed by exhaustion. The image was both moving and arresting but not, Stella thought, the sort of thing her friend would wish to have hanging on the wall.

"They are honest," Mr. Keller agreed, "and they are good. Very good. If you can produce something like these when you take the portraits for the story about the Great Smog and its aftermath, you'll have done well."

They stood side by side, together surveying her work, and then he nodded to a row of prints he'd hung on a lower wire. "Tell me about these."

"When I finished the portraits I still had the best part of a roll left. I didn't want to waste the film, so I went around the hotel and looked for interesting things."

She hadn't put much thought into the exercise, only looking for elements in the hotel's historic interior that seemed noteworthy: a set of initials painstakingly carved into the age-darkened oak paneling in the library; a pane of old glass that had caught and refracted the last of the afternoon sun; the worn stone lion on the carved plaque outside; the faded velvet and richly carved wood of a single chair, now set on a raised dais in the dining room, on which Elizabeth I had, if the legend was true, taken her ease while sheltering from a winter storm nearly four centuries earlier.

"I know the Blue Lion is not a living thing, but it seems to me that it has a character of its own. I wonder if . . ."

"Go on," he prompted.

"What if we were to do a story on the hotel? The world has changed a great deal in four hundred years, but the Blue Lion is still here. That is itself a story, is it not? There cannot be many other places like it left in London."

"Certainly there are fewer now than before the war." Mr. Keller squinted at the photographs, then frowned. "These are still damp. Better to fetch Kaz up here so he can look at them. Go on—it's your story. You need to be the one to convince him."

Stella hurried downstairs and along the hall to Kaz's open door. She knew better than to knock or otherwise interrupt her editor, whose attention was absorbed by a typewritten document festooned with annotations in red ink.

"Won't be a moment," Kaz muttered. "Almost done with this piece of tripe. What on earth was I thinking?" And then, flinging aside his pen, he sat up, stretched, and waved Stella forward. "Sorry about that. I asked a young MP from the northeast for an opinion piece on the nationalization of the coal industry. Don't know what came over me, and now I'm stuck with a thousand words of rubbish to wrestle into shape."

"I can come back later."

"No, no. I could use some time to clear my head."

"I have an idea," she said, still hovering at the door.

Kaz nodded, waiting for her to elaborate.

"Do you remember when you asked me to speak to Mr. Keller about the portraits for the story about the Great Smog? I did, and he told me to practice with the people I live with as subjects. Would you come with me to look at them?"

"Certainly." Kaz heaved himself to his feet and followed her back upstairs. "Hello, Win."

Stella waited for Mr. Keller to take over, but he stepped back and out of the way. "This is your idea, Stella. Go on."

Her heart was racing, but she couldn't be certain if it was due to nerves or excitement. Likely it was a bit of both. "These are the portraits I took of the people who work at the Blue Lion. That's where I live. This woman, here, is Edie Howard. The hotel was founded by her ancestors almost four hundred years ago, and now she owns it. And this"—here she pointed to her photograph of the timeworn chair on its little dais in the dining room—"is a chair that Elizabeth the First once sat upon when she was caught in a storm."

The idea was evolving and growing as she spoke. "London has changed so much since the coronation of the first Elizabeth. I thought that by telling the story of this one place, the sort of place most people pass by without ever knowing its history, we might also tell the story of London."

Kaz was frowning, but Stella recognized it as the good sort of frown that meant his interest had been piqued. He leaned forward, his attention focused on the handful of photos she'd taken of the hotel's exterior. "It doesn't look very remarkable from the outside. I'd have thought it no more than a century old."

"The outside was changed not so very long ago," Stella clarified, "but inside it is easy to see the old parts of the building."

"I understand. Are there any paintings or drawings of the exterior before it was changed?"

"There is one in the front hall, but I haven't looked at it closely," Stella admitted.

"Very well. Let's start with your sounding out Miss Howard. See if she's willing to let us do a piece on the hotel and her family's involvement. While you're at it, ask for permission to reproduce any historic images she has of the hotel. Paintings, drawings, old photographs. Let me know how you get on."

With that, he retreated back downstairs, leaving an astonished Stella in his wake.

"Why the look of surprise?" Mr. Keller asked. "Of course he liked your idea. It's good, you know." He briskly unclipped her photographs of the hotel and gathered them into a neat bundle. "Show these to Miss Howard. And good luck."

EDIE WAS SITTING at the front desk when Stella arrived home. At her inquiring glance, Edie smiled ruefully. "Mr. Brooks had to leave early, and Mr. Swan doesn't arrive until six o'clock. How was your day?"

"Very good. How was yours?"

"Busy. I think that's the best I can say for it."

"I had another question for you, but if you are tired—"

"No, no—go on. I'm fine."

"After I finished with the portraits, I still had some film left, so I took some pictures of the Blue Lion. They turned out very well—I'll show them to you in a moment—and they gave me an idea. Would you agree to *Picture Weekly* publishing a story about the Blue Lion? About its history, I mean, and the Howard family, and how it has changed over the centuries. My editor likes the idea, but we need your permission, and so I was hoping—"

"Of course you have it! Oh, Stella—thank you. Thank you *so* much for thinking of the hotel."

"You are most welcome. Would you like to see the pictures I took? I will take more, of course, and one of the writers will come to speak with you. Is that all right?"

"Certainly it is. Is there anything else you need?"

"There is." Turning, Stella pointed to the framed watercolor hanging across the hall. "Is that a picture of the hotel before the outside was changed?"

"It is. I'll come round and take it down for you." Edie rose from the reception desk and emerged from the adjacent door into the hall. Together they crossed to the far wall and inspected the little painting.

"It dates to the 1830s, I think," Edie explained. "You can still see the half-timbered exterior and the galleried first floor. Then, about twenty years later, my great-grandfather had two stories added, the gallery closed in, and the whole of the exterior covered over with brick to match the other buildings on the street."

The painting was charming, but Stella could see immediately that it would not do. There was water damage along its margins, and the pigments had faded badly. "It is very nice, but I am not certain that we will be able to use it. The condition . . ."

"I know. I keep meaning to have it restored, but I'm not sure who to ask. Perhaps Mr. Geddes might know."

"What might I know?" came a voice from behind them.

Edie whirled around, a delicate flush coloring her cheeks, but her voice was composed when she answered him. "Mr. Geddes! How helpful that you've returned at the exact moment when we need your advice. Stella is a photographer at *Picture Weekly*—perhaps you knew that already?—and they are thinking of doing a story about the hotel. She asked to see a picture of the original exterior, but I'm afraid this sad little watercolor is all I have."

Stella had encountered Mr. Geddes a few times before, though only in passing, but he'd seemed a pleasant and decent man. His reaction to Edie's news confirmed her fine opinion of him.

"That's splendid news! About the story, I mean. You could pay for a hundred advertisements and still not get half the attention that a story in a magazine like *Picture Weekly* will bring. As for the painting, I'm sure I can help."

"That's what I wanted to ask," Edie explained. "Can you recommend anyone who might restore it for me?"

"I can, but it would take some time, and it wouldn't be inexpensive. What if I were to copy it instead?"

But Edie was shaking her head. "No, I couldn't possibly ask that of you, not with all the work you have to do for your commission."

"It will only take me a few days at most if I do it up in pen and ink and a few washes of color. Would that suit your needs, Miss Donati?"

"I think so, although I would have to ask my editor."

"It's too much," Edie protested. "Really, it is."

Rather than answer, Mr. Geddes took Edie's hands in his, and he waited for her to look him in the eye, and then he smiled. "Let me do this for you. Please."

Edie nodded. Mr. Geddes took a step back, releasing her hands, and only then did he return his attention to Stella. "Let me know what your editor says. If he has any questions, I'd be happy to speak with him. Good evening, Miss Howard, Miss Donati."

"Good evening," Edie replied, her voice softly yearning. Could it be . . . ? But the other woman's expression, when she turned to Stella again, betrayed no evidence of anything more than professionally appropriate sentiments for a guest of the hotel.

"Well," Edie said, "that was fortuitous." And then, after glancing at her wristwatch, "Would you like to have your tea with me? We'll have to eat in my office, though, in case anyone stops by the reception desk."

"I would like that, yes."

"Oh, good. On busy days like this I usually end up bolting down a few sandwiches at my desk, but as long as I leave the door open we can sit in the easy chairs by the fire and take our time. Such a treat for me, and a lovely way to celebrate. Quite honestly, Stella, this is the best news I've had in ages. Let's pretend the tea is champagne, and we'll toast your magazine, and your editor, and Mr. Geddes, too. How lucky I am that fate brought you both to my door."

Chapter 12

JAMIE

Thursday, March 26, 1953

It was the smell that woke him, a noxious stench of damp and sweat and blood and cordite that clogged his throat and stopped his nose. His eyes were open, but the dark that enshrouded him was absolute, and though he struggled for long minutes, he couldn't free even a single limb from the invisible bonds that secured him.

It had been his decision alone, and his duty, to descend into the frost-rimed cellar of the ruined farmhouse not far north of Rome, and once there to defuse the UXB that had flattened the humble structure, and when he'd finished and his men had begun to haul it away, he had insisted on staying behind so he might shine his electric torch into the corners of the void to ensure no other live ordnance remained behind.

It was empty, apart from a tangle of broken timbers, wire, and burst sacks of dried corn. He'd turned, ready to climb out, but then his sergeant had called out, and a heartbeat later there had been more shouts, and Jamie had known. He had known what was about to become of him.

There had been no time to fear, only enough to hold his breath as a dull roar had signaled the collapse of the ground beneath him. He'd been carried away by the surge of noise and the storm of rushing debris, and when he had opened his eyes again he'd been greeted by silence and impenetrable darkness.

He was alive but alone. He was trapped in a hole deep below the ground. His grave, he supposed. He shouted for help, but none came, and after a while he stopped shouting because he couldn't be sure if any fresh air was getting in.

Smoke began to drift into the hole, so he covered his face with his shirt, but he was only able to take in shallow breaths without coughing. The smell was awful, but oblivion was not far away, not now. All he had to do was bear it a little longer.

Alone in the dark, he thought of the people he loved. His mother and father, brother and sister, the nieces and nephews destined to know him only through stories and photographs. He blinked, they vanished, and another face bloomed before his sightless eyes.

Edie Howard. Kind and lovely, stoic and selfless, funny and wise. She was the sort of woman he'd waited his entire life to meet, but it was too late, too late, and now she would never know.

The tomb around him shifted once more. He was falling, too surprised to shout or even struggle, and when he hit the ground the last of the air was knocked from his lungs. Yet oblivion did not follow, not then, nor for many seconds after. Encouraged, he reached out, expecting to touch hard-packed earth or cold stone, and instead found . . . carpet?

Jamie opened his eyes and recognized, in the feeble half-light of dawn, his room at the Blue Lion. He'd been dreaming, though the farmhouse and its infernal cellar were something like a thousand miles distant and a decade in the past. He must have fallen out of bed.

Rather than get up, he lay back and waited for his heartbeat to slow and his limbs to cease their trembling. He lay on the floor until he felt steadier, and then he got to his feet and went to the window. It was raining, the sky a leaden gray, and he was too tired and glum, he decided, to venture out on a walk just yet.

Instead he crossed the hall and had a brief and very hot bath, shaved, and got dressed. It was far too early for breakfast, so he went to his desk, switched on the light, and pulled out the portrait of the Blue Lion he'd begun the day before. And then, a measure of his hard-won equilibrium regained, he began to draw.

JAMIE MADE STEADY progress all day, stopping only for breakfast at seven o'clock and then, when his stomach began to grumble, a rather indigestible bacon sandwich from the Queen Bess for his lunch. It was getting on for five o'clock when he set aside the portrait of the Blue Lion and resolved to go on a proper walk before tea.

It occurred to him, as he put on his coat and began to descend the stairs, that he might ask Miss Howard to come with him on the walk. He lost and regained his nerve more than once on the short journey from his room to the front hall, but the sight of her by the reception desk, deep in conversation with the tiresome Ivor Brooks, propelled him forward.

She turned at the sound of his footsteps. "Good afternoon, Mr. Geddes. How are you?"

"Very well, thank you."

"I was about to take your advice and go for a walk. Would you like to come with me?"

For a long moment he simply stared at her, worried that he might have misheard. But she only smiled, and tilted her head a little, as if she were waiting for an answer, and he concluded that his ears had not misled him. "I would," he managed at last. "Thank you." He hadn't felt quite so much like a blushing schoolboy since he had been an actual schoolboy. Another one of her smiles and he'd forget his own name.

"Let me fetch my coat. I won't be a moment."

She retreated into her office, leaving him alone with Brooks, who had evidently listened to the entire exchange and, judging from his sour expression, was not best pleased by Miss Howard's plans for the next half hour. Perhaps the man disapproved of her fraternizing with the guests, though as the hotel's outright owner she might do as she pleased. Or perhaps—Jamie thought this far more likely—Brooks disapproved of the specific guest.

"Shall we go?" Miss Howard, now suitably prepared for the changeable weather, had returned to the hall, and the sight of her pushed Ivor Brooks from Jamie's thoughts entirely.

"Yes, please," he answered. "Do you have a destination in mind?"

"I do," she said as they left the Blue Lion behind. "One of my favorite places in London."

He followed her across Northumberland Avenue and along Great Scotland Yard, then down Whitehall to Downing Street, with a quick wave to the bobby on guard outside Number Ten, and last of all across Horse Guards Road to St. James's Park. The wind was a little too gusty, and the traffic too noisy, to allow for much conversation, so he had to be content with her smiles and the few words of direction she shared as they walked.

She stopped them at the park's entrance and directed his attention to a weather-beaten sign affixed to an adjacent railing. "I hope you'll agree to abide by the rules and regulations," she said, stepping aside so he might read them. There were the usual admonitions against picking the flowers and scattering rubbish about, as well as—

Visitors may not wash their clothes in the pond, nor may they dip their heads in the water.

"What do you think?" she asked, already laughing.

"I must say I am disappointed at the inflexibility of the rules. What if I wish to go for a brisk swim with the swans?"

"Perhaps it is still rather cool for such frolicking," she admitted, her eyes sparkling with delight.

"I suppose—but what will I do in July?"

"Oh, I don't know . . . perhaps you could dampen a handkerchief in the water and use it to wipe your fevered brow?"

He quite liked this silly side of Edie Howard, and for a moment he wondered who else, among her acquaintances, was fortunate enough to witness it. She was kind and patient with her employees but not, he suspected, the sort to share jokes at mealtimes. Assuming she even shared her meals with them. If not, did she eat alone in her room or at her desk? He hoped she didn't, for it could only serve to underscore the loneliness he sensed in her. And though he couldn't say he knew her well, at least not yet, he did recognize the solitary nature of her life.

"I thought we might walk over to Duck Island," she suggested. "Unfortunately, we're rather late for the pelican feeding, but there are some pleasant places to sit along the pathways."

"Pelican feeding?"

"Oh, yes. Mr. Hinton, the keeper, brings out a bucket of herrings for them at four o'clock each afternoon. It's quite fun to watch."

They crossed over a short wooden boardwalk and past an impossibly picturesque cottage where, Jamie assumed, Mr. Hinton the pelican keeper lived. Presently they came to the end of the path, and since there was a waiting bench and a pretty view across the lake to the old suspension bridge, they sat and watched a pair of swans glide past. The sounds of the city fell away, leaving only birdsong and greenery and peace.

"I could stay here for hours," she admitted.

"A long day?"

"Ever so long. It started at breakfast. Young Dolly is our scullery maid, and she simply adores the royal family, and of course I knew she would be very upset by Queen Mary's death. Unfortunately, she was so upset that she was in floods of tears all morning and quite useless to Cook and Ruth. Was driving everyone to distraction with her predictions that the queen will be brokenhearted and the coronation will be ruined."

"I was sorry to hear the news that Queen Mary had died, but I can't say I dwelled on it."

"Nor did I. It's not that I wasn't fond of the old dear. I was, of course. She seems to have always been there, in the background, hasn't she? But she was getting on, and she did have the sort of life where she wanted for nothing. Set against the world's ills, it's not what one would call a great tragedy, is it?"

"I suppose not. Though it must be hard for her family. She was a queen, but she was also someone's granny."

Miss Howard nodded. "I've always thought it must be a lonely life. Not without its consolations, naturally, but to know that one is always on view, always being watched . . ." She shuddered delicately. "I think I should hate it."

"The wealth and privilege part of it? That doesn't appeal at all?" he asked in what he hoped she recognized was a playful tone.

"Oh, I wouldn't say no to a smallish amount of riches. Enough to set the Blue Lion to rights, and to provide some security for my employees when they retire. Perhaps I should consider the football pools."

"I think the chances of any of us winning the pools is about the same as the queen doing cartwheels down the Mall on Coronation Day."

"Can you imagine?" She turned to face him, her smile wide and unaffected, her delight shining in her eyes, and Jamie was seized by the realization that his heart had become too large for his chest.

Rather than respond in a normal fashion, with a smile and some quip about being a betting man, he said the first thing that came into his head. "Will you call me Jamie? If it's not too bold of me to ask?"

She nodded, still smiling. "Only if you'll call me Edie in return. And only if you'll tell me how you spent your day."

"I was working on my portrait of the Blue Lion. I'm quite close to finishing it. Stella's editor doesn't need it straightaway, so I've been taking my time. Pen and ink can be rather unforgiving to artists who are in a rush."

"You're happy with it?"

"I am. So far, at least."

"Good. Only . . . I thought you seemed rather glum. Earlier, I mean, before we started our walk. I hope you don't mind my saying so."

"I . . . ," he started, but the pat explanation he was tempted to offer, kissing cousin to a lie, died on his lips. Edie deserved the truth, or something close to it. He respected her too much to fall back on his usual excuses.

"I had a bad dream. A nightmare. They happen now and again." He waited for her to answer with a polite fiction of her own, something about everyone having bad dreams now and again, and how wearying they were, and how she'd had her own share over the years.

"Go on," she said instead.

"Would you like the short and sanitized version, or the longer and rather more truthful accounting?"

"The latter. If you please." She then set her hand on his, and she waited for him to continue.

"I was an officer with the Royal Engineers during the war. Bomb disposal. I'd have joined one of the Scottish regiments, but the sergeant in the recruiting office put me off. Said I was too educated to join the other ranks, and 'too brown'—his words—to become an officer."

"Oh, *Jamie*."

"I was on the point of leaving, of trying my luck else-where, when he stopped me."

Even now, years later, Jamie could still picture the man's face; still hear his voice as he'd started to fire off questions.

"Educated man, are you?"

"Yes. I just sat my finals."

"How old are you?"

"Twenty. I'll be twenty-one in December."

"Would you consider the Royal Engineers? They need officers for bomb disposal. It's dangerous work, mind you. I wouldn't mention it to just anyone, but you have the right look about you. Nerves of steel. Able to think on your feet. You might do."

Jamie had known the man had been flattering him, but he hadn't cared. "Where would I be posted?"

"No way of knowing just yet. Likely here in England at first. If the Krauts do try to invade they'll start by softening us up with a round of bombing. Once that's past, though, you might end up anywhere. Even as far off as India. That might be nice."

Jamie had long since learned that it was easiest, sometimes, to say nothing and instead wait for people to explain themselves. So he'd looked at the man and waited.

"Isn't that where you're from?" the sergeant had asked after a lengthy and uncomfortable silence.

"No. I'm a Scot. I should have thought my accent was a dead giveaway," Jamie had answered, smiling, and the other man had smiled back, likely under the impression they were sharing a joke.

"I signed up then and there," he now explained to Edie.

"Started my training, and was out dealing with UXBs by the end of the summer."

"When was this?" she asked.

"September 1940. Just in time for the Blitz. I barely remember those months. We all worked more hours than we slept. Then we were sent to North Africa. I mostly remember the sand, and how cold it was at night, and how there seemed to be twice as many stars in the sky. And then on to the Italian campaign, and all the while I got better and better at my work. I had strong nerves and steady hands, and my men respected me. I was tired and homesick and scared to death most of the time, but it wasn't all that bad. Compared to what some lived through, it was easy."

Her hand tightened around his. "What happened?"

He ought to have known she would see past the anodyne fiction he had relied upon for so long that he almost believed it himself. It would be easy enough to lie to her. Insist that he was fine and slept as well as the next man. But he'd already come this far, and she deserved more from him.

"We were in Italy, not far from Rome. I'd gone into a cellar to defuse a bomb, and while I was there another one went off. Not close enough to kill me, but it brought down the rest of the building. That's what I dream about when I have my nightmares. Those hours when I was alone in the dark, trapped in a hole, waiting to die."

"Such a horror. I can't bear to think of it."

"It was a great surprise when they broke through and dug me out. Apart from burst eardrums, a bad concussion, and some scrapes and bruises, I was unhurt. Within a week I was back at work. And only then . . ."

This next part he had never told anyone, not even his father, and rather than examine his reasoning for telling Edie all of it, he carried on. "We were sent to look at a UXB that was lodged halfway down a well in a little village that was nothing but ruins. Nothing but collapsed buildings and desperate people who had nowhere else to go. I was all set to climb into the well and deal with the thing, but when I looked over the edge and got ready to go down, I realized I couldn't feel my hands. I could see them, so I knew they were there, but I couldn't feel them at all. It was the strangest thing.

"I can't remember how long I stood there, trying to figure out what to do, with all my men watching and likely wondering what had come over me. Jones, my sergeant, came over to see what was up, and when I tried to explain I couldn't talk, either. Not one word."

Even now, he could remember every moment of what had followed. Jones had been the sort of man who missed nothing, but rather than shame Jamie in front of the men he'd acted as if nothing was wrong.

Jamie could still remember every horrifying detail of what had happened next.

"It's not all that far down, sir, but I don't think you'll fit. Best to send someone down who'll have a bit more elbow room. Maybe Mr. Ogilvy could give it a go?"

Second Lieutenant Ogilvy had been barely twenty, as slight as a reed, and keen as mustard to prove himself. "Happy to try, sir," he'd said, and Jamie had nodded, and they'd only just begun to lower the kid down when the bomb had gone off.

There hadn't been enough of Ogilvy left to scrape out

of the well for a decent burial, and when Jamie had tried to write the obligatory letter home to the boy's mother he hadn't been able to hold the pen, and that was when his CO had got wind of things and had taken Jamie aside and told him he was done.

This he now explained to Edie, and rather than cringe away in horror or make some sort of well-intended comment about war fraying the nerves of even the bravest men, she simply squeezed his hand. Just that.

"They sent me back to England, to a convalescent hospital near Greenwich, and by the end of the war I was able to hold a pencil again. I spent VE Day in Trafalgar Square, watching other people celebrate while I tried to draw what I saw around me. Tried not to think of the men I'd left behind to finish the work I'd been too weak to do myself."

He waited for her reply, bracing himself for the same sort of carefully measured response that most people, even his parents, resorted to employing as they reacted to his story. But Edie surprised him yet again.

"I was in Trafalgar Square that day, too. How strange to know you weren't far away. We might have walked past one another. Danced together." Another moment of silence. "Have you been in London all this time?"

"No. I thought of staying, but my parents insisted I return to Edinburgh. So I did. It was the only way I could convince them I'd come back in one piece."

"How long were you there?" she asked, steadfastly ignoring the question of whether he'd ended the war as a whole or broken man.

"About two years. I ended up reading law, mainly to make my father happy. And, well, it gave me something to do."

"So why are you here? Why aren't you in a courtroom somewhere?"

"Because I hated it. It took me an age to confess the truth to my father—that I was miserable, and dreaded the thought of becoming a barrister, and wanted to toss aside two years of my studies and become an artist. But when I did confess it all, he was lovely about it. They both were. My mother cried, but only because she'd been so worried about me, and then she badgered me nonstop about applying to art school until I'd filled out the applications and put them in the post."

"Your parents *encouraged* you?" Edie asked, as if the entire notion was so farfetched she couldn't quite believe it.

"They did. I don't think I'd have made the leap without their giving me that first push."

Edie made no reply, and it seemed to Jamie as if she were lost in thought, or perhaps resurrecting memories of her own. "Are you all right?" he asked.

"Yes. Sorry. It's only that I can't imagine what it would be like to set one's heart on something and then go ahead with it."

"Did you never wish to do anything else with your life?"

"At one point I very much wished to be a prima ballerina, but that was only for a few months when I was seven or eight. I'd been taken to see Margot Fonteyn at Sadler's Wells, and it was heady stuff." She tried to smile, but it was unconvincing, and the light in her eyes had dimmed. "Before me, before I was born, my parents had two boys. They were killed in the Great War, and as my father was an only child . . . well. They had to try again."

"You must have been a great consolation to them," he

said. Empty words, but for the life of him he could not think of anything better.

"I hope I was. They seemed happy enough, though I know they'd hoped for a boy."

What might he say to *that*? How might he take the sting from such knowledge? There was nothing he could do, nothing at all, so instead he twisted round to face her, and took hold of her other hand as well, and held them tight. Only for a few seconds, and only so she might know that she had been heard.

She smiled up at him, and this time it was true, and his heart began to splinter in his chest.

"It's all in the past, though, isn't it?"

"You're right," he agreed. And then, because he couldn't bear not to say it, "thank you."

"For what?"

"Reminding me of the rules for visitors to the park. Letting me know about Mr. Hinton and the pelicans and their bucket of herrings. Listening."

"You're welcome, but—"

"I apologize for interrupting, but if you were about to say something about it not being a bother, or it's nothing special, or really it's the sort of thing that anyone might do, please don't. The sort of kindness you've shown me, and which I know you show others, deserves far more than a few words of thanks. So thank you for listening, and for giving me a home, and for taking care of all of us at the Blue Lion. You are a treasure, Edie Howard, and it's long past time that someone told you so."

APRIL

Chapter 13

EDIE

Thursday, April 2, 1953

The day after her walk with Jamie, Edie had received a telephone call from Mr. Kaczmarek, the editor of *Picture Weekly*. He'd agreed to her request that Stella take the photographs for the story about the Blue Lion, confirmed that the magazine would include Jamie's illustration, and suggested a date for an interview with one of his staff writers.

"Her name is Ruby Sutton," he had explained. "One of my best writers, and she and Stella work well together."

Now that day had come, and Miss Sutton was supposed to arrive any minute, and Edie hadn't managed to get a single thing done all morning. Stella had promised that it would go well, that the writer would be pleasant and friendly, and that the resulting article in *Picture Weekly* would show the Blue Lion in the best possible light. And Edie believed her. She truly did.

The difficulty was that it all rested on her. She had to be amusing and witty and insightful. She had to make the Blue Lion seem like the most charming, welcoming, and memorable hotel in London. And if she failed at any of it, the fault would rest upon her shoulders alone.

She'd given up on her typing after ruining three sheets of paper with one silly mistake after another. She'd paced the hallways, but they, along with the rest of the hotel, were already immaculate, without so much as a stray mote of dust to catch her eye. Now, with only five minutes to spare, she was roaming the main floor, though she was careful to stay within hailing distance of the front door.

In the lounge, she straightened the stack of newspapers and magazines on the side tables, plumped up cushions, and built up the fire in the hearth. Normally she wouldn't have one laid so late in the spring, but it was a cool and wet day and the fire added a welcome note of homeliness to the room. The library she left alone, for the professor was busy with his documents and the maids had already done a fine job of cleaning every part of the room excepting the table where he worked.

Back in the front hall, she set about tidying the tourist brochures in their rack, used her handkerchief to whisk away invisible specks of grime from the gilded frame of the timeworn watercolor of the hotel, and added a professional cleaning for it and the hotel's other artworks to her mental list of *Hotel To Do (Future)*.

At exactly three o'clock a merry trill sounded from the bell above the front door. Edie smoothed down her jacket and skirt, stood up very straight, and prepared to greet Miss Sutton, who came through the door in a flurry of rain-soaked umbrella, mackintosh coat, and oversized handbag.

There was an awkward moment as the other woman, wrestling with her umbrella, finally wrenched it shut and stuffed it impatiently into the waiting receptacle. "Wretched thing," she muttered, but then she looked up and smiled. "Miss Howard? I'm Ruby Sutton."

Rather startled by Miss Sutton's American accent, Edie shook her hand and smiled in return. "I'm delighted to make your acquaintance. Welcome to the Blue Lion."

"Thanks so much for agreeing to speak with me. I've really been looking forward to meeting you, and of course seeing the hotel. It has quite the history."

"It certainly does. Would you like me to take your mackintosh? I can hang it up in my office. I won't be a moment."

When she returned Miss Sutton had already taken a notepad and pencil from her bag and was busily making notes. "Please don't mind me. I thought of a few things on the way over and I just need to jot them down before I forget."

"I quite understand," Edie said. She felt oddly hesitant, for Miss Sutton, though perfectly pleasant, was not a guest of the hotel but rather a reporter, and in that capacity she might choose to write unflattering things about the hotel. "I'm not sure how to start," she said, deciding to begin with a measure of honesty. "Would you like a tour of the hotel? And then we can sit down and talk a bit more?"

"That's exactly what I hoped you would say."

Edie dutifully led Miss Sutton from room to room, beginning with the lounge, then a quick peek into the library, and upstairs to one of the guest rooms. As the Hons had not yet been dislodged from their rooms, Edie had asked the maids to freshen up a second-floor room directly above, for it had an excellent view of Northumberland Avenue, was close to the bath and WC, and had a bedspread, draperies, and carpet that, while far from new, were still very pretty. The furniture was a mix of Georgian and Regency pieces, plain and solid and shining with polish, and the room looked, Edie thought with satisfaction, like the sort of place one might happily stay for days on end. Miss Sutton made gratifyingly positive comments about the niceness of the decoration and the convenience of the hotel's location, all the while taking down everything Edie said.

"The sign by the door says it was founded in 1560," Miss Sutton said, having finished her inspection of the room. "Was it owned by your family even back then?"

"It was. Jacob Howard was the first proprietor, and I'm his direct descendant."

"And the name—is there a story behind it?"

"If there is, it's lost to history. A blue lion is associated with the heraldry of the dukes of Northumberland, but my family was connected to the dukes of Norfolk, and then in only the most distant way. I'm not sure their grand cousins ever knew they existed. Certainly there's no record of any of the dukes or their immediate family staying here."

"All right. Can you tell me more about the building itself? When was it built?"

"The original structure dates to the late 1300s. It was likely a farmhouse to begin with, and at first there were only two floors. The upper stories were added when the area was rebuilt about a hundred years ago, and the entire building was enlarged then, too."

"So back then, this was the countryside?"

Edie nodded. "Nothing more than hunting grounds and farmers' fields and the occasional manor house. But it wasn't in the middle of nowhere, either. Charing Cross was just to the west, and the Thames was only a few hundred yards to the east. By the time Jacob opened the inn, it was much busier here. The palace of Whitehall was nearby, and the roads themselves were getting better, and before long there were travelers coming and going from the stage-coaches near what is now Trafalgar Square."

Edie stopped short, conscious that she'd been providing far more historical tidbits than Miss Sutton likely needed or wanted. "I'm sorry. I do have a tendency to ramble on about the history of the hotel."

"Don't apologize. This is exactly the sort of stuff I want for my story. Let me just go back to what you said about the area being rebuilt. That wasn't because of the Great Fire, was it?"

"No—the fire was farther east. The streets around here were straightened out and modernized in the 1730s and again in the 1850s. That's when the Victorian facade was added. Have you seen the illustration that James Geddes did of the original exterior?"

"I have. It's very good. You can really get a sense of the age of the hotel from it."

"It can be hard to tell, you know, what with all the changes that have been made over the years. But the really old bits are still here. One just has to look a little harder for them. Some of the paneling in the hall downstairs is original, along with parts of the staircase, and here and there are some very old beams. Usually at just the right height for our taller guests to catch their heads if they aren't careful."

"Do you have any ghosts?" Miss Sutton asked, a thread of mischief in her voice.

"None that I've ever encountered."

"All things considered, that's probably a relief for your guests. You do have a legend attached to the hotel, though."

"Oh, yes. Elizabeth the First and the great storm of 1564."

"Go on."

"As legends go, it's fairly straightforward. The queen had gone out riding, and although the weather had been fair when she and her party left, a blizzard descended without much warning and they lost their way. Somehow they ended up on the Blue Lion's doorstep. Naturally they were welcomed in and showered with every comfort that Jacob Howard had at hand. Food, wine, a seat by the fire for the queen, and shelter for the horses, too. We still have the chair she sat in—remind me to show you when we're in the dining room."

"Did she stay the night?"

"No, sadly. They continued on their way as soon as there was a break in the weather. Jacob was sent a purse of coins to thank him, but they were soon spent. And that is the legend. No dragon, no miraculous path through the snow for the Virgin Queen. Only a warm seat by the fire."

"And it was your ancestor, Jacob Howard, who greeted her?" Miss Sutton asked, scribbling away.

"It was, assuming the legend is true. I'd like to believe it, but we've no actual proof, and it does seem rather improbable to me. At least in parts."

"Which parts?"

"It was the countryside then, but it was far from empty. There would have been any number of manor houses scattered around, all of them far more grand than the Blue Lion. For that matter, the palace of Whitehall was barely three hundred yards south of here. Why not simply press on home?"

"If the blizzard was a sudden one, they might have been desperate to find any shelter at all," Miss Sutton mused. "I grew up in New Jersey, and once or twice a winter we used to get storms where the snow was so bad it actually stung when it hit your skin. Maybe it was like that."

"Maybe it was," Edie agreed.

"I don't think it really matters if the legend is true, you know. It's a good story, even if there aren't any dragons or knights in shining armor or enchanted swords. Besides, the part of the story that *is* true, your family's connection to this place, is just as interesting as the queen's visit. At least I think so."

"You're very kind to say that."

"Does it make you proud, or would you say that it's a burden?"

It was the first of Miss Sutton's questions to flummox Edie. "I'm not sure . . . a bit of both, I think? I love this place, and I feel a great obligation to preserve it, and to care for the people who work and live here."

"I don't mean to put you on the spot. It's only that I can't imagine how I would cope if I were in your shoes. Have you ever thought of selling up?"

"Not seriously, no." It wasn't the entire truth, but if she were to admit to doubts and worries, let alone hint at the repeated offers from Mr. Bamford, she'd have to explain to her employees and guests, likely more than once, that she had no desire to sell the hotel, not if she could help it. "There have been offers over the years, but none worth considering. Running this hotel is my life's work." That part, at least, was true.

Miss Sutton nodded, still scribbling away. "Why don't you tell me about your plans for the coronation?"

"Well, we're very lucky to be located along the procession route, and have every room booked for the weeks before and after Coronation Day. Of course, anyone who wishes to stay with us later in the year can be certain of a warm welcome. We also serve a traditional afternoon tea each day, including Sundays, and nonresidents are most welcome." She checked her watch, and was gratified to see it was exactly half-past four. "For that matter, it's teatime now. Would you care to join me?"

"Yes, please," Miss Sutton said eagerly. "Though I hope you don't mind if I abstain from the tea-drinking part of things. I've lived in England for more than ten years, but your adoration of tea continues to mystify me."

Edie didn't forget to show Miss Sutton the queen's chair, now installed on a low platform next to the enormous hearth in the dining room, and as there was nothing much of interest about the chair, apart from its age and connection to royalty, they were soon seated at Edie's table by the door to the kitchens. The room was empty apart from the Hons, who, to Edie's relief, were absorbed in their conversation and barely looked up. Ginny hurried over the minute Edie and her guest sat down, plates of delicacies in hand, and that helped to soak up some of the awkwardness Edie felt at the lack of guests.

"Would you like some coffee?" Edie asked. "We make it strong, and it's real coffee. None of that bottled essence."

"Yes, please. But only if it isn't too much trouble."

Edie looked to Ginny. "One coffee, please, and a pot of tea for me. Thank you."

"Yes, Miss Howard."

"Do help yourself to everything," Edie said. "I'm sure you must be hungry."

"Thanks. It looks delicious."

"Cook works miracles for us, I must say. You'd never know that butter and sugar are still on the ration."

Ginny returned with the coffee and tea, and Edie and Miss Sutton doctored their cups, and then it was time for another round of conversation. Edie knew she ought to say something more about the hotel, but she'd been twittering on for ages and was feeling heartily sick of her own voice.

"You said earlier that you've been in England for—how long was it, again?"

"It's actually been almost thirteen years. I was only meant to stay for a year or so, but the city, and the people, got under my skin. I feel at home here in a way I never did when I was growing up in the States."

Edie then noticed Miss Sutton's wedding and engagement rings. "Is your husband a journalist as well?" she asked.

"Ha! No, Bennett is a barrister. We were introduced by his best friend, Walter Kaczmarek. My editor at *PW*."

"Oh, yes. I spoke to Mr. Kaczmarek just the other day."

"Bennett was the first person I met when I got here, if you can believe it, and the man made *quite* an impression." Miss Sutton smiled, as if prompted by fond memories. "Then

I hardly saw him for years. He was off doing mysterious things he's still not meant to talk about. But he survived the war, and he came home to me, and since then we've hardly spent a day apart."

"That sounds terribly romantic. Do you have any children?"

"We do. There's Victoria, who is five and a half, and Vanessa, who is just coming up to four. I stayed at home when they were little, but now that Victoria's in school, and her sister is in nursery school a few mornings each week, I've gone back to work."

Edie nodded, rather bowled over by the other woman's effervescent energy, and felt briefly envious of the aura of happiness that radiated from her. "I expect it was quite nice to have those years at home with them."

"Oh, it was. They're very sweet girls, though of course I'm biased, and there are days when I would much rather be at home reading them stories and going on long walks with the dogs and laughing when they try to imitate my accent. At the same time, I also want them to see that my work is interesting and important to me, just as their father's work is important and interesting to him. Does that make sense?"

It made perfect sense. "Your daughters are very lucky to have you as their mum," Edie said.

"Thank you." Miss Sutton glanced at her watch and frowned. "I'm so sorry, but I have to run. The girls are with their great-aunt for the afternoon, and I said I'd collect them at half-past five, and here it is, five o'clock already, and they're all the way over in Kensington." With this she downed what was left of her coffee, polished off her last bite of scone, and gathered up her notepad and pencil. "I think I have everything I need, but if I remember anything later on, do you mind if I ring you up?"

"Not at all. Let me fetch your coat."

They said good-bye, shaking hands, and Edie watched from the door as Miss Sutton ran out into the rain, her umbrella still furled, her bag slung any old way over her shoulder, her left hand clutched to her hat, as if she was expecting a sudden gust of wind might tear it from her head.

Edie waved good-bye, and then she retreated back inside, back to the warmth and comfort of the Blue Lion, its centuries of secrets, and her solitary life within.

Chapter 14

STELLA

Sunday, April 12, 1953

7 April

My dear Signorina Donati (or rather Stella, as I hope you will allow me to call you),

My Walter has told me so much about you, and I feel I cannot wait any longer to make your acquaintance. If you are agreeable I do hope you will come to dinner this coming Sunday evening.

We live in Hampstead but the journey is not a difficult one and I think you will find it a pleasant change from the city. Would you be able to join us as early as half-past five? The children eat at six o'clock and I should love for you to meet them, but if you prefer to dine later in the evening that is quite all right. Either way do let Walter know if you are

able to come, as I am eager to meet you and hear all about
your photographs that have so impressed my husband.

With my warm regards,
Miriam Dassin

Kindly written as it was, there was no doubt in Stella's
mind that Miriam Dassin expected her to be present
for dinner on Sunday. "I would be delighted to come to
dinner," she told Kaz later that day. "Is there anything I
may bring?"

"Only yourself, and a degree of tolerance for excitable
children who forget their manners in front of honored
guests."

Along with her invitation, Miriam had enclosed a detailed set of directions that specified, down to the meter,
the way to her and Kaz's home on a narrow lane called
Holly Walk. Compared to the busy and built-up streets
around Charing Cross, Hampstead felt like a much
smaller town, with winding streets, scarcely a motorcar
to be seen, and enormous old trees that cast a dappled,
green-gold veil over the pavements they overhung. The
house was set back from the road behind a low stone
wall, its rosy bricks curtained with ivy, its slate roof
mossy with age. The path to the front door was flanked
by beds of still-dormant lavender, nodding heads of fading daffodils, and pale pink tulips that were just coming
into bud, and a child's tricycle had been abandoned at
the bottom of the steps.

Stella straightened the tricycle, moving it to the side so
no one would trip over it later, and knocked on the door.

Kaz opened it promptly, his pale eyes brightly welcoming behind the thick lenses of his spectacles. A whimpering toddler was secured in the cradle of one arm. He smiled, and she smiled back, suddenly nervous, and he stepped out of the way so she might enter.

"Hello, Stella, and welcome." He nodded toward the little boy in his arms. "This young chap is my son, David. He was keeping watch from the front window, and I'm afraid that in his excitement to help answer the door he took a tumble."

"I am very sorry that you fell down. Are you all right?" she asked David.

He nodded, sniffling loudly. "Ow."

"Ow, indeed," said Kaz. "Do come in. Miriam's in the kitchen with Sarah. They made a cake in honor of your visit and they're just pulling it from the oven now."

A pleasing sort of homely chaos had taken over the front hall and what she could see of the house. There was a jumble of shoes and boots in the front hall, both enormous and very small, and the walls were shingled with framed photographs. She spied Miriam and Kaz on what looked to be their wedding day, as well as other less formal occasions: Kaz at his desk, the entire family on vacation at the seaside, and Miriam in an artist's studio, her back to the camera, her hands raised as she pinned scraps of material to a bulletin board.

Her attention fixed on the photographs, Stella almost missed the framed document on the opposite wall, its Hebrew text beautifully embellished with gold and jewel-bright details. Her parents' own marriage contract, their *ketubah*, had once hung in the sitting room of their flat in

Livorno; she would not have comprehended the purpose of the document otherwise. It had to mean that Kaz, or Miriam, or more likely both of them, were Jewish.

"You recognize it," Kaz said. "Not many people do."

"Did you know I am a Jew?" she asked.

"Not until now. Come along and meet my wife."

She followed him into the kitchen, and her first thought, upon entering, was of how much it reminded her of Zia Rosa's kitchen back in Mezzo Ciel. Not in its particulars, of course, for it was quite a different room, but more in the way it made her feel.

There was a big range instead of a hearth, and in the middle was a sturdy wooden table, an art project left half-done at one end. A black cat with white socks was snoozing in a lumpy armchair drawn close to the range, and by the back door was a wicker basket crammed with gardening tools and muddied gloves and a stack of small clay pots.

The garden itself was being swallowed up by the growing dusk, but through the kitchen's windows Stella could just make out brick walls trellised with rose canes and winter-bare vines, a patch of overgrown lawn, and a child's swing hanging from the gnarled branches of an apple tree. A greenhouse was set in the far corner, with a well-trodden flagstone path leading from its door back to the kitchen.

Miriam and her daughter, who looked to be about four years old, had been admiring their cake, but now they turned and came forward. Only then did Stella realize that the other woman was expecting a baby.

"At last, at last," Miriam said, and took Stella's hands in hers before leaning forward, a little awkwardly on account of her belly, to kiss her on both cheeks. "Children, this is

Miss Donati. She is a photographer at Papa's work. What do we say to new friends when we meet them for the first time? *En français, s'il vous plaît.*"

The little girl offered her hand so Stella might shake it. "*C'est un plaisir de faire votre connaissance, Mademoiselle Donati. Je m'appelle Sarah.*"

"*Merci bien,*" Stella replied. "*Piacere di conoscerti.* That is how we introduce ourselves in Italy."

David, still grizzling, now held out a small and very damp fist, and Stella shook it, too. "*Allô,*" he said gruffly.

Miriam smiled benevolently at her son. "Ah, well. We are trying, are we not?"

Miriam was younger than Stella had expected, no more than thirty or so, with a fresh, glowing complexion, bright hazel eyes, and lovely dark hair that she'd pulled into a loose bun at her nape.

"How was your journey?" she asked. "Were my directions easy to follow?"

"They were very helpful, thank you."

Stella had bought a bunch of bright orange tulips from a flower stall in Charing Cross station that afternoon, and she now presented them to Miriam. "These are for you," she said, feeling rather shy about her modest offering. The other woman reacted as if she'd been given a bouquet of hothouse roses.

"These are lovely, and such a delicious color. Thank you."

"Your house is beautiful," Stella said, watching as Miriam trimmed the tulips' stems and arranged them in a blue-and-white-patterned china jug.

"It is nice, isn't it? I'll show you around in a bit, but first let's sit down and have a drink. Would you like a glass of wine? I opened a bottle of claret to make the stew and there's most of it left."

"Yes, please," Stella said.

"Let's go through to the sitting room while Walter pours your wine. I'll take David"—here she plucked the boy from his father's arms and perched him on her hip—"and we'll bring Sarah, too, and they can play while we talk. Come, Sarah."

The sitting room was every bit as warm and welcoming as the kitchen. Overflowing bookcases stretched to the ceiling on either side of the chimney breast, a fire was burning merrily in the grate, and a pair of sofas with plump down-filled cushions faced one another at right angles to the hearth. A second cat, her fur a pretty patchwork of ginger, white, and dove gray, sat on the arm of a sturdy oak chair that faced the fireplace.

Miriam set David down and watched fondly as he joined his sister at a child-sized table in front of the room's big bay window. Sarah helped him clamber onto his little chair, and once he was settled she opened a box of brightly colored wooden beads, handed him a long shoelace knotted at one end, and proceeded to help him string the beads.

"She plays with him very nicely," Stella said.

"She does," his mother agreed, "although he'll get bored before long, and she'll become impatient with him, and they'll both come running back to me in about five minutes. All the more reason for us to make the most of these few moments of peace. Come and sit next to me on this sofa—Walter will want the 'Papa chair,' as David calls it."

"May I ask why you call him Walter when he is Kaz to everyone else?"

Miriam laughed. "Only because he has only ever seemed like Walter to me. Though I do not mind that others call him Kaz."

The subject of their conversation now returned with glasses of wine for himself and Stella and a drinking glass filled with fizzing water for his wife, and after Stella thanked him Miriam explained her unusual aperitif. "It is rather indelicate of me to admit, but this baby is giving me the most frightful indigestion. Soda water seems to help, though I do not like it nearly as much as wine."

"Do you have long to wait before the baby arrives?" Stella asked, then cringed at her audacity in asking something so personal.

But Miriam didn't seem to mind. "This one is due at the end of June. It seems very far away but also, somehow, much too soon. Fortunately, I do have help with the children in the mornings, and Sarah is wonderful with her brother."

"Most of the time," Kaz qualified. And then, turning his attention to his wife, "The story I was telling you about the other day, the one about the Blue Lion hotel, was Stella's idea. Ruby's writing it, and Stella took care of the photographs. I've my eye on it for the cover—only don't tell Miss Howard, if you please," he directed at Stella. "Just in case we have to bump it."

"I won't say a thing. I think it will be a nice surprise for her."

"Would you mind very much if we used James Geddes's illustration on the cover? Rather than one of your photographs?"

"No, not at all," Stella answered truthfully. Only a few

weeks earlier, one of her portraits of the people left bedridden by the Great Smog had been on the cover, so she could hardly begrudge Mr. Geddes the satisfaction of seeing his work so prominently featured.

"Tell me again how you came to live at the Blue Lion," Kaz asked. "Am I right in thinking you have some connection to Miss Howard? You mentioned something of the sort in our correspondence, I believe."

"I did. My parents became friends with Miss Howard and her family when they were working on their first guide to London. When you offered me the position at *PW*, I wrote to her and asked for advice on where I might live, and she invited me to stay at the Blue Lion. There are other boarders, you see, and it is very economical compared to a flat of my own."

"Of course. That does make sense. May I tell Miriam about your parents and their guides?" Kaz waited for her nod before continuing. "It has been some years now, but Stella's parents once published a splendid series of travel books called, if you'll pardon my execrable Italian, the *Guide di turistiche Donati*. It's fair to say that what the Michelin guides are to France, the Donati guidebooks once were to Italians. I remember seeing them everywhere when I was in Italy before the war, and in other countries, too—I'm not mistaken in that, am I?"

"You are not," Stella confirmed. "Their guides to Italy were published in eight languages, and they had just begun to publish a series of guides to other European countries when—"

The pain of it all was still enough, years later, to leave her breathless. The fear, too. It was dangerous to speak of what had happened, even in a place as safe and outwardly welcoming as England.

Only then did Stella remember the *ketubah*. Here, in this house, she could speak truthfully of what had happened to her family. Here, among these people, she was safe.

"The laws changed. It was before the war. The company was taken away from my family. Everything was taken. The printing presses were seized by the government, and my parents' employees were told they could not work for Jews, and the shops and museums and galleries that had once sold their guides were no longer allowed to carry them. Nor, I think, did most of those places wish to be associated with books written and published by Jews."

"How did you manage after that?" Miriam asked softly.

"We had a little money, but not much. It was very difficult. It was . . ."

She was conscious of the children's chatter, of a log falling in the grate, of the cat's contented purr. She waited for Kaz or Miriam to change the subject, or tell her she was a lucky girl to have survived, or offer up some other kind of ill-fitting bandage that would cover her wounds but do nothing to heal them.

Instead they waited, and they did not look away, and she knew without their needing to say so that they understood.

"When the laws changed, Edie's father tried to help us. He even found a way to send my father some money. So many of my parents' friends turned their backs, but Mr. Howard never did. I wrote to him after the war because I wanted to thank him, only Edie wrote back and explained that her parents had died. She said how very sorry she was about my parents, and we began a correspondence. Not so very many letters, for she is always so busy, but enough that I felt she had become my friend."

Just then, and rather to Stella's relief, the children came running over to clutch at Miriam's knees.

"When are we going to eat, Maman?" Sarah asked. "My tummy is emptyyyyy!"

"Yes, yes, I suppose it is time for supper," Miriam told them, popping kisses on their upturned faces. Turning to Stella, she made a face of apology, then heaved herself to her feet with the help of Kaz's promptly outstretched hand. "I have made a stew of beef in red wine," she explained, "and there is lovely fresh bread, and butter, and a salad, too."

"And my cake!" Sarah shouted.

"Most certainly we will eat your delicious cake, but only after we have finished the main part of our supper."

Back they trooped to the kitchen. Once there, Kaz set about slicing the bread and putting it in a basket, which he handed to Sarah with a solemn warning to wait until everyone was seated in the dining room before taking any for herself. Meanwhile, Miriam dressed a salad of endive and radicchio, which she gave to Stella to carry, and last of all retrieved a covered casserole dish from the oven.

The dining room was simply furnished and decorated, with plain white crockery on the table, lovely old silver flatware, and Stella's gift of tulips in their jug. Kaz put David in a high chair that had been pulled up to the table and Sarah seated herself on a chair with a fat cushion to boost her up. Though they used smaller plates and cutlery, both children were given the same food to eat as the adults.

Miriam's beef stew was the most delicious thing Stella

had eaten in months. Cook was very capable, of course, but the food she made was prepared with English tastes in mind, and Stella found it plain and rather boring. Not that she would ever say so and hurt Cook's feelings.

"This is wonderful," she said. "All of it is wonderful."

"Thank you. It is simple food but made with good ingredients. Fortunately, I have an excellent greengrocer and baker here in Hampstead, and that is a great help."

Over dinner Stella asked her friends how they had met, which led Kaz to explain, very charmingly, how Miriam had caught her shoe in a grate while crossing the street and he had come to her rescue.

"I thought him very gallant, and although I was rather wary at first, I agreed to have lunch with him soon after. That was six years ago."

"Very nearly to the day," he agreed. "The truth is that she saved me. I'd been wallowing in loneliness for years but didn't realize it until we met. It was Miriam who taught me to see the world with fresh eyes."

Buoyed by her friends' kindness, as well as the large glass of wine she had just finished, Stella talked of her life since the war. Of her zia Rosa and nonno Aldo, her friends Nina and Nico, of the ancient farmhouse where they lived and the beautiful countryside that surrounded them. She talked of how difficult it had been to leave, and how much she missed them still.

"Are you happy here?" Miriam asked.

"I am. I love my work, and I am not only saying that because you are listening, Kaz. I do. I have learned so much already from Mr. Keller and Frank and the others."

"You're the only one who calls him that," Kaz observed. "Likely he'd prefer that you call him Win."

"Do you know why he is called Winton? I thought his name was Winston, after Mr. Churchill, but he said there was no *s*, and that everyone gets it wrong."

"That's Win for you. He'll explain when he's ready."

Stella nodded, for she understood better than most the importance of secrets. "It was difficult to leave Italy behind, but I needed to begin somewhere new. Somewhere else. Does that make sense?"

"It does," Miriam said.

"When the war ended, I told myself I would regain all my parents had lost. All of it—their home, the guides, the factory where their books were printed. It was not long before I realized I would never succeed. Too much was lost."

"Yet you became a photographer all the same."

"At first it was to honor my mother. Then, because I enjoyed it. Now I continue because I am good at it, and there are stories I wish to tell with the photographs I take. Here in London, for now, and perhaps other places, too. But not just yet."

Kaz smiled approvingly. "I'm relieved to hear it. You've become quite indispensable, you know."

"You are kind to say so. And you need not worry. If I leave London, it will only be on holiday."

The mention of holidays was enough to draw Sarah's attention. "Will you go to the seaside? I *love* the seaside. We went last summer and we dug in the sand and looked for clams and had ice cream and Papa got a terrible sunburn because he forgot his hat."

"I may tend to forget my hat, but I never forget to eat my supper," Kaz told his daughter. "Why is there still so much salad on your plate? And yours, too, David? Three more bites, please, and then you may have some cake."

"Cake!" David shouted, then obligingly ate three tiny bites of his salad. His sister, grumbling, did the same.

"Well done," Kaz said. "No, Miriam—you and Stella can stay where you are. I'll clear the plates and return with the cake."

"What kind of cake is it?" Stella asked Sarah.

"It's apple cake, my very favorite, and the apples are from the tree in the garden. We picked them ages ago and Papa put them in a wooden box in the cellar where it is nice and cool. It was fun making the cake but cutting up the apples was rather a bother. Maman helped me with that part."

The children devoured their slices of cake enthusiastically and asked for more, but their father ignored their pleas, scooped them up in his arms, and announced that it was time for bed. "I started the moka pot, so listen for it singing. I won't be long," he told his wife as he bore them away.

Miriam began to gather up the dishes. "Will you keep me company while I do the dishes?"

"Yes, but only if I may help you."

As Miriam washed the dishes, Stella took them from her, dried each one carefully, and set it on the table. "I remember seeing moka pots in shop windows back in Italy, but we did not have one. Do they make good coffee?"

"Oh, yes. To my mind it is one of the greatest inventions of our time. Never mind things like radar or television or antibiotics. Being able to make a strong cup of coffee in my own kitchen is a wonder to me," Miriam said happily. "Oh—I was about to ask you this earlier but the children distracted me. We were talking about holidays. Are you thinking of taking a trip when the magazine has its summer break? It is only a fortnight, but that should be enough time to visit your family in Italy."

"I would like to see them, yes. If I take the train, I could stop on the way back and spend a day or two in Paris."

"Have you been before?"

"Yes, but not since before the war. My parents took me to visit our cousins in Colombes. It is very close to Paris."

"My goodness. That is where I grew up. Such a wonderful coincidence."

"They lived on the rue des Cerisiers. My father had told me it meant the street of the cherry trees, but when we visited there were no cherries to be found. I was very disappointed."

Miriam had gone very still. "Michele Donati—was that your uncle's name?"

"Yes. How—?"

"He and his family lived next door. I met your parents, Stella. I *met* them, and I cannot believe I did not realize until this moment. I can still remember it. We went next door to meet all of you, and my mother told me I was to be nice to the little girl who had come all the way from Italy. That was *you*, Stella."

"Can you remember anything else?" Her hands were trembling, so she set down the plate she'd been holding, the dish towel still wrapped around it. If Miriam could add but one detail, one more scrap of memory, it would be a gift beyond measure.

"We came for lunch, and we all sat around the big table in your aunt and uncle's kitchen, and your cousins were there, too, although they were older. I think they had finished school? But they still lived at home."

"Daniele and Carlo."

"Yes. I can't remember what we ate. Afterward we went into the garden, and we played bowls on the lawn, and then I pushed you on the swing. They still had a swing, even though their children were grown."

"I remember the swing. I remember the smell of the roses my aunt grew, and the peonies, too." A surge of emotion, sharp yet sweet, seized at her heart.

"Yes. My mother and your aunt both loved peonies. And now I know why you did not seem like a stranger when we met."

The moka pot began to hiss. Miriam dried her hands and pulled it from the heat, and then she took a handkerchief from her skirt pocket and pressed it into Stella's hand. "Come and sit and have your coffee."

Stella dried her eyes and caught her breath and drank the wonderful coffee Miriam had made for her. "I have never gone back to Livorno. I don't think I could bear it. To see again how everything they created had been stolen. Destroyed."

"I understand. I do."

"I survived the camps with the help of a friend. It is her family that took me in—her family by marriage, that is. They have been so good to me, have become so dear. But they only know me from *after*. In all the world, there is no one left who knows me from before. Does that make sense?"

"Yes."

"Yet I met you before. Long ago we met, before everything changed. Before I changed. I had never thought to have that again."

"Nor I," Miriam said, her voice so wonderfully gentle. "There are so few of us who can know, or understand, what it is like to have everything taken away. I do not mean material things. I speak of my sense of safety. My belief in justice. For a long time, too, my hope in the future. There have been many times, over the years, when I feared my anger would consume me."

"I feel so angry, too. Even on the brightest days I can feel it whispering in my ear. I hope that does not sound strange."

"Not in the least."

"What happened to your family?" Stella dared to ask.

"My parents and grandfather were arrested in 1942. They were sent to a place called the Vélodrome d'Hiver, along with many thousands of other French Jews. I think your uncle and his family were probably taken at the same time."

"I wrote to them after the war, but the letter was returned. How was it that you were not arrested, too?"

"I was working in Paris. My father had feared such a thing might happen, and he had helped me change my identity papers so it appeared I was a Gentile. I was able to hide in plain sight for months, and I even helped in a small way with the resistance. But I was captured and sent to Ravensbrück. Like you, I found friends there who helped me. I survived, and then I came to England so I might begin again."

"Did you ever learn what became of your parents?"

"I did. My Walter promised to find them, and as I'm sure you already know, he can be very persistent when something is important to him." A pause, and Miriam brushed away her own tears. "They were murdered at Birkenau."

"I was there," Stella whispered. "I was there, and I think that is where my parents were killed. I suppose the rest of my family, too. I have not yet tried to find out."

"Yet you survived when they did not?"

"The police did not find me when they came for us, not at first. I tried to hide, but I had no money. No food. I asked one of our neighbors to help me, but she turned me away, and then she called the police. I was sent to Bolzano for a while, and from there to Birkenau."

"And then?"

"There was a selection. I survived only because my friend told me to lie about my age. All the children and old people on our train were being sent to their deaths, so I said I was sixteen and they decided not to kill me straightaway. Instead they took away my name and replaced it with a string of numbers, and then they shaved my head and gave me a shift to wear that had been taken from the body of a dead woman. That was my first day at Birkenau."

"How old were you?" Miriam asked, her face a rictus of agony.

"Fourteen. But I was strong, and tall for my age, and they needed workers. They sent me to a camp in Germany. I was put to work in the foundry, making parts for weapons." She held out her hands so Miriam might see the constellation of tiny scars. "After a while I did not notice the sparks."

"I am so sorry," Miriam said.

"They do not bother me. But this," she said, unbuttoning her cuff and pushing back her sleeve, "this still hurts. The memory, I mean, not the tattoo."

Miriam stared at the numbers on Stella's arm, and then she set her fingers atop the markings. Her hand was warm and her touch was kind.

"I told myself I would not learn the number. I would refuse to carry it in my head. But I had no choice but to learn it, for they called it out at *appell*. They took away my name and replaced it with *this*, and now I cannot forget."

"My dear Stella. Oh, my dear. I am so very sorry."

"Thank you. It is good to talk to someone who understands. How . . . how do you live with it?" she asked her new friend.

"Imperfectly," Miriam answered, her own eyes bright with tears. "My husband is a patient man, and of course my children do not understand, not yet. And there is my work. My work has made all the difference. Would you like to see?"

They went through the kitchen door and along the path to the greenhouse, only it wasn't a greenhouse but rather a studio. Miriam switched on an overhead light and beckoned Stella forward. "This is my studio."

On the far side of the room, drawn close to a large window, was a sort of table without a top, and where the top ought to have been there was a panel of fabric stretched tight around a wooden frame. A group of people had been drawn on the fabric, or rather outlined in thread, and they were running down a street, pushed along by unkind hands, and at the center of their group a woman had stopped and was turning to face her pursuers.

The other figures were still ghostly outlines, but the woman was almost complete. She was constructed of delicately appliquéd pieces of fabric, and wondrously fine embroidered stitches brought life to her face. Stella could not look away, for the work before her, even unfinished, was the equal of anything she had ever seen in the galleries of London or Florence or Rome.

"I hardly know what to say. This is extraordinary. I thought, at first, that these were paintings. But they are made of fabric and thread."

"Until recently I was an embroiderer at the atelier of Monsieur Hartnell—perhaps you have heard of him? He is the couturier who is making the gown for the new queen's coronation."

"You no longer work there?"

"Not since Sarah was born. I still embroider, but it is for my own purposes now."

"The woman, here—was she your mother?"

Miriam nodded, as Stella had known she would. "Yes."

"I wish I had the words to explain how I feel. Your work is extraordinary," she repeated.

"Thank you. I wonder if you might consider doing the same."

"Embroidery like this? I could never—" Stella protested.

"I mean with your photography. I have only seen a few of your pictures, but they are the work of an artist. I am certain of it."

"Even if I am, what does it matter? I cannot change what happened. I cannot bring them back."

"You cannot. But you can tell their story, and your own, and that of others who have suffered and died."

"How?" Stella asked, feeling helpless in the face of Miriam's calm certainty.

"Only you can answer that question. Simply consider the idea, and imagine how you wish to tell your story, and the rest will come to you. Perhaps not tonight, nor tomorrow, but it will come. As one artist to another, I can promise you that."

Chapter 15

JAMIE

Friday, April 17, 1953

Of course it was raining, and of course he'd left his umbrella upstairs. He would just have to make a run for it.

He'd waited until the worst of the morning rush was past, but impatience had got the better of him and now it was five past nine and he couldn't be bothered to fetch his coat or umbrella. So he ran as fast as he might to the newsagents in Charing Cross station, and joined the end of a long queue of commuters who were buying their papers, and as he waited he tried hard to temper his expectations.

At last it was his turn. "Good morning, Mr. Patel. How are you?"

"Very well, thank you. I have them ready for you. Half a dozen copies, and so fresh I can smell the ink. I put them in a paper bag for you already—ah. Here it is. That will be one florin."

Jamie handed over his two shillings, accepted the bundle

of magazines, and briefly considered opening the bag and taking a peek. But no; it was better to wait a little longer. "Thank you."

Mick was waiting outside the hotel, and as soon as Jamie came around the corner he hurried forward to shelter him under his umbrella. "Morning, Jamie. Whyever didn't you take one of the brolleys from the front hall? Since I'll wager you left your own upstairs in your room."

"I'm afraid I did. I was in a rush to get to the news-agents. The new issue of *Picture Weekly* is out today."

Mick, having closed the umbrella, now followed Jamie inside. "So it's out already? The story that American gal was writing about the Blue Lion?"

Jamie took out his handkerchief and set about mopping the worst of the rain from his face and hair. "It is, and I bought extra copies so everyone might have a look. If it's all right, though, I'd like Miss Howard to be the first to see it."

"More'n all right," Mick agreed. He turned in the direction of the reception alcove, where Ivor Brooks was fussing with a stack of outgoing post. "You, there. Go on and tell Miss Howard that Mr. Geddes is waiting to see her."

Jamie had to suppress a laugh at Brooks's silently indignant response to being ordered about by Mick, but he found the man's next words rather less humorous. "Confound it, Nelligan. You know that Miss Howard is busy at the best of times. He can leave the magazines with me."

"No," Jamie said.

"I beg your pardon?"

"No," Jamie repeated. "I do not wish to leave the magazines with you." He raised his voice a fraction so it might carry a little farther, but not so much as to appear belligerent.

"If you could simply let Miss Howard know I have the new issues of *Picture Weekly* to show her?"

It worked. The door to her office opened and Edie appeared. "It's here?"

"It is indeed. Do you have a moment?"

"Of course—do come straight through."

It would have been satisfying to scowl at Brooks, but it was far better, he judged, to simply look through him as if he were invisible, and thereby give the man a taste of his own medicine. He did allow himself a mischievous wink in Mick's direction, and to his delight the doorman not only returned it, but also amplified the cheeky gesture with a wide grin.

Jamie shut the door to the office, for he didn't care to have Brooks listening in, and joined Edie where she stood by her desk. "Nervous?" he asked.

"A little. Miss Sutton was very nice, but one never knows how these things will turn out."

"I doubt very much it will be anything less than perfectly flattering."

"You haven't read it yet?"

"I haven't so much as peeked. I wanted us to have the chance to see it together. I mean . . . I hope that doesn't seem presumptuous of me."

"Not at all," she reassured him. "I'm glad you waited. Shall we?"

He nodded, and he pulled one of the issues from the bag and set it faceup on the desk. On the cover was his illustration of the Blue Lion, along with the question *Is This London's Most Historic Hotel?* He had not known, nor expected, that his work would be on the cover.

Edie was the first to break the silence. "I had assumed it would be Rab Butler and his new shoes."

"I expect this issue had already gone to press when the budget was announced," he said, almost reflexively, because he still wasn't sure if she liked it. He longed to know, but he couldn't bear to ask.

"Your painting of the hotel," she began. "It's perfect."

He let out the breath he hadn't realized he was holding. "Thank you. I hope I've managed to capture the hotel as it was in Jacob Howard's day."

Jamie had depicted the exterior of the sixteenth-century version of the Blue Lion in some detail, employing only sparing touches of color: a bright blue for the lion on the hanging sign, and dots of red, orange, and yellow to suggest the bounty of midsummer flowers in the surrounding gardens that had since been buried under centuries of progress and oceans of concrete. The result was an idealized version of the hotel, but not impossibly so, and if it meant a sacrifice in his artistic integrity, then so be it. The look on her face had been worth it.

"Shall we look inside?" he asked, and waited for her nod before opening the magazine. Walter Kaczmarek had given the story three full pages, generous by any measure, and along with Ruby Sutton's story there were Stella's photographs of the hotel and the people who worked there. The first, and largest, was of Edie standing at the Blue Lion's threshold, her usual jacket and suit abandoned in favor of a pretty blue dress.

Their heads nearly touching, they read the story, though it was hard to focus on the words rather than Edie's reaction to them. As he'd hoped, Ruby Sutton had captured the warmth and appeal of the Blue Lion without entirely glossing over the difficulties of operating a small hotel in a great city. Anyone reading the article would be tempted to at least visit for afternoon tea, which was described in loving detail, and the legend of Elizabeth I's snowy visit had also been recounted with care.

He knew Edie had finished reading when she let out a deep breath and looked up at him. "What do you think?" she asked.

"I think it's splendid. Both the article and Stella's photographs. Do you agree?"

"Oh, yes. I had been worrying about how it would turn out. Not that Miss Sutton would write anything unpleasant. More, I suppose, that the hotel would come across as horribly outdated or old-fashioned. Instead she's made it seem like the most charming place imaginable."

"I bought some extra copies," he remembered to tell her. "I thought you might like them for the staff, and even the guests."

"How thoughtful of you. Everyone is very excited, you know. Apart from the professor, that is. He got wind of it the other day and came to me in an absolute froth. According to him, the government is employing the coronation to convince ordinary people that all is well. 'Gilding the nation with false hope' was the phrase he used, and he accused me of being complicit by cooperating with the *Picture Weekly* article."

"Is there anything I can do to help? Perhaps try to reason with him?"

"I wouldn't dream of wasting your time in such a fashion. Besides, it's mostly bluster. I'll do my best to ensure the other guests leave him in peace, and I'll have Ginny bring his breakfast and tea to his room or the library. That should minimize any fractious moments."

Jamie had half a mind to seek out the professor and set him straight on a few matters. But that would only upset Edie. "He seems rather oblivious to the opinions and well-being of others," he said instead. "If that's not too harsh."

"Oblivious is a good way of describing him. He is a dear, but once he's got an idea into his head he can be relentless. Yesterday, for instance, it was the tunnel beneath the hotel. He'd been reading about timber construction in the 1400s, and it made him curious about the hotel's structural supports. He insisted that I allow him to inspect the support beams for evidence of scribe-framing, whatever that is, and he went on and on about hand-hewn beams and saw-hewn beams, and I'm afraid there was more but I stopped listening."

"There are tunnels beneath the hotel?" Jamie asked, trying earnestly to suppress his horror.

"Only the one that's still intact, and we haven't used it since the war. Not even for storage. I'm not certain the beams he was going on about are very secure, and it's far too dusty there, besides."

"Will you promise me something?" he asked, hoping she would not notice the sheen of perspiration on his brow. "Do not agree to go into the tunnel with Thurloe. No matter how often he asks, don't go. You're right to think it isn't safe, because it's not. Ancient structures like that are almost never safe."

"I promise. I do."

"I don't wish to seem as if I'm telling you what to do in

your own hotel. Far from it. It's only that I saw some things during the Blitz. Awful things." He shoved his hands in his pockets, hoping she couldn't see how they trembled. "I can't tell you how many people we pulled out of bomb shelters that had fallen in on them. Shelters they had been told were safe."

"I understand. Of course you're right to worry. I promise I'll stay away from the tunnel, and I'll have a surveyor in to inspect it, too."

"A sound idea," he said, but the discovery was already weighing upon him. He would fret about it for the rest of the day, and he could taste it, already, in the shape of his nightmares to come, and short of begging her to have the tunnel filled in with concrete, he would not stop worrying until he had left the hotel. And even then he would worry, for what if she were to venture down there a year from now, having forgotten his warnings, and be trapped, buried alive, just as he had once—

Enough. "I mustn't keep you," he said. "I expect you'll wish to hand out the copies to Cook and the others."

"Of course, but you must keep one back for yourself."

"Never mind me. I'll buy another one. You should have this one framed—or would you like the original? I mean the original copy of my illustration."

"Truly? I don't know what to say. I shall treasure it, of course." Her smile wide, her eyes alight with happiness, she rose on her tiptoes and pressed a soft kiss to his cheek. "Thank you, Jamie. Thank you ever so much."

He nodded, and then, before he could think better of it, "Would you like to come out for dinner with me one evening?"

"Yes" came her answer, so quickly he wondered if he might have misheard. "Yes, please," she repeated.

"Wonderful." And then, before he could think twice, "As far as where we might go . . . have you ever eaten Indian food?"

"I'm afraid I haven't. Not proper curry, that is. Only kedgeree and things like that. But I would very much like to try it."

"Excellent. There's a restaurant not far from here that I quite like. Will you let me know an evening that suits?"

"I will. Thank you again. For the magazines, of course, but most of all for your beautiful portrait of the Blue Lion."

Jamie followed her out of the office into the hall, and then he waited until she had vanished down the corridor before he turned to go upstairs. Though he knew Brooks was staring daggers at him, he ignored the man. In so doing he'd likely made an enemy, but he could not, in that moment, bring himself to care. Not with the memory of Edie's delight in the *Picture Weekly* story so fresh in his mind, and not with her happy acceptance of his invitation to dinner still ringing in his ears. His regrets would keep for another day.

Chapter 16

EDIE

Wednesday, April 22, 1953

Miss Howard? Edie? May I speak with you for a moment?"

Ivor stood at the threshold between Edie's office and the front desk, and he was holding an enormous bouquet of bright pink lilies.

"Of course. Where did those flowers come from?"

Ivor set the lilies, which were arranged in a rather nice cut-glass vase, on her desk. "They were delivered just now. I believe there's a card tucked into the greenery somewhere."

"I can't imagine who sent them," Edie said, rummaging through the forest of stems. The flowers were pretty, but their heavy scent was far too strong; she already had the beginnings of a headache. "Ah—here it is."

A token of my continuing regard

—David Bamford

Curse the man. Not only for his persistence, but also for his wretched taste in flowers. She might have forgiven him if he'd sent her some peonies.

"Where would you like me to put them?" Ivor asked warily.

In the nearest bin, she thought. "I'm not very fond of the scent," she said instead. "Let's see if the Hons will have them."

Ivor retrieved the arrangement and carried it through to the front hall, but rather than continue up to the Crane sisters' rooms, he placed the vase on the fireplace mantel and returned to Edie's office. "I'll take the flowers upstairs in a moment, but I wanted to ask you something first."

"Of course. I'm sorry I was distracted." He looked tired, the shadows under his eyes nearly purple with fatigue. "Is anything the matter?"

"No. That is, yes, something is the matter, but I don't wish to bother you."

"Ivor. Do tell me."

"My mother is ill. I'm hopeful she'll recover, but she has been asking for me, and as I've been away so long . . ."

"You must go. How long do you need? Is a week enough?"

"I'd never leave you for that long. I thought three days at the most? That should see her through until after the coronation."

"Do you need to leave now?"

"Only if it's convenient. Perhaps Mr. Swan might be able to come in a little early?"

He might, but Mrs. Swan wouldn't thank Edie for it. "We'll be all right. Off you go, and don't feel you have to rush back."

He hurried away, and Edie carried through the accounts ledger to the reception desk. It would be just as easy to sit there while she went through the past week's invoices, and if one of her employees passed by she could ask them to fetch her a cup of tea.

She had just begun to tally up the past week's outgoings, which sadly eclipsed the same period's income, when the bell above the front door trilled out its merry welcome.

"Detective Inspector Bayliss," she greeted the man who had come through the door and was even now approaching the reception desk. "It's been an age since your last stay."

"It has indeed. Do you have a moment to speak with me? In your office, if you can find someone to keep an eye on the desk?"

"It's quiet enough for the moment," she said. "I'll come round to open the door for you."

That accomplished, she went to her usual place behind her desk and waited for Inspector Bayliss to settle himself in the visitor's chair. He was a big man, broad rather than tall, with short-cropped ginger hair and a freckled face that made him look younger than he likely was.

"I don't wish to alarm you, but what I have to say is of a rather serious nature," he began.

A wave of catastrophic possibilities rushed through her head. It was one of the staff—one of the guests. Someone had been injured, or even killed, and the police had sent along someone she knew to break the news. "Is it . . . is it very bad news? Has someone from the hotel been hurt?"

"No, no. Nothing like that. I'd have told you so straight-away."

"Thank goodness."

"It is, nonetheless, quite serious." He reached inside his coat and produced an envelope, and from it he extracted a folded piece of paper. This he flattened upon the desk so she might read it.

A penciled note took up most of the page. The writing was in clear, somewhat childish block letters.

THE TRUTH MUST BE KNOWN. WE ARE A NA-TION OF BEGGARS, BROUGHT LOW BY THE WAR WHILE OUR ENEMIES FLOURISH ANEW. WE LIVE IN PENURY WHILE THE QUEEN AWAITS HER CROWN OF GOLD. BEWARE FOR IT IS A FALSE CROWN WROUGHT OF BASEST METAL AND GILDED WITH LIES.

LET THIS SERVE AS A WARNING TO OUR LEADERS THAT REPARATIONS MUST BE MADE AND NOT TO THE ENEMY BUT TO THE BRIT-ISH PEOPLE. WE ARE OWED A DEBT AND WE SHALL COLLECT COME CORONATION DAY.

But that wasn't the worst of it. The note, she realized with horror, had been written on a piece of the Blue Lion's letterhead.

"This note was delivered to the *Times* yesterday. Other letters with the same message, all written out on identical stationery, were delivered to the *Mail*, the *Mirror*, the *Telegraph*, the *Herald*, the *Sketch*, and the *News Chronicle*."

Her mouth had gone dry. "I don't know what to say. It's ridiculous. Some horrible prank."

"It may well be, but we can't discount it. Not so close to

the coronation. And since it's anonymous, and was sent to most of the papers at the same time, I feel bound to look into it. Never mind that experience tells me it's likely the work of some pathetic crank with too much time on his hands."

"I see."

"I am not accusing you of anything, but I am concerned that the person issuing these threats has chosen to do so on stationery from your hotel. This is your stationery, is it not?"

"May I pick it up?"

"Go ahead. We've gone over it for fingerprints."

Edie held it to the light, and then she opened her desk drawer and took out a fresh piece of letterhead. The watermark was the same on both pieces of paper, and the rampant lion at the top of each page, a simplified version of the hotel's ancient sign, was identical. For economy's sake the printing was in black ink, with the hotel name and address at the bottom of the page.

"Yes. It is the same as ours," she admitted.

"Do you provide a supply of stationery to hotel guests?"

"We do. A half-dozen sheets with two envelopes."

He had taken out a notebook and began to write down her answers. "And it's refreshed with each new guest?"

"Yes." And then, though it was mortifying to admit, she added, "We haven't been very busy in recent weeks."

"Are there desks in each room?"

"Yes."

"With a blotter beneath?"

"Yes."

"And how often is it refreshed?" he asked. "The blotter, I mean."

"Only if it's stained with ink."

"Apart from the guests themselves, who might have access to the stationery? Where is it stored?"

"There are several boxes of it in the storage closet—you can see the door over there. That's where the maids go when they need to refresh the supplies on their carts."

He nodded, still scribbling away. "So the maids—how many work here?"

"Four girls, all very steady and hardworking. I doubt very much they'd be behind this."

"As do I," he agreed, "but I may wish to speak with them at some point. It's possible one of them may have noticed something."

"I suppose so. But you won't frighten them, will you?"

"I will do my very best to appear as unthreatening as possible," he said. "To confirm—it's only the maids and yourself who have access to the stationery? Might anyone else have cause to fetch things from that office?"

"I suppose the assistant manager might. Ivor Brooks. He's away for a few days, but I expect him back soon. And there's our night manager, Arthur Swan, and our doorman, Mick Nelligan. He stores luggage in there from time to time. I think that's it."

"Very well. Without making too much of it, I'd like you to switch out the blotters and stationery in each room, even if it has been vacant for some weeks, and keep track of which room they come from. Probably easiest to mark the room number on the back in pencil as you go. In the meantime, can you move the boxes of stationery to a more secure spot? Ideally somewhere under lock and key."

She nodded, trying hard not to dwell upon the bother and expense of it all.

"We only need to look over the paper and blotters," Inspector Bayliss clarified. "I'll have everything returned as quickly as possible."

"May I ask why you need them? Is it to check for fingerprints?"

"The letters were written in hard pencil, so it's possible the writer left behind an impression on the sheets of paper beneath or the blotter itself."

"I should imagine he'd have thought of that."

At this the inspector smiled wryly. "Never underestimate the stupidity of the ordinary man. While I'm here, could I trouble you for a list of your past guests? I won't contact any of them just yet, but it will be helpful to know who has stayed here in the year or so since the queen's accession."

"Very well. Though I would prefer if you refrained from speaking with any of my guests, both present and past. I do have the hotel's reputation to consider. If word of this were to get out—"

"Word is already out, Miss Howard. Every newspaper editor in London knows that the threats were written on stationery taken from your hotel. I can keep it out of the news so long as there's a chance that it represents a genuine threat, but I can't stop people from gossiping."

"Is there anything else I can do?" she asked. "Apart from gathering up the blotters and keeping track of the stationery."

"You can let me know if you notice anything out of the ordinary. Grumbling about the coronation, republican sentiments, dissatisfaction with the government in general. That sort of thing."

"On any given day, I'd expect there to be half a dozen such conversations going on here in the hotel."

"I don't mean the usual whingeing," he clarified. "More like someone who talks as if they have an axe to grind. Someone whose talk is fueled by anger, not boredom."

"Oh. I see."

"Setting aside your overnight guests, what about your boarders? The Crane sisters and Professor Thurloe still live here, don't they?"

"They do," she confirmed, "as does a friend of my family, an Italian photo-journalist. She works at *Picture Weekly* magazine. And there's also James Geddes, an artist. He's staying here while he works on a commission for the Cartwrights' guild across the way."

"I know. I stopped by the Queen Bess not long ago and he and Mick were there. Seemed like a sound fellow to me."

"He is. I would stake the future of my hotel on it. As for the sisters and the professor, none of them is remotely capable of what you allege. Not least because it requires a level of stealth and cunning they simply don't possess."

"And the Italian woman?"

"Impossible. You have my solemn word on that. Stella Donati's character is beyond reproach."

"Fair enough. That still leaves two possibilities: Either the letters are from someone who filched some of your stationery when he stayed at the hotel, and used it because it was at hand, or the threats are the work of someone who used your stationery specifically because he hoped to land you in hot water." His voice was gentle, but his words felt like a slap across her face.

"Me? I can't have done anything to provoke such behavior."

"I'm not saying you did. I do want you to think about it, though. Is there anyone who might wish you ill or resent you in some way?"

"I don't know. I suppose it's possible . . ."

She would have to sift through every conversation she'd had for weeks and weeks, with every person who had crossed her path, and each time she would have to ask herself if that other person had been harboring ill feelings toward her. Could it be possible that, without realizing or intending, she had hurt someone? Hurt them so badly they felt compelled to retaliate in such a dramatic way?

"Don't let it get to you," Inspector Bayliss said, likely guessing the direction of her thoughts. "All the same, if anything does come to mind, ring me up straightaway. Here's my card."

"Thank you. I will."

"Good night, Miss Howard. Try not to worry."

They shook hands again, and she watched him go, and then she collapsed back into her chair, the edges of his card digging into her palm. And all she could do, in that moment, more alone than she had ever been, was to worry.

But worrying had never helped her before, and it wouldn't make a lick of difference now. Instead she would make a cup of tea for herself, strong and well sugared, and then she would get back to work.

MAY

Chapter 17

STELLA

Saturday, May 2, 1953

Every other Saturday, as soon as she had finished her work for the day, Stella went to the big post office at Leicester Square and purchased a money order for five pounds and ten shillings, which she then posted to her zia Rosa in Italy. For safekeeping she folded it within a long letter, written on sheets of foolscap over the course of successive evenings, and so far every money order she'd sent had reached her family without incident.

Had it been a fine day, she would have gone for a walk in the sunshine, or sat on a park bench and enjoyed an ice cream, but it had been raining steadily for hours, so instead she went to the National Gallery for the third or fourth time since she'd moved to London, since it was no more than a five-minute walk from the Blue Lion.

Before the war, before 1938 and the laws that had barred her family from Italy's art galleries and museums, she had loved to look at paintings, the older the better, and at her mother's direction Stella had often tried to picture the person who had taken pigments and oil, canvas and wood and glue, and made of them something entirely *other*. Later, when she'd only had the memory of the paintings to sustain her, she had still marveled at the continued existence of such fragile creations. How could it be, she had wondered, that their creators were long dead while their work lived on?

Generations lived and died, and all the while the earth continued to spin on its axis, never slowing, never resting. It had existed for aeons before her own life had blinked into existence, and it would continue on long after she and everyone she had ever met had turned to dust.

Such a thought ought to have upset her, and indeed she suspected most people would likely find it unsettling. Yet somehow it brought her comfort, as did her visits to the gallery. The artists whose paintings she admired had known nothing of the twentieth century, nothing of the terrible years she had somehow survived; and when she fell into their vanished worlds, one canvas after another, each of them entirely unburdened by the future, she felt a little of her sorrow lift from her shoulders.

There was no one to tell about the wonderful sense of lightness, of freedom, even, that the paintings gave her, for no one in London knew the full horror of her memories. Among those who loved her, only her friend Nina understood the length and breadth and depth of it all, for she had been at Stella's side from the night they had arrived at Birkenau to the day of their liberation, and far beyond, too.

But Nina was half a continent away, and busy with her

studies and her young children, and it had been some years since Stella had felt able to talk of her grief, her fury, and her loneliness with her friend. To share her memories, she still feared, would be to dive headlong into the depths of her loss, and risk the chance of never again surfacing.

For now, it was enough to visit the gallery as often as she could, immerse herself in the unknowing past, and then, on her way home, treat herself to a cup of coffee at the Café Milano, where the barman, taking pity on a fellow Italian far from home, only charged her two pennies rather than the posted sixpence.

Today, rather unexpectedly, she'd become captivated by a succession of Rembrandts. There was something so familiar about their subjects, for if she set aside their unfamiliar and occasionally alarming garments—the starched ruffs must have been a horror to wear—she saw much that she recognized in their earnest and rather anxious expressions.

Perhaps, she mused, some trick of magic now allowed them to see through their painted eyes, and they were alarmed by the world that greeted them. The twentieth century was surely bewildering, and not only because of the oddities of modern dress, speech, and manners. She felt a sudden urge to reassure them, to tiptoe toward the portraits and whisper words of comfort and hope.

It isn't all war and death and calamity, she wanted to tell them. *People still love. Babies are born and gardens are tended and choirs raise their voices in song. Artists still see beauty and immortalize it in paint and canvas.*

It was silly, of course, for the stolid merchants and their wives, together with Rembrandt and his Hendrickje, had been dead and gone for almost three hundred years, and they would forever remain ignorant of this century's horrors and glories alike.

"Stella?"

She looked around to discover Win Keller standing at her side. It was such a surprise to encounter him away from the office that she simply stood and blinked at him.

"Are you all right?" he asked.

"Yes. Sorry. I did not expect to see you here. That is all."

"I can go if you'd rather be on your own."

"No—I am pleased to see you. I was simply caught up in my thoughts."

He nodded, and they stood together and looked at *A Woman Bathing in a Stream*.

"What draws you to Rembrandt?" he asked suddenly.

"The ordinary faces, I think. His subjects look real. They have wrinkles and freckles, and bumps in their noses, and their hair isn't always tidy, and their clothes don't always seem very clean. Even their hands are real. A century earlier, people in portraits had hands that looked as if they'd never held anything heavier than a feather. But Rembrandt painted hands with chewed-up fingernails and brown spots and calluses."

She stopped short, realizing that she'd offered a much longer answer than he'd likely wished for or anticipated, and decided to ask a question of her own. "What did you come to see today?"

"Nothing in particular. I like to roam the galleries and see what catches my eye. I was on the point of leaving when I bumped into you."

"Would you like to have a coffee with me?" she asked impulsively, not caring to examine her reasons for the invitation. "Café Milano is not far."

"I know the place. If we go out the side entrance here we can chop a few minutes off the walk."

The café's front windows were foggy with steam from an enormous Gaggia espresso machine, and its tables were crowded with fellow refugees from the dismal weather, but Mr. Keller spotted a place at the counter near the back. "Now I remember why I don't often come here," he said as he helped Stella to her perch on one of the high stools. "The medical school attached to Charing Cross Hospital is just next door, which means it's always awash in students. Can spot them a mile away—they're the ones that look as if they've been raised from the dead. Poor sods. Now, tell me—what would you like?"

"May I have an espresso? Let me give you the money for it."

"Absolutely not. Would you like anything to eat? Perhaps we might share a currant bun?"

He soon returned with two small cups of espresso and the promised bun, which he cut neatly in half. "Do have some," he urged.

"Thank you. I will, but first I must have my coffee. It is nicest when it is very hot." She picked up the little cup, its handle so small she had to pinch it between her forefinger and thumb, and drank down the espresso in one wonderfully satisfying gulp.

She had, she suddenly realized, been starving for moments such as this. Fleeting moments of joy and inspiration and understanding that were as bold and vivifying as the delicious cup of coffee she'd just downed. She had been so hungry, but she hadn't known why until this very moment.

"Do you often visit the gallery?" she asked.

"Once or twice a month, if I can. I've learned a great deal about the composition of photographs by looking at paintings. I discover something new every time I visit. Today, for instance, I learned about Rembrandt and hands. So I thank you for that."

"You are welcome. Why are you called Winton?"

"Why do you want to know?"

"Because it is important to you. At least I believe it is."

"Very well." He bolted down his espresso, as if his resolve needed bolstering, and then he looked out the window, even though it was fogged over and there was nothing to see. When he began to speak, his voice was low and hesitant, as if the calmly decisive man she knew from work had been replaced by a stranger.

"When Germany annexed the Sudetenland, my family became refugees. We escaped to Prague, and because my father was certain that Hitler would not honor the Munich Agreement, he set about finding a place for my sister and me to go. We weren't wealthy people, and we had no connections abroad, and no one was interested in taking in Jews. He was desperate, he and my mother both. And then he learned of an Englishman who was making a list. The man was staying at the Hotel Europa, so we went and queued up in the cold, along with what seemed like every other Jew in the city. We were there for hours and hours, and all the while my parents were arguing in whispers. My mother was certain it was a hoax of some kind, but Papa insisted it was genuine. That the group of people the man represented wished only to help.

"At last we reached the front of the queue, and the Englishman was very kind. He truly was. He took down my name, and my sister's, and someone else took our photographs, and he said that he would do his very best to ensure we would be taken to England. To safety."

"And he did?"

"He did. A letter came, with tickets and details of the journey we children would take, and I remember that Mutti and Papa said it would not be for long. It would be a holiday, they promised. I was so excited that when we said good-bye I hardly paid any attention at all."

He blinked hard, still looking at some lost view beyond the window. "When Renata and I arrived in London we were sent to a sort of children's home, and after a week or so a man came to take our photographs for a magazine. For *Picture Weekly*. Kaz, you see, had promised to run a series of short articles about the children from the transports. I didn't meet him then, but his decision led to our being taken in by a retired bank manager and his wife in Lewisham."

"They were good to you?"

"Oh, yes. My sister still lives with them. Mr. Swakeley even paid for my schooling."

"How did you end up at *PW*?"

"As soon as I turned eighteen, I tried to sign up for active duty, but I was still considered a foreign national. Instead I was sent to an office not far from here and taught how to operate a darkroom. I spent the rest of the war enlarging aerial photographs of German industrial sites, which I still find rather ridiculous given my rejection from the armed forces on the grounds of my being a security risk."

"So after the war . . . ?"

"I showed up at the *PW* offices and begged for ten minutes with Kaz. I told him I would work for free until he saw for himself that he couldn't do without me. He hired me on the spot."

"You still haven't explained your name."

He sighed, and made a show of frowning at her, but she could tell he wasn't annoyed. Not really. "It used to be Wilhelm. Within half an hour of arriving in this country I had decided to change it. Only Adolf could have been worse. I was desperate to fit in, to lose my accent and learn English and leave everything behind."

"Why Winton?"

"He was the man at the hotel in Prague. Nicholas Winton. Foolish of me, really."

"Why? Because people think your name is Winston?"

"Yes. But also because I might just as easily have chosen Nicholas." He smiled, and the sight of it set her heart racing.

"Thank you for telling me."

"With most people I can't be bothered. At *PW*, only Kaz and Frank know the full story."

"Why Frank?"

Another fleeting smile. "He took my picture for that story."

She ought not to have pressed on, but she had to know. "What happened to your parents?"

"Dead. They must be dead, or they'd have come for us. I expect they were sent to the camps."

"Why confide in me?"

This time he did not look away. "It was a few days after you started at the magazine. You were reaching for some photographs that were clipped to the top row of wires. Your sleeve fell back, and I saw the numbers."

"But you said nothing."

"If you'd shown me, I might have asked. But it was an accident, my seeing the marks on your arm. It didn't seem right to question you."

"I wish I were the sort of person who is brave enough to speak loudly of what happened. To use my suffering to help others. But it feels such a private thing. I am not ashamed, not at all. It is only that my grief is something I do not wish to share with strangers."

"Then don't. And you are brave, you know. Never think otherwise. Words are not the only way to answer the world's questions. You already do so with your photographs."

"What would you say if I told you I wish to take the portraits of people, like us, who survived? Their faces, and also a picture of their hands as they hold something precious from their old life. A photograph of someone they loved, or a memento of some kind."

"I think it is a good idea. Would it be for the magazine?"

"One day. For now it would be for myself."

He fished in the pocket of his jacket and retrieved a small object, which he now presented to her on his open palm. "This is my memento. My treasure." It was a carved wooden cat, curled into a tidy ball, and was both simple and beautifully made. "My father was a cabinetmaker," he explained. "He had to leave behind all his tools, but he still managed to carve this with only his penknife. He gave it to me a few days before I left. I told him I didn't like it. I was thirteen, and I told him it was something you would give to a baby. I only found it later, tucked away in the bottom of my rucksack, when I thought I might die for missing him and Mutti. I would hold it in my hand each night as I fell asleep."

Win put the cat back in his pocket, patting the fabric to ensure it was secure. "What about you?"

"I have nothing from before the war. It was all stolen, or destroyed. I don't even have a single photograph of my parents."

At this, his serious expression became intensely woeful. "Stella. I am so sorry. I didn't think."

"I don't mind. I hardly ever talk about them, but now, with you, I can. I know you will understand."

"I'm honored."

"If I could have one thing back, I think it would be my mother's sketchbook. She and Papa wrote travel guides, and when they came home from one of their trips she would show me the views she had painted. I asked her, once, why she didn't put any of the drawings in a frame, and she told me they were meant to stay in the book. They were a sort of diary, she told me."

Perhaps the diary still existed somewhere. Perhaps the drawings had been taken from the book and put into frames and sold to tourists. Perhaps, one day, if she saw enough of the world, she might come upon one of them hanging upon a shop wall, or at an antiques stall in a market, and recognize her mother's hand, and so regain something of the lost life they had once shared.

"I have the memory of them still," she said at last. "Of Mamma and Papa, and the places they visited, and the pictures she brought home for me. And that is enough. For me, for now, it has to be enough."

Chapter 18

JAMIE

Friday, May 8, 1953

At six o'clock Jamie set down his pencil and began the serious work of getting ready for dinner with Edie. Normally he spared no more attention to his appearance than a cursory check that his flies were buttoned, his tie was free of stains, his socks matched, and his hair was brushed flat, but tonight he had to look his best.

The boiler, for once in a cooperative mood, spat out just enough hot water for him to shave and have a quick bath. He'd set aside his best shirt, still fresh from the laundry, for the occasion. His socks definitely matched. His suit was pressed. His tie, a birthday present from his brother, was made of silk and looked it. All excellent auguries for the evening ahead, he judged.

It helped that they would be dining in an Indian restaurant, for the chances of being stared at, or a passerby letting him know what they thought of a brown man sitting with a white woman, would be significantly decreased. Even so, he would have to be on his guard. It had been a risk to ask her out in the first place; and though he did not and would not regret it, he had no desire to see Edie embarrassed or humiliated as a consequence. It also helped that he was tall, and sufficiently broad across the shoulders to discourage all but the most ardent of bigots, but that alone would never be enough. If someone wished to let him know he was unwelcome or resented or feared or even hated, there was little he could do to stop them.

He had been about six years old, possibly a little younger, when he'd learned that other people saw him in a different light from most children, his siblings included. It had been at a family gathering, likely over Christmas, and he'd been absorbed in a book he'd been given. It had been a history of Scotland, with beautiful illustrations, and he'd hardly looked away from it all day. Nevertheless, at some point he'd become aware that the grown-ups nearby were talking about him.

"Such a shame that he takes after Shilpa. Poor child," Aunt Morag had murmured. That part had confused Jamie, for his mother was the prettiest woman he had ever seen. His aunt had to be mistaken.

"It's a puzzle, it is. Fraser and Fiona look so like their father you'd never know they were mixed. And then *he* came out looking brown as a berry. Must have been a shock for Colin. Not that he'd ever admit it, not with James being the apple of his eye and all. But still." The other woman had been a neighbor. He couldn't remember her name.

"He's that bright, he is, but what chance does he have of getting on in the world? Not looking like that, he won't," his aunt had stated with a calm sort of finality, and she had heaved a great sigh, and in that moment he had both hated and feared her. Twenty-five years later, or something close to it, he still resented the woman, for she'd taken the last of his childhood from him.

From that moment on he had seen, and he had *known*, and things that had once made no sense had suddenly slotted into place. The boys at school who kept saying that he needed a good scrubbing to clean him up. The schoolmasters who looked through him, even when his hand was raised and no one else had the answers. The neighbors next door who never said hello, and who refused to let their son play with him.

He was reasonably confident that Edie did not look at him and see a man who was diminished by his race. He had yet to scent so much as a whiff of bigotry from her, nor did he think it likely he ever would. Yet how could he be certain? She might be happy to accept him as a valued and even esteemed guest, and she might have begun to think of him as her friend, but would she ever be able to think of him as *more*? For that was what he wanted from her, and it was time he admitted it, if only to himself.

Edie was waiting for him in the front hall. Rather alarmingly, she was kneeling by one of the upholstered chairs that flanked the fireplace, and was using a pair of pliers to wrench a length of decorative fringe from the bottom of the chair. She looked up, smiled ruefully, and returned to her task.

He crossed the hall and crouched next to her. "I confess I hadn't expected to find you engaged in emergency surgery on a chair."

"I won't be a minute." She yanked off the last of the fringe, her nose wrinkling at the aroma of ammonia that rose from its tangled strands, and turned her attention to a few stubbornly clinging staples. "Mrs. Hemmings stays for a week every May and September, and has done as long as I can remember, and she always has a pair of little dogs with her—not the same dogs, naturally, but they always *look* the same, like little brown footstools—"

"Pekingese?"

"Yes. Sweet-natured things but they wee *everywhere*. And Mr. Swan informed me that one of Mrs. Hemmings's Pekingese relieved itself upon this very chair not a half hour ago. He tried to mop it up, but there was no hope for the fringe. Tomorrow I'll pop on some ribbon to cover up the edge, but this will do for now."

"You had better give the other chair a haircut," he advised. "They look a bit mismatched."

She inspected one, then the other. "I suppose you're right."

"Would you like me to do it? I'm an old hand at pulling out staples from frames and canvases."

She considered his offer for a moment before nodding decisively. "Yes, please. That would be enormously helpful."

Although Jamie's nose was at least a yard away from the second chair, its fringe smelled rather ripe; he suspected it, too, had been anointed by a Hemmings Pekingese. "We'd best put all of this with the other rubbish," he said, gathering up the mess.

"Thank you. The big bin is at the back, and we can wash our hands in the scullery."

He followed her down the corridor, aware that it was a rather unusual way to begin a dinner date, but equally aware that he didn't mind one whit. At her direction he stuffed the fringe into the large, lidded bin by the door, then insisted on waiting his turn at the scullery sink.

"There," she said, drying her hands. "I am sorry about that. I honestly thought I'd be finished before you came downstairs. I hope I haven't made us late."

"Not at all. It's only gone seven now, and the restaurant isn't far. We can take a taxi if you like."

"Is it near enough to walk? I was at my desk all afternoon."

"Only a half mile at the most. And I could do with some fresh air, too."

Having helped her with her coat, Jamie stepped away so she might speak with Mr. Swan without his looming over the two of them.

"I don't think I'll be late back in, Mr. Swan," she said.

"Very good, Miss Howard. I hope you have a lovely evening. Oh—Mr. Geddes—I meant to warn you."

"Yes?" Jamie answered warily. "Is anything the matter?"

"Oh, heavens no. I only meant to say you had best take an umbrella," Mr. Swan advised, his homely face animated by nothing more than honest concern.

"Thank you. How kind of you to remind me," Jamie said, and hastened to fetch an umbrella from the stand by the door. Thus equipped for the journey, he turned to Edie. "Shall we go?"

As they walked toward Trafalgar Square, Jamie was careful to keep a proper distance from her, for it was still full light outside, and it would be so awfully easy for their evening to be spoiled before it had even begun. Not that they'd been bothered on their afternoon walks, but there, again, he'd always been careful to keep a certain distance between them.

"How was your day?" she asked.

"Productive. I spent most of it working on some preparatory sketches of the gold state coach. It's rather a difficult thing to capture in paint."

"Nothing but gold, I expect."

"Yes. Gold and more gold, and I'm nervous it will look like Cinderella's pumpkin if I'm not successful."

"That I very much doubt," she said with certainty. "Not in the hands of a painter as gifted as you."

"Thank you," he said, though his response seemed entirely inadequate for such a meaningful compliment. "What of your day? I did promise I would ask."

"Hmm," she considered. "I suppose you know the low point already."

"Pekingese versus chair?"

"Yes. On the other hand, I was able to convince Cook to plan a coronation-themed menu for afternoon tea. She was reluctant, but I prevailed in the end."

"What new delicacies will she be concocting?" he asked, hoping they wouldn't skew toward the dainty and insubstantial. He quite liked the hearty afternoon tea at the Blue Lion, not least because Cook always gave him extra sandwiches.

"It's not so much a case of new things, but rather new names. The gingerbread cake will become the Gâteau de Couronnement, and the curried chicken salad will be Poulet Reine Élisabeth. You may have already noticed that it contains very little curry. Cook likes to say she adds 'just enough to give it some color.'"

"I wouldn't dream of complaining," he said truthfully.

They walked on, dodging pigeons as they crossed Trafalgar Square, and presently they passed the National Gallery and continued north toward Leicester Square. Their talk was pleasant and not especially memorable. She spoke of the plan to install a television in the lounge and the rumors that sugar would be coming off the ration. He talked of the books he had read in recent weeks, nearly all of them borrowed from her excellent library, and his hopes to visit his family in Edinburgh after he'd finished the Cartwrights' commission.

Their conversation may have been inconsequential, but the feeling of walking next to her, simply being near her, was not. She'd put on some perfume, a delicate scent that was exactly right for her, and she had on a pretty frock beneath her coat, its dark inky blue the exact color of the sky where it met the horizon at sunset.

Before long they turned the corner onto Gerrard Street. "Here we are," he told her. "I know Veeraswamy claims to be the oldest Indian restaurant in London, but Shafi's has been around a good long while. It's not as grand inside, but the food is excellent."

Shafi's was impossible to miss, for its facade was painted a stark white and the name was picked out in angular black letters. They were greeted by the usual doorman, who wore a tailored topcoat, an immaculate turban, and had a snow-white beard and moustache. He opened the door with a nod, his expression rather solemn and watchful. Edie beamed up at him, murmuring her thanks, and

Jamie watched as the man, evidently entranced, returned her smile.

Inside they were met by the maître d'hôtel. "Good evening, and welcome to Shafi's."

"Good evening. I have a reservation for half-past seven. The name is Geddes."

"Yes, of course. If you will first allow me to take your coats?" These were carried away to a curtained alcove. "And now, if you would kindly follow me to your table."

The maître d'hôtel pulled out Edie's chair, presented her with a menu, and then did the same for Jamie. "May I interest you in an aperitif to begin? Madam?"

"May I have a glass of tonic water?"

"But of course, madam. Mr. Geddes?"

"I'll have a pint of lager. Tennent's, if you have it." Another reason he preferred the more casual atmosphere at Shafi's.

"Very good. Your waiter shall be with you promptly."

Jamie watched Edie as she read over the menu, earnestly hoping she would see something she liked. "Is there anything that catches your eye?" he asked.

Her expression, when she looked up from the menu, was uncertain. "I'm not sure what to order. There are some English dishes here, but I would rather try something Indian. It seems a shame to come to a lovely place like this and have roast chicken and mashed potatoes."

"It's quite usual to order a number of dishes for the table, and then take a little of each. I think you might enjoy one of the curries—perhaps the lamb or pigeon? They don't seem to have chicken tonight. No matter which kind you pick, the meat will be cooked in a sauce, so it will be very tender. And the sauce itself is mild. I'm not sure of the exact ingredients, but they're likely to include tomato and yogurt and things like ginger and garlic, along with some spices. But nothing too spicy, I promise."

"That sounds lovely."

"Good. I'll also order some chana masala, which are chickpeas cooked in a sauce, and some rice with vegetables, and some samosas. They're a sort of pastry with vegetables in the filling. And we'll want some poppadoms with mango chutney."

"I'm sure it will all be delicious," she said.

A white-jacketed waiter quickly returned with their drinks and departed with their dinner order in hand. Jamie picked up his beer, and was on the point of taking a great gulp of it, but remembered just in time that he was no longer a sweaty undergraduate but a grown man at dinner with a woman he wished to impress. Instead he restrained himself to a single refreshing sip before setting down his glass.

"I've been meaning to ask about your name," he began, thinking that it was a good sort of question to launch their dinnertime conversation. "On the badge you wear on your lapel, your initials are *E* and *D*. Is Edie derived from them? A sort of nickname?"

"Do you know, I'm not certain. I've always been Edie, which is rather a good thing as my first name is Edwina and I've never much liked it."

"It's a lovely name," he said. "It suits you."

"Thank you. What about your name? I noticed that you sign it A. J. Geddes. What does the *A* stand for?"

"Alexander. After my grandfather, but my family has always called me Jamie."

"For a moment I thought you might say the *A* signified a terribly unusual or old-fashioned name," she said, a thread of laughter gilding her voice. "Augustus, say, or Archibald."

"Good Scottish name, that." And then, daringly, "It might just as easily have been Aadiyapadham. My maternal grandfather's first name."

"And a very nice name it is," she said. "Although you'd probably have to spell it endlessly for people, and then correct them when they got it wrong."

"There is that."

"From time to time we have guests whose names aren't English. I mean the language of their name, not their nationality."

"Of course," he said, though there was no "of course" about it. Few people he knew would bother to make such a distinction.

"I do try to ensure I pronounce their names correctly," she went on, "and if I'm not sure I ask. Quietly, so as not to embarrass them. I don't want them to think they've done something wrong, you see, for I'm the one who needs to learn. And I do feel it's important to get things like that right."

"That's decent of you. Most people don't care, or they put up a fuss if they're corrected. I expect that's why my parents gave us conventional names. Well, conventional if you're British."

"Yes, but who's to say what is conventional? There are any number of English names—English-*language* names, I mean—that are quite out of the ordinary. I remember, years and years ago, we had a guest arrive, and he introduced himself as Mr. Fanshaw. He then offered to spell it out for me, and I was ever so surprised—it was completely different to what I'd expected. I'd have pronounced it 'feather-stone-huff' if I hadn't known."

"I expect he was used to the confusion. I knew a boy at school with the surname of Mingus. Only years later did I learn it was actually spelled *M-e-n-z-i-e-s*. I've no idea why it was pronounced in such a way."

Their conversation continued on in a similar vein for another fifteen minutes or so before their food arrived. The waiter deftly arranged the dishes before them and then, at Jamie's direction, served out portions of everything they'd ordered.

Jamie held his breath as Edie took her first few bites. "What do you think?"

"I think I ought to have come here for dinner long before now," she said, grinning, and his heart turned over in his chest.

"I'm so glad," he said.

"Does your mother cook this sort of food at home?"

"To be honest, she isn't much of a cook. She grew up in a rather grand family where there were servants to do everything, so I'm not sure she ever saw the inside of a kitchen before she was married. She did try to learn, but her heart was never in it. I suppose she was too interested in her work."

"What does she do?"

"She's a professor of mathematics. During the war she was involved in some very secret goings-on. Not that she's ever said a word about it."

"My heavens."

"When I was growing up, we had a housekeeper who took care of all the domestic sorts of things. Cooking and the laundry and cleaning the house. Mrs. Beild, but we called her Billy. Lovely woman. She retired after the war and my mother has never quite got over it."

"Did Billy make curry for you?"

"Oh, no. We ate nothing but the plainest and sturdiest Scottish fare at home. When we felt like eating proper Indian food, we would go to a restaurant."

"This is such a treat for me," Edie said, helping herself to another portion of chana masala. "Not only the food, but having the time to really savor it."

"Does the hotel keep you too busy to have many evenings out?"

"I'm afraid it does. I had dinner out a few times earlier this year, but it was all to do with the hotel. It wasn't with a proper friend, you see." Her cheeks grew pink, and he realized, suddenly, that she was speaking of the odious man he'd once seen with her in the hotel's front hall.

"I hope you don't think of tonight in the same way."

"Goodness, no. This, tonight, with you, is different. I promise it is."

"I'm very glad to hear it. What about time away from the hotel?" he asked, prudently changing the subject. "When was your last holiday?"

"Not since before the war, I'm afraid."

He very nearly dropped his glass of beer. "Are you telling me that you haven't had a holiday for fourteen years? Your employees are given time away from work, aren't they? Certainly you deserve the same."

"I suppose so. But my parents died at the end of 1940, and I've had the running of the hotel ever since."

"Were they killed in the Blitz?" he asked, and immediately wished he'd swallowed his tongue instead.

"Yes—no. I mean, it was during the Blitz, but they weren't killed by a bomb. They were crossing the Strand in the blackout, and they were run down. It was an ambulance that hit them, if you can believe it. He said he didn't see them, and he was going fast enough that they likely didn't see him, either. I suppose I should be grateful for that."

"I'm very sorry."

"My brothers were killed in the last war, before I was born—I did tell you that, didn't I? And as my father was the only surviving child in his family, that meant I was the last of the Howards. That's how I ended up with the hotel." She was fidgeting with her glass, turning it round and round.

"I ought not to have asked. I'm sorry."

"It's quite all right. It was a long time ago."

"Will you tell me about your parents? How did they meet?"

At this she smiled. "My mother's parents ran a guesthouse in Margate, and every year my Howard grandparents would stay there on their annual holiday. That's how they met—as children each summer. They were quite young when they married—I think Mum was only nineteen."

"Did they always live at the Blue Lion once they were married?"

"Oh, yes. I think, back then, they were quite happy. My

brothers were only a year and a bit apart, and the hotel did well in those days."

"And your brothers?" he asked, unable to stop himself.

"Killed at the Somme. The telegrams arrived on the same day. Edwin had just turned twenty, and Duncan was eighteen. My mother was never the same after that. Or so I've been told."

Edwin. Duncan. "You were named for them," he said, and she nodded bleakly.

It was all he could do, in that moment, to hide his reaction. Her whole life, every single day of it, had been spent in perpetually indentured service to her brothers' memories. What on earth could her parents have been thinking? Why could they not have remembered and honored their sons in a way that did not require the sacrifice of their daughter?

But he was only just getting to know Edie, and he wasn't about to criticize two people he'd never met for a decision they had made when still undone by grief. Instead he swallowed down his horror and cast about for something to say. "The men I commanded during the war were of an age with your brothers. Hardly any were older than twenty or twenty-one. For that matter, I was only twenty when I was given my own section and put in charge of fifteen other men. My knees were knocking with fright those first few weeks."

"It's a lot to ask of a young man," she said.

"We grew up quickly, just as you had to do."

"When my parents died? It was a shock, I suppose, but I'd been working at the hotel since I was a girl and I knew the work well enough. Besides, I wasn't doing anything dangerous. I certainly wasn't defusing bombs for—how long was it?"

"Something like three and a half years."

"It's a miracle you survived."

"If I believed in such things I might agree with you. I think it was more along the lines of luck, pure and simple. I knew men who were far better at the job than I, with steadier hands, steadier nerves, and then they'd come up against some fiendish new wiring device . . ."

He was a fool to have burdened her with the knowledge of such things. He wouldn't blame her if she got up and left. He—

Her hand covered his, cool and delicate, and he could breathe again.

"I beg your pardon," he managed, and would have blundered on if salvation, in the form of their pudding, had not arrived. He hadn't even noticed that they'd both cleared their plates, focused as he'd been on Edie and Edie alone.

"With the compliments of our chef, Mr. Geddes," their waiter explained. "Our special preparation of rose and pistachio kulfi."

"Thank you very much."

Edie immediately picked up her spoon and, without questioning him as to the ingredients or flavor of the frozen confection, took one bite, then another. "This is delicious," she said between mouthfuls. "I thought it was ice cream at first, but it's not, is it?"

"No, but it's similar enough. It comes in many flavors, but this is one of my favorites."

"I'm not surprised. Now . . . where were we? Ah—we'd begun to talk about you. Shall we continue?"

Please, no, he thought. *No more questions about the war.*

"Do you have any brothers or sisters?" she asked instead.

Yet again she had surprised him. "One of each. My brother, Fraser, is four years older. He's a barrister at my father's chambers. His wife is Mary and they've three boys. My sister, Fiona, is two years older. She was a nurse in the war. Married one of the doctors she worked with and they have two children now. A girl and a boy."

"Your parents must be in heaven with five grandchildren already."

"Oh, aye," he said, deciding to keep his mother's avowed desire for additional grandchildren to himself. "Do you have any other family?"

"On my father's side, no—as I said before, I'm the last of the Howards. My father was an only child, and my grandfather's siblings died years ago. I think my father may have mentioned some cousins, but I never knew their names. I feel as if, perhaps, there was some sort of falling-out? But it was long before I was born, and no one has popped out of the woodwork since then."

"Do you have anyone on your mother's side?"

"Some aunts and uncles, but I never see them. They used to stay at the hotel all the time when my parents were alive, sometimes for weeks on end, but they never paid a penny for their rooms or meals. After my parents died, I stopped it. I didn't want to, but it was costing a fortune, and I couldn't afford it. And that was that. Not so much as a Christmas card since."

"No doubt you're better off without them," he said. "But still."

"But still," she echoed. "It can be rather lonely at times.

The guests come and go, and the staff . . . I'm very fond of them, of course, and I've known some of them since I was little, but I'm not friends with any of them. Not really."

"Is there anyone you can talk to when you're having a hard day?"

"In a pinch I could talk to Cook. Or Mick, I suppose. But it wouldn't be fair. They have their own problems. I wouldn't wish to burden them in any way."

"I wonder," he said, his heart hammering away so loudly it was a wonder she didn't remark on it, "if you might turn to me. When you feel worried or frightened. For I would be very happy to listen."

"Thank you, Jamie." Her voice was soft, and the look in her eyes, when she met his questioning gaze, was solemn and trusting.

"I mean it, too. I never make promises that I don't intend to keep."

"I believe you. Didn't you promise that I would enjoy my supper? And here we are, and I've polished off every last bite while we've been talking, and it was wonderful, Jamie. Just wonderful."

It was raining as they began their journey home, so he opened the umbrella he'd borrowed from the hotel, and she tucked her hand in the crook of his elbow, and he was more content, in those minutes, than he'd felt in years, if not decades.

They'd just turned onto Little Newport Street when a car came round the corner at some speed and sent a great wave of water sheeting toward them. Jamie reacted instinctively, moving in front of Edie so her coat and pretty frock wouldn't be splashed. She was close to him, so close, and for an endless moment he simply looked down at her, mesmerized by the expression in her lovely eyes.

She was happy, too. She didn't mind that he was touching her arms. Holding her so near to him.

She rose up on tiptoes and brushed her mouth against his, and he nearly expired from the shock and delight of it. Once he'd regained some control of his senses, he returned her kiss, and after he'd drawn away he traced the curve of her cheek with his fingertips, memorizing her beautiful face. And then he took her arm in his once again, and together they walked home to the Blue Lion.

Chapter 19

EDIE

Thursday, May 14, 1953

Tea would help.

That thought alone had propelled her from her office to the kitchen, had kept her voice calm as she asked Cook for a tea tray and said no, she could certainly carry the tray back to her office, and yes, it was quite all right and please let's not bother Ruth, and no, she simply had a bit of a headache after a long day at her desk.

She had made it safely away from the kitchen and across the dining room, the tea tray growing heavier with every step, and was halfway across the front hall when Jamie came through the front door. Though she tried very hard to return his smile, her face refused to cooperate, and her eyes welled up with tears that were impossible to wipe away because her hands were busy with the tray and its rattling contents.

She hadn't cried in front of anyone else since the day of her parents' funeral, so why now? Why should the sight of his kind and wonderfully familiar face make the last of her courage ebb away?

He crossed the hall in a heartbeat and took the tray from her shaking hands. "Good evening, Miss Howard. If I might carry this through to your office?"

She nodded and held the door open for him, and once inside he set the tray on the table next to the armchair where she never had time to sit. Then he took her arm and gently propelled her across the room and into the chair.

"How do you take your tea?" he asked.

"Black. Thank you."

"Can you bear to have it with some sugar? I think that might help."

She nodded. He added two heaping spoonfuls, stirred it well, and made certain she had a firm grasp of the cup and saucer before he relinquished them. Only then did he draw out the footstool and sit on it.

"Drink your tea," he told her.

She took one hesitant sip, and another, and another, and presently she began to feel a little less shaky. She set the cup and saucer on her lap and reminded herself to breathe.

"Tell me," he said.

"I don't know where to begin. What to think. I was having a nice day, too, until the telegram arrived. I think it must have been just past five o'clock. It was from California. From Mrs. Daley. She and her husband live in Santa Monica and they are coming for Coronation Week. I expected the telegram to be a special request. Could I make reservations for them at a certain restaurant, or would I arrange for a car to collect them at the airport. They fly all the way here, if you can believe it."

"What did the telegram say?" he prompted.

"I have it here. In my jacket pocket." She extracted the now-crumpled form and handed it to him. She already knew it word by word.

TODAY RECD CANCELLATION LETTER OF OUR STAY AT BLUE LION. NO NOTICE OR EXPLANATION GIVEN. OUR HOLIDAY RUINED. DEMAND EXPLANATION. MRS. FRANK DALEY

"You canceled her reservation?"

"No, of course not. I did send a letter to confirm everything, but that was last August. I put through a trunk call to California so I might speak to her and find out what had happened. It took ages for the operators to line everything up, and when Mrs. Daley did answer I could hardly hear her. I told her there had been a terrible mistake and we certainly had not canceled her reservation, and in fact were looking forward to welcoming her. But she said she'd received the letter directly from me, *signed* by me, and it was on the hotel's letterhead. She said she'd already arranged to stay elsewhere and that it was awful of me to do such a thing, and then she hung up."

"Oh, Edie."

"I went to Mr. Brooks and asked if perhaps he might have canceled the reservations, but he knew nothing about it. I actually had to explain more than once before he grasped what I meant. I even asked Mr. Swan when he got here, and he was just as surprised, too."

"Is it usual for either of them to handle reservations?"

"Only over the telephone, and even then I always confirm them. It's the only way to make sure we don't double-book the rooms. After that I couldn't think of what to do. I sat at my desk for a while, and tried to make sense of it all, and then it occurred to me to check the other reservations for that week."

"Very sensible of you," he said.

"The call to California was more than sixteen pounds—*sixteen* pounds, Jamie—so I thought I had better start with some of the reservations from England. I decided to ring up Colonel Arbuthnot, because he and his wife have always been so kind to me, and they've been guests here for years and years. He was very understanding, but he was also terribly confused, because he, too, had received a letter from me, on the hotel's letterhead, saying that regrettably I had to cancel his reservation."

"He didn't think to ring you back?"

"Well, he doesn't much like the telephone, and he admitted that he hadn't been keen on coming to London for the coronation—it was Mrs. Arbuthnot who had insisted. I told him that we would certainly hold the room for him if he still wanted it. He asked if there had been a mistake, and I said there had been, and I was very sorry, and he said he understood and he would speak with Mrs. Arbuthnot and let me know if they still wished to come up from Cornwall."

"How many of the guests with reservations for Coronation Week have you spoken to today?" he now asked. He was so calm. So reasonable. Perhaps he would be able to help her make sense of it all.

"Ten," she answered. "They all got the letter. My signature, or what appeared to be my signature, was on each one."

"Ten out of how many reservations?"

"Thirteen. The other three live abroad. One in Canada, another in New York, and the last in Malta."

Jamie nodded, but rather than ask her another question he took her cup and saucer and filled it with fresh tea and another small mountain of sugar. "First this. Drink it all, if you can."

"I do apologize for all of this," she said between sips. "Taking up your time, and keeping you from your plans for the evening."

"Edie? *Edie*. Will you look at me?"

She set the cup and saucer on the table, and then, gathering up the last of her courage, she met his gaze. In his eyes she saw nothing but understanding, patience, and sympathy.

"Are we not friends?" he asked.

"Yes."

"Good. Now, when a friend receives alarming or upsetting news, how do you normally respond? With indifference? With, I don't know, irritation that they've interrupted you in some important task?"

"No, not at all. It's only . . ."

He waited, and after a moment he took her hands in his.

"I've never had many friends," she admitted. "Not in the way you mean. Not even when I was younger. My life was always here, at the hotel. I had some friends at school, but none of them were very close. I expect they found it odd that I lived in a hotel, you see, and I wasn't able to go out and do things with them very often, since I was expected to help at the reception desk, and then my parents were killed . . ."

"Edie. That was almost thirteen years ago."

"I know. I know. But ever since, you see, my life has been nothing but this hotel. I've had no time for any of the things I used to dream about doing when I was a girl. Going out dancing, or to the pictures, or for a cup of tea and a bun at Lyons—"

"I'm not sure I'd call a visit to Lyons *fun*," he said, his voice gently teasing.

"No? I think it would be lovely."

"You may not be able to get out and do those things, but that doesn't mean you're without friends. I've seen you with the other people who work here, Edie. I know they like you. Everyone likes you. Aren't they your friends?"

"How can they be? I pay their wages, I decide their hours of work, and from time to time I even have to give one of them the sack. There will always be that gap between us, and it's not because I think I'm better than them. That's not it. It's only . . . how can they be at their ease when I'm sitting there?"

He nodded, his expression solemn and a little sad. "I see. I think I understand."

"Thank you."

"Do you feel a little better? Did the tea help?"

"It did. Only I'm not sure what to do next." It was mortifying to admit such a thing, but she was almost certain that Jamie would understand.

"I can't say that I do, either, but I'm sure we're capable of figuring it out together. Let's start with the canceled reservations. Were you able to reconfirm any of the bookings?"

"Not all, but some. Five sets of guests will be coming as agreed, three are thinking about it and will let me know, and two, including Mrs. Daley from California, have booked elsewhere."

"So that leaves two rooms at the least to rebook, and possibly an additional three if the remaining foreign guests don't come. Will it be very difficult to find guests to take those rooms?"

"I shouldn't think so. I do have a list of people who had expressed interest in a room if one should become available. A sort of waiting list. I could ring them up."

"Excellent plan."

"I only wish I knew *why*. Why would anyone do such a thing?"

"When I was a law student, one of my lecturers was fond of asking 'cui bono'—who profits? Is there anyone who might profit from the hotel having difficulties?"

All of these difficulties and troubles? They're only going to get worse. It had been months since her evenings out with David Bamford, but she still remembered his prediction. Or perhaps it had been a promise?

"Late last year I was approached by a man named David Bamford. A businessman. He wanted to buy the hotel. I went out to dinner with him several times, mainly because he was so persistent, but I was very clear that I would not sell the hotel. I'm afraid I was rather rude to him the last time we spoke."

"Has he contacted you since?" Jamie asked sternly.

"Not directly. I asked him to leave me alone, and he has, but he did send me flowers. Horrid lilies that made the hotel smell like a funeral parlor. But he hasn't tried to speak to me."

"Based on your conversations with him, do you think Bamford is the sort of man who might do such a thing?"

"No. He was self-absorbed and not especially attentive, but he didn't seem at all malicious. Besides, I can't see how he'd have been able to obtain details of our reservations, or the stationery we use."

"If he'd had help from someone here, I expect it would have been straightforward. But you raise a fair point: Apart from you, who has access to the reservations ledger?"

"If I'm away from my office, both Mr. Swan and Mr. Brooks are allowed to take reservations. They mark them down in pencil and leave me a note. I then confirm the reservation with a letter to the guests. I always do that part myself."

"Might it be one of them?" Jamie asked.

On that point she felt quite certain. "No. Arthur's been here for years, and I trust him entirely."

"And Brooks?"

"I haven't known him quite so long, but he, too, is indispensable."

"How did he come to work here?"

"It was rather a lucky thing," she said, remembering her first conversation with Ivor almost five years ago. "He was staying at the hotel for a few days, I think because his flat was being painted. The previous assistant manager, Mr. Jephson, had just retired, and I hadn't had much success in finding his replacement. Mr. Brooks heard about the vacancy and asked if he might apply. His CV was very impressive. He'd worked in hotels before the war, and I think at a chemist's, too, and his service record from the war was exemplary. I checked his references and they were good, so I took him on for a trial period. By the end of the first week I couldn't remember how I'd managed without him."

Jamie nodded, taking it all in. "All right. For now, I think you should lock up the reservations ledger whenever you're away from your desk. Does anyone else have a key to the safe?"

"No," she confirmed. There had only ever been one key, and it lived on the key ring that she carried everywhere. At night it sat on her bedside table, and during the day it was in her jacket pocket.

"Good. Don't tell anyone else about this, not just yet. If Brooks or Swan asks you about the reservations, just say you're looking into it."

"I will."

"I also think you ought to talk to the police. Not long ago, Mick introduced me to a detective at Scotland Yard. Gordon Bayliss. He seemed a decent fellow. Perhaps you could speak with him."

"I know Inspector Bayliss," she said readily.

"Oh, of course. From when he stayed here during the war."

"Yes, but he also came by to see me about three weeks ago. Someone had sent threats to the newspapers. Something about the coronation and how the people were owed and debts had to be paid, and they were written out on pieces of stationery from the hotel. I would have told you, but he said that I wasn't to mention it to anyone. So I didn't. I am sorry."

"You don't owe me an apology. It was none of my business, to begin with, and it was sensible of Bayliss to tell you to keep it quiet."

"Do you think the cancellations could be related to the threats? They were both sent on hotel letterhead."

"I think it's possible, and all the more reason for us to speak with Inspector Bayliss. How about I ring him up now? If we're lucky, I'll catch him before he goes home for the day, and we can meet him somewhere nearby—the Queen Bess, for instance."

She realized he was waiting for her to agree. "Yes," she said, and she went to her desk and moved the telephone so it was closer to the visitor's chair. He sat down, dialed, and as he waited for the call to go through he smiled at her reassuringly.

"Good evening. Could you put me through to Detective Inspector Gordon Bayliss? You can tell him it's James Geddes from the Blue Lion. Oh, good. Yes, I'll wait . . . Inspector Bayliss? James Geddes here. We met at the—oh, good. You remember. Are you free to meet me and Edie Howard in a bit? Is half an hour all right? Not at the hotel— the Queen Bess is better. Fifteen minutes, then. Good. See you there." He replaced the receiver on the telephone's cradle and let out a satisfied huff.

"He didn't ask you why?" she asked.

"No need. We'll be seeing him soon enough."

"He said fifteen minutes . . ."

"Aye. Does that give you enough time to get ready?"

"I don't know," she said worriedly. "I've never been to a public house."

"Not even the Queen Bess?"

"Not once. Should I change?"

"No need. You're perfect as you are."

THE INTERIOR OF the Queen Bess was warm and convivial and not so very different from the dining room at the Blue Lion, Edie thought, excepting of course the mahogany bar with its bottles and taps and rows of glasses, and the choking fug of smoke that stung at her eyes, and the sheer number of occupants, mostly men, many of them familiar faces from the neighborhood. She recognized the landlord, who brought his wife for afternoon tea at the Blue Lion on her birthday every year, and he greeted her and Jamie alike with a cheerful halloo.

Jamie steered them to a table in a dim corner, took her order, and returned with one small glass of tonic water and two enormous glasses of beer. "One's for Bayliss," he explained. "A single pint is about my limit."

Inspector Bayliss arrived a few minutes later, coming straight to their table after Jamie hailed him and pointed at the waiting pint of beer on the table. "Already ordered for you."

"Kind of you, Mr. Geddes. Good evening, Miss Howard."

"Good evening, Inspector Bayliss."

He sat, drank deeply from his beer, discreetly stifled a belch, and fixed a very policeman-like stare on Edie, then Jamie. "So. Tell me."

"Go on, Edie," Jamie said. "He'll want to hear it from you."

"I discovered this afternoon that all—well, I think it's likely all—of the reservations for Coronation Week have been canceled by someone pretending to be me. Everyone with reservations was sent a letter on Blue Lion stationery, with what appeared to be my signature, saying that their reservation had been canceled."

"Have you seen any of the letters?" the inspector asked calmly.

"No, but Colonel Arbuthnot has promised to send his back to me. He's in Cornwall, so it should arrive tomorrow afternoon."

"Edie told me you've been looking into threats that were also written on the hotel's stationery," Jamie said.

"Yes. As it happens, I've had some news on that front. The threats appear to have been written on the blotter that came from Professor Thurloe's room. They were written in hard pencil, and it left multiple impressions on the blotter beneath."

Impossible. It was impossible. "I can't believe it. I won't believe it," Edie insisted. "What motivation would he have to do such a thing?"

"I didn't say the professor was the author of the threats," Inspector Bayliss clarified, "only that the blotter on which they were written was found in his room. While it's possible he wrote the letters, it's also possible that someone else placed the blotter there to cast suspicion upon him."

"Oh, good. Because I'm certain he would never hurt anyone."

"I'm glad to hear it, but that doesn't rule him out. We all

know he can be a bit obsessive when he decides something is bothering him. What is it this month—noise from the Hoover? His tea not hot enough?"

"I wouldn't call him obsessive," Edie protested. "He's very particular, that's all."

"Even if it is Thurloe, it might have nothing to do with you. He might simply be upset about the expense and bother of the coronation itself. In that, I can tell you, he's far from alone. Only look at the letters to the editor in any given newspaper and you'll have your answer."

"So what do we do now?" Jamie asked. "Presumably you can't do anything about Thurloe without further proof."

"No, we can't. For the moment, I'm inclined to think both the letters and the cancellations are the work of a disaffected crank. Possibly someone with a connection to you, Miss Howard, or the hotel, but as I've no solid proof, nor any evidence beyond a single blotter that might have been placed in the professor's room at any time, I can't do more than ask you both to keep a close eye on things."

"You truly don't think there's any danger?" Edie asked anxiously. "I couldn't bear it if one of my employees or guests were frightened or hurt."

"I don't. In my experience, ninety-nine times out of a hundred these sorts of threats are the work of some lonely soul who gets an idea fixed in his head that he's been wronged, and this is how he responds. Not directly, because confronting the person who's upset him takes a certain amount of courage, and practically never with an act of violence. This is the type that works off his rage by writing excitable letters to the editor and popping them in the post."

Inspector Bayliss drained the last of his beer and pushed back his chair. "I'd better go. I didn't remember to ring my wife before I left, and she'll be none too pleased if I'm late getting home." He leaned across the table to shake their hands. "Setting aside every bit of what I said just now, if something doesn't seem right, I want you to call me straightaway." He reached into his breast pocket, retrieved two business cards, and handed them to Edie and Jamie. "My home address and telephone number are written on the back. Just in case you need to reach me after hours."

"I'm sure it won't come to that," Edie protested.

"I agree. But I still want you to promise that you'll call if you notice anything amiss. Better to be wrong and feel a bit foolish than to be right, say nothing, and suffer the consequences."

They sat in silence after the inspector left, and though Jamie had finished his drink ages ago he didn't seem to mind that she was taking her time with her tonic water. Despite the unsettling circumstances, she had enjoyed her visit to the Queen Bess. Perhaps they might venture down the street on another evening, and sit together as other couples were doing, and share a quiet hour of conversation together.

"Shall we go?" he asked, noting her empty glass.

"Yes. Yes, of course. I was woolgathering there."

Jamie smiled. "One of my favorite occupations." He came round to help her with her chair, and as they left he called out a friendly good night to Pete the landlord, and then they were standing alone, under the acid glare of the streetlight, in the abrupt chill of a too-cool evening.

She was wishing they'd gone somewhere farther away so

she might stretch out her walk with Jamie, and simultaneously was considering what pleasant thing she might say, if only to end their evening on a happier note, when two men stepped out of the shadows. Even from a distance of three yards or so she could see, and smell, that they were both thoroughly pickled by drink.

"Oi there! You with the white girl!" one of them called out. Jamie's arm tightened around Edie's, but his step didn't falter.

"Talkin' to you, I am!" the lout went on, his anger seemingly heightened by Jamie's indifference. "Ya gonna lishen ta me *now*?" Moving surprisingly fast for someone so inebriated, the man rushed forward to stand no more than a yard in front of them.

His friend followed rather more slowly, swaying on his feet as he came to stand at the other's side. "We's talkin' to you!"

"I can see that you are," Jamie said calmly.

The first man now turned his head to stare at Edie, his gaze moving greasily over her face and figure. "Whassa gal like you doin' wi' *that*?"

She wanted to answer, but fear had taken hold of her tongue, freezing it solid. Before she could will it to thaw, Jamie took her hand and gently guided her to stand behind him.

"I'll thank you not to speak to the lady. If you have anything to say, say it to me. But watch your language."

"Fair 'nuff," the first man acknowledged. "How 'bout this? Get off home, why doncha?"

"Like 'e said!" the second man chimed in. "We fought a war so's to keep out the likes o' you!"

Still Jamie didn't flinch, nor did he retreat by as much as an inch when the men advanced ever closer, their hate and the drink they'd guzzled lending them false notions of courage.

"Which one?" Jamie asked them.

"Whaddya mean?" answered the first man, his expression almost comically befuddled.

"Which war? Because I fought in the last one. And when I was commissioned as an officer in His Majesty's Forces, I do not recall being told that the war, or my service in it, had anything to do with keeping a man like me, born and educated in Britain, out of my own country. So which war, precisely, are you talking about?"

The men now exchanged frantic glances. "We din' mean anythin' by it," the second one mumbled uneasily.

"You did. You always do." Still Jamie stood his ground, unbending, unwavering, and only when Edie started to feel lightheaded did she realize she'd forgotten to breathe. She took in a great gasp of air, and this alone broke his concentrated focus on the loutish pair.

"If you will excuse us, the lady and I will be on our way. Miss Howard?"

Edie took his arm once more, and together they sidestepped the men and continued down the street as if nothing had happened and no one stood behind them. "Jamie, I—"

"Best to wait until we're safely home," he said, his voice perfectly steady.

Her heart racing almost out of her chest, Edie steeled herself against a rush of movement from behind, but the men, now reduced to mere grumbles of disdain, didn't attempt to follow.

In no time at all she and Jamie crossed the threshold of the hotel; without a further word, she took his hand and led him through the door by the front desk and into her office. To Mr. Swan she offered only a smile and a nod.

"I need a glass of sherry," she said, going straight to the drinks cabinet. "But would you prefer a whisky? I've the best part of a bottle of Laphroaig here."

"I'd love some, but only enough to cover the bottom of the glass. Otherwise I'll be up half the night with bad dreams."

She poured their drinks, and they sat in the chairs that flanked the little hearth, and rather than sip at her sherry like a lady she downed it in one bracing gulp.

"I'm sorry about all of that," Jamie now said. "I ought to have said nothing. Normally I wouldn't have answered back, but when he spoke to you I couldn't stop myself."

"You don't owe me an apology. Not at all. It's those, those . . ." She tried to think of a term that would convey her disgust, but her vocabulary was singularly lacking in the sorts of rude words that would match her feelings. "Those cretins were at fault. Not you. And I wish I had said something. Told them they ought to be ashamed of themselves."

"It wouldn't have helped. It never does."

"I expect not." She watched as he swallowed the single mouthful of whisky she'd given him. "Will you be able to sleep?"

He shrugged, his expression inscrutable. "I'll be all right. And you?"

"I'm used to my worries keeping me awake." She tried, and failed, to offer up a believable smile.

"Try not to dwell on it. Same goes for the mystery of the cancellations. Only do promise me one thing—if you notice anything amiss, let me know straightaway. Just as you promised Inspector Bayliss."

"But you're so busy with the commission," she protested. "I couldn't possibly."

His own smile was rueful, and not a little bit sad. "Not so busy that I can't help a friend in need. Promise you'll let me know. If only so I can sleep tonight."

"Very well. Would you like some tea? I can go into the kitchen and—"

"No, thank you. I'll go on up to bed now. Thank you for standing by me tonight. It meant the world to me."

She watched him slip out of the office, the door shutting softly in his wake. Her sudden realization that she was in love with him, quite hopelessly so, was a truth she could not ruminate over now. Not until the coronation was over and done, the hotel was back on an even keel, and she had time to think, and dream, and wonder. Only then, and possibly only after Jamie had moved on, could she let herself dream of what her future might hold.

Chapter 20

STELLA

Sunday, May 17, 1953

The rehearsal for the coronation procession, complete in nearly every particular save the presence of the queen herself, had begun at dawn, but Stella hadn't minded having to get up early to photograph it from several different vantage points, among them the forecourt of the Blue Lion, the wide expanse of the Mall, and the steps of the Victoria Memorial. The first set of pictures, taken while standing on a stepladder propped against the front wall of the hotel, would be of little use to *PW* but might, she hoped, be helpful to Mr. Geddes as a reference for his grand painting of the queen as she passed by the ugly building on the far side of Northumberland Avenue.

Not that he had asked; he was not the sort of man to demand favors of others. Edie, instead, had gently inquired if Stella might have a few minutes to take some photographs as a surprise for Mr. Geddes, and with Mick's help—he had procured the ladder and then steadied it while she perched at its top—it had been easily done. The subsequent rushing about to capture views of the procession had been rather more troublesome, but at last the job was done and she was home again and might spend the rest of the day at her leisure.

Stella trudged up the stairs, her attention focused on her room and the promise of a long bath and brief nap, and she was halfway along the corridor before she realized she wasn't alone. Mr. Brooks was standing in the shadows outside Professor Thurloe's room at the far end of the hallway, and his unexpected presence was enough to startle her from her reverie.

"Mr. Brooks?" she asked, taking a hesitant step toward him. "What are you doing here? The professor is never in his room at this time of day."

He looked around, startled, and turned to face her. As he did, a book fell from under his arm to the floor. "Miss Donati? I'm sorry—I didn't see you there."

"Were you looking for him? Professor Thurloe?"

"Oh, no. No, it isn't that."

Only then did she notice the key in his hand. "Were you going into his room just now?"

He turned to look behind him, then craned his neck to look over her head. Satisfied, he beckoned her closer. "To be perfectly honest, I was just leaving his room. I, ah . . . it's a rather delicate matter."

"I cannot imagine what reason you might have for entering his room without permission."

"Normally I would never dream of doing such a thing, but I was worried. The reservations ledger went missing earlier, and I looked and looked and wasn't able to find it anywhere." Bending, he retrieved the book at his feet and held it up so she might see the handwritten label on its front cover: *Blue Lion Hotel - Record of Reservations - 1953*. "I had a hunch that he might have taken it, and I wanted to make sure before I said anything to Miss Howard."

"Why should he wish to have such a thing? What interest could he have in it?"

Again he surveyed the empty hallway. "She doesn't wish the staff to know, but I don't think it matters if I tell you. We found out on Thursday that someone pretending to be Miss Howard canceled all the bookings for Coronation Week. If we hadn't discovered the ruse, the hotel would have been all but empty for the coronation."

"That is awful, but I do not see what it has to do with the professor. Surely he would not have done such a thing."

"It's not so much that I suspect him—the police do. They've been keeping an eye on him for weeks, if not months. I think they're worried that his annoyance over the coronation has become obsessive, and that he's upset with Miss Howard for the disruption to his routine that her preparations have caused."

Stella was tired, and more than a little irritated by Mr. Brooks and his furtive manner. "So now that you have the ledger, you are going to return it to Miss Howard? And tell her what you know?"

"I would rather keep it quiet for the moment. You can't possibly understand, but Miss Howard has so many worries. It wouldn't do her any good to tell her, not now."

"I disagree. I insist that you tell her."

"You don't know her as I do," he all but spat out. "You've

only lived here for a few months, but I've been at her side for years and years. No one cares about the Blue Lion as I do. *No one*."

Stella took a step back, suddenly wary, for they were alone in the corridor and he was on the verge of losing his temper entirely. "I do beg your pardon," she said. "I certainly did not intend any offense. All the same, I do insist that we tell her. Either I can go on my own, or you may come with me."

"Fine," he said, and then, as if only just remembering that he had been addressing a guest of the hotel, "I do beg your pardon for my outburst just now. I was, ah, overcome by an excess of concern for the Blue Lion. And Miss Howard, too."

"I understand. Shall we go down now?"

The little sign and bell were on the reception desk when they returned to the hall. "You stay here. I'll fetch Miss Howard," Brooks instructed.

Edie hurried into the hall a few minutes later, with Brooks not far behind. "Stella—is anything the matter? Mr. Brooks says that you and he have something upsetting to tell me, but I can't imagine what it could be."

"I think we ought to go into your office," Stella answered. "Only so we may discuss this problem in private."

"Very well," Edie agreed, her expression so bleak and weary that Stella's heart pinched in sympathy.

"After you told me about the cancellations I was terribly concerned," Mr. Brooks began as soon as they had filed into the office and shut the door. "Before I went on my morning break, I decided to take a close look at the reservations ledger. I know you've been keeping it locked up at night, and I was sure I'd seen it on your desk this morning, but when I went to look I couldn't find it anywhere. Not on your desk, nor anywhere else in your office."

Edie glanced at the ledger, which Mr. Brooks had only just placed on her desk. "You seem to have found it."

"Yes. And here I must confess something. In my agitation, I did something rather, ah, imprudent."

"Go on."

"I had an idea, you see, of who might have taken it. And while I ought to have come straight to you, in the heat of the moment I took it upon myself to find the ledger as quickly as possible."

Edie looked to Stella, her expression questioning. "Why is Stella here, then?" she asked.

"As a witness. She was there, in the hall, when I discovered the ledger in Professor Thurloe's room."

"The professor's room?" Edie repeated, a frown etched deep into her brow.

"Yes. He'd left it on the table by the window. He hadn't even troubled to hide it."

Edie breathed in deeply, as if she were attempting to steady herself, and exhaled with deliberate calm. "You know how strongly I object to hotel staff entering the guests' rooms without their express permission. I have given other employees the sack for doing just that."

"I understand, of course I do, and in ordinary circumstances I would never dream of doing such a thing. But I was very nearly certain that I would find it in the professor's room."

Edie nodded, and for a moment it seemed she might say something more. Instead she drew the ledger toward her and set her hands on top, as if hoping to divine its secrets through touch alone.

"You need to tell Inspector Bayliss," Mr. Brooks demanded. "Is that not why he was here the other week? Something is going on, and I feel certain the professor is at the heart of it all."

"I can't say anything, Ivor. Not yet."

"Might someone else have placed the ledger in his room?" Stella asked softly, and was taken aback by the furious expression that Mr. Brooks directed at her. She blinked, and he looked away, and his voice, when he next spoke, was measured and calm. Perhaps she had been mistaken.

"It seems unlikely," Mr. Brooks replied. "Although . . . I suppose it could have been one of the maids. Do you think one of them might have done it?"

Miss Howard shook her head decisively. "Of course not. And I'm not ready to go back to Inspector Bayliss. Not yet. I think Stella is right. Anyone might have placed it in his room. We have no real evidence of his wrongdoing, and suspicions alone are not enough to convince me to displace a long-term resident of the hotel."

"But he stole the reservations ledger—"

"No. It was found in his room, which is a different thing altogether. Don't forget that my reputation, and that of the hotel, is also at risk here. If we accuse him falsely, he would be well within his rights to accuse us of slander. I need to consider the best course of action, and in the meantime I insist you say nothing to the other staff."

"I understand. And I do apologize, again, for putting you in this position. I probably ought to have spoken to you first."

"What's done is done. And now, if you wouldn't mind returning to the desk, I have something to say to Stella."

"Of course, Miss Howard."

He withdrew, very much on his dignity, and shut the door behind him, and Stella suppressed the childish urge to make a face at his retreating back. She hadn't believed one bit of his story, but she could not, unfortunately, think of a reasonable explanation as to why he might have been trying to put the ledger in the professor's room. Perhaps he had hoped to come across as some sort of hero to Edie, whom he evidently worshipped? Or perhaps he held a grudge against the professor, and hoped to discredit him in some way.

Her musings were interrupted by Edie's gentle voice. "Stella? Are you all right?"

"Yes. I was only woolgathering. Is that the correct idiom?"

"It is, and such a useful one. I asked you to stay so I might wish you a happy birthday, although I must apologize for being a day late. I had every intention of seeking you out, but the hours seemed to slip through my fingers yesterday, and it was midnight before I had a moment to think straight. Were you able to celebrate in proper fashion?"

"Not yet, but soon. My editor and his wife are taking me to dinner tonight."

"How lovely. I do hope you enjoy yourself. And please don't worry about the professor. Mr. Brooks is very helpful, and I believe he is trying to help, but he's rather muddied the waters with his accusations."

"Do you believe Professor Thurloe took the ledger?"

"No. He can be difficult, but that's true of hundreds of

guests who have stayed here over the years. Yourself very much excluded." Edie closed her eyes and sighed, but a moment later her usual expression of determined good cheer was back in place. "I do hope you have a wonderful time tonight."

WHEN KAZ CAME to collect her for dinner that evening, Stella's spirits were fizzing with excitement. It was the first birthday she had spent away from Mezzo Ciel since the end of the war, and though she was a little homesick still, and missed her family there dreadfully, what little unhappiness she felt had been more than tempered by her delight at the prospect of a dinner out with her new friends.

"Hello, Stella, and happy birthday," he greeted her.

"You already said so at work yesterday."

"Yes, but that was as Kaz your editor. Tonight it's as Kaz your friend. Miriam's outside in the taxi—shall we go?"

"Yes, please," she said, and followed him outside to the car. He opened the door for her, ever the gentleman, and, after encouraging Stella to sit next to his wife, squeezed himself into the fold-down seat across from them. The taxi sped into traffic, and Stella sat back and tried to get her bearings. She hadn't thought to ask where they were going, but perhaps it was meant to be a surprise.

"May I ask what it is like, the restaurant? Or is it a secret?"

"Not at all. It is an Italian restaurant, one that Walter and I visit often, and the food is always very good. Simple but good. The people that own it are Italian, although they have lived in England for many years."

"We're almost there," Kaz observed. "Just turning onto Charterhouse. Had no idea traffic would be so light this evening. Makes a nice change."

"Walter detests cars. Both driving them and riding in them," his wife explained. "We have one at home, but I decided we would have a far more pleasant evening if we left it in the garage tonight."

"I doubt there'd have been anywhere to park the wretched thing," he added. "Seems like there are more cars than people in London these days."

The taxi turned off the main road onto a quieter street, turned again, and pulled to a stop about halfway down the road. "'Ere we are!" the driver called back.

The exterior of the restaurant was painted white, with red trim around the windows and half barrels filled with red geraniums on either side of its door. In lieu of a sign, *The Victory Café* had been painted in grandly scrolling letters on its large front window. Inside it was noisy and crowded and the air smelled intensely of delicious things, wonderful things, and Stella knew, without even seeing the menu or sampling a single bite of food, that their dinner would be splendid.

Kaz now turned to Miriam and Stella. "I see Jimmy at the back—he's waving us on. He'll have set aside a table for us there."

Stella followed in his and Miriam's wake, and as there wasn't much space between the tables she had to watch her feet, and even then she wasn't able to see past Kaz's broad back.

"Here you all are!" the man named Jimmy called out. "Is

this the guest of honor?" he asked, reaching over to shake her hand. "*Buona sera, signorina.* Happy birthday, and welcome to the Victory Café."

He beckoned her forward, and Kaz stepped aside, and only then did Stella realize that three people were already sitting at the table: Edie, James Geddes, and Win. They had come to celebrate her birthday. They were there for her.

She blinked hard, determined to banish her tears, happy though they were, and sat down, and accepted their best wishes and compliments. Jimmy himself served their meal, and every part of it was exactly right: linguini in a tomato and anchovy sauce for *primo*, pollo alla Fiorentina for *secondo*, and for *dolci* there was an almond cake studded with dried cherries. With this they drank red wine, although Stella was sensible and limited herself to two small glasses, and when the cake was served Jimmy also brought out an enormous moka pot full of espresso for the table, and when all of the plates had been cleared away and the last of the wine and coffee had been drunk, Miriam put a small box wrapped in silver paper in front of Stella.

"For you," she said, and Stella opened it carefully, not wishing to spoil the lovely paper. Inside was a change purse made of blue felted wool, and it was decorated with a beautifully embroidered wreath of twining white flowers. "Star jasmine," Miriam explained. "Because of your name."

"You *made* this?"

"I did, and it gave me great pleasure to do so."

"Thank you. I will treasure it."

Win had a present for her, too: a catalogue raisonné of Rembrandt's portrait etchings. She stammered out her thanks, for she would never have expected a gift from him, nor indeed from anyone else that evening. The meal they had shared was more than enough.

Then Edie brought out yet another parcel. "There's a bit of a story behind this, so I hope you'll bear with me," she began. "In 1932, as you know, your parents came to London to work on the first of their guides to the city, and not only did they include a splendid description of the Blue Lion in the guide, but they also became fast friends with my father. They remained in touch with him, and two years later my parents went to Italy on holiday. While there, they visited your family.

"Now, my father always took a camera with him on his trips, but he nearly always took pictures of things rather than people. I have albums full of photographs of old buildings and ruins and bridges and so forth, but with hardly a human face to be seen. So I was cautious when I went looking for the pictures he'd taken on his visit to Italy. But I was also hopeful."

Edie picked up the gift and, reaching across the table, put it in Stella's hands. "Go on," she said encouragingly.

Somehow Stella managed to undo the ribbon bow and fold back the layers of tissue to reveal a framed photograph of her family. Mamma and Papa and her own four-year-old self.

They were younger than she remembered them, but happier, too. She was in their arms, held tight, safe and happy. Her legs were dimpled and bare, her hair was caught up in wispy pigtails, and she was laughing.

"It has been so long," she managed to say. "I have not seen them in so many years."

"You don't have any other pictures of them? Oh, my goodness. Had I known, I would have looked for this—I would have *found* it—months ago," Edie fretted.

"Please do not apologize. You have already given me so much." And then she could say no more.

"Come here, *ma belle*," Miriam urged. Pulled into the comforting circle of her friend's arms, Stella allowed herself to cry for a few minutes before she sat up straight, accepted a handkerchief, dried her eyes, and blew her nose as discreetly as she could. The others, rather to her relief, were also wiping their eyes. Even Win, stoic Win, had resorted to pinching the bridge of his nose.

"I worried that I was forgetting them," she explained. "Each night I would close my eyes and try to remember, but it has been so long, and I could not be sure that my memories were true. But now, with this picture, I can see them again. I can remember them clearly. And my heart is full."

Chapter 21

JAMIE

Monday, May 25, 1953

At the start of his second meeting at Cartwrights' Hall, Jamie was invited to take a seat at Master Owens's desk. The Gainsborough still hung on the wall behind, and from where he sat Jamie was able to make out the brushstrokes on the canvas. He hoped the painting wouldn't end up hanging in some out-of-the-way corridor when his own, comparatively humble work of art displaced it in some months' time.

"How have you been getting on?" Owens asked. "As it's been some months since we heard from you, I thought it might be wise to check in, as it were."

"It's no trouble at all," Jamie said easily.

Last week Archibald Owens had sent a note to Hugh Campion, asking if Jamie might have time to advise the Cartwrights as to his progress on the commission. Hugh had forwarded it to Jamie, who had seen no reason to refuse, promptly agreeing to meet Owens at ten o'clock on Monday morning. He had then spent nearly all the weekend going through his preparatory drawings and paintings before selecting the best examples to show Master Owens and any other guild members who came to the meeting.

To Jamie's relief, Owens had been joined by only one of his colleagues—Mr. Mallory of the nicotine-stained moustache. One naysayer he could manage easily; a boardroom full would have been a different story altogether.

"I've brought along some examples of the preparatory work I've done so far," Jamie now explained. Opening his portfolio, he selected several charcoal drawings he'd made of the building itself. "Here are some sketches of the hall, done at intervals of about a month apart. As the trees came into leaf, they began to obscure parts of the facade, but they also softened it and added a sort of brightness that was missing in the early spring."

Mallory was already shaking his head. "I scarcely recognize the hall in these drawings. Surely we're not paying two hundred guineas for something so ill-formed. These look like the sort of thing one might find hanging at the Tate."

"I'd be honored to have my work on display there," Jamie replied, the threads of his composure beginning to fray. "That aside, these are preparatory works. I made them so I might become acquainted with the way light and shade fall across the facade on sunny days as well as rainy ones."

"I have no doubt it will be fair on Coronation Day," Mallory said with pompous certainty. Jamie was tempted to advise him that rain would make for a more interesting painting, but he suspected his explanation would fall on stony ground.

Owens was frowning over the drawings now, and Jamie braced himself for yet another objection. "Is anything the matter?" he asked.

"Not at all. It's only that I've been trying to work out where you were standing when you made these. You were too close to have been on the pavement outside, and you also seem to have been rather higher up. Did you copy this from a photograph?"

"I have been making use of photographs, not only of the hall but also the coach and the queen herself. But these drawings were made in my room at the Blue Lion across the way. I've been living there for several months. I can see all of the hall, without any foreshortening, and on Coronation Day I won't have to fight the crowds to see the procession itself."

"Goodness me. I had no idea there was a hotel across the street," Owens said.

"It's small but well run, and the location is ideal for my purposes." He'd have been happy to sing its praises, but neither man was likely to care or remember.

"If we might return to the subject at hand?" Mallory asked. "You're saying these sketches are all you've done? It's been four months."

Jamie had been patient and polite, and he had tried to retain his composure in the face of Mallory's disdain, but he was no longer inclined to sit back while the man attempted to browbeat him. "There is no clause in my contract that requires me to undertake any amount of preparatory work. *At all*. That I have done so at my own discretion, taking time away from my other work, is something I am not, in any way, obliged to do. Nor, may I add, was I required to come here today. Do I make myself understood?"

Mallory's only response was an odd sort of sputtering noise that reminded Jamie of a rusty kettle coming to the boil. It would have been funny if it hadn't been so tiresomely familiar.

"Once again, Mr. Geddes, I must beg you to take no notice of my colleague," Owens intervened. "I, for one, am delighted by what you've shown us."

"Thank you. I do, in fact, have a number of other preparatory pieces to show you. Here, for example, is a view, done in oils, of the hall on a rainy day." Jamie waited for Mallory to make a comment about the inevitability of fair weather, but the man was still grizzling over Jamie's rebuttal. "See how the colors are heightened by the absence of sunshine? If it does rain on Coronation Day, this is the sort of palette I expect I'll employ."

The painting, hardly larger than a sheet of typing paper, had turned out well. Jamie was especially pleased with his depiction of the hall's architectural details, which he'd subtly heightened where they contributed to the whole, and let recede into the background where they proved distracting or diminishing. The result was a version of Cartwrights' Hall that was indefinably more interesting and striking on canvas than it was in reality, but still recognizably itself.

Next to it he set another work in oils, this time on a large gessoed board. "Here are some details of the gold state coach's structure and decoration. The abundance of gilding, along with the sheer volume of ornate carving, makes it a surprisingly difficult thing to paint. I was worried it might overtake the entire composition, but I've now spent enough time on these elements to feel rather more confident."

Last of all he set out three pencil drawings of the queen herself, each embellished with delicate washes of watercolor. A fourth portrait, slightly larger than the rest, was done in oils.

"You've captured her likeness very well," Owens enthused. "I *am* pleased."

"But she isn't wearing her crown," Mallory said, having rediscovered his voice.

"Well, no. She'll be passing by the hall on the way to her coronation. *Before* her crowning, not after."

"And?"

"The queen will only wear the crown for the part of the procession that takes place after the coronation ceremony. On her way to the Abbey she'll be wearing the George the Fourth state diadem. The same one she's wearing in my portraits here. The same diadem she's wearing on every coin that's been struck for the past year or more."

But Mallory had decided to dig in his heels. "I think we really ought to have the crown. Otherwise how will people know it was painted on the day of her coronation?"

"I should think it would be obvious. She'll be wearing her robes of state and riding in a coach that's hauled out of mothballs only once or twice a century, the pavement will be thronged with well-wishers, and there will be enough Union Jacks to stretch from here to Gibraltar. What part of that doesn't signal a coronation to you?"

"Gentlemen, gentlemen," Owens implored, his air of genial bonhomie rather diminished. "Do as you see best, Mr. Geddes. It's unfortunate she won't pass by on the way back from the Abbey, but I suppose we're fortunate to be on the route in the first place. Certainly none of the other guilds can boast of *that*. With that said, when do you think it will be ready?"

"It will likely take me several weeks to complete the painting, and the oils will need another month or so of drying time after that. Shall we say six weeks at the earliest, but more likely by the end of July?"

"That seems entirely fair to me," Owens said, and Jamie shook not only his hand but also Mallory's when the man offered it. Altogether the meeting had gone better than he'd feared, if rather worse than he'd hoped, but it was done and over and he could now put their expectations out of his mind.

He made his escape without lingering. As he approached the Blue Lion, he called out a cheery hello to Mick, who was still wearing his heavy doorman's overcoat despite the warm weather. The reception desk was empty—he always checked, just in case Edie happened to be minding it while Brooks or Swan was absent—and he was about to charge up the stairs when someone called out his name.

"Jamie, lad—there you are!"

He whirled around and nearly dropped his portfolio when he recognized the speaker. It was his father, comfortably ensconced in one of the chairs flanking the hearth, and the sight of him was at once so unexpected and welcome that Jamie could only stand and stare.

"I was beginning to worry you might have left for the day, but Miss Howard felt certain you'd be back before long."

"I was just across the street," Jamie answered. And then, suddenly anxious, "Is it Mum? Has something happened?" His father hardly ever traveled, hated sleeping anywhere but his own bed, but if there were bad news to share he wouldn't have left it to the telephone or a letter.

But his father was shaking his head, his smile as broad as ever. "Your mother is quite well, never you fear. Won't you come here and give your old dad a hug?"

Jamie closed the distance between them in two quick strides. He was a few inches taller than his father, but the comfort of being held by him was as strong and sustaining as it had ever been.

"Everything is all right, then?" he asked, reluctantly stepping back.

"Yes. I ought to have written, but it was a last-minute sort of thing."

"How last-minute?"

"Ah. Well. Your mother and I were talking at supper last night, and she happened to express some concern. Were you eating and sleeping properly, were you happy with your work. That sort of thing. And I said, really without thinking, that I could always pop down on the train to see for myself, and would you know—she held me to it. I was out the door with hardly more than the clothes on my back before I could blink. Took the sleeper train and arrived not a half hour ago."

"I'm that glad to see you, Dad, but I truly am fine. More than fine."

"I'm happy to hear it. I was thinking of staying the day and taking the train back tonight, but I don't want to interrupt your work."

"I'm not so busy I can't spend a day with my own father. Let's go up to my room so I can drop off my portfolio. You can leave your case there, too."

Had he known his father would be visiting, Jamie would have made at least a smallish effort to clean up his room. Fortunately, he'd made his bed that morning, and his clothes were hung up properly, but his desk was a disaster, its surface entirely covered by a mess of drawings and bundles of pencils and page after page of scribbled notes.

Naturally his father made a beeline for the desk. "Your handwriting wasn't always so atrocious."

Jamie shrugged. "Mum can read it easily enough."

"Hmm," his father said, for his attention had been captured by a pencil sketch Jamie had made of Edie just the other day. It was a slight thing, hardly more than a few curving lines, but it had turned out well enough. "There she is again. A lovely girl."

Jamie knew better than to lie to his father, whose barrister's nose could sniff out a falsehood with the ease of a bloodhound. "She is," he agreed. "Everything about her is lovely."

Apparently content with Jamie's answer, his father went to the window. "Which one of those dull heaps of stone is the guild hall you're going to immortalize?"

"The one with the rounds of leaded glass in the front doors. They're meant to look like wagon wheels. There's also an inscription in Latin on the lintel above the door. Can you make it out from here?"

"*Discere faciendo*, I believe. 'Learn by doing.' Very worthy of them. I thought you said they're marking their five-hundredth anniversary, but this building can't be much older than I am."

"The original was lost in the Blitz. Built in the fifteenth century, survived the Great Fire and God knows what else over the centuries, but one direct hit from the Luftwaffe flattened it."

He would not think of the beautiful buildings he'd seen destroyed. He would not think of the broken bodies he'd come across in their ruins, nor of the hours he had spent in his own tomb as he had waited for the mercy of oblivion. He would not think of such things today.

"Rather a comedown for the guild, I expect. From high medieval magnificence to what might pass as the head-quarters for an insurance company."

"They don't seem to mind, and the street will be decorated for the coronation. Banners hanging from light poles and boxes of flowers in every window. Besides, the real focus of the painting will be the queen in her golden coach."

"Monstrous thing," his father observed, his nose wrinkling in disdain. "I've always thought it looks like a Bernini sculpture that someone put on wheels and dipped in a vat of gold paint. Better than an open-topped motorcar, though, as if she were the wife of an American politician."

"I doubt anyone would mistake the queen for Mamie Eisenhower, Dad. Besides, I'm looking forward to the challenge. Do you want to see how I've been experimenting?" He went to his portfolio, which he'd tossed on his bed, and pulled out the gessoed board he'd shown to Owens and Mallory not a half hour earlier. "Getting the color right is the really hard part. The gilding needs to look old. Soft, somehow, and not nearly as shiny or reflective as one might think." Now he pointed to a group of rococo swirls and curlicues of gold. "Here—this part. This is right. This is what I have to capture."

"I'm proud of you," his father said. "Ever so proud."

"You might not be when you see how this turns out," Jamie joked, but his father frowned and fixed him with the exact look he always employed when one of his children said something inane or imprudent. When he was a child, that look had turned Jamie's knees to jelly. It still did.

"Alexander James Geddes. I should be very grateful if you would allow me to express my admiration for your achievements without rushing to invalidate my sentiments. It is ill-mannered and selfish, and I expect better of you."

"Yes, sir. I do beg your pardon."

"In that case, let me say it again. I am very proud of you. We both are, your mother and I. We are immensely proud of the man you've become."

"Thank you," Jamie acknowledged, and then, risking another scolding, "I know this isn't what you wanted."

"Perhaps not at first. I had my hopes you'd join me in my work, just as your brother has done. But I got over it. Or, rather, your mother made sure I got over it. All that matters, now, is your happiness. And it's clear to me that you're happier here, in this place, than you've been for many years."

THEY SPENT A pleasant day together, one of the nicest Jamie could remember. They went out for breakfast, and then walked along the Embankment, across the river at Westminster, and back through the festival grounds. They lunched together at Rules, and then his father read while Jamie worked on his preparatory drawings. And then it was time for another walk, this time only as far as his father's favorite bookshop in London, Marks & Co on Charing Cross Road. They spent a wonderful hour browsing happily through its stacks of books, and Jamie could scarcely believe his luck when he unearthed a copy of *Anatomy of the Horse*.

"I've been going to the library at the V&A to look at their edition, but having my own is much better," he told his father. "I'll go and pay up now."

He was greeted by Mr. Doel, whom he hadn't seen for years but who had recognized Jamie and his father alike when they'd first come in. "Good afternoon, young Mr. Geddes. I see you found the 1899 edition of the Stubbs. Not so fine as the original, but rather better than the one from 1938. Will you be taking it with you today?"

"Yes, please. How much is it?" Jamie asked, praying it would not be beyond his means. If he had to put it back his father would surely insist on buying it for him. Bad enough that he'd already insisted on treating Jamie to breakfast and lunch.

"Twelve and six. Is that agreeable?"

It was indeed, for Jamie had been bracing for a price of twice or three times the amount. "Oh, yes. Quite."

He then waited while his father's purchases were paid for and wrapped up, and then they set off for home and afternoon tea and, he hoped, a few minutes of Edie's company.

She was in the dining room already, crouching between the Crane sisters as they expounded on some urgent matter, but she saw him enter and her smile was undoubtedly for him. He tilted his head, his question unvoiced but unmistakable, and she nodded right away.

It was a few more minutes before she excused herself and came across the room to Jamie's usual table.

"Good afternoon. How have you been enjoying your day in London, Mr. Geddes?" This she directed at Jamie's father.

"It has been splendid. Would you care to join us?"

"I should love that, although I may not be able to stay for long. Has Ginny been by to take your order?"

"She has, and my son tells me I'm in for a rare treat. The best afternoon tea in all of London, he says, and I'm inclined to believe him."

"You're both very kind," she said, her cheeks pinkening. "Oh—here comes the tea. Thank you, Ginny."

Edie stayed with them for half an hour, and though their conversation was engaging and pleasant, it never once strayed from the conventional. They spoke of the weather, the railways, the influx of tourists for the coronation, the weather once more, and finally the continued difficulties of rationing, and all the while Jamie was unable to look away from her. He was aware of taking part in the talk around the table, of drinking his tea and eating his sandwiches and cake, but all the while his thoughts turned and returned to one subject only: Edie, and the abrupt and clarifying realization that he loved her.

He loved her, but he could not be certain of her feelings for him, not yet. He watched her closely, searching for some spark of insight into her hidden, inner self, but her veneer of polite reserve remained intact, and if she detected any part of his true feelings she gave no sign of it.

It was pointless for him to expect anything else, especially given the presence of his father, but it did not stop him from hoping for more. By the time she made her apologies and returned to her office, he was feeling as giddy, uncertain, and self-doubting as a schoolboy.

His father's train left at seven o'clock, which left them just enough time for a round at the Queen Bess. It was pleasant to be greeted with real warmth by Pete the landlord and a few of the regulars, who now recognized him as a boarder at the Blue Lion and a friend to both Edie and Mick. He found a table in a quiet corner, fetched his father a half and himself a pint of bitter, and settled in for one more stretch of time with the man he admired most in the world.

They resembled one another in certain respects, for Jamie had inherited both his father's height and the leanness of his build, along with his high-bridged nose that would, he knew, become increasingly beaklike as he aged. But the similarities, at least in appearance, ended there, for his father's hair was a sandy brown gone quite white at the temples, his eyes an arresting shade of sky blue, and his skin was so fair and freckled it invariably burned in the summer sun.

Hardly anyone noticed their similarities. Most focused, instead, on their differences. On Jamie's brown skin, dark eyes, and black hair. They saw someone who appeared exotic at best and alien at worst. They saw someone who could not possibly be Colin Geddes's son.

"You're here until June?" his father asked, pulling Jamie away from his unhappy ruminations.

"I think so. Maybe a little longer. It depends on how long it takes me to finish the painting. But I've done a lot of preparatory work, so that should help."

"And after that?" His father's voice was gentle, but Jamie wasn't fooled.

"I don't know. I truly don't."

"You haven't considered the possibility of staying on?"

"Dad. How can I?"

"I should think Miss Howard would be reason enough."

"She is, but there's a very real chance she will have to close the hotel. The place was barely solvent when she inherited it. Since then she's worked miracles to keep it open, but she's exhausted and with no solution ahead I think she may decide to sell up."

"Doubtless the property is worth a considerable amount," his father said mildly.

"It likely is. I don't think she cares." And there was another problem—if Edie did sell the hotel, she would become a woman of means. A woman who could do far better for herself than a near-penniless artist.

"At tea she seemed hopeful enough. What with the wealthy Americans coming to stay."

"That will help," Jamie agreed, "but only for so long."

Rather than reply straightaway, his father sipped at his beer; and Jamie, who knew better than to prod him along, did the same.

"You care for her," his father said at last.

"I do." She had become as essential to him as air and water and sunshine, and when he thought of home he now thought of Edie and the Blue Lion.

"Does she share your feelings?"

"I hope so, but I can't be certain. Not yet. Not with her so busy with the hotel, and my hands full with the commission. I've barely had time to say hello to her for days now—today was the first time we've exchanged more than a few words in nearly a week. I hope it will be easier once the coronation is over."

"Based on my observations of the two of you at tea earlier, I feel quite confident in saying she does care for you. The question, of course, is to what degree. Is she willing to take on all that comes with it?"

Jamie did not need his father to specify what, precisely, Edie would have to endure if she chose to link her future to his. Disdain, insolence, incredulity, rejection—and that from people she knew well. From strangers, he knew from bitter experience, she would receive even more galling treatment. The encounter with the pair of louts outside the Queen Bess had upset her badly, but there would always be another bigot waiting, another back turned away in disgust, another volley of abuse to endure.

"I'm not sure. How did you know?" Jamie now asked. "With Mum, I mean. You've never spoken of having doubts, or of worrying what others would think, or how it might affect your future."

"I was all of twenty-one when I fell in love with her. Of course I didn't have doubts. She was the most beautiful girl I'd ever seen, and quite honestly I was astonished that she felt the same way." His father smiled in fond reminiscence. "Remember that her parents were very grand people— there was a maharajah not so many generations back on your grandmother's side. In every respect that mattered, she was marrying down. Others may not have known it, but I certainly did."

"What about the things people said? The way they treated her then? Now? Doesn't it make you angry?" Jamie gulped at his beer, hoping to stem the tide of rage that now rose in his chest, but it was no use. "If you only knew how many times people have told me it's a shame I take after Mum. They might as well shove a knife between my ribs."

"You think they don't say the same things to me? About you and your mother both?"

"How do you answer?"

"I say that my son is exactly as he ought to be, and his mother is the most wonderful woman I have ever known, and perhaps they might wish to retract their words while they are still able to speak with some degree of lucidity. That usually does the trick."

In that moment, Jamie could not have loved his father more. "Good for you. Normally I just stare them down."

"I won't deny that it's maddening," his father went on. "Especially since none of those people are worth so much as a single hair on your mother's head. Naturally I try my best to protect her, and our friends provide a sort of insulation, and there's Fraser and Fiona and their families, too. And of course there's you."

"Me?" Jamie asked.

"Where do I even begin? You left Oxford with a double first. You served your country for nearly the entire war, doing the most terrifying work imaginable, and you were decorated for it. You had the wisdom to listen to your gut when it told you that the law was no home for you. You gained a place at England's most prestigious art school and excelled there. Your work has been exhibited at the Royal Academy, and you've been awarded an important commission to paint the queen on the day of her coronation. You must know that you have made your mother and me, and indeed your entire family, very happy and terribly proud."

"Oh, Dad," Jamie mumbled, blinking hard. Not that his

father would give him a hard time if his son did cry. He'd only hand over a handkerchief, advise him to blow his nose while he was at it, and pat him on the shoulder when he was done.

"I'm a sentimental old duffer," his father said, and he set his hand on Jamie's shoulder, and its weight was so comforting and necessary that Jamie had to blink hard yet again. "And now I need to go home to your mother. You will come to see us soon?"

"I will. Later this summer, if I can."

"Good. I'm glad."

"Seeing you today has been a great help. Thank you, Dad. Thank you for everything. I think I can see a way forward now."

Chapter 22

EDIE

Wednesday, May 27, 1953

Edie considered herself a strong woman, capable of responding to even the most harrowing news with discretion, composure, and even a measure of acceptance. But Inspector Bayliss's newest revelation was almost too much to bear, coming, as it did, after a horrendously trying day.

It had taken hours to move the Hons across the hall, for the short distance involved had been of little consequence in the face of the sisters' obstinate refusal to allow even one of their possessions to be packed up in anticipation of the change in rooms. And that had been a problem, for every vertical surface of the two rooms they had occupied for more than thirty years was layered with fragile things. On the mantel above the hearth, the pair of étagères that flanked it, and the occasional tables at either end of the settee, the sisters proudly displayed an eye-watering array of painted and gilded porcelain, china figurines, photographs on metal stands, cut-glass oil lamps, sprays of wax flowers under glass domes, and one rather pathetic stuffed monkey, all of them sitting atop crocheted doilies, rounds of Bruges lace, and embroidered cloths. And that had only been the one room; their bedchamber had been just as bad.

It had taken Edie and all four housemaids nearly six hours to cart the sisters' things across the hall, help Mick to haul over the furniture, and then reassemble and rearrange every last one of the sisters' possessions to their satisfaction. All the while the elderly ladies had fussed and complained and exclaimed over Edie's unkindness, and only pots of tea and plate after plate of lemon biscuits had kept their tears at bay.

Edie would very much have liked to collapse upon her bed and spend the next twenty-four hours there, prostrate, never mind that she hadn't eaten a thing since breakfast and was close to expiring for want of a strong cup of tea. She was at her desk, wondering if she had time to nip over to the kitchen, when Ivor knocked at her door and informed her, in a knowing fashion that was oddly irritating, that Detective Inspector Bayliss had arrived and wished to speak with her.

The inspector wasted no time, once she had ushered him in and firmly shut the door, in acquainting her with yet more dispiriting news.

"There's been another round of letters to the papers. Once again, they're on Blue Lion stationery. No fingerprints. Postmarked Monday, so probably rules out anyone who checked in after that day. I'm sorry, I am, but I will have to search the hotel."

"May I see the letter?" Edie asked wearily.

"Of course. Similar enough to the previous round that it seems likely they were written by the same person." He pulled a sheet of paper from one of the envelopes he was carrying and handed it to her.

OUR ENEMIES HAVE PREVAILED AND THE BATTLE FOR ENGLAND SHALL SOON BE LOST. THEY SEEK TO PLACE A FALSE CROWN UPON ELIZABETH'S HEAD. HER PEOPLE ARE WRETCHED AND HER REALM IS UNDER SIEGE. A RECKONING AWAITS AND THEY SHALL PAY IN BLOOD FOR ALL THAT HAS BEEN STOLEN.

She read it, and reread it, and even then it seemed so strange as to be impossible. How could such a thing be happening? "You need to search the hotel today? Now? Whatever will I say to the guests?"

"You're under no obligation to tell them anything. In fact, I would prefer you say as little as possible," Inspector Bayliss instructed. "Simply say the police are inspecting the buildings along the parade route for purposes of public safety. As a way of ensuring, ah . . ."

"That no malcontent has set up shop?" she finished, not unaware of the irony.

"Exactly. If they object, refer them to me. I'll shake my head and mutter something about defense of the realm, and that should be enough."

"Do you think it's Professor Thurloe?" She dreaded even asking the question, but she had to know.

"It's possible, but I can't be certain. I am prepared to

confide that we've had him under surveillance for a few weeks now. Simple enough to arrange, since the man barely sets foot outside the hotel. And that's the thing—he hasn't left the premises since last week. Well before this last batch of letters was posted."

"He did tell me that he was finding the crowds of tourists rather disconcerting. Said he's planning to hide away like a badger in its sett until the whole thing is over and done with."

"I don't blame him. Still, I'll need to search all the rooms. His especially, but yours and James Geddes's as well. Can't be seen as playing favorites."

"I understand. May I come along? It might help to stave off any complaints."

"You may. Before we begin, we'll need to let people know we'll be searching their rooms. Would you mind telling your staff? We'll speak to the guests as we go along."

"Very well. Only . . . I don't wish to be untruthful in any way."

"You only need tell them it's a routine police matter. Something to be expected in light of the hotel's position along the procession route. It's the truth, after all, if not quite all of it."

"I suppose. But what about the professor? He's in the library now."

"I'll take care of it. Don't fret—I won't upset him."

The ordeal of telling her long-serving, hardworking, and loyal employees that the police would shortly be searching the hotel, their private rooms included, was an experience she hoped never to repeat. They were frightened, as was she, and more than a little wary of the reasons for such a search, but no one raised an objection or asked for further explanation.

"You have the right to be present as your room is searched," she told them, "but you certainly don't have to be there. I will remain with Inspector Bayliss and his officers the entire time, and I give you my word that the search will be conducted properly, and that your belongings will not be damaged."

Edie returned to the front hall to await the inspector. When he rejoined her, he seemed puzzled and even rather amused.

"I told the professor we'd be searching his room."

"And?"

"He said to go ahead, but on no account to disturb his papers."

"That was all?"

"I advised him that it was in his best interests to be present as I conducted the search, but he said he was occupied with his work and he trusted you to keep me on my toes."

"Oh, dear," Edie said. "You don't think I should try to persuade him?"

"No. I gave the man fair warning, and he understood me well enough. Better to just get on with things."

Up they went to the top floor, Edie and the inspector and two alarmingly youthful police constables, and within the first fifteen minutes she learned that supervising a police search was an exceedingly tedious business. The officers were careful to leave the occupants' belongings undisturbed, and the few documents they presented to Inspector Bayliss were promptly replaced in the same position they'd been found.

She was glad that she'd made her bed that morning, though she could have done without the sight of the downy-cheeked constables sifting through the dresser drawer that held her undergarments.

Jamie's room was spotlessly tidy, and though she'd half expected him to talk with Inspector Bayliss during the search, he instead stood calmly by, to all appearances a stranger to the man.

Only when Edie said hello, and explained the reason for the search—for the constables' benefit, she told herself—did his composure waver in the slightest. He nodded at Inspector Bayliss, and readily agreed to the search, but his gaze, when his eyes met hers, was troubled. He was worried, she realized, but not for himself. For her. He knew what this was costing her, and he both understood and cared.

"Done here, sir," one of the constables announced.

"Very well. Are you all right to continue on with the floor below, Miss Howard?"

"Yes, of course."

They came to Professor Thurloe's room, and she unlocked it and stood back so the police officers might enter, and then she could only stand at the door and watch, her hands damp with perspiration, her heart racing, as they conducted their search.

"I'm afraid he doesn't allow the maids to touch anything on the tables in here," she explained, more than a little mortified by the state of the room, which appeared to have been picked up and shaken roughly only moments before their arrival.

"I understand," Inspector Bayliss said, his smile brief

and businesslike. "If you don't mind waiting by the door, we'll get on with things."

So she stood back and tried not to eavesdrop on their hushed conversation, and when they began to gather up some of the papers and put them in envelopes she grew even more apprehensive, and by the time the inspector turned to her, his expression grave, she knew.

"What is it?" she asked anxiously. "Can you tell me?"

"We need to search the remaining rooms. When we're done, you and I will have a talk."

Numbed by dread, Edie followed them from room to room, and though normally she would have laughed at the sight of the young constables moving gingerly about the Hons' overcrowded rooms, she was unable to focus on anything besides the horrifying possibility that Professor Thurloe was, in fact, connected to the bizarre occurrences of the past few weeks.

At last it was done. While the constables stood guard in the front hall, presumably to prevent the professor from bolting if he chanced to look up from his books and realize what was taking place, Edie followed Inspector Bayliss back into her office.

"Do you mind if I sit at your desk?" he asked.

"Not at all. Let me switch on the light for you."

He had brought in several bulging envelopes, the first of which he now upended on the desk. Slipping on a pair of thin cotton gloves, he held up one of the items. It was a small, softcover notebook, with a black cardboard cover and dog-eared pages. "Do you recognize this?"

"It looks like one of the professor's notebooks. He uses

them to keep track of his ideas. Stray thoughts, avenues of research he wants to pursue. Those sorts of things."

"Hmm. Along with his concerns and complaints about a number of subjects. The hotel among them."

"It's only that he likes things done a certain way. I can't fault him for that."

"Such as?"

"Well, noise is a problem. He detests unexpected noises, and he can't bear the sound of the vacuum cleaner. We accommodate him as best we can."

"Would you say he's an angry man?" the inspector asked, still paging through the notebook.

"Not at all," she insisted. "Certainly he's never been rude or aggressive to me."

"Perhaps not, but would that be true of his dealings with others here at the hotel? The maids, for instance?"

"Not to my knowledge."

Inspector Bayliss nodded, still reading, and from time to time he huffed softly, as if he'd come across something unexpected.

"What is it?" she asked, unable to bear the uncertainty any longer.

"This is . . . disturbing stuff. I don't know how else to describe it. Here, for example. He's written: 'Blood shall run through the streets like water through the Thames.' And then there's this bit: 'Someone shall soon make an end of the queen's majesty, and all will be well.'"

"I always thought of him as harmless. An eccentric, to be sure, but not a revolutionary. But this . . ."

"I know. It's bad. Not least because some of these

passages remind me of the anonymous letters. Do you remember how, in the first letter, the writer talked of a false crown that was gilded with lies? Or something along those lines? Because here, under his entry from the middle of April—the sixteenth, to be precise—he's written, 'The Coronation is a tableau for the masses, wrought of base metal and gilded with false hope.'"

It was, unfortunately, all too familiar. "It was the budget that upset him," Edie confirmed. "It was the same week that the article about the hotel was printed in *Picture Weekly*. That's why I remember."

"What did he have to say?"

"He was incensed that the government had decreased the purchase tax on things like cosmetics and television and motorcars. He felt that luxuries ought be taxed at a higher rate and the money raised be used for postwar rebuilding."

"Incensed enough to predict, or rather promise, that blood would soon run through the streets of London?"

She collapsed into one of the visitor's chairs. "Who among us hasn't said or written things while in a temper? Things we would never dream of actually *doing*."

"Not many would have troubled to send anonymous letters to the papers that threatened the life of the queen."

Edie nodded, and then it hit her: She would have to tell the inspector about the reservations ledger. "There is something else. I didn't tell you because it wasn't anything I could prove, and I knew you were terribly busy already. For that matter, I'm still not convinced that he did it."

"Go on," Inspector Bayliss prompted.

"Last week, last Sunday, in fact, my assistant manager

told me that he'd noticed the reservations ledger was missing. He then admitted that he had gone directly to Professor Thurloe's room to look for it, and having let himself in, he then searched the room. The ledger was sitting on a table in the professor's room."

"You believed him?"

"I had no reason not to. Another one of my guests came across him in the hall just as he was leaving."

"God almighty," the inspector said, rubbing away at his temples. "As if I haven't enough on my plate right now."

"I am sorry."

"None of this is your fault. All the same, I am going to have to take the professor in. Question him properly."

"Because of the ledger?"

"No. We didn't find it there, and we've no way of knowing if anyone else placed it in his room. These notebooks are enough, and we've yet to look at his papers in the library. Better, I think, if we move him and the evidence over to the Yard."

"He's very sensitive—promise you won't be unkind to him?"

"I'm not going to stretch him on the rack, but I'm not going to treat him like a schoolboy who threw a ball through a window, either. He's under suspicion of some very serious offenses."

"It's only that he's lived here for so long," she explained. "He has no one else."

"You aren't the slightest bit upset with the man? Not at all?"

"If there were any certain evidence against him, perhaps. If he'd been seen posting the letters, for instance, or if you'd caught him in the act of sending the cancellation notices. But it's all so circumstantial."

"I don't disagree with you. But I also have to act on anything that seems like a credible threat. And the man lives a stone's throw from the parade route, the coronation is a week away, and I've enough here to keep him on remand for at least forty-eight hours, if not until after the queen is safely crowned."

"I understand," she said, and she did. The evidence may have been entirely circumstantial, but it was damning all the same.

"The thing is, Edie—do you mind if I use your Christian name?"

"Not in the least."

"We now have the letters on your hotel's stationery. We have the rash of cancellations that were made, again on hotel stationery, but this time using your forged signature. We have the reservations ledger that was found in Thurloe's room. And now we have a second round of letters to the editors of a half-dozen newspapers. I could argue that Thurloe is the link between all these things. I could, and that's how I'll explain it to my superiors. Never mind that I don't truly believe he is the actor behind all of this. But do you know what does link everything together? *You*."

"I would never—"

"I don't mean that you are personally responsible for any of this. Quite the opposite. I mean that you may be the target. Not the queen, not the government, but you. Now, I know I've asked you this before, but can you think of anyone who might wish you harm?"

"No one." She had to focus on his questions. Simply

focus, and listen, and answer him truthfully. There would be time to fall to pieces after he was gone.

"Have you had to sack anyone recently?"

"Not for ages. I'm careful about who I take on, and I pay people well. My employees stay with me for years."

"Someone with whom you do business, then. Perhaps a dispute over money?"

She shook her head, but even that small movement left her feeling dazed. "I don't think so. I've had to dig into my savings at times, but better that than to owe money to anyone."

"Can you think of anyone else? Anyone who's been difficult to deal with—anyone who has given you trouble in any way?"

"Earlier this year I met with a man who wished to buy the hotel. We had dinner together several times. But it's been ages since I last heard from him. David Bamford. I have his card somewhere."

"Good. I'll copy out his details in a minute. Has anyone else shown interest in the property?"

"No, not for some time. Do you . . . do you think someone wishes to hurt me?"

His answer was reassuringly prompt. "I don't think you're in physical danger, no, but I think they might wish to do harm to you by harming the hotel. As a business, I mean. If your losses exceed your profits you might be forced to sell up. I'll look into this Bamford fellow and let you know if I find anything concerning. In the meantime, I do have to take the professor with me."

She stood, ready to follow, but the inspector shook his head. "No. Best if you stay here."

"Promise you won't upset him?"

"I'll do my best. I am sorry about all of this, Edie, but the sooner we sort it all out, the sooner that life at the Blue Lion can return to normal."

Edie attempted to smile, but the result, she feared, was more akin to a pained grimace than anything else. She trailed after him as far as the door to her office, watching as he vanished from sight, listening intently for any signs of a commotion from the library. But all was silent. No shouting, no sounds of a scuffle, no cries for help.

"Edie," came a whisper from behind.

She whirled around, a scream at the ready, but suppressed it when she saw who stood behind her. "Ivor. You startled me."

"I beg your pardon. May I ask what is going on? Why is Inspector Bayliss here again?"

"It appears that someone at the hotel has been threatening to disrupt the coronation. Letters written on our stationery were sent to the newspapers."

His eyes grew round with surprise and horrified fascination. "One of our guests? Here at the Blue Lion?"

"He couldn't be certain. That's why he had the hotel searched." She ought to have taken Ivor aside earlier, but she'd been so focused on managing the reaction of her live-in employees, not to mention her actual guests, that she'd quite forgotten.

"Was it the professor?"

"They think so. The letter to the newspapers seemed to echo some things he's been writing in his notebooks. And of course there was the matter of the reservations ledger in his room."

Just then, the inspector emerged from the corridor, and at his side was Professor Thurloe, who was talking a mile a minute and appeared not in the least distressed. She forced herself to stay where she was, hovering at her office door, until they had vanished through the front door, but even then she felt profoundly uneasy, as if her own grandfather had been taken away.

"To threaten the queen," Ivor whispered, his breath tickling her nape, "and to be so careless as to do it on hotel stationery. If that isn't the act of a madman, I don't know what is."

"There's to be no talk of this. If anyone asks, you're to say the police officers were here as a matter of routine. No more."

"What if they ask about the professor being arrested?"

"He wasn't arrested, for a start. Inspector Bayliss simply wished to speak with him discreetly, and as you and I were the only witnesses to his departure I doubt it will be a problem. I'll let Cook and the maids know that he'll be away for a few days."

"And after that?" Ivor pressed. "Surely you won't let him return."

"That depends on what the inspector is able to learn. If the professor is innocent, there's no reason why he can't return."

"But—"

"I don't know," she snapped, her patience in tatters. "I don't have answers for any of this, and I don't wish to speculate just yet."

"I understand. May I fetch you a cup of tea? This must be terribly upsetting."

"Yes, please. Thank you for offering."

She retreated into her office, but the thought of sitting at her desk and continuing on as if nothing had happened, all the while waiting for the telephone to ring, or for Ivor to knock at the door to tell her the police were back again was intolerable. She needed . . . she needed what, exactly?

And then, suddenly, she knew.

Forgetting Ivor and his promise of tea, she ran up the stairs, one flight after another, until she was at Jamie's door. A few seconds to catch her breath, and then she knocked.

"Come in!"

She opened the door, suddenly apprehensive, and took a single, hesitant step inside. He was sitting at the window, a sheaf of brushes in his hand, but he set them down when he saw her.

"Edie?"

She could not think of what to say, not a word, so she shrugged, and blinked helplessly as her sight was dimmed by tears, and then he was there, before her, his arms open. Another step and he had her, one big hand cradled against her head, the other spread wide across her back.

"There, there," he soothed. "I've got you. Come, now. Come and sit and tell me what's the matter."

He steered her toward his upholstered chair, and once she was settled he pulled his desk chair over and arranged it so he was facing her. Then he took her hands in his, and he smiled such a tender smile, and he listened while she told him what had happened.

He listened, and he didn't interrupt, not once, and when she came to the end of her story he asked, "Do you want to talk about it some more? No? Then what do you say to keeping me company for a wee while?"

"I should like that," she said, and a little of her fear began to drain away. She was safe here, with Jamie, with the rain tapping softly against the window and skylight, his voice so reassuringly steady and sure.

"At tea yesterday I heard one of the maids say that Cook was in a lather about the menu for Coronation Week," he began. "Only I thought you'd said that you wouldn't be changing afternoon tea."

Remembering her conversations with Cook was almost enough to make Edie smile. "It's breakfast that has her fussing. All the 'foreign food' she's expected to make—and by 'foreign food,' she means American food."

"Surely not hot dogs and hamburgers?" he asked, feigning horror at the prospect.

"More along the lines of orange juice, breakfast cereal, and streaky bacon. You'd faint if I told you how much the orange juice is costing me."

"Is it only breakfast that's affected?"

"We did add a few items to afternoon tea. Some little jam-filled doughnuts, and also a sort of chocolate cake. A brownie, I think it's called." Then, warming to the subject, "What nearly put Cook in her grave was a request from the Americans who are staying in the Crane sisters' rooms. Mr. and Mrs. Harding, and Mr. and Mrs. Ivey. Very nice people from Georgia. They asked for sweet tea at breakfast."

"Can't they simply add sugar?"

"That's what I wondered. So I went to Mrs. Harding, and asked her, and she explained that they meant cold tea, served over ice, with sugar added to it. She even wrote out the recipe for me."

"What happened when you told Cook?" Jamie asked.

"She looked at Mrs. Harding's recipe and told me it was, and I quote, 'an abomination.'"

"I can't say I disagree. Did she agree to make it?"

"She did, after I reminded her, delicately of course, that we are charging Mrs. Harding and her party a king's ransom for their rooms. And then I promised her a fortnight's paid holiday in July."

"That seems more than fair."

Simply mentioning the summer, and holidays that she herself would never be able to take, was enough to flatten her mood once more. "I can't wait until all of this is over," she admitted.

"You aren't excited?"

"No. I haven't had time. In a day or two we'll be full up for the first time in years, but we've barely enough staff to keep on top of things. I haven't been able to sleep for worrying."

"Things will return to normal before long," he said, and though he meant to reassure her, it had the opposite effect. For normal meant hardly any guests, and it might also mean the departure of the man at her side. A man who had, in the space of only a few months, become her favorite person in the world.

"Edie? Stay with me a little longer. Set it all aside, if you can."

On any other day she might have been brave enough to ask him if he meant to stay. But she didn't think she could bear the disappointment of hearing him admit that he would soon leave the Blue Lion. Better, instead, to focus on the problems that had been laid on her doorstep that afternoon. "I'm sorry. It's only that I'm worried about what Inspector Bayliss said. That this might be aimed at me."

"I know, but you also told me that he thinks someone may be trying to put the hotel out of business. Not that anyone wishes to hurt you."

"I know. All the same, it's frightening."

"Of course it is, but Bayliss knows what he's doing. I'm confident he'll get to the bottom of it."

"What shall I do?" she asked.

"Remember what he told you when we met at the Queen Bess a few weeks ago? Keep your eyes and ears open. Trust your instincts. And if something seems wrong, come and find me. Whatever you do, don't keep it to yourself. Promise me?"

"I promise."

Chapter 23

STELLA

Saturday, May 30, 1953

She hadn't expected all of it to be so exciting. Guests had been arriving for days, most of them British, although there were also Americans and Canadians and Australians and even one family from Argentina. Now the hotel was full up, and its once-quiet corridors were calm only at night, and the dining room was packed full at breakfast and tea, and Stella was enjoying every part of it.

The guests themselves were fascinating. The Americans were friendly, tipped lavishly—Stella thought perhaps they weren't quite aware of the value of the coins they left for the waitresses and pressed into Mick's hand every time he hailed them a taxi—and ate their enormous breakfasts with real gusto. The Canadians were slightly more reserved, though still very nice, and keen that she not confuse them with the Americans. All had come to London with the express purpose of seeing the queen on Coronation Day.

That was the part that still confused her, since the ceremony was being broadcast on television around the world, and the wireless, too, and within a few days would be running at the cinema and chronicled meticulously in newspapers and magazines, *Picture Weekly* included. The difference between watching the coronation that way, in relative ease and comfort and without the expense and bother of travel, and instead standing shoulder to shoulder with strangers pressing close for hours on end, only to catch a glimpse of the queen in her coach, simply made no sense.

The young queen was an inescapable presence, of course, and had certainly become much more familiar to Stella since she'd come to England. Her face was on so many things, from banknotes and postage stamps and biscuit tins to china mugs and imitation silk scarves, and most places, the Blue Lion included, had a framed photograph of her on display. But recognizing her face was not at all the same as *knowing* her.

Perhaps that was why the guests had come to London. Perhaps they felt that by watching the queen pass by, and possibly even catching her eye for a fleeting second or two, they might have a true and honest connection with her. It would give them the chance to tell their children and grandchildren they had seen the queen in her golden coach on Coronation Day, and had waved at her, and she, improbably but indisputably, had smiled and waved back. It would be a good story to tell when they were old and memories of the day had grown faded and distant for most other people.

And now, quite to her surprise, Stella would be one

of those who could say, in years to come, that they had been present in Westminster Abbey when the queen was crowned.

Spaces for journalists in the Abbey had been allotted months ago, long before Stella's arrival in London, and while Ruby had been accorded a place in one of the banks of seating along the nave, Frank had been given one of the coveted photographers' spots in the triforium, which could only be reached by way of a tightly winding spiral staircase. The access point was so confined, in fact, that the television cameras and other apparatus for filming had been winched into place some months earlier.

No one had thought anything of it until Frank had arrived at the journalists' rehearsal on the morning of May 29 and found he was quite unable to make it up the stairs to the triforium, and as there was no possibility of having him winched into place on Coronation Day itself, Kaz had requested that another photographer be allowed to take Frank's place on the day.

That photographer was Stella, for no one else, it seemed, was keen on the job. "It'll be a squash inside, and hot as a blast furnace, and you'll need to arrive long before and stay put for hours. And I haven't been able to get a straight answer from the Earl Marshal's office on the question of lavatory facilities. Nor will you be allowed more than one small bag of equipment," Kaz had explained.

Stella had been unfazed, for she already had an idea of the sort of photos she wished to take, beyond the usual run of documentary images that Kaz would require.

"Do you remember the pictures I was experimenting with a few weeks ago? The ones in Trafalgar Square?" she asked Win, who'd barely raised an eyebrow when she'd run upstairs to tell him that she would be in the Abbey on the second of June.

"Of the flower seller and the pigeons? I do. What of them?"

It had been late in the day, not long before dusk, and Stella had been drawn to the crowds milling about in the great square, and had spent some time messing about with the shutter speeds on the Leica, reducing them to one-tenth, then one-fifth of a second. Nearly all the photographs she'd taken had been rubbish, but one had stood out from the rest.

An old lady, to all appearances *in situ* since the turn of the century, had been selling bread crumbs to the tourists, and the circle of pigeons around her, startled by some unseen disturbance, had spread their wings and erupted into the sky. The woman, likely used to the birds' murmurations, had scarcely moved; the pigeons, their wings flapping wildly, had become a swirl of gray and white in the long exposure that Stella had taken.

"This is what I want to capture at the coronation. I do not know the queen, but I believe she is a calm sort of person, even when all around her others are flapping their wings. Just like these pigeons."

"Yes. I see what you mean."

"Do you think it will work?"

"I do. Frank is a fine photographer, and I'm sorry for him that he won't be at the Abbey for the ceremony, but I hope—I believe—you will return with something extraordinary for me."

It was late by the time Stella returned home, having

talked for hours with Win, and even though she'd been absorbed in their discussion she had also struggled to suppress a series of increasingly romantic thoughts about the man. They worked together, to start with, and he had yet to indicate anything other than a strictly professional interest in her. To press for more, she knew, would risk ruining their working relationship, and likely put Stella's position at *PW* in jeopardy.

All the same, her heart was aglow when she walked through the Blue Lion's front door in search of Edie. Not only was she excited to share her news, but she also had a more practical question for her friend: What was Stella to wear to the coronation?

Mr. Swan waved her through to Edie's office, and once she had shared the news about the triforium and Frank's knees and Kaz's decision that Stella would go instead, she made her request for help. "There is a dress code, and with only a few days to go, I am not sure what to do."

"I'm sure we can find you something smart to wear. Oh, Stella—this is so exciting! Come with me. I've some things that might do."

"I do not believe it needs to be a floor-length frock," Stella said as they stood in front of Edie's open wardrobe and assessed its contents. "The invitation referred to 'afternoon dress,' though I am not certain what that means."

"It means that a nice frock will do. You won't need a coat, nor will you have room for one. And you won't want to be fussing with a long skirt while you're working. What do you think of this?" Edie held out a pretty wool gown, its tailoring softly feminine, its color a delectable shade of dark blue. "I've a hat that matches it nicely."

"The dress code says that hats are not allowed. Here—it is written on this card that came with my invitation."

"'A light veiling falling from the back of the head,'" Edie read out, her nose wrinkling in disapproval.

"Does that mean a veil like a bride would wear?" Stella asked.

"I should hope not! Let's have you try on the frock first, just to make sure it fits, and then we'll see about something for you to wear instead of a hat."

Edie's frock fit Stella well, and though it was a little loose at the waist, they agreed that it would not be noticed, and would likely make it more comfortable. Edie then pulled down a hatbox from the top of her wardrobe and extracted from it an airy crescent of woven black straw that was meant to perch upon the wearer's head like an Alice band. "I've a scarf of a very fine black voile somewhere . . . here it is. If we pin it to the crescent, it will cover just the back of your head and no more. There—what do you think?"

Stella inspected her makeshift headdress in a mirror that hung from the inside of the wardrobe door. "It is very nice. Thank you, Edie."

"I'm happy to help. What are you planning on doing with your hair?"

"I thought I would set it myself," Stella admitted. "I won't have time for anything more."

"Your hair always looks nice, so I'm sure you'll be fine. But do use plenty of lacquer. You'll only need to brush it out, pop on this hat that isn't a hat, and head off to the Abbey."

BEFORE GOING DOWNSTAIRS for tea, Stella dropped off the frock and the not-a-hat in her bedroom, along with her camera bag and other work things. She was gone no more than an hour, but when she returned she knew, instantly, that someone had been in her room. The door, which she had closed but not locked, had been left ajar, and there was a lingering scent in the air, too faint to identify but foreign all the same.

Nothing had been taken: Her handbag and the few coins within it were untouched. Her camera was similarly undisturbed. Her battered old copy of the *Guida Donati* to London had not been moved from its place on her nightstand.

Only when she switched on the overhead light did she see what had been done. The photograph of her parents had been removed from its frame, and then it had been torn to pieces. The fragments were so small she could not put them together. She had lost her parents' faces once more.

She was still kneeling by her bed when Mr. Geddes found her, for in her misery she'd failed to notice her door was wide open to the corridor beyond. "Miss Donati? Are you all right? I was coming up the stairs, and I heard you crying. Tell me what is wrong."

"My photograph. The only one I have of them, the one that Edie gave me for my birthday. It is gone," she wept. "It is destroyed."

"May I see?" he asked, and at her nod he came into the room, and when he saw for himself he sighed, and rubbed at his face, and sat next to her on the floor. "This is awful. It's just awful."

"I thought the Blue Lion was my home. I felt safe here. But now . . ."

"Has anyone been unkind?"

"No. Not here."

"No nasty talk as you pass by? The sort that fades away just as you approach?"

"I am not sure I understand," she said, although it was more the case that she did but couldn't bear the thought of talking of it just then.

"Really? You haven't overheard people grumbling about foreigners stealing good English jobs, how things were better in the old days, how half the time on the bus you can't make out heads or tails of what people are saying because they're jibber-jabbering away in some foreign tongue?"

"I have, yes," she admitted. "Though not often. I think because people cannot tell I am a foreigner until I speak to them, and they cannot see I am a Jew unless I show them the numbers on my arm. For you, I think, it is not so easy."

"It isn't. I've the hide of an elephant, but I'm not insensible to it. Nor, I'm sure, are you."

"I thought I was. I decided, after I was liberated, and the war was over, and I was safe in Mezzo Ciel with my friends, that I was beyond such hurts forever. What could anyone do to me that had not already been done in the camps? What more could be stolen from me? Yet it still hurts. *This* hurts," she said, touching the confetti that had once been her precious photograph. "I wish I knew how to armor myself against it all."

"No elephant hide?" he asked softly.

"Not for me, no. But perhaps it is for the best. If I put a wall around my heart, and say to myself that I will not let it hurt me, that it is better to forget, then I will lose all that is left of my mother and father. I must hold on to my memories, both the good and the bad. For their sake, and for mine." She fell silent, suddenly conscious of how passionately she'd been speaking to a man who was little more than a stranger. "I beg your pardon," she whispered. "I would never have told anyone. Only you asked."

"Don't apologize. Thank you for telling me. For trusting me. I cannot say I can truly understand what you endured during the war, but I . . ."

"Go on," she encouraged.

"Only that I know a little of what it's like to be seen as someone who doesn't belong, and not because of anything I've done or said, but only because of my ancestry. It's no good saying that my father's forebears stood alongside Robert the Bruce at Bannockburn, nor that my mother's ancestors were far more distinguished than any of the Geddes clan, with a family tree that stretches back for something like a thousand years. All that means nothing to people like them."

Moving slowly, his exhaustion evident, he rose to his feet. "It's late, and you need your sleep. Will you let me have the pieces of the photograph? I'd like to see if there's anything I can do."

Mr. Geddes took a folded handkerchief from his jacket pocket and, stooping, held it out so she might deposit the fragments upon the square of fabric. He tucked them away with the utmost care and returned the bundle to his pocket.

He paused at the threshold. "Lock your door tonight, and put the chair under the knob. Just in case. And remember that my room is directly above this one. If anyone disturbs you, shout out and I'll be here in a shot."

"Thank you, Mr. Geddes."

"Jamie will do, aye? Sleep well, and I'll check in on you tomorrow."

By the time she had undressed and got into bed, having secured her door as Mr. Geddes—Jamie—had asked, she felt better. Knowing he was nearby was a comfort, and it helped, too, that he had offered to mend the photograph. It seemed unlikely, for it had been torn into so many pieces, but the offer alone had been wonderfully kind.

She climbed into bed and drew the covers up beneath her chin, and the moment she closed her eyes she could see them. Mamma and Papa, exactly as they had been on a gorgeous July day so long ago, when life had been an endless summer afternoon filled with sunshine and laughter and the bluest of blue skies.

She slept well, and had dressed and was brushing her hair before she happened to notice the envelope pushed under her door. For an instant her heart seized in dread, but then she saw the name at the left-hand corner of the envelope. *A. J. Geddes.*

Inside was a drawing. It was the image from her photograph, only now it was better, for something of Jamie's genius as an artist had infused the whole. There was also a note.

Dear Stella,

Edie showed me the photograph when she first came across it. I was struck then by its composition, and of course the joyful expressions on your faces. I hope I have managed to capture a good likeness of your parents, but if I have been less than successful I will certainly rework the drawing to ensure it is as good a match as possible to the photograph that was stolen from you. In the meantime, remember that you have many friends here at the Blue Lion, myself included.

> *Yours faithfully,*
> *Jamie*

Chapter 24

JAMIE

Sunday, May 31, 1953

He hadn't slept at all the night before, for he'd been driven to restore some version of Stella's photograph to her. He'd finished the drawing just as the sun was rising, and after putting it in an envelope and slipping it under her door, had decided to press on with his day. A hot bath had helped, and then he'd set out on a long walk along the Embankment. In two days' time it would be a sea of smiling faces and waving flags, and he would be in his eyrie overlooking Northumberland Avenue awaiting the queen in her coach, and rather to his surprise he realized he was looking forward to it.

Back in his room, he made the mistake of stretching out on his bed. Only for a few minutes; only long enough to rest his eyes. Instead he was catapulted back to the cellar, to the weight of the tomb that surrounded and suffocated him. He was alone in the dark once more, and though he tried to break free, the endless night held him ever closer.

"Jamie."

The voice came from far away, but he could hear it clearly, and that gave him hope.

"Jamie? I'm here. Open your eyes. Come to me now."

A hand emerged from the darkness, slim and clean and wonderfully strong. He grasped hold of it, and suddenly he was on his feet again, blinking in the light of day, and Edie stood next to him. She had found him in the darkness. She had rescued him.

"There you are," she said. "Safe and sound."

"Where are we?"

She looked over her shoulder, her smile ever so wide. "Home," she said. "Can't you see? I've brought you home to the Blue Lion."

SOMEONE WAS KNOCKING at his door. Jamie sat up, heaved his braces back onto his shoulders, and rubbed the grit from his eyes.

"Yes?" he answered.

"Jamie? If you're busy, I'll come back later."

Edie. He was at the door in two long strides. He opened it, beckoning her forward, but she only stood and frowned at him. "I woke you. I'm sorry."

"I didn't mean to fall asleep, only I was up too late last night. And I'm that glad you're here. Can you stay on for a bit?"

"I can, but would you like to go for a walk? Before the rain sets in?"

"I would. Shall we visit the pelicans?"

"I'm not sure I can be away for as long as that. Will the Embankment gardens do instead?"

"They will."

They walked side by side along Northumberland Avenue to the river and the Embankment gardens, and the peace of being with her, of having time with her alone, was a far more effective balm to his spirits than any amount of sleep or introspection.

"Are you all right?" she asked.

"A bit tired, that's all."

"Would you like to hear about the television set that now takes up about a quarter of the lounge? It was delivered this afternoon by a very nice man from Empire Wireless and Television Services. The delivery part of things took about two minutes. The setting-up part of things took far, far longer."

"Temperamental?"

"The television certainly is. The deliveryman was perfectly pleasant. He spent something like half an hour tuning the thing, and all the while promised that it only needed to warm up and settle in, and just as I was about to lose hope it started barking at me. Well, not the television. It was Rin Tin Tin who was responsible for the barking. A few seconds later, the picture came on, and there he was. The dog, I mean."

"So it works?"

"It does. There's only the one program for now, so all I have to do is turn it on and let it warm up. But enough of my coronation preparations. How are yours coming along?"

"Good. I'm all set for Tuesday. My sketch pads are at

the ready and my materials are laid out like a surgeon's instruments. The only thing that remains is to capture the feel of things as they happen. I know I can paint Cartwrights' Hall and the gold coach with my eyes closed, so they aren't a concern. The queen, too. Even the horses. I've been studying a book on equine anatomy that I bought when my father was here."

"I'm so glad I was able to meet him," she said. "You're very alike, you know."

"Thank you. That's high praise indeed."

"Did the two of you have a pleasant day? I've been meaning to ask, only I feel we've hardly seen each other in days."

"I know you've been busy, Edie. And I'm glad you asked. Seeing him . . . well. It made me think."

She said nothing in reply, instead choosing to wind her arm through his, and it was all the encouragement he needed.

"It made me think about the life he has built for himself. He's a successful man by any measure, but he is also happy. He's truly content, and it has very little to do with how others regard him. If you were to ask, I'm sure he'd tell you the central joy of his life is his family. Not his work. Not any material thing he may have earned through that work. Only the people he loves."

Edie nodded, her expression solemn, and waited for him to continue.

"I've also been thinking about what happened a fortnight ago. The men outside the Queen Bess. I know it was upsetting, and I expect a wee bit frightening, and it makes me sick that you had to witness it. But things like that happen to me all the time. Most often it's straightforward rudeness, or someone shrinking away, but sometimes it's overt. And I can't stop it. Do you see? There's nothing I can do to prevent it."

"Oh, Jamie. I keep thinking about that night, you know, and how I ought to have said something. Told those louts what I thought of them."

"It wouldn't have helped."

"I know. But would it help, now, if I tell you that I will always be on your side? *Always*. Because you are the best and bravest man I have ever known, and you are worth a thousand of those horrid men, and I can't bear that anyone should be unkind to you."

He was still absorbing the truth and weight of her words when she gasped, clutching even tighter to his arm. "You must tell me—has anyone at the hotel ever treated you in such a way?"

"No," he said, unwilling to add to her worries. Brooks was rude and disdainful, but that didn't amount to outright bigotry. Compared to most places he'd lived, the Blue Lion was an oasis of goodwill. "Your hotel is a haven," he assured her. "I feel entirely at home there."

"I'm so glad," she said, her relief palpable.

They walked on, and he willed himself to say more. To lay bare his heart, and in so doing learn if her feelings matched his own. She had called him a brave man, but he felt weak-kneed at the prospect of the risk he was about to take. But what was courage, apart from a willingness to face one's fears head-on? He had been sitting on the truth of what he wanted since his conversation at the Queen Bess with his father, and that truth had grown and bloomed, and it was enough, now, to push aside the last of his fear.

"When I saw my father, we talked about the life he and my mother have made together. How they support each other, and together are able to keep the bigots at bay. And it made me realize . . ." Jamie paused, willing his voice to a steadier cadence, praying his next words would manage to convey the sincerity of his feelings. "It made me realize that these past months, living at the Blue Lion, I have been happy, and I believe that much of my happiness is because of you. Because of what you have come to mean to me."

"Oh, Jamie—"

"I don't expect you to answer me now," he hastened to add. "Not when you have so much else to think about and do and plan. But perhaps, once the coronation is over, we might talk of this again?"

She halted abruptly, letting go of his arm so she might turn to face him. She was so beautiful, her eyes shining, her smile so wide and true. His hope-stricken heart skipped a beat as he waited for her reply.

"What if I want to answer you now? Because I do. I care for you, too, and once the queen has been crowned and the nice Americans have gone home, and life is rather closer to normal, I hope we can talk about what comes next. To begin with, I very much hope you will stay at the Blue Lion. That's all I can think of just now. Only that I wish for you to stay."

"I'll stay," he promised.

"I'm glad. Now will you walk me home? It's almost teatime, and I've a hotel full of guests to ply with gingerbread and scones and, heaven help us all, enormous glasses of iced tea. Will you join me?"

"For tea, and for tomorrow, and as long as you'll have me. On that you have my word."

CORONATION DAY

Chapter 25

EDIE

When Edie opened her eyes at four o'clock in the morning, her first thoughts were of Jamie, the things he had said to her on Sunday afternoon, both wonderful and sad, and the knowledge that he cared for her. He cared for her, and he hoped for a future that included her, and all she had to do was get through the next few days.

Then she woke up a little more, and clarity descended like an anvil, and she remembered it all. The pile of invoices on her desk for things like orange juice and peanut butter and smoked salmon and champagne—she had no memory, none, of ordering two dozen bottles of champagne—and the truly shocking figure of seventy-five guineas for the purchase, delivery, and installation of a television set that she doubted anyone would care to use after the coronation was over.

The absence of any news from Inspector Bayliss about Professor Thurloe worried her, too, though she ought to have preferred no news at all. If evidence were found that linked the professor to the bizarre goings-on, she would feel awful about it, not least because she had missed the signs of his distress and failed to protect him from his worst impulses. If, however, the professor were cleared of any suspicion, she would be delighted for him—and exceedingly anxious for herself and the hotel, since the author of the threats would still be at large and, she could only assume, still bent on upending Coronation Day in some unspecified fashion.

Even the boiler had seen fit to unleash its own form of chaos. When Dolly had gone down to stoke it yesterday morning, there had been water all over the cellar floor. Edie, once roused, had aimed her electric torch at the bottom of the behemoth and there discovered a small but steady stream of water coming from beneath its main tank. Mr. Pinnock, duly summoned, had agreed to an emergency visit, though not before insisting upon and receiving a twenty-five-pound deposit. Having poked and prodded and hummed and hawed for a good half hour, he had informed Edie that the boiler had sprung a leak.

"Of that I am quite aware, Mr. Pinnock. There was a small pond in my cellar this morning. Could you possibly tell me *why*?"

"I'll know better once we dig it out. Likely a case of corrosion at the bottom. No concrete pad underneath, you see. That's a problem."

"Was it not your own grandfather who supervised the installation of this boiler?" Edie had asked, not bothering to hide her irritation.

"Times change, Miss Howard, and even the best-quality boiler will need to be replaced at some point."

"I cannot afford to replace it now, nor indeed in the immediate future, so perhaps we might talk instead of repairs. Can you fix it?"

"Not without draining it first and then digging down around the main tank."

"I cannot manage without hot water. Not until after the coronation. Is it not possible to put in a patch of some sort?"

He considered this, and he hummed and hawed some more, and then he agreed it might be possible. "Only I'll need to pull up the first row of hearthstones there. Just to get at the edge of that corroded bit. Might make a bit of a mess."

"Do what you must. Just so long as I have hot water for my guests."

The remainder of Monday had been a blur, and she'd not slowed down, or even paused for a cup of tea, until well past ten o'clock that night. The staff had organized a small party for themselves in their dining room, which she'd been happy to encourage in light of how hard they'd all worked, and she'd popped her head round the door to say good night and thank you to everyone.

Mick had been about to open several bottles of champagne, which someone had explained was the gift of a guest, only no one could remember which guest, exactly, as the card had gone missing. Another crate of the stuff had been delivered to the kitchen, with instructions that it be delivered to the guests in residence. Even now, Cook explained, Ivor was making the rounds from room to room.

"That's lovely, but I don't recall ordering champagne for the guests. It's far too dear for me to be quite so generous."

Cook had shrugged, and Mick had shrugged, and

Edie had decided that it was a problem best dealt with on Wednesday, after the coronation was over and done with and she and the others weren't so tired they were about to fall over sideways.

"Won't you stay?" Cook had asked Edie, and the others had chimed in, too, although she suspected they were only being nice and didn't truly wish her to remain.

"Thank you, but I still have a number of things to see to this evening. Have a lovely time—and don't forget that we all need to be up early."

She might easily have gone to bed at that point, but instead she'd returned to her office, set aside the tedious invoices, and had set about responding to requests for reservations. There had been an increase, although only a modest one, and she feared the profits would scarcely be enough to keep the wolf from the door. But that, too, was a problem for another day.

At one o'clock she'd gone up to her room, by which time the hotel had been quiet, its corridors empty, and she'd been quite alone as she'd had her bath and got ready for bed, taking care to first set out her clothes for the morning and double-check her alarm.

Now it was four o'clock and she was awake and so alert there was no chance she'd fall asleep again. So she switched off her alarm, got out of bed, and drew back the curtains. It was full dark still, and angry needles of rain were beating against the window.

She went to the sink and brushed her teeth, then took up her hairbrush and began to smooth the tangles from her hair. Catching a glimpse of her face in the mirror, she was taken aback by how exhausted she appeared. Her eyes were dull, and the skin around them felt tight and heavy. A hot compress, she decided; that would help, and it would also soothe her incipient headache. She turned on the hot water tap, letting it run, but it was still cold when she dipped her fingers into the stream of water a few minutes later.

"No," she whispered. *Not today.*

It had to have been the champagne. Dolly wasn't used to the stuff, and she had probably been a bit tipsy when she'd gone up to bed, and consequently had forgotten to stoke the boiler. That was all. As long as Edie dealt with it now, there would be hot water in time for morning baths.

She changed into her siren suit, only pausing to gather her hair back with an elastic band and a handful of Kirby grips. Then she hurried downstairs, not bothering to switch on the corridor lights, for the lamp by the back door was more than sufficient to see her to the top of the cellar steps.

She opened the cellar door and was about to switch on the light when, alarmingly, she heard a voice from below. There was no reason for anyone to be in the cellar at such an hour, no one apart from Dolly, who as far as Edie knew was fast asleep upstairs. And it had been a man's voice she had heard.

Edie would have called out to ask who it was, but something, some instinct, told her that it was better to be quiet. She stood at the door, considering what to do, and when the man began to speak again she gathered up her courage and stepped down into the darkness.

She was almost at the bottom of the steps when the voices become clear, just as Rin Tin Tin's barks had so abruptly emerged from the ruinously expensive television set only a few days before.

"But I'm not allowed to go into the tunnels. Miss Howard says it isn't safe. She'll be cross if we go against her wishes."

It was Professor Thurloe. Had he escaped? Had he returned to the hotel in search of revenge?

Another voice drifted out of the darkness. "I know, but I thought you would wish to see for yourself. We only need to go a little farther."

Ivor? Why were he and the professor in the tunnel together? It made no sense, for he knew it was unsafe, and it was the middle of the night, besides, and he ought to have been asleep at his own flat at such an hour.

"What is that?" the professor asked, his reedy voice rising in alarm. "What have you done? What on *earth*—"

Edie stood in the darkness, paralyzed, and tried to make sense of what she was hearing. Someone was thrashing around, and then something heavy was being dragged, she thought, and then, even more horrifyingly, there was only silence.

She had to escape. She had to get to Jamie. He would know what to do. He would help her.

She began to creep back up the stairs, her heart in her throat, her eyes still frantically searching the darkness. The door had swung shut behind her, blocking out the light from the corridor. She had only to reach it—a few steps more, only a few—and then she would be safe. She would lock it from the other side and run to Jamie.

She was almost there, she had to be, but then a rush of

air came out of the void, a smothering weight was pressed over her face, a wretchedly sweet and nauseating smell filled her nose and mouth, and she fell down, down, and into the dark.

WHEN EDIE WOKE from her nightmare there was a disagreeable taste in her mouth, and she had an awful headache, too. She was cold and her bed was hard and strangely lumpy. She decided to pull up the covers, but her hands would not move. They were, she understood after several long minutes of fruitless effort, tied securely behind her back.

It was dark in her room, only it was not her room. She was in the cellar, for she recognized the close, musty smell of the place. It was dark, but she could just make out some flashes of light, and it seemed they were not so very far away.

"Hello?" she called out, and only then did she remember.

The cellar. The stairs. Professor Thurloe. *Ivor.*

The light came closer, ever closer, and something nudged at her ribs. A man's foot, prodding at her.

"Awake?" the man asked.

"Ivor? Is that you?"

The man crouched by her head, his shoes crunching on the limestone screening. "You might as well call me Cousin Ivor. We're past pretending now, aren't we?"

The light was so strong, and it hurt her eyes so badly. "I can't see. Where am I?"

Suddenly the light swung upward, pointing at the ceiling, and she was able to see the man. It was Ivor, and for some reason he wore a sort of head lamp, as a miner might do. It was rather comical, though there was nothing funny at all about the chilly look of irritation on his face.

"You couldn't help yourself, could you? That bloody boiler. You just had to come down and check on it. Never mind that I'd have fetched you down before too long. At least you saved me a trip upstairs."

With the light out of her eyes she was able to see a little better, and as she turned her head she noticed that Professor Thurloe was lying only a yard or so away, his eyes shut, his hands bound.

"Why are you doing this to me? To the professor? I don't understand."

"Of course you don't. You haven't the *least* idea of what is going on around you." Ivor smiled, but it was a mechanical gesture quite devoid of warmth. "You really have made it so easy. Stupid, naive Edie, who is very much *not* the last of the Howards, despite what you claim to believe. Or have you truly forgotten those of us who were disinherited so your grandfather might deprive his own sister of her birthright?"

"I've never met, let alone heard of, a single Howard cousin," she insisted, and even as she said it she remembered the whispers and rumors of a rift that had happened long before her own father's birth.

"Of course you have. My grandmother was five years older than her brother, your grandfather, and twice as smart, besides, and even though she knew everything about this hotel and its workings, her own father chose to cast her aside when she married my grandfather."

"I agree that sounds most unfair, Ivor, and had I known—"

"You knew. You all did. He cut her off, not so much as a penny to her name, and my mother grew up in a poor man's house in South Shields while your father set about running this place into the ground."

"Not deliberately, he didn't. And I've done my best to set things right since I inherited the hotel. Surely you can see that."

"I suppose I do. Not that it matters now."

"Ivor. Listen to me. I swear, on my honor, that I did not know that your grandmother was unfairly disinherited. Had I known, I would certainly have made amends. Not only because it would have been the right thing to do, but also because I never wished to be the last of the Howards. You know how lonely I've been all these years. Why did you never tell me? I wouldn't have pushed you away. I'd have *welcomed* you."

For a moment he seemed to consider what she had said, but then, his frown deepening, he shook his head. "So what if you had? It's too late now."

In that moment, Edie knew that he would not let her live. "What are you going to do?" she managed to ask.

"Nothing so dramatic as you might think. I've made a smallish bomb—you can't see it from here, I'm afraid, but it should be enough to bring down the tunnel and just enough of the forecourt to alarm the authorities. I'll knock you out again before I set it off, and when the tunnel comes down I promise you won't feel a thing. Consider it a kindness from your long-lost cousin."

Far away, at the other end of the cellar, there came

a sound. Was it a creak on the stairs? The cellar door
swinging open? She gathered her breath, ready to scream,
but Ivor was too fast. He stuffed a rag into her mouth,
pushing it so deep she had no hope of spitting it out, and
sprang to his feet.

"I'll be back in a moment. Don't go anywhere."

Chapter 26

STELLA

It was the sound of firecrackers that startled her out of sleep. Merrymakers, she supposed, not caring who they disturbed as long as they had their fun. She lay in bed for a while, but it was no use. She was awake now, and thirsty besides.

Stella put on her robe and set off down the corridor to fetch a drink of water from the washroom. Passing by the Crane sisters' temporary bedroom, she noticed that the door was ajar and the light was still on. "Miss Polly? Miss Bertie?" she whispered, and when neither woman answered she dared to peek inside.

Miss Polly was asleep, lying on top of her bedcovers, and she was still wearing her party dress from the night before. Her sister was snoring in the easy chair on the opposite side of the room, her feathered aigrette headband drooping low on her forehead. Suddenly fearful, Stella approached Miss Bertie and touched her shoulder. She was warm, and she was breathing, but she was so terribly still.

An open bottle of champagne was sitting on the table in the sisters' adjoining sitting room, and from the look of it neither of the women had consumed more than a glass. Certainly not enough to have left both of them in such a stupor. Perhaps they had fallen ill? It was the middle of the night, and Miss Howard would be sleeping, but Mr. Swan would be at the front desk. He might be able to help.

She dressed in a rush and ran downstairs to the front hall, only Mr. Swan wasn't at the reception desk. Daring to open the office door, she peeked inside, hoping to find him there. "Mr. Swan?" she called out softly, but she was answered by silence.

Retreating from the office, she glanced behind the reception desk—and there was Mr. Swan, lying on the floor, and he, too, was sleeping so soundly he could not be roused.

What to do, what to do? She ran down the corridor that led to the kitchen, but it was dark and still, and so, too, was the staff dining room. And then, just as she ran past the cellar door, she heard it. A voice. A man was in the cellar, and from the sound of it he was furiously angry.

She pushed the door open, but only a little. Only enough to hear what the man was saying.

". . . bloody boiler. You just had to come down and check on it. Never mind that I'd have fetched you down before too long. At least you saved me a trip upstairs."

It was Ivor Brooks, but why was he at the hotel in the middle of the night, and in the cellar? And why was he so upset about the boiler?

Another voice answered him. It was a woman—it was *Edie*, and she was terrified. "Why are you doing this to me? To the professor? I don't understand."

"Of course you don't," Brooks said, and the way he spoke to Edie, his every word dripping with disgust and contempt, made Stella's blood run cold. "You haven't the *least* idea of what is going on around you. Stupid, naive Edie."

It made no sense, none of it made any sense at all, but the worst thing she could do, now, was to lose her head. She could not hope to overpower him on her own—she needed help.

Jamie would help.

Stella closed the door as carefully as she could and scurried down the hall, but succeeded only in bumping against the umbrella stand by the kitchen door. She froze, praying that Brooks hadn't heard, but it was no use.

Footsteps sounded on the cellar steps, relentless, terrifying, and she knew she had only seconds to hide. But where? Where? The scullery was close by, its door ajar, and the big hampers of laundry might be large enough to conceal her. She darted across the corridor and squeezed behind one of the tall wicker baskets.

She held her breath, waiting, waiting. The footsteps came closer, ever closer. She was breathing so heavily, and the drumbeat of her heart was so very loud.

The footsteps stopped. Had he come into the scullery? Or was he still in the corridor? Endless seconds ticked past, but then, finally, just as Stella thought she might faint from the effort of keeping so still and silent, Brooks grunted in annoyance and swore under his breath.

He retreated back along the corridor. The cellar door swung shut. A key, turning, grated in a lock.

Stella forced herself out of her hiding place and along the corridor and up the stairs, running so fast she tripped and bruised her shins more than once, but soon she was at Jamie's door, and she hammered on it wildly, not caring if she woke the entire hotel. For all she knew, they had all been drugged, just like the Crane sisters and Mr. Swan.

What if Jamie, too, had been knocked out? What would she do? A telephone call to the police? But the only telephones were on the main floor, at the reception desk and in Edie's office, and if she were to use one of them Brooks would surely hear.

"Jamie!" she called, her voice rising. "Jamie—please come! I need your help! There is something very wrong! Oh, *please*—"

The door opened to reveal Jamie, who was very much awake though still in his pajamas. "What is it, Stella?"

"I cannot wake the Crane sisters, and Mr. Swan, too, he is lying on the floor, and I heard someone in the cellar. It is Ivor Brooks, that wretch, and he has Edie with him, and he is so very angry, and I think he is going to hurt her. I think he heard me, and now he has locked the cellar door, and I do not know what to do. Please help me!"

"I will," he said, and she believed him. "Do you know how to use the telephone here?"

"I do, but I was worried he might hear me. I thought it would be better if I came to you first."

"I'm glad you did. I think you'll be all right if you use the one in Edie's office. As long as you shut the door, and speak softly, Brooks won't hear. Dial zero for the operator, and when she answers tell her to put you through to Detective Inspector Gordon Bayliss on Gairloch Road in Southwark. Got that? Gordon Bayliss, Gairloch Road,

Southwark. He'll answer. Tell him Brooks has Edie cornered in the cellar. Can you do that for me?"

"Yes."

He set off at a run down the stairs. "I'll deal with Brooks," he called back.

"But the cellar door is locked!"

"I know—I have another plan."

Chapter 27

JAMIE

Jamie considered his options as he ran down the stairs and out the back door into the courtyard. It was full dark still, though not for long; enough time, all the same, for him to slip into the cellar without Brooks noticing. Now he only had to pray the coal chute was big enough for him to squeeze through.

It was. Long ago, it must have been another entrance, for its door was set into the ground at an angle, and was wide enough for two men to pass abreast. Now he knelt before it and forced himself to reach for the handle. His hands were shaking, and his chest felt so tight that he might as well have been deep-sea diving, but he could not allow fear to prevent him from helping Edie.

He opened the door, dreading the squeak of rusty hinges, but someone had kept them well greased. God bless them, whoever they were. He slipped through the opening, letting his arms bear his weight, unable to see anything at all in the encompassing dark.

The coal store beneath was nearly empty, and it was easy, in bare feet, to nudge aside the few lumps that remained and find his footing on the gritty floor. He reached out, feeling for the edge of the store, and swung one leg over, then the other.

Then he stood in the darkness, letting his eyes adjust, waiting for his heartbeat to slow. After a minute or so he was able to make out a light in the distance. It was bobbing about, rather as if an enormous firefly had found its way into the cellar, but it was just enough to guide him forward.

Jamie edged closer, ever closer, determined to catch Brooks unaware. He had no weapon, an oversight for which he cursed himself, but he did have the advantage of surprise.

Brooks was talking, and it beggared belief to hear the wretch go on as if he were standing at a party, cocktail in hand, gossiping about the neighbors. "I've any number of plans for the hotel once you're out of the way. A complete redecoration, for a start, and good-bye to that pair of old bags you've let molder on for years. While I'm at it, the rest of the staff can go. Useless pack of duffers."

The headlamp Brooks wore cast a pool of bright light wherever he faced, and as he swung about and looked down, Jamie saw her, his darling Edie, and it was all he could do not to rush forward and gather her in his arms. She lay on her side on the cold, hard floor, her hands tied behind her back, a rag shoved into her mouth. Professor Thurloe lay not far away, his eyes closed. He, too, was bound and gagged.

"Nothing to say for yourself?" Brooks asked her. "Oh, right. I forgot about the gag." He crouched down and pulled it roughly from her mouth. "If you scream I'll push it down your throat until you choke on it."

"What makes you think you'll get the hotel once I'm dead?" Edie asked, her voice hardly more than a whisper. "My will leaves the hotel to my employees, and the proceeds are divided according to length of service. You'll be left a few thousand pounds, but no more."

"Stupid, stupid girl. That was your *old* will. In your new will, the one the police will find in your safe, you leave everything to your beloved long-lost cousin. Among my other talents, I'm a dab hand at forging your signature. Of course, I've had years to practice."

"I suppose it was you who sent out the cancellations," Edie said wearily, and the despair in her voice tore at Jamie's heart.

"I did, but that was just for fun."

"And the threats to the papers?"

"Guilty as charged. All the better to set the stage for what comes next. Professor Thurloe here will be blamed for the bomb, I will be the hero of the hour, and my reward will be this hotel."

"Jamie will stop you," Edie bravely insisted.

"He will do nothing," Brooks snarled, and he pulled at her hair so savagely that she screamed in agony. "He will do *nothing*, for he's asleep in his bed, he and everyone else at this hotel. All it took was some doctored champagne— would you believe he even thanked me for it?" Once more Brooks tore at Edie's hair, and the sound of her piteous cry was more than Jamie could bear.

"I thanked you," he said, stepping forward, "just as any gentleman would. But I didn't drink it. I hate champagne.

Always have. If you'd brought me a pint of Tennent's . . . well. But you didn't think of that."

Brooks whirled around, and only then did Jamie realize the mistake he had made in revealing himself, for the light of the headlamp, aimed directly at him, was utterly blinding.

He staggered back, felt a rush of air, and was just able to make out a shadow scything toward him. He raised his arms, bracing himself for a blow, and it was worse than he'd imagined, for Brooks was hammering at him with a metal bar, and each blow was savage enough to rattle the teeth in Jamie's head. Blow after bruising blow rained down on his arms and shoulders and chest, and though he was bigger, and likely far stronger, it was only a matter of time before Brooks broke his arm or collarbone or worse.

There was another telltale hiss of air as the weapon sliced toward him, but this time, instead of blocking it, Jamie caught hold of the thing, pulled it sharply forward, and, with Brooks so close he could smell the man's acrid breath, he reached for the light, caught hold of the headlamp, and tore the contraption off his head.

His enemy staggered back, still waving what Jamie now saw was a pry bar. They had retreated from the tunnel and were back in the cellar, were almost at the stairs, and it was far darker there. So dark that Jamie didn't see the lump of rubble until he tripped over it and fell hard on his back.

Brooks raised the pry bar above his head and swung it down, his face twisted in a rictus of hate, but Jamie managed to roll away so the blow landed on his shoulder instead of his skull. He scrabbled at the floor, desperate to find his feet again, and when Brooks lunged forward once more Jamie scooped up a handful of dust and pebbles and flung it at the other man's face.

Brooks shrieked, stumbling away, and tripped on the same piece of rubble that had upended Jamie moments before. He fell to his knees, hard, but before he could rise again the cellar door opened with a bang and a figure came rushing down the steps. It was Stella, and she now leaped forward and jabbed something into Brook's back. It was, of all things, a furled umbrella.

"This gun is pointed at your heart," she snarled. "If you move, if you so much as *blink*, I will kill you. That is a promise."

Jamie pulled the pry bar from Brooks's grasp, tossed it across the cellar, and twisted the man's right arm behind him until he was a breath away from dislocating his shoulder. He had him prostrate on the floor a moment later, both arms secured, and though he knew his father would have disapproved, Jamie found it grimly satisfying to grind his knee into the small of the other man's back.

"Is there anything I can use to tie his hands?"

"There's some rope over here," Edie answered, and Stella ran over to fetch it, along with a pocketknife that Brooks must have dropped earlier. It was a good thing the wretch hadn't thought to make use of it as well.

Jamie fastened the rope around Brooks's wrists, rather more tightly than he ought to have done, and then he cut a second length of rope and tied together the man's feet, just to be sure, before turning him onto his back. It wouldn't do for him to expire from asphyxiation before he could be brought to trial.

And then he remembered the bomb.

He ran to Edie's side, dropped to his knees, and untied the rope that Brooks had wrapped around her wrists. "He spoke of a bomb—where is it?"

"In the tunnel. I'm not sure how far."

Brooks's abandoned headlamp was nearby, and Jamie used it now to guide him as he advanced into the encompassing void of the unlit tunnel. It was an effort to continue on, step-by-step, into the dark unknown, his legs shaking, his every breath an effort, and when he did find the device that Ivor Brooks had constructed, the last of Jamie's courage threatened to desert him.

Brooks had spoken of wanting the hotel for himself, and had even changed Edie's will so he'd be sure to inherit it, but the device in front of Jamie was capable of flattening the Blue Lion and every other building in a fifty-yard radius. Not only did it appear to incorporate at least fifty pounds of dynamite, but the alarm clock rigged as a timing mechanism was ticking steadily away, and the hour hand—the others had been removed—was creeping toward a contact wire that had been secured in place with a blob of melted wax. At the speed the timer was advancing, the bomb would detonate within the quarter hour, if not sooner.

He rushed back to the cellar and, crouching next to Brooks, wrenched the man's head around to face him. "I don't know who told you how to build a bomb, but a single stick of dynamite properly placed would have been more than enough to bring down the tunnel and do away with Edie and the professor. Instead you've wired up enough goddamn explosive to bring down this entire hotel and most of its neighbors. What were you thinking?"

Brooks's eyes widened in disbelief. "You're lying. I was told I needed at least a hundred sticks to bring down the tunnel."

"By the man who sold it to you? For a hundred times the price of the amount you actually needed? Let me guess: Was he the one who showed you how to wire it up, too?"

Jamie considered himself a peaceable man, but the display of greed, heartlessness, selfishness, and stupidity he was witnessing made it intensely difficult for him to resist the urge to throttle Brooks on the spot. It was with great difficulty that he refrained, but that was only because he needed to learn how Brooks had put the device together.

"Listen," he began, affecting a tone of sympathy that was in no way sincere. "I can understand your feelings. I'm sure you have your reasons for all of this. I'm also sure the authorities will be lenient once you've had a chance to explain. But if you don't help me now, we are all dead. Tell me you understand."

But Brooks, his mouth pressed into a thin, bitter line, said nothing.

"Did you build in a way to deactivate the thing if you changed your mind? People will *die*. You do understand, don't you? Innocent people, complete strangers. Hundreds of people. There are *children* in the crowds above us—does that mean nothing to you?"

Brooks shrugged, his gaze fixed on a point over Jamie's shoulder. "I've no chance of getting the hotel now, and life in prison is what I'm facing if I do survive. Better a quick death to the alternative."

It was no use; Jamie would get nothing from the man.

"Stella?" he called out, marveling at how composed he sounded. "Has Inspector Bayliss arrived?"

"I do not know."

"All right. Please go upstairs, and if he's here, let him know that Brooks has planted a bomb that's big enough to level this entire building and put an enormous hole in the middle of today's coronation route. If Bayliss hasn't arrived, run through the hotel and do your damnedest to clear the place out. Edie, see if you can wake the professor. But don't take too long. I need you out of this cellar and as far away as your legs can carry you."

That accomplished, he ran back into the tunnel, his only tools a dull penknife and the miner's headlamp he'd taken from Brooks.

He crouched before the bomb, knowing he should do nothing until he had properly assessed every component and gained some understanding of what he was facing. The sticks of dynamite, strapped into bundles, were divided between two open suitcases that had been arranged side by side on the ground. Perched atop the explosives in the right-hand case was the alarm clock that Brooks had modified so clumsily. It was wired to an electric detonator, which in turn was connected to a set of six-volt lantern batteries. The connecting wires were a uniform gray, and the location of the entire contraption, set back against the open lid of the suitcase, made it impossible for Jamie to assess the rear or underside for evidence of a booby trap. If Brooks had simply wired one element to the next, it would be a straightforward matter of severing the connection between the timer and the detonator—the penknife he held would do the job in an instant. But there was every chance the bomb was booby-trapped with a hidden antitamper circuit that would detonate if he started rummaging around. There was no way of knowing, and there was no time to lose, not now. Dozens of lives—hundreds, even—depended on Jamie, but it had been years since he'd matched his wits and nerves to an explosive device, and the last time he'd tried didn't bear thinking about.

"Is it something you can sort out?" Edie asked in a voice so calm she might have been asking about a lightbulb that needed changing. Only then did he realize that she'd been standing at his side all along.

"Oh, aye. Nothing to it. Only I can't begin until you go. Please, Edie."

"If I go, there will be no one to hold the light while you work."

"I'm begging you. We're almost out of time. You *must* go."

"Look at me for a moment," she asked. "Thank you. I want you to know that I believe, truly believe, you can and will defuse this bomb. I have complete confidence in you. And that is why I am going to stay here and hold the light so you have both your hands free to deal with this wretched thing. You have a coronation procession to paint, and I have a hotel full of guests who will be wanting their breakfast before long, and I have had enough of Ivor Brooks and his antics to last me a lifetime."

"I can't persuade you to go?"

"No. When we leave this cellar, it will be together."

He had never loved her more. "Right, then. I won't be a moment."

Chapter 28

EDIE

Of course she was afraid. She was standing next to an enormous bomb, one that would level the Blue Lion if it exploded, kill or maim hundreds of bystanders, bring down the street above, ruin the coronation, and not incidentally end her life and that of the man she loved.

She was afraid, but she had complete confidence in Jamie's ability to defuse the bomb. So she remained at his side, and held the light for him, and watched as he bent close and examined the parts of the device that Ivor had assembled—a nonsensical collection of batteries and wires and an alarm clock missing all but one of its arms, and most alarmingly stick after stick of dynamite that looked exactly like something out of a Hollywood film.

After what felt like hours, but likely had only been a few minutes, he stepped back, took a deep breath, and smiled at her. "Done."

"We're safe?" she asked, hardly daring to breathe. "What did you do?"

"Since Brooks didn't have the faintest idea of how much explosive to use, I reasoned he likely didn't have the knowledge to build in a booby trap. So I simply clipped the wires connecting the timer to the detonator. It was a risk, but I had to take it."

"Is it safe now?"

"Safe enough. I'll happily explain the whys and wherefores, but would you mind if I do so upstairs? I've had about as much of this cellar as I can take."

Her heart clenched in sympathy, and not a little guilt at having forgotten how unbearable it was for him to be underground. "I don't blame you one bit. Let's see if we can get the professor moving."

The poor dear was stirring already, and with a little help he was able to sit up, and then, once he wasn't quite so dizzy, Jamie heaved him to his feet.

"Good heavens. What on earth has happened?"

"Rather a lot," Jamie answered. "Let's get you upstairs."

"But the beams! Mr. Brooks told me that he'd found evidence of scribe-framing. I really must have a look."

"Another time," Edie answered firmly. "After you've seen a doctor, and after Mr. Brooks has been dealt with by the authorities, and after the coronation, then I'll let you have a look."

"Very well. I do have rather a nasty headache, come to think of it."

"I'm not surprised," she said. "A nice cup of tea is just what you need. Come along, now."

With Jamie taking the professor's right arm and Edie his left, and guided by the waning light of the headlamp she still held, they made their way, one shaky step after another, out of the tunnel and across the cellar. Ahead, a line of light appeared and grew steadily wider as someone opened the door at the top of the stairs.

"Sorted?" Inspector Bayliss called down.

"Sorted," Jamie called back.

"Good man. Need some help?"

"God, yes."

The inspector came down, and together he and Jamie carried the professor out of the cellar, and Edie, for a moment, was left alone. She was halfway up the steps before she thought to look back.

Ivor lay on the floor, forgotten, though presumably the police would return for him before too long. He glared at her, and although she was curious to learn how, exactly, he had put his awful plans in place, she didn't much care to listen to him ever again. And she had better things to do than spend another moment in his company.

"I'm off to watch the coronation," she told him. "I don't expect I'll see you again. Excepting at your trial, of course. Consider yourself sacked."

STELLA

After Professor Thurloe, still woozy from his ordeal, had been taken to the hospital, and Brooks, in shackles, had been led to a waiting police van, brought in through the back courtyard as the streets in front of the hotel were quite impassable, Stella remembered that she was expected to be in her place at the Abbey by no later than eight o'clock, and it was already half-past seven.

"No need to panic," Edie soothed. "I'm sure we can find a way to get you there on time. Just do your best to get dressed as quickly as you can."

Fortunately, Stella had always been the sort of person who had difficulty falling asleep if she was not prepared for the day to come, which meant her camera bag was already packed and her frock, ironed to perfection by Edie herself the day before, was laid out and ready for her to cast aside her pajamas and dressing gown.

With the Speed Graphic and its large-format film secured in her satchel, her Leica slung around her neck, and her press pass, identity card, and official pass to the Abbey tucked into the front pocket of her bag, Stella deemed herself ready.

Edie and Jamie were waiting for her, along with Gordon and one of his uniformed policemen. "Constable Timms here'll see you through to the Abbey," Gordon explained. "I'm off back to the Yard to see what I can get out of Brooks. If he admits to anything significant I'll let you know."

"And after that?" Edie asked. "Will you keep him in custody?"

"No chance of him getting out. Not today, and not for a long while. Try to enjoy Coronation Day, if you can."

"I'll do my best," Edie said brightly. And then, turning to Stella, "These are for you." She held out a packet of sandwiches wrapped in wax paper. "Cook was worried you might get hungry while you're waiting for everything to start."

Stella tucked the sandwiches into one of the exterior pockets of her camera bag, and then, impulsively, pulled Edie close for a brief but heartfelt hug. It was not a day for restraint, she had decided. "Please thank Cook for me."

A police car was waiting in the cobbled yard behind the hotel. Gordon opened the rear door and waited, showing no sign of impatience, as Stella settled herself on the rear seat. Constable Timms went around the bonnet of the car and took the front passenger seat.

"Thank you for this," she told Gordon. "I'm not sure how I would get to the Abbey otherwise."

"Least I can do in light of your actions this morning. You were very brave."

"I only did as Jamie told me," she protested. "He was the one who went into the cellar."

"I mean the umbrella. Jamie told me about it while you were getting ready. Not sure as I'd have thought of it myself."

"I was in such a panic. I didn't even think."

"I disagree. You kept your head, and you helped to prevent Brooks from blowing the entire hotel, and most of Northumberland Avenue, to kingdom come. Speaking as someone who would have spent the rest of his working life embroiled in the aftermath if that cretin had managed to set off his bomb, and also as an Englishman who wants to see his queen crowned today, I am very, very grateful for what you did. Now, tell me: You've got your pass? All your bits and bobs? Good." He shook her hand, shut the car door, and thumped on the roof. "Off you go, and good luck."

The driver reversed out of the courtyard onto Craven Street, but then, rather than turn left onto the Strand, he turned right.

"Streets are all blocked off," Constable Timms explained, correctly sensing her alarm at the direction they were taking. "So we're heading for Waterloo Bridge. There's a police mooring point nearby, and we've a boat waiting for you. From there it's straight along the river to Westminster Pier. We'll be there in no time at all."

Within five minutes, no more, they were passing by the pier at Charing Cross, and from there onward the riverbank was a mass of jubilant crowds and waving flags and voices raised in song.

"They'll wear themselves out," Constable Timms observed. "Hours yet until the procession."

The boat pulled in at Westminster Pier soon after, and together Stella and the constable hurried up the stairs and across Bridge Street. She had expected a certain degree of chaos—how could it be avoided with thousands of people all vying for the chance to see the queen pass by?—but the crowds were polite and orderly, and not a single person complained when Constable Timms told them to step aside and make way.

Straight ahead were the Houses of Parliament; to their right was Westminster Abbey, its western end engulfed by a starkly modern annex. They continued on and presently came to a barrier that was guarded by a pair of uniformed soldiers.

"Got a press photographer here," Constable Timms explained.

"You was supposed to be in your place hours ago," one of the soldiers protested.

"None of your guff, if you please," said Constable Timms. "She was helping Scotland Yard with some inquiries."

"Why didn't you say so straightaway? Let's see your

pass—no, it's the reverse I need. It'll show me where you're meant to go."

"I believe it is called the triforium," Stella said, hoping to expedite matters.

"Good thing you wore sensible shoes. The triforium it is, and you'd best brace yourself for a climb. You'll be going in through the entrance next to Poets' Corner. It's straight ahead, just before the chapter house. Show this to the usher when you come to the door."

She said good-bye to Constable Timms, who promised to wait for her, and hurried onward, almost missing the path to the entrance in her haste. It was narrow and rather overshadowed, and led beneath the flying buttresses of a high round structure to the promised door. A short queue of men and women were waiting for admission, and as several among them had camera bags slung over their shoulders she felt confident she was in the right place.

Her passes and identification duly vetted, Stella followed the other journalists to a small wooden door, through which was a steep and tightly winding set of stairs. Up and up she climbed, not at all certain where she would end up, but as the man in front of her had said he was a writer for *Time* magazine it seemed sensible to follow.

They emerged onto a sort of mezzanine set high above the floor of the Abbey, and rather like the attic of an old house, it, too, was cluttered with the detritus of centuries. Several rows of chairs had been set close to the edge of the triforium, with a slender, waist-high metal rail offering only nominal protection against a long and presumably fatal fall.

It took her a while to inch past the other journalists and

photographers, whispering brief hellos to the ones she knew from photo-calls, trying all the while not to let herself dwell on the twenty meters or more of empty air between the triforium and the marble floor below. When she did sit down she had scarcely enough elbow room to open the Speed Graphic, load it, and set it on her lap. Fortunately, she had no need for a flash, since the lights set up for the newsreels and television would brighten the dim interior even better than direct sunshine.

Next she took the Leica from its case, removed the lens cap, and slung it over her shoulder so it sat just under her arm. That way it would be easy to access when she needed it, but also secure if anyone were to bump her arm.

She glanced at her wristwatch; it was almost nine o'clock, with more than two hours remaining before the ceremony began in earnest. Now was a good time to eat at least one of the sandwiches Cook had prepared. She extracted the packet from her camera bag, unfolded the paper just enough to wiggle loose one triangle of sandwich, and as she took her first bite she caught the eye of a woman in one of the galleries across the way. She, too, was eating a sandwich, and rather amusingly was using her upturned coronet as a makeshift bowl. They exchanged smiles, and when Stella lifted her camera, the woman nodded and raised what looked to be a bottle of ginger beer in a silent toast. That was an image worth capturing, no matter that the ceremony had yet to begin.

The Abbey filled with people as the minutes crept by, the noise steadily rising, and when the television lights switched on, a collective gasp of delight swept through the crowd. The music began not long after, gradually swelling and rising, and with it a sense of scarcely contained antici-pation. Coronation Day had come at last, and the queen was on her way.

JAMIE

There was time enough, once Gordon and Stella had left, for Jamie to run upstairs and shed his filthy pajamas, run a quick bath, shave, and dress in a decent shirt and trousers. He was rolling back his sleeves and contemplat-ing the emptiness of his stomach, together with the late-ness of the hour, when someone knocked at his door.

It was Edie, and she had brought him tea and toast and marmalade. "I wasn't sure if you felt quite up to a full breakfast. Will this do? I can run down and fetch you some eggs and bacon if it isn't enough."

"It's exactly right. Thank you. I was just thinking how much I'd like a cup of tea."

"You've plenty of time, you know. It's only just gone half-past nine, and there's no sign of the procession yet."

He forced himself to drink his tea slowly, and then, once its sugary warmth had begun to work its magic, he ate three pieces of toast, each of them spread with nearly a jam jar's worth of marmalade, and with each bite he felt a little better, a little stronger and steadier, and by the time he'd finished he very nearly felt like a new man.

"There," Edie said. "Now I won't fret about you keeling over while you're working today. I had better go and see how everyone is managing downstairs."

"Will you stay? Only until the procession has gone by?"

He knew it was unfair to ask, but he badly wanted her at his side.

"Of course I will. I'd have asked, but I didn't want to impose. Are you ready? Is there anything else I can bring you?"

"I'm ready," he assured her. And he was, for he had just then dared to pick up a piece of vine charcoal, and his hand had been steady. He tried again, this time with a freshly sharpened pencil. Not so much as a tremor.

He went to the window and arranged his easel just so, and Edie stood at his side, and together they waited. The roar of the crowd outside grew louder and louder, and then, quite suddenly, it all began.

First came scores of guardsmen in their red coats and bearskin hats, followed by the household cavalry, their golden helmets topped with swinging horsehair plumes, and then, at last, the great gold coach lumbered into view, moving far more slowly than Jamie had expected, its team of eight Windsor Greys sweating and straining as they plodded forward, and beside them marched liveried grooms and Yeomen of the Guard in lavishly embroidered tunics and Tudor caps.

The queen herself, dressed in bridal white and festooned with diamonds, was an improbably small and delicate figure. Though she sat on the far side of the coach, with Prince Philip to her left, Jamie was able to see her quite clearly, for she was leaning forward, looking from side to side, and all the while she waved to the adoring masses, her arm as elegant as a ballerina's, her smile heartfelt and unwavering.

He made sketch after sketch, working quickly but not

frantically, and once the queen and her coach had vanished from sight he added color to his drawings and made notes in the margins, endeavoring to translate the swirl of images in his mind's eye into something that was truthful as well as beautiful.

It was a long while before he sat back, and rubbed at his eyes, and stretched his aching back until his bones crackled in protest.

"Done?" Edie asked.

"For now."

"What did you think of it all?"

"I'm not quite sure. When I was planning it all out, the elements of the procession never quite made sense to me. They seemed too much, somehow. Does that make sense? Only today, just now, I couldn't help thinking that everything *did* fit together. I'd been worried I'd find it ridiculous, but it wasn't. And I'm not entirely sure I understand why."

She considered what he'd said, but rather than press him on it, she instead asked, "Would you like to come down and watch the ceremony on television with me?"

"I would, but I want to look through my sketches first. Make sure everything is fixed in my mind." In the distance, bells began to chime. "That's the queen arriving at the Abbey. Best join the others so you don't miss the ceremony. I'll be down before long."

He waited until she was gone, and then he arranged the sketches upon his desk, and he looked them over, one by one, absorbing every line and shadow and wash of color until he could see it, the painting he'd imagined for so long, the painting he had yet to create, as clearly as he now saw the sketches arrayed before him.

He was tempted to make a start, but he'd promised Edie he would watch the coronation ceremony with her. A half hour's separation was all he could bear for now, with the memory of Brooks and the bomb and the cellar so fresh in his mind. He needed to stand at her side and see that she was safe and well. He needed to know that no part of his nightmare had come to pass.

In the dream that had haunted him for so many years, he was always alone. Always. But today, in the cellar, with everything at stake, with everything to lose, Edie had been at his side. Darling Edie, a beacon of goodness and hope and love, and she was waiting for him, and that meant he was, quite to his surprise, a lucky man after all.

Chapter 29

EDIE

The lounge had been cleared of its sofas and easy chairs for the occasion, and in their place were rows of chairs from the dining room, set up like a small theater, with the television screen at center stage.

Edie's guests and employees alike had filled the room to bursting, and though she'd been nervous of their reaction, for she herself ought to have taken on the task of smoothing ruffled feathers and fractured nerves, rather than leave it to Gordon and his officers, she was greeted with cheers and hurrahs and no end of hearty handshakes and congratulations, for Gordon had explained that Edie, Jamie, and Stella had saved Coronation Day from certain disaster, though the precise nature of that disaster, beyond its connection to the doctored champagne many of them had consumed, was a subject best left for another day.

Cook had rallied, a magnificent breakfast had been served, and the hotel's street-side windows had been crowded around with guests and employees alike as the procession had rolled past in its stately, opulent, and arguably antediluvian magnificence.

And now they were all together in the lounge, tight as sardines, to watch the great occasion on the television. Even Edie had to admit that it was exciting to watch the ceremony as it unfolded, and to know that millions of other people, all over the world, were fellow spectators, too.

The procession had just arrived at the Abbey when Jamie reappeared at her side. "Did I miss anything?"

"No, you're just in time."

The lounge fell silent as a rising tide of music from the television heralded the queen's entrance. A fanfare of trumpets sounded, the Abbey's great organ thundered ever louder, and the massed voices of the choir rang out in welcome. "I was glad," they sang, and the echo of it rang deep and true in Edie's heart, for in spite of everything that had happened in the cellar, and all that Brooks had done, she was happy. Here, in her home, with Jamie at her side, she was happy at last.

STELLA

High above the coronation theater, Stella watched as the queen was led to King Edward's chair for her anointing, the ritual's sacred mysteries hidden from view by a golden canopy. The choir sang of Zadok the priest and King Solomon, and Stella, quite to her surprise, had to blink back sudden tears. It was a wondrous thing to behold, as was the moment when the queen, engulfed in robes of cloth of gold, was led to a second throne and was handed, in succession, various swords and orbs and scepters.

And then, in perfect silence, the ponderous weight of Saint Edward's Crown was placed upon her head, and she was crowned.

At that exact moment, the hundreds of lords and ladies surrounding the queen raised their arms and set their own coronets upon their heads, and the only point of stillness was the slight figure of the monarch herself, serene and dignified and utterly alone.

"God save the queen! God save the queen!" came the acclamation of thousands of voices, and though it was tempting to look around and attempt to take in the larger spectacle, Stella did not move. Instead she gently squeezed the shutter on her Leica, which was resting on the metal barrier before her, and took one photograph, then another, then another, not daring to blink or even breathe.

The ceremony continued on for at least another hour, the language so arcane and unfamiliar that Stella didn't even attempt to understand what was taking place. Instead she let her eyes guide her, using both the Speed Graphic and the Leica to capture moments of beauty and calm amid the noise. She went through roll after roll of film, and when, at last, the queen had been borne away in her enormous gold carriage, and the thousands of guests had begun to vacate their coveted seats, she heaved a sigh of relief and set about packing away her cameras.

It was a long while before she and the other journalists were able to descend the perilous stairway and leave the Abbey by way of the half-hidden door by Poets' Corner, and it was a wonderful relief to be free at last of the searing lights and stifling warmth of the great church's overstuffed interior.

"Miss Donati!"

She'd quite forgotten that Constable Timms had promised to wait for her, and she was ridiculously glad to see him now, for she hadn't, until that moment, considered how she would find her way back to the *PW* offices. "How was it?" he asked. "Did you get any good snaps?"

"Oh, yes," she said. "Only I am not sure how I will return to my work. It is still so busy."

"Where do you need to go? Fleet Street, I expect? That's easy enough. We'll run you along to Blackfriars Bridge. From there it's not far at all."

Forty minutes later she was racing up the stairs to the photographers' eyrie at *PW*, still a little out of breath after running nearly the whole way from the river.

Win was waiting for her. "Did you get it?" he asked.

"I think so. I used the Leica, just at the moment she was crowned, with the Ilford 125 film. I set the shutter speed to one-fifth of a second." She dug in her bag, looking for the single canister she'd tucked into the same pocket as her press pass; there hadn't been time to write anything on the label. "Here it is. I think maybe the second or third exposure?"

"Good. Wait here for a bit. I won't be long."

He retreated into the darkroom, leaving her alone, and though she knew it would only be a half hour or so until the red light switched off and he'd finished working his magic, it was agonizing all the same to have to wait and fret and wonder.

The light above the darkroom door clicked off. "Stella?" came Win's voice from within.

"Yes?"

"You can come in." It was the first time she'd been invited inside—the first time, as far as she knew, that anyone other than Win had been allowed past the door. "Sit on that stool," he directed, his features looking faintly demonic in the red glow of the overhead light. "The film's still drying."

After five minutes or so, Win opened a small cabinet and retrieved a strip of negatives. "They're good," he said. "Sit tight while I make a contact sheet."

She couldn't see what he was doing, for his back was turned and he'd told her to stay where she was, but the quiet and near dark of the space was wonderfully soothing. If she hadn't been so eager to see her photographs, she'd have been tempted to take a nap.

"Let's go to the table outside," Win said at last. "The light's better there."

He cleared an empty space on the big table and set down the contact sheet. "You'll want to look through them all, but I fancy this is the one." He pointed to the second image on the contact sheet. "Go on," he encouraged, and handed her a magnifier.

She crouched low over the contact sheet, set the magnifier over the image Win had indicated, took a deep breath to steady herself, and looked.

As she'd imagined and hoped, the long exposure she'd employed had captured the lonely figure on the throne in perfect focus, while the people around her receded into an impressionistic swirl of light and dark. The queen was the radiant center of the image, her regalia aglow under the glare of the television lights, her cloth-of-gold robes gleaming warmly even when rendered, as here, in shades of gray.

"Yes," she said. "That is what I hoped for all along."

"Good." He took the magnifier from her and began to examine the contact sheet in earnest.

"I wasn't sure I would be able to do it," she admitted. "I didn't get much sleep last night."

"Nerves?"

"No. There was a bomb, you see. At the hotel."

Win tossed aside the magnifier and spun around to face her. "You weren't hurt, were you?"

"No. It didn't go off—I should have said so. It was one of the clerks. A horrid man named Ivor Brooks. He knocked out nearly everyone with some sort of drops he put in the champagne, and then he trapped Edie in the cellar. I overheard him, and so I ran upstairs and found Jamie—do you remember him from my birthday dinner? He stopped Mr. Brooks from setting off the bomb, and then the police came, and they helped me get to the Abbey. We went along the river." She stopped short, fretting at how nonsensical her story must seem, and was taken aback by the expression of torment on Win's face. "Oh, Win—you mustn't worry. I am fine. Truly, I am."

"I feel like an ass. I didn't even say hello when you arrived, let alone ask how you were."

"There's no way you could have known. Please, Win. You mustn't worry."

He reached out to cradle her face in his hands, inspecting her features as intently as he'd examined the contact sheet only moments before. "Will you sit with me while I do up the enlargements?"

"It won't distract you if I stay?"

"Not at all," he insisted. "You can tell me about the ceremony while I work. I listened to some of it on the wireless, but I'd like to know what you thought of it."

"I didn't think you were all that interested in the coronation."

"I'm not. I am, however, very interested in you. Not only are you a gifted photographer, but you are also an intelligent and amusing woman, and I am trying very hard not to dwell upon what nearly happened to you this morning. I should also tell you that if we were not standing in our place of work I would ask you for a kiss."

"I understand," she said. "What about this evening?"

"I beg your pardon?"

"Once you've finished the enlargements and shown them to Kaz and got through the rest of your work for the day, and you've taken me to dinner and escorted me back to the Blue Lion, then will you ask to kiss me?"

"Put like that, how can I refuse?"

JAMIE

Jamie returned to his room as soon as the coronation ceremony was over, for Edie was determined to make the rounds of her guests and ensure they were happy and well and suffering no aftereffects from the doctored champagne. He made more drawings, each time focusing on an element of the procession that he wished to fix in his memory: the goldwork on the queen's mantle, the reflection of the coach in the puddles of rainwater upon the pavement, the kinetic energy of the jubilant crowds.

When he next thought to look away from his easel, the sun was fading and the streets beyond were all but empty. He came down the stairs at a run, but there was no sign of Edie in the lounge or dining room or any of the other public areas on the main floor of the hotel.

"She's in her office," Mr. Swan explained, having noticed Jamie's agitation. "The inspector has just arrived. Shall I let her know you're here?"

"Yes, please."

A moment later Edie came into the hall. "I was just about to come looking for you."

Together they returned to her office, and at her direction he sat next to her, and then they waited for Gordon to tell them what he had learned.

"I'll start by telling you that I still have no idea what drove Brooks to act as he did. Above and beyond straightforward greed and jealousy, that is. He seems to have had some trouble finding steady work after the war; perhaps that's what brought him south in the first place. He was curious about the Blue Lion, too, and when he learned there was a position vacant he put himself forward and you hired him on.

"Before long, he decided he wanted the hotel for himself, but he knew you well enough, by then, to realize you'd never sell up, not unless you were desperate. He also knew you hadn't much capital left after paying the death duties when your parents were killed, and he was well aware that your expenses often outstripped your takings, especially in the slower months when fewer guests came to stay. So he started to turn away guests as often as he could without your taking notice."

"But how?" Edie asked. "I've always insisted on confirming each reservation as it comes in."

"Only the ones you know about," Gordon clarified. "He was a dab hand at steaming open envelopes that looked as if they might come from prospective guests. If the letter was from someone who'd never stayed at the Blue Lion— that was easy enough to check, since you've a card file with your regular guests' preferences—he responded by return post, in your name, saying the hotel was unfortunately fully booked, but the Cranbourn Hotel in Leicester Square was likely to have rooms available.

"It was the same when people rang up and asked for a room. If you were in your office, and there was a chance you might overhear, he'd put through the call. But if you weren't nearby, he'd tell the callers the same thing: The hotel was full up, but the Cranbourn might well have room."

"How much were they paying him?" Jamie asked.

"Half a crown per reservation. I expect he made a tidy sum for himself over the years. It also had the added benefit of making it that much harder for Edie to stay in business. He seemed to believe, at least until recently, that you might be driven to sell up if you couldn't keep the hotel profitable. He even enlisted an old friend from Newcastle to try and persuade you. Jack Turnbull. Man's been in and out of prison half a dozen times for all manner of offenses."

"I don't know anyone by that name," Edie said.

"He used an alias. David Bamford."

"My heavens. I never suspected."

"What if Edie had agreed to sell the hotel to Bamford? What then?" Jamie asked.

"I doubt Brooks ever got that far. He definitely didn't have the cash to buy it outright. In any event, you soon sent Bamford packing, and that's when Brooks's plans changed."

"When he decided to kill me," Edie said flatly.

"Yes. He seemed quite proud of his little plot, if you can believe it, and surprised as anything that it unraveled so easily."

"How did he get hold of the explosives?" Jamie asked.

"From a neighbor back in South Shields. Seems to be the sort of type who likes to rabbit on about his dangerous job handling dynamite for the local colliery. Brooks got him talking, asked if anyone would notice if a smallish quantity of mining explosive were to go missing, and promised he'd pay well for the stuff, no questions asked. Said he needed it to collapse an old bomb shelter in a property he'd bought. The neighbor convinced Brooks that bigger was better, and sent him back to London with two suitcases in hand, each with twenty-five pounds of dynamite packed inside, neat as pie."

"So he fetched the explosives when he was home visiting his mother?" Edie asked.

"Yes, only she wasn't sick, and he didn't visit her. Went straight there and back, and spent the rest of his time off in his bedsit here in London. I expect that's when he prepared the other parts of the device. The alarm clock needed modifying, and he had to wire up the batteries and solder the terminals and so on."

"He told me his father was a chemist," Edie now said, so

calm that Jamie could scarcely believe it. "Is that where he got the knockout drops for the champagne?"

"His father was a miner, but Brooks himself worked for the local chemist when he was still in school. Sweeping the floor, fetching and carrying, delivering parcels. I managed to get the name of the place out of him. Wouldn't surprise me to learn that he paid a visit not so long ago, and that a bottle of chloral hydrate, or something not so very different, has since gone missing. As for the ether he used to knock you out, he might have bought it anywhere."

"My goodness. It just gets worse and worse," Edie fretted.

"Stella's photograph," Jamie remembered. "Was it Brooks who tore it up?"

"I expect so. He had no shortage of nasty things to say about her. And you, as well, though I won't insult you by repeating any of it."

"Is that all?" Jamie asked wearily.

"Just about. The threats to the papers came from Brooks—I think he already confessed to that when you were in the tunnels with him."

"How did the professor end up back at the hotel?" Edie now asked.

At this, Gordon flushed brick red. "That was my fault. Do you remember the threats we found in his notebooks? About rivers of blood and so forth?"

Edie winced. "How could I forget such a thing?"

"It turned out they weren't threats. They were translations, taken from letters written by supporters of Mary Queen of Scots. Apparently he'd come across the letters some years ago, in the archives where he used to work, and he'd only just begun to translate them from the original

Scots and French. It was pure chance that they sounded so similar to the threats concocted by Brooks. It was enough for me to let him go, though I did have one of my constables take him to another hotel. I suppose he must have returned here in the wee hours."

"So that's it?" Jamie asked.

Gordon shrugged. "Just about. It all fits together, at least from what I can tell."

"What happens now?"

"Now I get down to the hard work of putting together a case against him, although he's made my job that much easier by providing me with so much evidence. Would you believe he didn't even bother with gloves while he put together the bomb? I expect you'll both be called upon to give evidence at his trial, but that won't be for some months. He'll remain on remand, so you don't have to worry about him showing up at your front door."

"Thank goodness for that," Edie said, glancing at her watch. "Good heavens—it's a quarter past nine. We've missed the queen's speech on the wireless."

"I'm sure they'll repeat it on the news tomorrow," Jamie reassured her. "And we haven't missed the fireworks."

They said good night to Gordon, and then Edie insisted on making the rounds through the dining room and lounge and library, and only once she was certain her guests were in need of nothing did she agree to put on her raincoat and walk with Jamie to the river.

"A walk will do us both good," he insisted.

"Very well. But only because I'm not ready for this day to end."

Hand in hand they hurried along Northumberland Avenue, its streets still thronged with merrymakers, and though the Bailey bridge was jam-packed Jamie was still able to find a spot for them.

The fireworks had just begun when Edie rose on her tiptoes and spoke directly in his ear. "I ought to have told you before, although I think you already know. I love you."

"Your insisting on staying with me while I dealt with the bomb did rather tip your hand," he teased. "I love you, too. May I kiss you now?"

Her eyes were shining as she looked up at him. "Yes," she said, and she set her hand over his heart, and he bent his head and kissed her as strangers squeezed by, and the river flowed on, and the coronation fireworks boomed and bloomed in the rain-swept skies so far above.

Epilogue

EDIE

November 19, 1953

It was to be a private visit; on that point The Palace had been exceedingly clear. After the event, naturally, Her Majesty the Queen's decision to join Miss Howard and her colleagues at the Blue Lion for afternoon tea could be shared with the press, but certainly not beforehand.

In the weeks since her first communications with The Palace—she had taken to thinking of it as such, with initial capitals and a distinct personality of its own—Edie had learned a number of things. She now knew how to address the queen properly ("Your Majesty" upon first introduction, then a broad, rather American-sounding "ma'am" thereafter); how to converse with her (no direct questions, no attempts at overfamiliarity, no requests for her signature or endorsement, and absolutely no touching of the royal person, beyond Her Majesty's hand when it was offered, and then only as a light grasp, remembering that H.M. was expected to shake many hands over the course of the day and an overhearty grip would lead to discomfort); and how to prepare the Blue Lion for the private and unofficial royal visit (one room with facilities should be set aside for Her Majesty's express use; the chair provided for H.M. at teatime should be of the same style and disposition of the other guests' chairs, with a firm seat and supportive back, and a low stool or table at its side where H.M. might deposit her handbag).

Edie had asked if she, and Cook, might be acquainted with Her Majesty's preferences in regard to afternoon tea, but The Palace had responded with maddening obliqueness, saying only that H.M. would be perfectly happy with a conventional English afternoon tea, and the only foodstuffs to be avoided were shellfish, excessive spice, garlic, and onions (excepting spring onions, which were acceptable in moderation).

Together Edie and Cook had decided upon a simple menu of two types of sandwiches (cucumber and egg-and-cress) and two varieties of scone (one plain, one with currants). The scones would be served with strawberry jam and clotted cream, and last of all there would be a loaf of the hotel's traditional gingerbread, decorated for the occasion with a small paper banner, strung between wooden skewers, that was inscribed (rather shakily) with *WELCOME H.M. QEII TO THE BLUE LION*.

This embellishment flouted The Palace's rules, which had specified no excessive decorations, but it had been made particularly for the occasion by Dolly, who was so excited and nervous that Edie had taken the precaution of unearthing an ancient bottle of smelling salts from the first-aid box in her office and securing them in her jacket pocket.

In a few minutes the queen herself would arrive for tea at the Blue Lion, and in anticipation of that moment Edie now stood outside its front door, which had been carefully propped open so as to facilitate to-ing and fro-ing. The street had been blocked off an hour or so earlier, and something like a dozen policemen now stood guard at intervals along the pavement. Edie was flanked by Dolly and Mick, and in Dolly's trembling grasp was a small posy for the queen, a pretty confection of carnations and gypsophila.

The poor dear's hands were shaking so badly that the bouquet was in danger of losing its petals, and after sending a silent prayer to the heavens that the girl would not faint at the queen's feet, Edie looked to Mick and whispered, "If she . . ."

"I'll catch her. You carry on with Her Maj."

Before she could thank him, three motorcars turned onto the street and drew to a stately halt, and as they did so every one of the surrounding policemen stood to attention as if magnetized by some great external force. The second of the cars was an enormous claret-colored Rolls-Royce that bore a small heraldic shield above its windscreen. A man came from nowhere to open its rear passenger door, startling Edie, and suddenly the queen was *there*, approaching Edie, and she was smiling and extending her elegantly gloved hand in greeting.

There she was, Queen Elizabeth herself, no longer Gloriana on her Coronation Day but a young and very pretty woman dressed in a gorgeously tailored jacket and full skirt, a smart little crescent of ink-blue straw and netting perched upon her head, a triple strand of gleaming pearls at her throat, and pinned to her lapel a brooch of diamonds that framed an enormous oval sapphire.

"Good afternoon, Miss Howard. How do you do?"

Edie took the queen's hand in hers and sank into what she hoped was a reasonably steady curtsy. "I am very well, thank you. Welcome to the Blue Lion, Your Majesty. May I introduce you to Miss Dolly Withers, our youngest employee?"

By some miracle Dolly had recovered her sangfroid, or more correctly had discovered it, and she now swept into a curtsy that Margot Fonteyn herself might have envied. "Welcome to the Blue Lion, Your Majesty," she said as she presented the little bouquet. "We are all of us very honored by your visit."

"Thank you very much, Miss Withers. How very kind."

"May I also introduce you to our doorman, Mr. Michael Nelligan?" Edie continued.

"How do you do, Mr. Nelligan?"

Mick had been standing at military attention but now executed a flawless bow. "I am well, Your Majesty. Thank you."

The queen, followed by her lady-in-waiting, now entered the hotel, with Edie just behind. The rest of the staff were waiting in the dining room, along with her residents and two additional guests: Detective Inspector Bayliss and Archibald Owens, Master of the Worshipful Company of Cartwrights and Wainwrights, whose only condition for lending Jamie's painting of their guild hall on Coronation Day had been an invitation to meet the queen.

There was just enough time for the royal guest to shake

hands with each of Edie's employees, though regrettably not to converse with them, with a few precious minutes set aside for her to meet Professor Thurloe, who had promised Edie not to air his complaints about the expense of the coronation and related festivities during the visit, as well as the Honorable Leopoldine Crane and the Honorable Albertine Crane. The brief moment of introduction left the sisters in a state of almost incandescent happiness.

Next was Master Owens, who took up rather too much time explaining the Cartwrights' decision to commission a portrait of Her Majesty and her procession as a way of commemorating their own five-hundredth anniversary; but the queen listened patiently, granted him a smile that left him blinking in amazement, and moved smoothly on to the next person in line.

"This is Miss Stella Donati, ma'am," Edie explained. "She is a photojournalist at *Picture Weekly*, and also one of the people who helped to prevent the, ah, unfortunate occurrence on the day of your coronation."

"How do you do, Miss Donati? I believe you also took that splendid photograph of my crowning that appeared on the cover of your magazine. How terribly clever of you to have captured it so well."

"Thank you, ma'am. It was truly an honor to be a witness."

Detective Inspector Bayliss was next, his freckled face engulfed in blushes, his hamlike fist trembling as he shook the queen's hand. "All in the line of duty, Your Majesty," he replied when she thanked him for his gallantry. "It was this man, here, Mr. Geddes, who was the hero of the hour. Him and Miss Howard together. I only came along once they'd risked their lives to make sure everyone was safe."

Edie had moved to stand next to Jamie, and it took an earnest effort not to join in, at that moment, and sing the praises of the man she loved. She refrained, though, for it would embarrass him as well as reduce the increasingly narrow window of time that was left for afternoon tea.

But the queen was not to be rushed. "I believe my father decorated you for gallantry during the war, Mr. Geddes."

"Yes, Your Majesty."

"From the looks of this painting, you are a talented artist as well as a courageous man."

"You are very kind, ma'am. Thank you."

Jamie had taken his time in completing the commission, steadfastly ignoring the requests of Master Owens and the other guild members when they begged for updates or a peek at the work in progress. When Jamie had finally deemed it ready for viewing, Master Owens had declared it a triumph, as had the Royal Academy, which had already secured its loan for the Summer Exhibition of 1954.

Edie had no technical understanding of the manner in which Jamie worked, nor did she have more than a passing knowledge of the history of artistic conventions and approaches, but she could, she believed, tell the difference between something that was good and something that was truly great. And *Second of June* was, she believed, a masterpiece.

Although Jamie had watched the procession from the top floor of the hotel, he had adopted the point of view of someone standing at eye level to the queen in her golden coach, but at a distance, with the surrounding crowds an impressionistic blur. Of the great, shining baroque globe of the coach he had made a frame in which the queen, as beautiful as any fairy-tale heroine, was the enchanting center. Behind her rose the mass of Cartwrights' Hall, which was recognizably itself yet somehow better, if such a thing were even possible, its stolid lines ennobled by Jamie's flattering interpretation of its late-Victorian facade. The dull skies and rain-soaked pavement of the day had heightened the contrast between the sober dress of the crowds and the splendor of the royal procession, and he'd also managed to capture a sense of movement within the whole, as if at any moment the horses might again walk on, the queen might continue to wave, and the countless gems embedded in her diadem, jewelry, and gown might continue to dazzle and delight.

One of the waiting men in dark suits, whom she suspected was a courtier from The Palace, although he might possibly be a policeman of some description, now caught Edie's eye and made a discreet show of tapping on his wristwatch.

"Would Your Majesty care to take tea with Mr. Geddes, Miss Donati, Detective Inspector Bayliss, and myself?" she asked.

"I should like that very much, thank you."

They moved to the largest of the tables, the only one set for tea that afternoon, and waited while the queen and her lady-in-waiting took their seats, and then they sat down, with Edie to the queen's right and Jamie to the left of the lady-in-waiting, and as they did so the rest of the Blue Lion's staff, as well as the Hons and the professor, quietly departed the dining room. The teapot had already been filled, the tiered trays already set out in preparation, and as they waited the queen removed her gloves and tucked them into her handbag, which she set on the little table next to her chair.

"Shall I be mother?" the unnamed lady-in-waiting asked, gesturing to the teapot.

"Oh, do," said the queen, and selected several sandwiches and pastries from the delicacies arrayed before her. "I understand there is a legend about the hotel that involves my predecessor?"

"Yes, ma'am," Edie began, and recounted the story of Elizabeth I and the storm, and the chair that the earlier queen had used, now displayed on its platform nearby. "We did wonder if we might employ it again for your visit, but when we tested it the other day it felt, ah, a little shaky." It had, alarmingly, all but collapsed under Dolly's slight frame; hence the note of warning that now sat on the chair's moth-eaten velvet cushion.

"How very sensible of you. These scones are delicious, by the way. Do pass on my compliments to your cook."

"I will, ma'am. Thank you."

"I gather that the individual who caused the difficulties here at your hotel has since been tried for his crimes. Is that correct, Detective Inspector Bayliss? May I ask what prompted him to take such an unfortunate course of action?"

"He is a distant cousin to Miss Howard, totally unknown to her, of course, and had become convinced that their shared ancestor had disinherited his branch of the family. It seems that he hoped to regain control of the hotel as a result of his schemes."

"I see. Well, distant cousins can sometimes prove quite troublesome. I believe the first Elizabeth knew something of that."

"Yes, ma'am. Fortunately, Miss Howard, Mr. Geddes, and Miss Donati were able to get the better of him. He has since been convicted of attempted murder, assault, fraud, theft, and a number of other lesser charges."

"But not treason?" the queen asked, and Edie couldn't be certain if the question was meant to be serious or playful. A glint in the monarch's eyes made her decide upon the latter.

"I pushed for it, ma'am, but there were concerns it might draw undue attention from the press."

"I quite understand. How very fortunate that Miss Donati is employed by a respectable publication."

"Yes, ma'am," Stella agreed.

According to Stella, the question of *Picture Weekly* running an insider's account of Ivor Brooks's plot to take over the Blue Lion had been rejected from the outset by Walter Kaczmarek, who deplored what he termed "gutter journalism." Brooks's recent trial had, admittedly, fanned the flames of interest, but within a few weeks the country's attention had been diverted by other scandals and stories.

"Nor, I believe, have you sought to make hay of the incident," the queen stated, casting her bright blue gaze upon Edie.

"No, ma'am. Although, in all honesty, word does seem to have got out. We've never had so many people for afternoon tea, and even now, in the low season, we're almost fully booked."

"I am very glad to hear of it. May I also offer my congratulations on your and Mr. Geddes's engagement?"

One week after he had finished *Second of June* and delivered it to Master Owens, and one day after he'd learned from his art dealer that enough requests for commissions had come in to keep him occupied for several years, Jamie had suggested to Edie that they go on a walk. He'd then led her to the same bench in St. James's Park where they had first become friends, and he had knelt on the pebbled ground in front of her, taken her hands in his, and asked if she would do him the honor of consenting to become his wife.

She had said yes straightaway, naturally, and once she had admired her ring and they had exchanged a series of delightful kisses, he had explained why he hadn't asked her earlier.

"I wanted to have some assurance that I wouldn't be a burden. No—hear me out. You are a successful woman in your own right, and the hotel is yours alone to own and to manage, and that is why I wanted to know that I have some hope of success as an artist. So you will know there is someone in this world who wishes to care for you simply because you deserve it."

"Oh, Jamie. I'd happily marry you if neither of us had tuppence to spare."

"I know, and it's one of the reasons I love you. But only one of many."

The ring had also been the cause of a small delay in his proposal, for Jamie's mother had been adamant that it be fashioned out of jewels from her own wedding finery. The stones, which his mother had secretly shown Jamie on an impromptu visit to London, had then been sent back to India to be set by her family's preferred goldsmith. Altogether the process had taken so long that Jamie had nearly gone ahead and proposed, ring or no ring. Edie was very glad, now, that he had accepted his mother's guidance, for the result—a cushion-cut sapphire (blue for the Blue Lion) set in filigreed gold, with a surround of brightly sparkling emeralds—had quite literally left her breathless when he'd placed it on her finger.

Jamie had moved out not long after their engagement, though only to a set of rooms above the Queen Bess. There was no view to speak of from the small windows in his little flat, and she worried the pub was too noisy to let him sleep properly, but he was unyielding.

"I can't bear the thought of your having to endure gossip on my account. I'll stay put until we're married, and then back I'll come to the Blue Lion."

"When are you to be married?" the queen now asked.

"On the twelfth of February, ma'am," Jamie answered. "The first anniversary of the day we met."

"We're planning on a quiet wedding," Edie added, "then a honeymoon in Scotland. I've never been."

This provoked a broad smile from the queen. "You're a brave man, Mr. Geddes, to introduce her to your home-land in the middle of winter."

The lady-in-waiting, having glanced at her wristwatch more than once, now cleared her throat discreetly. The queen answered with a slight nod, after which she took up her handbag, retrieved her gloves, and put them on. One of the men in dark suits came forward to pull back her chair. Everyone stood.

"Thank you very much for this splendid tea, Miss How-ard, and for your courage, and that of everyone here. I am most grateful."

The queen shook hands with Edie and the others once

more, and they exchanged a round of good-byes, and off she went, and that was that. The royal visit was over, and Edie could breathe again.

"How very extraordinary," she said, once she was sure the front door was firmly shut and the queen had been driven away. "I felt as if I was in the presence of someone who is immortal. I know she isn't, of course, but she doesn't feel entirely attached to this mortal plane, either."

The others agreed; they, too, admitted they had felt a little dazed by the experience, with the exception of Stella, who had behaved throughout with her usual demeanor of unflappable aplomb. "I must return to work, if only to tell my friends there what it is like to take tea with the queen. I am sure Kaz will find it very amusing to know that she described *Picture Weekly* as a 'respectable publication.'"

"I'll be off, too," said Gordon, who had been on a first-name basis with Edie and Jamie since Coronation Day. "Need to ring up my missus and let her know how it all went. Then it'll be back to my usual stock-in-trade. Burglary and assault, and if I'm lucky not so much as a whiff of treason. You'll let me know if you've any trouble?"

"I will," Edie promised, "but things have never been so good at the Blue Lion. So there's no need to worry on my account."

It was true. With Brooks's scheme to divert bookings away from the hotel no longer an impediment, and with heightened interest in the hotel bringing a steady stream of guests to their door, the Blue Lion was on a far better footing than it had ever been. Its accounts had been steadily in the black for months.

Brooks's mother had known nothing of his machinations,

though she had admitted to expressing some bitterness over her disinheritance and the relative penury in which she had been raised. The neighbor who had procured the dynamite for Brooks had been convicted on lesser charges and sentenced to prison, though for a far shorter length of time than the man he had entrusted with enough high explosive to turn Buckingham Palace into a smoking ruin.

At his trial, Brooks had insisted that he hadn't intended, at least not at first, to kill Edie and the professor; his sole intention had been to convince her to share in its ownership or, presumably by enticing her into a romantic entanglement, to gain control by marriage. Fortunately, the judge had dismissed his claims and sentenced Brooks to something very close to a life sentence in prison. With good behavior, he might hope to be free in time for the queen's silver jubilee.

He was part of her past; Jamie was her future. Their wedding would indeed be small, with only Jamie's family and their closest friends in attendance. Among them would be Stella and Win Keller—who had become, in recent weeks, "my Win" when Stella spoke of the man—along with Walter Kaczmarek and his wife, Miriam. Soon Coronation Year would be at an end, and she and Jamie would begin their lives together in earnest.

The comforting weight of his arm settled upon her shoulders, bringing her thoughts back to the present. "What now?" he asked.

"I've no idea," she admitted. "I haven't been able to think of anything but the queen's visit for weeks."

"Shall we go on a walk?" He held out her coat and hat, and he waited patiently as she put them on, found her gloves in her pockets, and retrieved her scarf from the sleeve of her coat.

"I'm ready," she said. "Where are we going?"

"Onward, my darling Edie. Ever onward."

"I can't imagine anything better," she said, and she looped her arm through his, and together they stepped into the welcoming light of their bright and beckoning future.

Author's Note

Since the publication of *The Gown* in 2019 I've received many emails and letters from readers who wish to know where they can see, or learn more about, the embroideries created by Miriam Dassin. The difficulty, of course, is that since Miriam was a product of my imagination, so too were her artworks; and while I did briefly address this fact in my historical notes at the end of that book, I fear that I was not explicit enough in my explanation. Mea culpa—and my apologies to anyone who has spent time in a fruitless search for the Vél d'Hiv embroideries.

Rather than risk sending any of you on a wild-goose chase in search of the Blue Lion, the paintings of A. J. Geddes, or Stella Donati's photograph of the crowning of Queen Elizabeth, I'm going to be honest and admit something right now: I made stuff up for this book. Quite a lot of stuff, in fact.

I didn't make up, or indeed alter, anything really significant as far as known historical events are concerned. The late Queen Elizabeth II really was crowned at Westminster Abbey on June 2, 1953, and the events of that day, as

I've described them in *Coronation Year*, really did happen. That's all part of the historical record and easily verified—and if you'd like to learn more, you can find a list of further reading on my website.

Where I let my imagination run wild was in respect to the people who live at the Blue Lion, their actions, their work, and the hotel itself. They are, without exception, products of my imagination, and for that I make no apology; this is, after all, a work of historical *fiction*.

That said, I think it's worth adding some context to my decisions; and if, after reading, you still have questions, please do feel free to contact me via my website or on social media.

I think I had better begin with the place at the heart of this book. The Blue Lion, as described in *Coronation Year*, does not exist, nor did it ever exist in the past. If you are in London and go looking for the Blue Lion, you will find a lovely old building at the end of Northumberland Street, but it is now—and has been for many decades—occupied by the historic public house the Sherlock Holmes. While the building itself does bear a superficial resemblance to the Blue Lion, unlike my fictional creation it is not built upon an ancient predecessor; it, together with most of its neighbors, is only a few centuries old.

You may reasonably ask, having seen the illustration at the beginning of this book, how the Blue Lion can be depicted in so much detail if it never existed. Where the illustration is concerned, I relied upon the artistic talent and architectural acumen of my friend Charisma Panchapakesan, who is a Toronto-based fine artist and architect. I may once have had a vision of the Blue Lion that differed from the illustration you see here, but the wonderful version created by Charisma has since displaced it. Every detail I specified in *Coronation Year* is present and exactly as I imagined—from the hanging sign to the ancient plaque by the door to the pot of primroses on Jamie's windowsill. Together (with the lion's share of the work falling to Charisma!) we were able to create a version of my fictional hotel that is not only possible, in that the structure and general architectural design are what one would expect for that part of London, but also plausible. I hope you will agree that our Blue Lion is the sort of place that might, had history taken a few minor turns, actually have existed.

Since the Blue Lion is fictional, I should also specify that the legend of Queen Elizabeth I taking shelter there is untrue, and moreover is not derived from any existing legend. If that makes you wonder if Queen Elizabeth II ever came to tea at the Blue Lion . . . I think you already know what I'm going to say.

Having declared more than once that I would never include the late queen as a character in one of my books, I now must ask forgiveness for breaking my promise. In my defense, I felt that the events of the book, had they actually occurred, would have merited a visit from the monarch; and where I have put words in her mouth, I have taken care to ensure they are consistent with Elizabeth II's recorded utterances and opinions, with only a touch of whimsy on my part (specifically when she refers to troublesome relations).

The Worshipful Company of Cartwrights and Wainwrights is fictional, together with Cartwrights' Hall on Northumberland Avenue. The City of London's livery companies (both guilds and trade associations) do exist, however, with 110 of them at most recent count. The oldest, the Worshipful Company of Mercers, dates to 1394; the newest, the Worshipful Company of Arts Scholars, was established in 2014.

Jamie's paintings, notably *Trafalgar Square* and *Second of June*, do not exist, but I was inspired in my description of them by the work of notable midcentury artists such as Julian Trevelyan and Terence Cuneo.

Picture Weekly never existed, though it will be familiar to readers of *Goodnight from London* and *The Gown*. It was inspired by *Picture Post*, a groundbreaking weekly newsmagazine (1938–1957), and some of the stories I mention as appearing in *PW* have their origins in the pages of *Picture Post*.

The *Donati Guides*, too, are fictional; they had no real contemporary equivalent, but were borne of my decision, when writing *Our Darkest Night*, to make Stella's parents the proprietors of a small publishing house that specialized in travel guides. I had no notion, then, that Stella would end up appearing in *Coronation Year* as well.

One element of *Coronation Year* is, sadly, very much grounded in truth: the racism and abuse experienced by Jamie and his family. In researching his story, I drew upon the memoirs and oral histories of British people of Indian, Pakistani, and Sri Lankan ancestry. I also submitted my manuscript to three friends whose backgrounds differ, but who, as people of color, with families whose ancestors emigrated from the Indian subcontinent to white-dominated communities in Britain and Canada, share an understanding of the challenges that Jamie faced which I cannot truly understand. These readers all suggested amendments to

Jamie's story that not only improved *Coronation Year*, but also deepened my understanding of the racism that afflicts every aspect of our society, and I am sincerely grateful for their careful assessment of my work.

The events of Coronation Day unfolded as I've described them, with the exception of the bomb plot engineered by Ivor Brooks. While authorities were alert to the possibility of an attack on the queen or other dignitaries, and in fact conducted multiple sweeps of buildings along the route, there is no official record of any attempts to harm the queen or anyone in the procession on the day itself. The only disappointment of the day was the weather, which was, as I've described (and Jamie predicted) unseasonably cold and rainy.

Acknowledgments

It has been a strange few years indeed, and one constant that sustained me as I researched and wrote *Coronation Year* was the kindness and support of the readers who bought or borrowed my books, read and reread them, and sent me kind messages that warmed my heart and buoyed my spirits many, many times. I am so fortunate to have such devoted readers, and I thank you sincerely.

In the course of researching this book, I relied upon the digital collections of a number of libraries and archives. I would specifically like to acknowledge the Bodleian Library at the University of Oxford, the British Newspaper Archive, the Mass-Observation Archive at the University of Sussex, the Museum of London, the National Archives (UK), the National Library of Scotland, the New York Public Library, the Royal Collection, and the Toronto Public Library.

Charisma Panchapakesan was instrumental in bringing my vision of the Blue Lion to life, and I thank her for the beautiful illustrations she contributed to this book. Thanks as well to Brian Hagood for answering my questions related